Pearl
Maiden

CENTENNIAL EDITION
1903–2003

TO

GLADYS CHRISTIAN

A DWELLER IN THE EAST

This Eastern Tale is Dedicated

BY HER OWN AND HER FATHER'S FRIEND

THE AUTHOR

DITCHINGHAM :
September 14, 1902

Pearl Maiden

A Tale of the Fall of Jerusalem

H. Rider Haggard

Revised and Edited
by
Christopher D. Kou
and
Michael J. McHugh

Christian Liberty Press
Arlington Heights, Illinois

General editorship by Michael J. McHugh
Revised and edited by Christopher D. Kou
Cover painting by Timothy Kou
Original book illustrations by Byam Shaw, edited by Christopher Kou
Layout and graphics by Christopher and Timothy Kou at
imagineering studios, inc.

A publication of
Christian Liberty Press
502 West Euclid Avenue
Arlington Heights, IL 60004
www.christianlibertypress.com

ISBN 1-930367-89-9

Printed in The United States of America

Centennial Edition

CONTENTS

ABOUT THE AUTHOR

Sir Henry Rider Haggard was born in England on June 22, 1856. He was the eighth of ten children and received most of his primary and elementary education at home through private tutors and occasionally at a local grammar school. His parents took him on frequent trips to the Continent during his childhood days.

In 1875, when Haggard was nineteen, he traveled to South Africa to work as a secretary for the newly appointed governor of Natal. Three years later, the young Englishman resigned his post at the high court of Pretoria to take up ostrich farming in Natal.

Haggard visited England in 1880 and was married on August 11 to Mariana L. Margitson, a Norfolk heiress. The newlyweds soon returned to their farm in Natal to resume the business of farming. In his spare time, Haggard began to work on his first book project and also began to take up the study of law. In 1882, the Haggard family sold their farm in Natal and returned to England.

Henry Haggard completed his law studies in 1884 and accepted a call to the bar of attorneys in London where he worked as an assistant to a chief judge. It was during this time that he made use of what he describes as his "somewhat ample leisure time in chambers" to write his first successful novel *King Solomon's Mines*. This book, as he put it, "finally settled the question of whether to pursue a legal or literary career." Henry Haggard proceeded to write over sixty-six novels and numerous papers, producing nearly one book for each year of his life.

Haggard traveled extensively throughout the world during much of his married life. His knowledge of the culture and terrain of Italy and Palestine enabled him to complete one of his grandest novels, *Pearl-Maiden,* in 1903. The recognitions of his contributions as a writer were crowned in the year 1912 when Henry Rider Haggard was knighted.

Sir Haggard died in London on May 14, 1925, at the age of sixty-eight.

Michael J. McHugh

EDITOR'S NOTE

Pearl-Maiden was originally published in 1903 and has for one hundred years led a relatively obscure existence compared to Haggard's other more celebrated works, among them, *King Solomon's Mines*. Now, through this new centennial edition, the publisher and I hope to reintroduce this little known classic to a whole new audience.

We believe that the 1st century A.D. era described in this novel is of vital importance to the Church and too often an overlooked period of history. Few today even realize the continuing impact the fall of Jerusalem and the destruction of the Temple have had in history. Fewer can describe the period leading up to that momentous event. It is our hope that *Pearl Maiden* will help to bring to light this critical event of Christian history so that we might better appreciate God's sovereign work of Providence both in the past and for the future.

To this end I have thoroughly revised and edited the original text to make the story clearer and more enjoyable for modern readers. Grammar and word usage have been changed and updated, and much of the dialog has been rephrased. Some Latin terms have been restored in lieu of the contemporary Victorian English equivalents found in the original text. Most of these changes are superficial in nature, but readers familiar with the 1903 edition will also note two new scenes near the final pages of this version: The preaching of Bishop Cyril to Marcus, and the final storm that threatens to sink the *Luna*.

Some historical errors and inconsistencies have been corrected. For instance, the reader will find that in this edition, the character Marcus is often called by his *cognomen,* or nickname, Fortunatus, while those who are closer to him tend to use his first name. His family name, Carius, is new to this edition entirely, and has been added to make the character more authentic. Hence, he now has a proper Roman name, Marcus Carius Fortunatus.

Finally, there were, in the original text, some fundamental biblical inconsistencies that needed to be addressed. The original version implied that it is lawful for a Christian to marry a non-

Christian, and it was only the command of Miriam's parents that forbade her. However, the Bible is very clear that those who are in Christ are not to be "unequally yoked" with unbelievers (2 Cor. 6: 14). Intermarriage is a problem as old as the Noahic flood when the sons of God took wives of the daughters of men (Gen. 6:1,2). Throughout history, intermarriage between Israel, God's covenant people, and the pagan world was always an occasion for God's chastisement. The call for purity of faith in marriage has always been a resounding command. Nothing has changed in that respect for the New Testament era. Christians are not to intermarry with unbelievers.

That being said, Haggard's original work does highlight an important principle of Christian marriage. In our story, Miriam refuses Marcus, even when he offers to convert to Christianity for her sake, and so must young adults today be cautious where matters of marriage and faith are concerned. One cannot trust a hasty conversion to Christianity when desire for marriage is the motive. Miriam's faith and regard for her parents' wishes were more important than her feelings and emotional attachment to an unbeliever, and young Christians would do well to learn from that example set forth in this book.

Notwithstanding all the revisions, the storyline structure of the original remains intact, as does the essential message that was always at the heart of the story—the message of God's grace and eternal love for His called out people and His sovereign working in history.

The *Pearl Maiden* project has been a great pleasure to work on, and I would like to thank Michael McHugh, director of Christian Liberty Press, for the opportunity to have a major part in it. It is my prayer and the prayer of all those involved that God will use this book for the furtherance of His Kingdom on Earth and the building up of His Church.

Ad maioram Dei gloriam, to the greater glory of God.

Christopher D. Kou
Prospect Heights, Illinois
2003

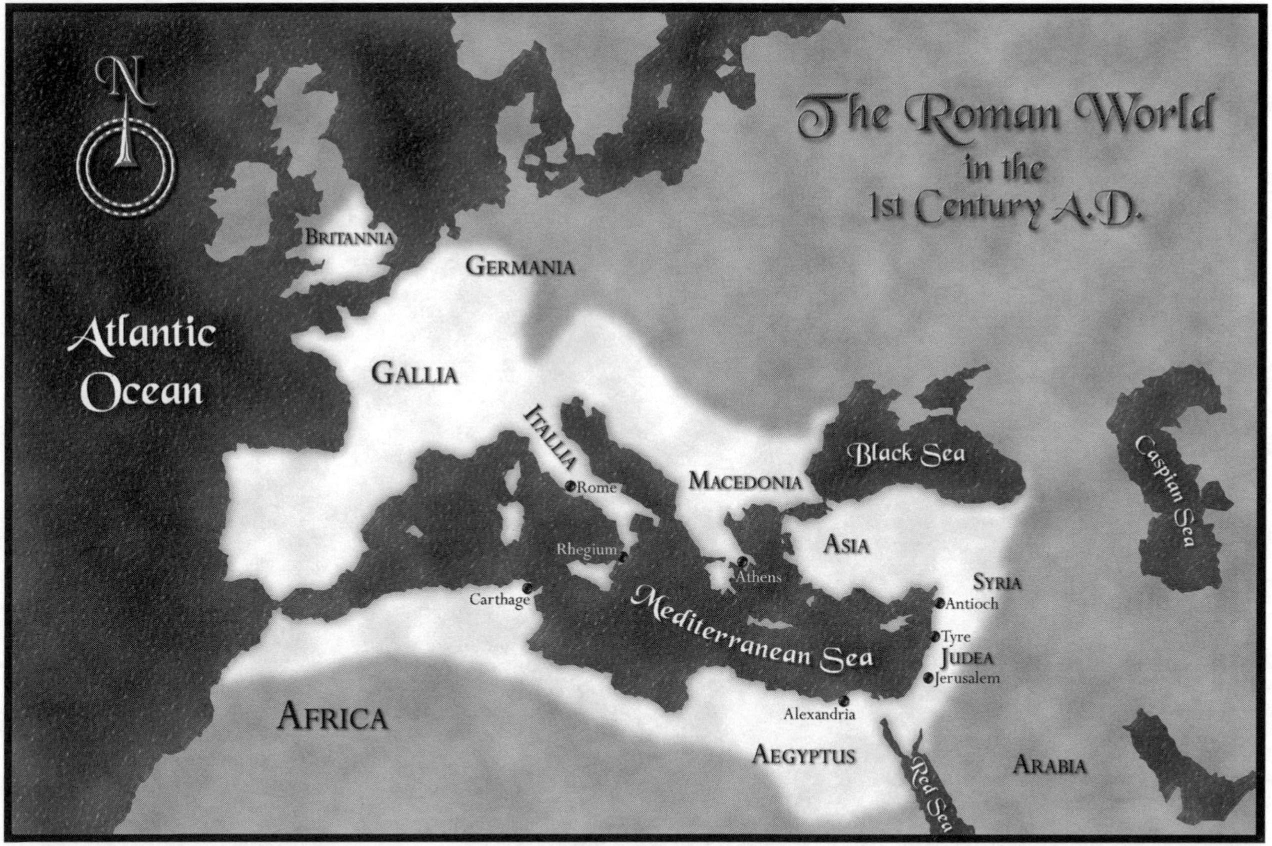

The Roman World in the 1st Century A.D.

Atlantic Ocean

BRITANNIA

GERMANIA

GALLIA

ITALLIA

Rome

Rhegium

Carthage

MACEDONIA

Athens

Black Sea

ASIA

Caspian Sea

Mediterranean Sea

SYRIA

Antioch

Tyre

JUDEA

Jerusalem

Alexandria

AEGYPTUS

Red Sea

ARABIA

AFRICA

TYRE

Mediterranean
Sea

Caesarea Maritima

Pella

Apollonia

Joppa

Jericho
JERUSALEM
Essene Village

Dead Sea

Judea
in the
1st Century A.D.

Masada

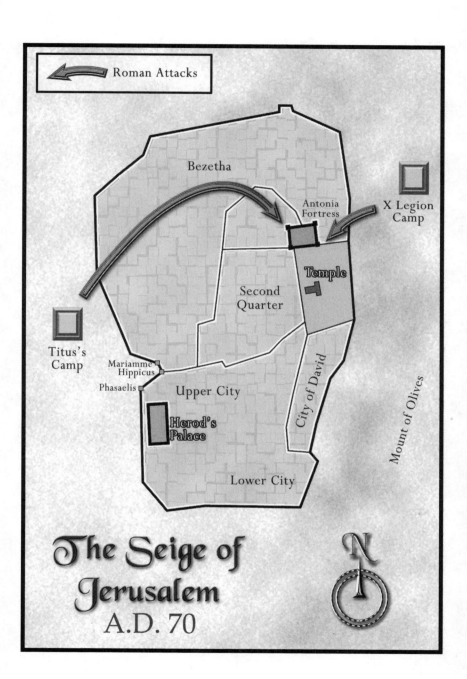

The Seige of Jerusalem A.D. 70

Chapter I
The Prison of Caesarea

It was two hours after midnight, but many were still awake in Caesarea, gem of the Syrian coast. Herod Agrippa, King of all Palestine by grace of the Romans, now at the very apex of his power, was celebrating a festival in honor of the Emperor Claudius, to which had flocked all the mightiest in the land and tens of thousands of the people. The city was full, and the camps of travelers were set upon the seashore for miles around. There was no room at the inns or in the private houses, where guests slept on the roofs, the couches, the floors, and in the gardens. The great town hummed like a hive of bees disturbed after sunset, and though the louder sounds of reveling had died away, parties of feasters, still crowned with drooping roses, passed along the streets to their lodgings, shouting and singing. As they went, those who were sufficiently sober discussed the incidents of that day's games in the great circus and offered or accepted odds upon the more exciting events of the morrow.

The captives in the prison, a frowning building of brown stone set upon a little hill, divided into courts and surrounded by a high wall and a ditch, could hear the workmen at their labor in the amphitheatre below. All were fixated upon the sounds drifting up to them, for many of those who listened were doomed to take part in the spectacle of this new day. In the outer court stood a hundred men called malefactors, most of them Jews convicted of various political offences. They had been condemned to fight against twice their number of desert Arabs taken in a frontier raid, unarmored savages mounted and armed with swords and lances. The malefactor Jews, to make the fight even, were to be protected with heavy armor and large shields. Their combat was to last for twenty minutes by the sandglass, after which, unless they had shown cowardice, those who were left alive of either party were to receive their freedom. Indeed, contrary to custom, by a kindly decree of King Agrippa, a man who did not seek unnecessary bloodshed, even the wounded were to be spared if any would undertake the care of them. Under these circumstances, since life is dear, all had determined to fight their best.

In another section of the great hall was collected a very different company. There were no more than fifty or sixty of them, and the wide arches of the surrounding cloisters gave them sufficient shelter and even privacy. With the exception of eight or ten men, all of them old or well into middle age, this little band was made up of women and children. The younger and more vigorous males had already been carefully drafted to serve as gladiators. They belonged to the new sect called Christians, the followers of one Jesus, who, according to report, had been crucified as a troublemaker by Pontius Pilate, the Roman governor of Judea. In his day Pilate was unpopular with the Jews, for he had seized the treasures of the Temple at Jerusalem to build waterworks, causing a tumult in which many Jews had been killed. Now he was almost forgotten, but very strangely, the fame of this crucified Jesus seemed to grow. There were many who had come to accept his teachings and the claim of his followers that he had risen from the dead. They made him to be a kind of god, preaching doctrines in his name that were contrary to Roman law and offensive to every Jewish sect.

Pharisees, Sadducees, and priests, all called out against them. All petitioned to Agrippa that they should be rid of them, these apostates who profaned the land and proclaimed in the ears of a nation awaiting its Messiah, the Heaven born King who would break the Roman yoke and make Jerusalem the capital of the world, that this Messiah had already come in the guise of an itinerant preacher and had perished with other malefactors.

Wearied by their incessant pestering, the King consented. Like the cultivated Romans with whom he associated, Agrippa had no real religion. In Jerusalem he embellished the Temple and made offerings to Jehovah; at Berytus he embellished the temple and made offerings there to Jupiter. Before the world, he was all things to all men, and in private, merely another licentious holder of public office. As for these Christians, he never troubled himself about them. Why should he? They were few and insignificant; not a single man of rank or wealth was to be found among them. To persecute them was easy, and it pleased the Jews. Therefore he persecuted them. One James, a disciple of the crucified man called Christ, who had wandered about the country with him, he had seized and beheaded in Jerusalem. Another called Peter, a powerful preacher, he threw into prison, and of their followers he slew many. A few of these were given over to be stoned by the Jews, but most of the men were forced to fight in the arenas of Berytus and elsewhere. The women, if young and beautiful, were sold as slaves, but if matrons or aged, they were cast to the wild beasts in the amphitheater.

Such was the end reserved for these poor victims in the prison on this very day of festival. After the gladiators had fought and the other games had been celebrated, sixty Christians, it was announced, old and useless men, married women and young children that nobody would buy, were to be presented in the great amphitheatre. Thirty lions made fiercely ravenous by hunger and mad with the smell of blood, were then to be set loose among them. Even in this act of judgment, however, Agrippa wished to be seen by all as gentle-hearted, and of his kindness he had decreed that any whom the lions refused to eat were to be given clothes, a small sum of money, and released to settle their differences with the Jews as they might please.

Such was the state of public feeling and morality in the Roman Empire, that this spectacle of the feeding of starved beasts with live women and children, whose crime was that they worshipped a crucified man and would offer sacrifice to no other god, either in the Temple or elsewhere, was much looked forward to by the population of Caesarea. Great amounts of money were wagered upon the event, and he who drew the ticket marked with the number that the lions left alive would take the entire sum. Some gamblers of foresight who had drawn low numbers had already bribed the soldiers and wardens to sprinkle the hair and garments of the Christians with valerian water, a mixture intended to attract and excite the appetite of these great cats. Others, whose ticket numbers were high, paid handsomely for the employment of concoctions calculated to induce in the lions an aversion to the treated subject. The Christian woman or child who was to form the *corpus vile* of these ingenious experiments was not considered except as the fisherman considers the worm on his hook.

Alone under a stone arch, not far from the great gateway where the guards, their spears in hand, could be seen pacing up and down, sat two women. The contrast between the pair was striking. One, no more than twenty years of age, was a Jewess, too sallow and thin for beauty, but with dark and lovely eyes, and bearing in every limb and feature the mark of noble blood. She was Rachel, the widow of the Greco-Syrian Demas and the only child of the highborn Jew Benoni, the richest merchant in Tyre. The other was a woman of remarkable appearance, about forty years of age. She was a native of the coasts of Libya, where she had been kidnapped as a girl by slave traders, and passed on to Phoenician merchants, who had sold her upon the slave market of Tyre. She was a noble Arab without any trace of African blood, as could be seen by her copper-colored skin, prominent cheek bones, abundant black hair, and untamed, flashing eyes. In frame she was tall and spare, agile, and full of perilous grace in every movement. Her face was fierce and hard; even in her present dreadful plight she showed no fear, though when she looked at the lady by her side it grew anxious and tender. She was called Nehushta—*copper* in the Hebrew tongue—a name that Benoni had given her many years ago when he bought her upon the marketplace. In her native land, however, she had been named Nou, and by this name she was known to her dead mistress, the wife of Benoni, and to his daughter Rachel, whom she had nursed from childhood.

The moon shone radiant in the vacant sky, and by its light an observer could have watched every movement and expression of these women. Rachel, seated on the ground, was rocking herself to and fro, her face hidden in her hands, deep in her prayers.

Nehushta knelt by her side, resting the weight of her body on her heels, and stared sullenly into nothingness.

Presently Rachel dropped her hands to her lap, looked at the unfeeling sky and sighed. "Our last night on earth, Nou," she said sadly. "It is strange to think that we shall never again see the moon floating above us."

"Why not, mistress? If all that we have been taught is true, we shall see that moon forever and ever. However, for my own part I don't intend that either of us should die tomorrow."

"How can you prevent it, Nou?" asked Rachel with a faint smile. "Lions are no respecters of persons."

"Yet, mistress, I think that they will respect my person, and yours, too, for my sake."

"What do you mean, Nou?"

"I mean that I do not fear lions. They are country-folk of mine and I listened to their roar when I was still in the cradle. My father was called Master of Lions in our country because he could tame them. When I was a little child I fed them and they fawned upon us like dogs."

"Those lions are long dead, Nou. And the others will not remember such days."

"I am not sure that they are really dead. Blood will call to blood, and their brothers will know the smell of the child of the Master of Lions. Whoever may be eaten, we shall escape."

"I have no such hope, Nou. Tomorrow we shall die horribly, that King Agrippa may do honor to his master, Caesar."

"If you think that, mistress, then let us die at once rather than be rent limb from limb to give pleasure to a stinking mob. See, I have poison hidden here in my hair. Let us drink of it and be done. It would be swift and painless."

"Nay, Nou, it would not be right. I will lift no hand against my own life, and even if I would, I have another life to think of."

"If you die, the unborn child must die also. Tonight or tomorrow, what does it matter?"

"Sufficient to the day is the evil thereof. Who knows? Tomorrow Agrippa may be dead, not us. And then the child might live. It is in the hand of God. Let God decide."

"Lady," answered Nehushta, setting her teeth, "for your sake I have become a Christian, yes, and I believe. But I tell you this. While I live, no lion's fangs shall tear your dear flesh. I would sooner stab you there in the arena."

"Please, Nou," she murmured, covering her eyes. "Take no such sin upon your soul."

"My soul! What do I care about my soul? You are my soul. Your mother was kind to me when you were but an infant, and I a slave. I rocked you upon my breast. I spread your bridal bed, and if need be, to save you from worse things, I will lay you dead before me and myself dead across your body. Then let God deal with my soul. At least, I shall have done my best and died faithful."

"You should not speak so," sighed Rachel. "I know it is only because you love me. I too wish to die as easily as may be, so I may join my husband. Then I might see even my child, and all three of us may dwell together eternally. Nay, not all three, all four, for you are well nigh as dear to me, Nou, as husband or as child."

"That cannot be, I do not wish that it should be, for I am but a slave woman, the dog beneath the table. Oh! If I could save you, then I would be glad to show them how this daughter of my father can bear their torments."

The Libyan ceased, grinding her teeth in impotent rage. Then suddenly she leaned towards her mistress, kissed her fiercely on the cheek, and began to sob, slow, heavy sobs.

"Listen," said Rachel, silencing her. "The lions are roaring."

Nehushta lifted her head, alert, like a hunter in the desert. From near the great tower that ended the southern wall of the amphitheatre echoed short, coughing notes and fierce whimpering, followed presently by roar upon roar, as the lions joined in their fearful music. The air shook with the boom of their voices.

"Aha!" cried a voice at the gate. It was not one of the soldiers who marched to and fro unconcernedly, but the jailor, Rufus, clad in a padded robe and armed with a great knife displayed prominently in his sash. "Listen to them, the kittens. Don't be greedy, little ones—be patient. Tonight you will purr upon a full stomach."

"Nine of them," muttered Nehushta, who had counted the roars, "all bearded and old, royal beasts. To hearken to them makes me young again. I can smell the desert and see the smoke rising from my father's tents. I hunted them as a child. Now they will hunt me; it is their hour."

"I need water!" gasped Rachel, sinking against her.

With a guttural exclamation of pity Nehushta bent down. Placing her strong arms beneath the slender form of her young mistress, and lifting her as though she were a child, she carried her to the center of the court, where stood a fountain, a remnant of the days when the jail had once been a palace. Here she set her mistress on the ground with her back against the stonework and dashed water in her face until she was herself again.

While Rachel sat, a gate swung open, and several persons, men, women, and children, were thrust through it into the court.

"Newcomers from Tyre in a great hurry not to lose the lions' party," jeered the warden of the gate. "Pass in, my Christian friends. Pass in and eat your last supper according to your custom. You will find it over there, bread and wine in plenty. Eat, my hungry friends. Eat before you are eaten and enter into Heaven—or the stomachs of the lions."

An old woman, straggling at the back of the party, turned around and pointed at the buffoon with her staff.

"Blaspheme not, you heathen dog!" she said, "or rather, blaspheme and go to your reward! Thus saith my God by the mouth of Anna that you have *already* eaten your last meal on earth. You claimed to be a Christian once and, therefore, are doubly guilty."

The man, a half-bred Syrian who had abandoned his faith for profit and now tormented those who were once his brethren, uttered a furious curse and snatched a knife from his girdle.

"You draw the knife? So be it, perish by the knife!" said Anna. Then without heeding him further the old woman hobbled on after her companions, leaving the man to slink away white to his lips with terror. He had been a Christian and knew something of Anna and of her gift of prophecy.

The path of these strangers led them past the fountain, where Rachel and Nehushta rose to greet them as they came.

"Peace be with you," said Rachel.

"In the name of Christ, peace," they answered, and passed on toward the arches where the other captives were gathered. Last of all, at some distance behind the rest, came the white-haired woman, leaning on her staff.

As she approached, Rachel turned to repeat her salutation, then uttered a little cry and said, "Mother Anna, do you not know me? I am Rachel, the daughter of Benoni."

"Rachel!" she answered, starting. "Alas! Child, how came you here?"

"By the paths that we Christians have to tread, mother," said Rachel, sadly. "But sit. You are weary. Nou, help her."

Anna nodded, and slowly, for her limbs were stiff, then she sank down on the base of the fountain.

"Give me to drink, child," she said. "They brought me from Tyre on the back of a mule, and did not think to give me water."

Rachel cupped her hands and held water to Anna's lips, which she drank greedily, emptying them many times.

"For this refreshment, God be praised. What said you? The daughter of Benoni a Christian! Well, for that God be praised also, even here and now. Strange, that I should not have heard of it. But I have been in Jerusalem these two years and was brought back to Tyre last Sabbath as a prisoner."

"Yes, Mother. And since then I have become both wife and widow."

"Who did you marry, child?"

"Demas, the merchant. They killed him in the amphitheatre at Berytus six months ago," and the poor woman began to sob.

"I heard of his end," replied Anna. "It was a noble one, and his soul rests in Heaven. He would not fight with the gladiators, so Agrippa ordered him beheaded. But cease weeping, child, and tell me your story. We have little time for tears before we shall be done with them."

Rachel dried her eyes.

"It is short and sad," she said. "Demas and I met often and learned to love each other. My father was no friend to him, for they were rivals in trade, but in those days Demas followed the faith of the Jews, and because he was rich, my father consented to our marriage. They became partners in business. Within a month of our wedding the apostles came to Tyre, and we attended their preaching—at first, because we were curious to learn the truth of this new faith against which my father railed—of all Jews, he is the most stubborn—and then because our hearts were changed. So in the end, we believed. We were baptized, both on one night, by the very hand of the brother of the Lord. The apostles departed, blessing us before they went, and Demas, who would play no double part, told my father of what we had done. Oh, it was awful to see! He raved, shouted and cursed us in his rage, blaspheming our Lord. When we refused to forsake Christ, he denounced us to the priests, the priests denounced us to the Romans, and we were seized and thrown into prison. My husband's wealth, except what the priests and the Romans took, stayed with my father. We were held in prison here in Caesarea for six months. They took my husband to Berytus, to be trained as a gladiator, and the rest you know. I have been here since then with this beloved servant, Nehushta, who became a Christian to follow our path, and now, by the decree of Agrippa, it is my turn and hers to die today."

"Child, weep not for that. Nay, be glad for you will find your husband and your Savior."

"Mother, I am glad for that. It is for my child's sake I weep, that will never be born. It is a cruel world, and full of tribulation, but I would have seen my child live. But now, it cannot be."

Anna looked at her with her piercing eyes.

"Have you, then, also the gift of prophecy, child, who are so young a member of the Church, that you dare to say that this or that cannot be? The future is in the hand of God. King Agrippa, your father, the Romans, the cruel Jews, those lions that roar, and we who are doomed to feed them, are all in the hand of God, and that which He wills shall befall, and no other thing. Therefore, let us praise Him and rejoice, and take no thought for tomorrow, unless it be to pray that we may die and go to our Master, rather than live on in doubts and terrors and tribulations."

"You are right, Mother," answered Rachel, "and I will try to be brave, whatever may befall. Listen, they call us to partake of the Sacrament of the Lord—our last on earth." And rising, she began to walk towards the arches.

Nehushta stayed to help Anna to her feet. When she judged her mistress to be out of hearing, she leaned down and whispered, "Anna, you have the gift. It is known throughout the Church. Tell me, will the child be born?"

The old woman fixed her eyes upon the heavens, then answered, slowly, "The child will be born and live out its life, and I think that none of us are doomed to die this day by the jaws of lions, though some of us may die in another fashion. But I think also that your mistress goes very shortly to join her husband. It was better that I showed her nothing of what is revealed to me."

"Then it is best that I should die also, and die I will."

"Why?"

"Because I go to wait upon my mistress."

"Nay, Nehushta," answered Anna, sternly. "Stay to guard her child, for this would be her desire, as well as the Lord's. When all these earthly things are done, you will give an account to God."

Chapter II
The Voice of a God

King Agrippa was a Roman in practice. Rome was his model; her ideals were his ideals. After the Roman fashion, he built amphitheatres in which men were butchered to the exquisite delight of vast audiences. And without the excuse of any conscientious motive, however insufficient or unsatisfactory, he persecuted the weak because they were weak and because their suffering would give pleasure to the strong or to those who chanced to be in strength at the moment.

The season was hot, and it was arranged that the great games in honor of Caesar should open each day at dawn and come to an end an hour before noon. From midnight onwards crowds of spectators poured into the amphitheatre, which, though built to seat over twenty thousand, was not large enough to contain them all. An hour before dawn, the place was full, and already latecomers were turned back from its gates. The only empty spaces were those reserved for the king, his royal guests, the rulers of the city, with other distinguished personages, and for the condemned Christians who were to sit in full view of the audience until the time came for them to take their share in the spectacle.

When Rachel joined the other captives, she found that a long rough table had been set beneath the arcades, and on it at intervals, bread and cups containing wine purchased from the guards at a great price. Round this table the old and the weak among the company were seated on a bench, while the rest of the number, for whom there was no room on the bench, stood behind them. At its head was an old man, a bishop among the Christians, one of the five hundred who had seen the risen Lord and received baptism from the hands of John the Beloved. For some years he had been spared by the persecutors of the infant Church on account of his age, dignity, and good repute, but now at last his end seemed to have overtaken him.

The service was held, the bread and wine, mixed with water, consecrated. When all had eaten from the platters and drunk from the rude cups, the bishop gave his blessing to the company and addressed them. This, he told them, was an occasion of peculiar joy, a love feast indeed, since all who partook of it were about to lay down the burden of the flesh and, their labors and sorrows ended, to depart into eternal bliss. He called to their memory the supper of the Passover, which had taken place within the lifetime of many of them, when the Author and Finisher of their faith had declared to the disciples that He would drink no more wine until He drank it new with them in His kingdom. Such a feast it was that lay spread before them this night. Let them be thankful for it. Let them not quail in the hour of trial. The fangs of the savage beasts, the shouts of the still more savage spectators, the agony of quivering flesh, the last terror of their departing, what were these? Soon, very soon, they would be done. The spears of the soldiers would dispatch the injured, and those among them ordained to escape would be set free by the command of the Caesar's representative, that they might continue the work until the hour came for them to pass on the torch of redemption to other hands. Let them rejoice, therefore, and be thankful, and walk to the sacrifice as to a wedding feast. "Shall we not rejoice, my brethren?" he asked. With one voice they answered, "We rejoice!" Yes, even the children answered thus.

Then they prayed again, and again with uplifted hands the old man blessed them in the holy Triune Name.

Scarcely had this service, as solemn as it was simple, been brought to an end when the head jailer, his blasphemous mocking since Anna's reproof replaced by a look of sullen venom, came forward and commanded the whole band to march to the amphitheatre. Two by two, the bishop leading the way with the woman Anna, they walked to the gates. A guard of soldiers was waiting to receive them, and under their escort, they threaded the dim, narrow streets until they came to the door of the amphitheatre used by the participants of the games. At a word from the bishop, they began to chant a solemn hymn and, singing thus, were thrust along the passages to their appointed seats. This was not, as they expected, a prison at the back of the amphitheatre, but a spot between the enclosing wall and the podium, raised a little above the level of the arena. Here, on the eastern side of the building, they were to sit until their turn came to be driven by the guards through the gate into the arena, where the starving beasts of prey would be loosed upon them.

It was now the hour before sunrise. The moon had set, and the vast theatre was plunged into gloom, relieved only here and there by stray torches and cressets of fire burning upon either side of Agrippa's lavish, but as yet unoccupied, throne. The gloom seemed to oppress the crowding spectators. No one shouted or sang, or even spoke above a murmur. They addressed each other in muffled tones, and the air seemed to be full of mysterious whisperings. Had this poor band of condemned Christians entered the theatre in daylight, they would have been greeted with scornful cries and tauntings of "Dogs' meat!" and with requests that they should work a miracle and let the people see them rise again from the bellies of the lions. But now, as their solemn song broke upon the silence, it was answered only by a great resonant hum that seemed to shape itself to the words, "The Christians! The doomed Christians!"

By the light of a single torch the band took their places. Then on they sang, and in that chastening hour, the audience listened with attention that approached respect. Their chant finished, the bishop stood up and began to address the mighty throng, though they were hidden from each other's eyes by the darkness. Strangely enough they hearkened to him, perhaps because his speech served to while away the weary time of waiting.

"Men and brethren," he began, in his thin, piercing notes. "Princes, lords, peoples, Romans, Jews, Syrians, Greeks, citizens of Idumaea, of Egypt, and of all nations here gathered, hearken to the words of an old man destined and glad to die. If it be your pleasure, hear the story of one whom some of you saw crucified under Pontius Pilate. Knowing the truth of that matter can at least do you no hurt."

"Be silent!" cried the voice of the renegade jailer, "and cease preaching your accursed faith!"

"Let him speak," answered other voices. "We will hear this story of his. We say—let him speak."

Thus encouraged the old man spoke on with an eloquence so simple and yet so touching, with a wisdom so deep, that for fifteen full minutes none cared even to interrupt him. When he had finished a faraway listener cried, "Why must these people, who are better than we, die?"

"Friend," answered the bishop, in ringing tones that in the heavy silence seemed to search out even the recesses of the ampitheatre, "we must die because it is the will of King Agrippa, to whom God has given power to destroy us. Mourn not for us because we perish cruelly, for this is the day of our true birth. Mourn instead for Agrippa, at whose hands our blood will be required, mourn for yourselves, O people! The death that is near to us perchance is nearer still to some of you. How will you awaken who perish in your sins? What if the sword of God should empty that throne? What if the voice of God should call on him who fills it to make answer of his deeds? One day, it will call on him and you to pass into eternity, some in your age, others by the sharp and dreadful means of sword, pestilence, or famine. Already those woes that He whom you crucified fore-told knock at your door, and within a few short years not one of you who crowd this place in thousands will draw the breath of life. Nothing will remain of you on earth save the fruit of those deeds that you have done—these and your bones, no more. Repent, therefore, repent while there is time. For I, whom you have doomed, am bidden to declare that the judgment is at hand. Even now, though you see Him not, the Angel of the Lord hangs over you and writes your names within His book. Now while there is time I would pray for you and for your king. Farewell."

As he spoke those words "the Angel of the Lord hangs over you," so great was the preacher's power, and in that weary dark-ness so sharply had he touched the imagination of his strange audience, that with a sound like to the stir of rustling trees, thousands of faces were turned upwards, as though in search of that dread messenger.

"Look, look!" screamed a hundred voices, while dim arms pointed to some noiseless thing that floated high above them against the background of the sky, which grew gray with the coming dawn. It appeared and disappeared, appeared again, then seemed to pass downward in the direction of Agrippa's throne, and vanished.

"It is that magician's angel," cried one, and the multitudes groaned.

"Fool," said another, "it was but a bird."

"Then for Agrippa's sake," shrilled a new voice, "let us hope it was not an owl."

At that some laughed, but the most were silent. All knew the story of King Agrippa and the owl, and how it had been foretold that this spirit in the form of a bird would appear to him again in the hour of his death, as it had appeared to him in the hour of his triumph.

Their speculations were interrupted by the sound of trumpets, blaring from the palace to the north, and a herald, speaking on the summit of the great eastern tower, calling out that it was dawn above the mountains and that King Agrippa drew near with all his company. The preaching of the old Christian and his tale of a watching Vengeance were instantly forgotten. Presently the stately notes of the trumpets grew louder and clearer, and in the gray of daybreak, through the great bronze gates of the Triumphal Way thrown open to greet him, advanced Agrippa, wonderfully attired and preceded by his legionaries. At his right walked Vibius Marsus, the Roman Governor of Syria, and on his left Antiochus, King of Commagena. After him followed other kings, princes, and great men of his own and foreign lands.

Agrippa mounted his golden throne with great pomp, and while the multitude roared a welcome, those of his company were seated around and behind him according to their rank.

Once more the trumpets sounded, and the gladiators of various arms, led by the *equites* on horseback, numbering in all more than five hundred men, were formed up in the arena for the preliminary march—the salutation of those about to die to their emperor and lord. Now, that they might take part in the spectacle, the band of Christian martyrs were thrust through the door in the podium, marshaled two by two to make them seem as many as possible in number.

Then the march began. Troop by troop, arrayed in their shining armor and armed, each of them, with his own familiar weapon, the gladiators halted in front of Agrippa's throne, giving to him the accustomed salutation of "Hail, King, we who are about to die, salute you," to be rewarded with a royal smile and the shouts of the approving audience. Last of all came the Christians, a motley, wretched-looking group, made up of old men, terrified children clinging to their mothers, and ill-clad, disheveled women. At the pitiful sight, the very mob that a few short minutes before had hung upon the words of the bishop, their leader now, as they watched them hobbling round the arena in the clear, low light of the dawn, burst into peals of laughter and called out that each of them should be made to lead his lion. Quite heedless of these scoffs and taunts, they trudged on through the white sand that would soon be red, until they came opposite to the throne.

"Salute!" roared the audience.

The bishop held up his hand and all were silent. Then, in the thin voice with which they had become familiar he said, "Oh King, we who are about to die . . . have pity on you. May God do likewise."

Now the multitude ceased laughing, and with an impatient gesture, Agrippa motioned to the martyrs to pass on. This they did humbly, but Anna, being old, lame, and weary, could not walk so fast as her companions. She reached the saluting place alone after all had left it, and halted there.

"Forward!" cried the officers. But she did not move or speak, but leaning on her staff she looked steadily up at the face of Agrippa. Some impulse seemed to draw his eyes to hers. They met, and he turned suddenly pale. Then straightening herself upon her tottering feet with difficulty, Anna raised her staff and pointed with it to the golden canopy above the head of Herod. All stared upward, but saw nothing, for the canopy was still in

the shadow of the velarium, which covered all the outer edge
of the dais, leaving the center open to the sky. It would appear,
however, that Agrippa did see something, for he who had risen
to declare the games open, suddenly sank back upon his throne,
and remained there lost in thought. Then Anna limped forward
to join her company, who once more were driven through the
little gate in the wall of the arena.

For a second time, with a visible effort, Agrippa lifted himself
from his throne. As he rose, the first even rays of sunrise struck
full upon him. He was a tall and noble-looking man, and his
dress was glorious. To the thousands who gazed upon him from
the shadow, set in that point of burning light, he seemed to be
clothed in a garment of glittering silver. Silver was his crown,
silver his vest, silver the wide robe that flowed from his shoulders to the ground.

"In the name of Caesar, to the glory of Caesar, I declare these
games open!" he cried at last.

Then, as though moved by a sudden impulse, the multitude
rose as one body shouting, "The voice of a god! The voice of a
god! The voice of the god Agrippa!"

And Agrippa did not gainsay them. The glory of their worship thundered at him from twenty thousand throats, making him drunk. For a while he stood there, the newborn sunlight playing upon his splendid form while the multitude roared his name, proclaiming it divine. His nostrils spread to inhale this incense of adoration; his eyes flashed and slowly he waved his arms, as though in benediction of his worshippers. Perhaps there rose before his mind a vision of the wondrous event whereby he, the scorned and penniless outcast, had been lifted to this giddy pinnacle of power. Perhaps for a moment he believed that he was indeed divine, that nothing less than the blood and right of godhead could thus have exalted him. He stood there, denying nothing, while the people adored him.

Then suddenly the Angel of the Lord smote. An intolerable pain seized upon his vitals, and Herod Agrippa remembered too late that he was but mortal flesh. He knew that death was near.

"Alas!" he cried, "I am no god, but a man, and the common fate of man is on me now."

As he spoke a great white owl slid from the roof of the canopy above him and vanished through the unroofed center of the dais.

"Look! Look! My people!" he cried again, "the spirit that brought me good fortune leaves me now, and I die!" Then, sinking upon his throne, he who a moment ago had received the worship of a god, writhed there in agony and wept.

Attendants ran to him and lifted him in their arms.

"Take me from here to die," he moaned.

Now a herald, at a loss for how to continue the celebration, cried out to the crowds, "The king is smitten with a sore sickness, and the games are closed. To your homes, Oh people."

For a while the multitude sat silent, stricken with fear for their own lives. Then a murmur rose among them that spread and swelled until it became a roar.

"The Christians! The Christians! They prophesied the evil. They have bewitched the king. They are sorcerers. Kill them, kill them, kill them!"

Instantly, like waves bursting through a ruptured dam, thousands of men began to flow towards the place where the martyrs sat. Sweeping aside the guards, the crowd surged against them like water against a rock, but the walls and palisades were to high for them to climb. Those in front began to scream, those behind pressed on. Some fell and were trodden underfoot, others clambered upon their bodies, in turn to fall and be trampled.

"Our death is upon us!" cried one of the Nazarenes.

"No, life remains to us," answered Nehushta. "Follow me, all of you, for I know the road." Seizing Rachel about the waist, she began to drag her towards a little door. It was unlocked and guarded by one man only, the apostate jailer Rufus.

"Stand back!" he cried, lifting his spear.

Nehushta made no answer, but drawing a dagger from her robe, she dropped close to the ground, then suddenly sprang up beneath his guard. The knife flashed and went home to the hilt. Down fell the man screaming for help and mercy, and there, in the narrow way, his spirit left him. Beyond lay the broad passage of the ampitheatre entrance. They gained it, and in an instant were mixed with the thousands who sought to escape the panic. Some perished, some were swept onwards, among them Nehushta and Rachel. Three times they nearly fell beneath the feet of the multitude, but the fierce strength of the Libyan saved her mistress, until at length, they found themselves on the broad terrace facing the seashore.

"Where now?" gasped Rachel.

"Where shall I lead you?" answered Nehushta. "Anywhere but here. Be swift."

"But the others?" said Rachel, glancing back at the fighting, trampling, yelling mob.

"God guard them! We cannot."

"Leave me," moaned her mistress. "Save yourself, Nou. I am spent," and she sank down to her knees.

"But I am still strong," responded Nehushta, and lifting the fainting woman in her sinewy arms, she fled on towards the port, crying, "Way, way for my lady, the noble Roman. She has fainted!"

The multitude made way.

CHAPTER III
THE GRAIN STORE

When they had passed the outer terraces of the amphitheatre in safety, Nehushta turned down a side street and paused in the shadow of the wall to think what she should do. So far they were safe, but even if her strength withstood the strain, it seemed impossible that she could carry her mistress through the crowded city and avoid recapture. For some months both of them had been prisoners, and the custom of the inhabitants of Caesarea, when they had nothing else to do, was to come to the gates of the jail, to study the prisoner through the bars, sometimes even with the permission of the guards, to walk among them. The faces of a Jewish girl and a Libyan woman would not be forgotten by many. As soon as the excitement caused by the illness of the king had subsided, soldiers would be sent to hunt down the fugitives who had escaped from the amphitheatre. They would search especially for Nehushta and her mistress, for by now it must be known that one of them had stabbed the warden of the gate, a crime for which they would die by torture if taken. Where could they go? They had no friends, and all Christians had been expelled from the city.

There was but one chance for them—to conceal themselves.

Nehushta looked round her for a hiding place, and her search finally proved worthwhile. The street in which they stood had been built upon an inner wall of the city, now long dismantled. At a distance of a few yards from where Nehushta had stopped rose an ancient gateway, unused except by the occasional beggar who slept under it. The outer arch of the gateway was bricked up. Into this gateway Nehushta bore her mistress unobserved, finding to her relief that it was quite untenanted, though a fire still smoldered, and a broken amphora containing clean water evidenced that folk who could find no better lodging had slept there recently. It would be scarcely safe to hide here, as the tenants or others might come back. Nehushta looked around again. In the thick wall was a low archway, stretched out over a staircase. Setting Rachel on the ground, she ran up it, lightly as a cat. At the top of thirty steps, many of them broken, she found an old oaken door. With a sigh of disappointment, the Libyan turned to descend again. Before leaving, she pushed at the door, almost in afterthought. To her surprise it shifted inward on its hinges. Again she pushed, and it swung open. Inside was a large chamber, lit by archers' portholes pierced into the thickness of the wall. The room had been converted into a grain merchant's storehouse, and it was clear that it now served no military purpose, for in a corner lay a heap of barley sacks, and strewn about the floor were wineskins and tanning animal hides.

Nehushta examined the room. No hiding place could be better—unless the merchant happened to come to visit his store. Well, that must be risked. Down she sped, and with much toil and difficulty carried her exhausted mistress up the steps and into the chamber, where she laid her on a heap of sacks.

Again, in afterthought, she ventured to descend, this time to fetch the broken jar of water. She returned to the lower room and closed the door, wedging a piece of wood underneath. She sat and began to rub Rachel's hands and sprinkle her face from the jar. Presently the dark eyes opened and her mistress sat up.

"Is it over, and is this Paradise?" she murmured.

"I would not call the place by that name, lady," answered Nehushta dryly, "though perhaps in contrast with the hell that we have left, some might think it so. Drink!" and she held the water to her lips.

Rachel obeyed her eagerly. "Oh, it is good," she said. "But how did we escape the rushing crowd?"

Before she answered, muttering "After the mistress, the maid," Nehushta swallowed a deep draught of water in her turn, which, indeed, she needed sorely. Then she told her all.

"I thank you, Nou," said Rachel. "But for you I should be dead."

"But for God, you mean, mistress. I believe He sent the knife-point home."

"Did you kill the man?" asked Rachel.

"I think that he died by a dagger thrust as Anna foretold," she answered evasively. "And that reminds me that I had better clean the knife. A bloody blade can be evidence against its owner." Then drawing the dagger from its hiding place, she snatched a handful of dust from one of the abandoned loopholes, rubbed it onto the blade, and polished it bright with a piece of hide taken from an empty wineskin.

Scarcely was this task accomplished to Nehushta's satisfaction when her quick ears caught a sound.

"For your life, be silent," she whispered. Then she laid her face sideways to a crack in the cement floor and listened. The voices of soldiers—she counted three—carried into the room.

"That old fellow swore he saw a Libyan woman carrying a lady down this street," said one of them to his companion, "and there was but a single brown-skin in the lot. If they aren't here I don't know where they can be."

"Well," grumbled one of the others, "this place is as empty as a drum. We may as well be going. There'll be fun back there, and I don't want to miss it over lion fodder."

"It was the black woman who knifed your friend Rufus, wasn't it—in the theatre there?" asked the third soldier.

"They say so. But he was trampled as flat as a roof board, and they had to take him up in pieces. It's difficult to tell what really happened. Anyhow his mates are anxious to get the woman, and I'd be sorry to die as she will when they find her, or her mistress either. They have leave to finish them in their own fashion."

"Hadn't we best be going?" said the first soldier, who evidently was anxious to keep some appointment.

"Wait!" exclaimed the second, a sharp-eyed fellow. "There's a stair here. We'd better have a look."

"No use. That's old merchant Amram's grain store there, and he isn't the sort to leave it unlocked. Have a look if you like."

Then came the sound of footsteps on the stair, and presently a man could be heard fumbling at the other side of the door.

Rachel shut her eyes and prayed. Nehushta, drawing the knife from her bosom, crept towards the doorway like a tigress and pressed her left hand against the stick that held it shut. Presently the soldier gave a savage push that might easily have caused the wood to slip on the cemented floor if she had not been there. Satisfied that it would not open, he turned and went down the steps.

With a gasp of relief, Nehushta once more set her ear to the crack.

"Locked," reported the man, "but it might be a good idea to get the key from Amram and have a look anyway."

"Friend," said the officer, "you must be in love with this black lady. Or is it her mistress you admire? I shall recommend you to the cohort for the post of Christian-catcher. We'll try that house at the corner, and if they are not there, I am off to the palace to see how his godship is getting on with that stomachache and whether it has moved him to order payment of our wages. If he hasn't, I'll tell you now that I mean to help myself to something, and so do the rest of the lads. They're just as mad at the stopping of the games."

"It would be much better to get that key from Amram and have a look upstairs," put in the other soldier reflectively.

"Then go to Amram, or to Pluto, and ask for the key of Hades for all I care!" replied the first irritably. "He lives about a league off at the other end of the town."

"I do not wish for the walk," said the conscientious soldier. "But as we are searching for these escaped Christians, by your leave, I do think it would have been much better to have got that key from Amram and peeped into the chamber upstairs."

Thereon the temper of the first soldier, already ruffled by the events of the morning and the long watch of the preceding night, gave way, and he departed, consigning the Christians, escaped or recaptured, Amram and the key, his colleague, and even the royal Agrippa who did not pay his debts, to every infernal god of every religion with which he was acquainted.

Nehushta lifted her head from the floor.

"Thanks be to God! They have gone," she said.

"But, Nou, will they not come back?"

"I think not. That sharp-nosed rat has made the other angry, and I believe that he will find him some harder task than the seeking of a key from Amram. Still, there is danger that this Amram may appear himself to visit his store, for in these days of festival he is sure to be selling grain to the bakers."

Scarcely were the words out of her mouth when a key rattled, the door was pushed sharply, and the piece of wood slipped and fell. The hinges creaked, and a shrewd-faced, middle-aged Phoenician entered, closed the door behind him, and locked it, leaving the key in the lock.

It was Amram. Like most Phoenicians of that day, he was a successful trader, this grain-store representing only one branch of his business. He was clad in a robe and cap of subdued colors and appeared to be unarmed.

Having locked the door, he walked to a little table, beneath which stood a box containing his accounting tablets, and came face to face with Nehushta. Instantly she slid between him and the door.

"Who in the name of Moloch are you?" he asked, stepping back in astonishment. His eyes flashed toward Rachel, seated on the heap of sacks. "And you," he added. "Are you spirits, thieves, ladies in search of a lodging, or—perchance those two Christians whom the soldiers are looking for?"

"We are the two Christians," said Rachel desperately. "We fled from the amphitheatre and have taken refuge here, where they nearly found us."

"This," said Amram solemnly, "is what comes of not locking one's office. Do not misunderstand me. It was no fault of mine. My apprentice is to blame, and I shall have a word to say to him. In fact, I think that I will say it at once," and he stepped towards the door.

"Indeed you will not," interrupted Nehushta.

"And pray, my Libyan friend, how will you prevent me?"

"By putting a knife into your gizzard, as I did through that of the renegade Rufus an hour or two ago! Ah! I see you have heard the story."

Amram considered, then replied, "And what if I also have a knife?"

"In that case," said Nehushta, "draw it, and we will see which is the better, man or woman. Merchant, your weapon is your pen. You have not a chance with me, an Arab of Libya, and you know it."

"Yes," answered Amram, "I think you are right. Desert folk are so reckless and athletic. And to be frank, as you may have guessed, I am unarmed. So what do you propose?"

"I propose that you get us safely out of Caesarea. But if you prefer, that we can all die together here in your grain store, for by whatever god you worship, Phoenician, before a hand is laid upon my mistress or me, this knife goes through your heart. I owe no love to your people. They bought me, a king's daughter, as a slave, and I shall be quite happy to close my account with one of them. Do you understand?"

"Perfectly, perfectly. Why show such temper? The affair is one of business. Let us discuss it in a business spirit. You wish to escape from Caesarea. I wish you to escape from my grain store.

Let me go out and arrange the matter."

"In a box! And not otherwise unless we accompany you," answered Nehushta. "Man, why do you waste words with us. Listen. This lady is the only child of Benoni, the great merchant of Tyre. Doubtless you know him?"

"To my cost," replied Amram, with a bow. "Three times has he overreached me in various bargains."

"Very well. Then you must also know that he is rich and will liberally pay the one who rescues his daughter from great peril."

"He may do so, but I am not sure."

"I am sure," answered Nehushta, "and for this service my mistress here will give you a bill for any reasonable sum drawn upon her father."

"Yes, but the question is—will he honor it? Benoni is a prejudiced man, a very prejudiced man, a Jew of the Jews, who does not like Christians."

"I think that he will honor it still. But that risk is yours. A doubtful payment is better than a slit throat."

"Quite so. Your logic is excellent. But you desire to escape. If you keep me here, how can I arrange the matter?"

"That is for you to consider. You do not leave this place except in our company, and then at the first sign of danger, I drive this knife between your shoulders. Meanwhile my mistress is ready to sign any reasonable payment upon her father."

"It is not necessary. Under the circumstances I think that I will trust the generosity of my fellow trader Benoni. Meanwhile I assure you that nothing will give me greater happiness than to fall in with your views. Believe me, I have no prejudice against Christians, since those whom I have met were always honest and paid their debts in full. I do not wish to see you or your mistress eaten by lions or tortured. I shall be very glad to think that you are following the maxims of your peculiar faith to an extreme old age—somewhere outside of my grain store. The question is, how can I help you do this? At present I see no way."

"The question is—how will you manage to keep your life over the next twelve hours?" answered Nehushta grimly. "Therefore

I advise you to find a way." To emphasize her words she turned, and, having made sure that the door was locked, slipped its key into the bosom of her dress.

Amram stared at her in undisguised admiration. "I would that I were unmarried," he said, "which is not the case," and he sighed. "For then, upon my word, I should be inclined to make a certain proposal to you . . ."

"Nehushta. That is my name—"

"Nehushta—exactly. Well, it is out of the question."

"Quite."

"Therefore I have a suggestion to make. Tonight a ship of mine sails for Tyre. Will you honor me by accepting a passage on her?"

"Certainly," answered Nehushta, "provided that you accompany us."

"It was not my intention to go to Tyre this voyage."

"Then your intention can be changed. Look you, we are desperate, and our lives are at stake. Your life is also at stake, and I swear to you, by the Holy One we worship, that before any harm comes to my mistress, you shall die. Then what will your wealth and your schemes avail you in the grave? It is a little thing we ask of you—to help two innocent people to escape from this accursed city. Will you grant it? Or shall I put this dagger through your throat? Answer at once, or I strike and bury you in your own grain."

Even in that light Amram turned visibly paler. "I accept your terms," he said. "At nightfall I will conduct you to the ship. It sails two hours after sunset with the evening wind. I will accompany you to Tyre and deliver the lady over to her father, trusting to his liberality for my reward. Meanwhile, this place is hot. That ladder leads to the roof. It is well walled, so that those sitting or even standing there cannot be seen. Shall we ascend?"

"If you go first. And remember, should you attempt to call out, my knife is ready."

"Of that I am quite aware—you have said so several times. I have given my word, and I do not go back upon my bargains. The stars are with you, and, come what may, I obey them."

Accordingly they ascended to the roof, Amram going first, Nehushta following him, and Rachel bringing up the rear. Projecting inward from the wall of the rooftop was a sloping shelter once used by lookout sentries in bad or hot weather. The change from the stifling store below with its stench of half-cured hides, to this lofty, shaded spot, where the air moved freely, was so pleasant to Rachel, weary as she was with all she had gone through, that she quickly fell asleep, not to wake again until evening. Amram and Nehushta, who did not sleep, employed themselves in watching the events that passed in the city below. From this height they could see the great square surrounding the palace and the strange scenes being enacted there. It was crowded by thousands of people, for the most part seated on the ground, clad in garments of sackcloth, and throwing dust upon their own heads and upon their wives and children. From the multitude a voice of supplication rose to heaven, which, even at that distance, reached the ears of Nehushta and her companion in a murmur of sound, constant and confused.

"They pray that the king may live," said Amram.

"And I pray that he may die," answered Nehushta.

The merchant shrugged his shoulders. "It matters little to me either way, provided that the peace is not disturbed to the injury of trade. On the whole, however, he is a good king who causes money to be spent, which is what kings are for—in Judea where they are but feathers puffed up by the breath of Caesar, to fall if he ceases to blow. But look!"

As he spoke, a figure appeared upon the steps of the palace and made some communication to the crowd, whereon a great wail went up to the very skies.

"You have your wish," said Amram. "Herod is dead or dying, and now, I suppose, as his son is but a child, we shall be ruled by some accursed thief of a Roman procurator with a pocket like a bottomless sack. That old bishop of yours who preached in the amphitheatre this morning must have had a hint of what was coming from his familiar spirit. Or perhaps he saw the owl and guessed its errand. Trouble must be brewing for others besides Herod, since the old man said as much.

"What became of him and the rest?" asked Nehushta.

"Oh, a few were trampled to death, and others the Jews stirred up the mob to stone, saying that they had bewitched the king, which they, who were disappointed of the games, did gladly. Some, however, are said to have escaped, and, like yourselves, lie in hiding."

Nehushta glanced at her mistress, who was now fast asleep, her pale face resting on her arm.

"The world is hard for Christians," she said.

"It is hard for everyone. Were I to tell you my own story, even you would admit it," he sighed. "At least you Christians believe in something beyond," he went on. "For you death is but a bridge leading to a glorious city, and I imagine that you may be right. Your mistress is quite frail, is she not?"

Nehushta nodded. "She was never very strong, and sorrow has done its work with her. They killed her husband at Berytus yonder, and—her trouble is very near."

"Yes, yes, I heard that story, also that his blood is on the hands of her own father, Benoni. Ah! Who is so cruel as a zealous Jew? Not even we Phoenicians, of whom they say much evil. Once I had a daughter"— here his hard face softened—"but let be, let be! Look you, the risk is great, but I will do what I can to save her, and you also, friend. For, Libyan or no, you are a faithful woman. Nay, do not doubt me. I have given my word, and if I break it willingly, then may I perish and be devoured of dogs. My ship is small and undecked. Your mistress shall not sail in that, but a big galley weighs for Alexandria tonight, stopping at Apollonia and Joppa. You shall make your passage on that, saying that the lady is a relative of mine and that you are her slave. This is my advice to you—go straight to Egypt. There are many Christians there who will protect you for a while. From there your mistress can write to her father and, if he will receive her, return. If not, at least she will be safe, since no writ of Herod stands in Alexandria, and there they do not love the Jews."

"Your counsel seems good," said Nehushta, "if she will consent to it."

"She must consent, who is in no position to make other

plans. Now let me go. Before nightfall I will return again with food and clothing, and lead you to the ship."

Nehushta hesitated.

"I say to you, do not fear. Will you not trust me?"

"Yes," answered Nehushta, "because I must. My words are not kind, I know. But we are in a desperate state, and it is strange to find a true friend in one whom I have threatened with a knife."

"I understand," said Amram gravely. "Let the issue prove me. Now descend so you may lock the door behind me. When I return I will stand in the open space yonder with a slave, making pretence to rebind a burst bundle of merchandise. Then come down and admit me without fear."

When the Phoenician had gone Nehushta sat by her sleeping mistress and waited with an anxious heart. Had she done wisely? Would Amram betray them and send soldiers to conduct them, not to the ship, but to some dreadful death? She could only pray, and pray she did in her fierce, half-savage fashion, never for herself, but for her mistress whom she loved, and for the child that, she remembered thankfully, Anna had foretold would be born and live out its life. Then she remembered that this same holy woman had also said that its mother's hours would be few, and at the thought Nehushta wept.

CHAPTER IV
THE BIRTH OF MIRIAM

Time passed slowly, but none came to disturb them. Three hours after noon Rachel awoke, refreshed but hungry, and Nehushta had no food to give her except raw grain, from which she would not eat. Clearly and in few words she told her mistress all that had passed, asking her consent to the plan.

"It seems as good as any other," said Rachel with a little sigh. "I thank you for making it, Nou, and the Phoenician, if he is honest. I do not wish to see my father again—at least, for many years. How can I, after the evil he has brought upon me?"

"Do not speak of that," interrupted Nehushta hastily, and for a long while they were silent.

It was about an hour before sunset when at length Nehushta saw two figures walk onto the patch of open ground she had watched continually for the better part of the day. Amram and a slave who bore a bundle on his head. Just then, the rope that bound the bundle seemed to come loose; at his master's command, the man set it down and they began to retie it, then advanced slowly towards the archway. Nehushta descended, unlocked the door and admitted Amram, who carried the bundle.

"Where is the slave?" she asked.

"Have no fear, friend; he is trustworthy and watches outside, though he has no notion why. Come, you must both be hungry, and I have food. Help me loose this cord."

Presently the package was opened, and within it appeared two flagons of old wine wrapped with meats more sumptuous then Nehushta had seen for months, rich cloaks and garments made in the Phoenician fashion, and a robe of white with colored edges, like those worn by the body slaves of the wealthy among that people. Finally, Amram produced from within his own robe a purse of gold, enough to support them for many weeks. Nehushta thanked him with her eyes and was about to speak.

"Say nothing," he said quickly before she could voice her mind. "I gave my word, and I have kept it, that is all. And on this money I shall charge interest; your mistress can repay it in happier days. Now listen. I have made arrangements, and an hour after sunset we will board the ship. Only I warn you, do not let it be known that you are escaped Christians, for the seamen think that such folk bring them bad luck. Come. Help me carry the food and wine. After you have eaten, both of you can retire here and robe yourselves."

Presently they ascended the roof.

"Lady," said Nehushta, "we have done well to put trust in this man. He has come back, and see what he has brought us."

"The blessing of God be on you, sir, who help the helpless!" exclaimed Rachel, looking hungrily at the tempting meats, which she sorely needed.

"Drink," said Amram cheerfully, as he mixed wine and water into cup. "It will cheer you, and your faith does not forbid the use of the grape. I have heard you called the society of drunkards."

"That is but one bad name among many, sir," said Rachel, as she took the cup.

Then they ate and were satisfied, and afterwards descended into the grain store to wash with the remainder of the water and clothe themselves from head to foot in the fragrant, beautiful garments that fit so well that they might have been made for them.

By the time that they had dressed, the light was dying. They waited a while for the darkness, and then, with a new hope shining through their fears, crept silently into the street, where the slave, a sturdy, well-armed fellow, kept watch.

"To the harbor," said Amram, and they walked onward, choosing the most quiet and isolated streets. It was now known throughout the city that Agrippa's sickness was mortal; many of the soldiers were already in a state of mutiny and inflamed with wine, parading the marketplaces and central streets, shouting and singing obscene songs, and breaking into the liquor shops and private houses, where they drank health to Charon, who was about to bear away their king to the underworld. They had not yet begun brawling to avenge their personal grudges. That would come later.

The party encountered no trouble on their way to the wharf, where a small boat with two Phoenician rowers was waiting for them. They embarked, all except the slave, and were rowed out to board a large galley that lay anchored half a mile or more away. The air hung heavy, and jagged clouds—*wind breeders* they were called—lay thick upon the horizon. On the lower deck of the galley stood its captain, a sour-faced man, to whom Amram introduced his passengers. "They are," he declared, "relatives of my own, proceeding to Alexandria."

"Well enough," said the captain. "Show them to their cabin. We sail as soon as the wind rises."

They descended to the cabin accordingly, a comfortable place supplied with all that they could need. But as they entered it, Nehushta overheard a sailor who held a lantern saying to his companion, "That woman looks much like the one I saw in the amphitheatre this morning when the condemned gave the salute to King Agrippa."

"The gods forbid it!" answered the other. "We want no Christians here to bring evil fortune on us."

"Christians or no Christians, there is a tempest brewing, if I understand the signs of the weather," muttered the first man.

In the cabin, Amram bade his guests farewell.

"This is a strange adventure," he said, "and one that I did not look for. May it prove to the advantage of us all. I have done my best for your safety, and now we part."

"You are a good man," replied Rachel, "and whatever may befall us, I pray that God may bless you for your kindness to His servants. I pray also that He may lead you to a knowledge of the truth as it was declared by the Lord and Master we serve, that your soul may win salvation and eternal life."

"Lady," said Amram, "I know nothing of your doctrines, but I promise you this: that I will explore them and see whether or not they commend themselves to my reason. I love wealth, like all my people, but I am not altogether a money-seeker. And I have lost those whom I desire to find again."

"Seek and you will find."

"I will seek," he answered, "though, perhaps, I may never find."

Thus they parted.

Presently the night breeze began to flow off the land, the great sail was hoisted; driven by oars worked by slaves, the ship cleared the harbor and set her course for Joppa. Two hours later the wind failed, and they could proceed only by rowing over a dead and oily sea, beneath a sky that was heavy with clouds. Lacking any stars to steer by, the captain wished to cast anchor, but the water proved too deep. So they proceeded slowly, until an hour before dawn a sudden gust rose up and struck them, causing the galley to tilt at a precarious angle.

"The north wind! The black north wind!" shouted the helmsman, and the sailors echoed his cry dismally, for they knew the terrors of that wind upon the Syrian coast. The gale began to rage. By the colorless daylight that reached them through the gray sky, they could see the waves running high as mountains. The wind hissed through the rigging, driving them forward beneath a small sail. Nehushta crawled out of the cabin and saw far away the white walls of a city built upon the shore.

"Is that not Apollonia?" she asked of the captain.

"Yes," he answered, "it is Apollonia sure enough, but we shall not anchor there this voyage. It is Alexandria or the bottom of the sea for us."

So they rushed past Apollonia and forward, climbing the slopes of the rising seas.

About midday the gale became a squall, and in spite of all efforts they were driven forward, until at length they saw the breakers forming on the coast. Rachel lay sick and prostrate, but Nehushta went out of the cabin to watch.

"Are we in danger?" she asked of a sailor.

"Yes, accursed Christian," he replied, "and you have brought it on us with your evil eye."

Then Nehushta returned to the cabin where her mistress lay almost senseless with seasickness. On board the ship, the terror and confusion grew. For a while they were able to steer out to sea, until the beating wind snapped the mast like a twig, hurling it into the water. Then the rudder broke and, as the oars could not be worked in the fearful tempest, the galley began again to drive shoreward. Night fell, hiding the rocky doom that awaited the overwhelmed vessel. All control of the ship was now lost, and she drove onwards at the whim of the wind and the sea. The crew, and even the oar slaves, retreated to the wine cellars and strove to drown their terrors in drink. Thus inflamed, some of them came twice to the cabin, threatening to throw their passengers overboard. But Nehushta barred the door and called through it that she was well armed and would kill the first man who tried to lay a hand upon her. So they went away, and after the second visit they grew too drunk to be of any danger.

Hours seemed like days. Again the dawn broke over the roaring, foaming sea and revealed the fate that awaited them. Not a mile away lay the gray line of shore, but between the ship and the shore the water broke upon a sharply jutting reef. Now the men grew sober in their fear and began to make ready the lifeboat that the galley carried. Before they could flee the doomed vessel, the galley struck the reef prow-first and was driven up by the sea onto a great flat rock where she wallowed, with the waves seething about her. Knowing that their hour was come, the crew made ready to launch the boat on the side of the ship sheltered from the wind, and began to clamber into it.

Now Nehushta came out of the cabin. "Take us with you, Captain! There is room enough in the boat. At least save my lady."

Whereon he answered her, "Neptune take you, black one! All this bad luck is of your doing! Stop; come no closer. If you or your mistress try to enter this boat, we will kill you and offer you to the storm god. Maybe then the storm will end."

So Nehushta struggled back to the cabin, and kneeling by

the side of her mistress, with tears she told her that these black-hearted sailors had left them alone upon the ship to drown. Rachel answered that she cared little, but only desired to be free of her fear and misery.

As the words left her lips, Nehushta heard the sound of screaming. She crawled to the bulwarks and looked out to see a dreadful sight. The boat, laden with a great number of men fighting for places with each other, had loosed from the lee of the ship and was floundering among the breakers, which tossed them up as a child throws a ball. Even while Nehushta gazed, the craft capsized, casting the sailors into the water, every one to be dashed against the rocks or drowned by the violence of the waves. It was over quickly, not a man of all that ship's company came living to the shore.

Giving thanks to God for bringing them out of that danger against their wills, Nehushta crept back to the cabin and told her mistress what had passed.

"May they find pardon," said Rachel, shuddering. "But as for us, it will matter little whether we are drowned in the boat or in this galley."

"I do not think we shall drown," answered Nehushta.

"How are we to escape it, Nou? The ship lies upon the rock, where the great waves will batter her to pieces. Feel how she shakes beneath their blows, and see the spray flying over us."

"I do not know, mistress. But we will not drown."

Nehushta proved right, for after they had remained fast a little longer, they were saved. The wind dropped, then rose again in a last furious squall, driving before it a very wall of water. This vast billow, as it rushed shoreward, caught the galley in its white arms and lifted her not only off the rock where she lay, but over the further reefs, to cast her down again upon a bed of sand and shells within a stone's throw of the beach, where she remained fast, never to shift again.

Now, as though it knew its work was done, the gale ceased and, as is common on the Syrian coast, the storm promptly died. By nightfall it was calm again. Three hours before sunset, if both of them had been strong and well, they might have escaped to the land by wading. But this was not to be, for now what Nehushta had feared befell, and when she was least fitted to bear it, being worn by anguish of mind and weariness of body, the birthing pains took sudden hold of Rachel. Before midnight, there, in that broken vessel upon a barren coast where no man seemed to live, a daughter was born to her.

"Let me see the child," said Rachel. So Nehushta showed it to her by the light of the cabin lamp.

It was a small child, but very white, with blue eyes and dark hair that lay upon her head in matted curls. Rachel gazed at it long and tenderly. Then she said, "Bring me water while there is yet time."

When the water was brought, she dipped her trembling hand into it and placed her palm upon the babe's forehead, baptizing her in the name of the Triune God, christening her Miriam, after her grandmother, to the service and the company of Jesus, the Christ.

"It should have been at the hands of a bishop, but who can say when one will be found? I have faith that God in his mercy will accept. And now," she said, "whether she lives an hour or a hundred years, this child has the sign and seal of Christ upon her. Nou, you are now the foster mother of her body and her soul. Whatever befalls, when she comes to the age of understanding, see to it that she does not forget the rites and duties of her faith. Lay this charge on her also as her father commanded, and as I command, that should she be moved to marriage, she wed none who is not a Christian. I would not that my child were unequally yoked to any man, and I fear the temptation will be great. Tell her, not only was this the will of those who begat her, but that the Lord himself commands it. If she is obedient to this command, the blessing of her parents shall be upon her all her life's days, and with it the blessing of the Lord she serves."

"Oh," moaned Nehushta, "why do you speak thus?"

"Because I am dying. Do not say no. I know it well. My life ebbs from me. My prayers have been answered, and God has preserved me to give this infant birth. Now I go to my appointed place, to one who waits for me, and to the Lord in Whose care we will be in Heaven, as we were in His care on earth. Do not grieve. It is no fault of yours, and I think no physician's skill could have saved me. My strength was spent in suffering, and for many months I have walked the world bearing a broken heart in my breast. Give me of that wine to drink—and listen."

Nehushta obeyed and Rachel went on. "So soon as my breath has left me, take the babe and seek some village on the shore where it can be nursed—you have the means to pay for such a service. Then when she is strong enough, travel not to Tyre, for my father would bring the child up in the strictest rites and customs of the Jews. Go instead to the village of the Essenes upon the shores of the Dead Sea. There find out my mother's brother, Ithiel, who is of their religion, and present to him the tokens of my name and birth, which still hang about my neck. Tell him our story, keeping nothing back. He is not a Christian, but he is a gentle-hearted man, and he thinks well of Christians. He is grieved at our persecution, and he wrote to my father reproving him for his deeds towards us and strove, in vain, to bring about our release from prison. Say to him that I, his kinswoman, pray of him, as he will answer to God, and in the name of the sister whom he loved, to protect my child and you. To do nothing to turn her from her faith, and in all things to deal with her as his wisdom shall direct—for so may peace and blessing come upon him."

Thus spoke Rachel, but in short and broken words. Then she began to pray, and, praying, fell asleep. When she woke again the dawn was breaking. In her weakness she could not speak but beckoned to Nehushta to bring Miriam to her. She gazed upon her earnestly in the newborn light, then placed her hand upon the infant's head. Her lips formed silent words of blessing. Nehushta she blessed also, thanking her with her eyes and kissing her hand. Then again she seemed to fall asleep, and presently, as Nehushta looked at her, she died.

Nehushta understood and gave a great and bitter cry, for after the death of her first mistress, this woman had been all her life. She had nursed her when but a child, when a maiden shared her joys and sorrows, when a wife and widow toiled day and night fiercely and faithfully to console her in her desolation and to protect her in the dreadful dangers through which she had passed. Now, at the end, it was her lot to receive her last breath and to take into her arms her newborn infant.

Then and there Nehushta swore that as she had done for the mother so would she do for the daughter until the day when her labors ended. All her days had been hard—she who was born to a great place among her own wild people far away and snatched away to be a slave, set apart by her race and blood from those into whose city she was sold—she who would have nothing to do with base men nor become the plaything of those of higher birth, she who had turned Christian and drunk deep of the tribulations of the faith, she who had centered all her eager heart upon two beloved women and had lost them both. All her days had been hard, and here and now, by the side of her dead mistress, she might have wished all her labors ended. But the child remained, and while it lived, she would live.

But Nehushta had no time for grief, for the babe must be fed, and within the day. Yet, as she could not bury her departed mistress and would not abandon her to the sea, she gave her mistress a royal funeral after the custom of her own Libyan folk. Fire was close at hand, and what pyre could be grander than this great ship?

Lifting the body from its couch, Nehushta carried it to the deck and laid it by the broken mast, closing the eyes and folding the hands. Then she loosened from about the neck the tokens Rachel had spoken of, packaged some food and garments into a bundle and, carrying the lamp with her, went into the captain's cabin amidships. Here she found an open moneybox, filled with gold and jewels that the sailors had abandoned in their haste. She took them, adding them to her own store and securing them about her. Then she fired the cabin, and passing to the hold, broke a jar of oil and set it to flame. She fled back again as the cabins were engulfed in the blaze, knelt by her dead mistress and kissed her, took the child, wrapping it warmly in a shawl, and by the ladder of rope that the sailors had used, let herself down into the quiet sea. Its waters did not reach higher than her waist, and soon she was standing on the shore and climbing the sand hills that lay beyond. At their summit, she turned to look, and lo! Yonder where the galley was, already a great pillar of fire shot up to heaven, for there was much oil in the hold and it burnt furiously.

"Farewell!" she cried, "farewell!"

Then, weeping bitterly, Nehushta walked on inland.

Chapter v
Miriam is Enthroned

Presently Nehushta found herself out of sight of the sea and among cultivated land, occupied by vines and fig trees grown in gardens fenced with stone walls. Patches of ripening barley and of wheat in the ear covered the rest of the landscape, here and there trodden down by grazing cattle. Beyond these gardens she came to a ridge, and when she had passed over she found a village of many houses built of green brick, some of which seemed to have been scorched by fire. She walked boldly into the village, and the first sight that met her eyes was that of many dead bodies, upon which the dogs were feeding.

On she went up the main street, until she saw a woman peeping at her over a garden wall.

"What has happened here?" asked Nehushta, in the Syrian tongue.

"The Romans! The Romans!" wailed the woman. "The head of our village quarreled with the *publicani* and refused to pay his tax to Caesar. The soldiers came a week ago and slaughtered nearly all of us. They took the sheep and cattle and our children for slaves. Such are the things that chance in this unhappy land. But, woman, who are you?"

"I was shipwrecked!" answered Nehushta, "and I bear with me a newborn babe—nay, the story is too long to tell you. But if there is anyone in this place who can nurse the babe, I will pay her well."

"Give her to me!" said the woman, in an eager whisper. "My child perished in the slaughter. I will nurse her. I ask no pay."

Nehushta looked at her. The woman's eyes were wild, but she was still young and healthy, a Syrian peasant.

"Is your house still standing?" she asked.

"It stands," she nodded, "and my husband lives. We hid in a cave, but our child was out with the child of a neighbor, and we lost her. Quick, give me the babe."

So Nehushta gave Miriam to her, and thus she was nurtured at the breast of one whose offspring had been murdered because the head of the village had quarreled with a Roman tax collector. Such was the world in the days when Christ came to save it.

After she had suckled the child, the woman led Nehushta to her house, a humble dwelling that had escaped the fire. There they found the husband, a winegrower, mourning the death of his infant and the ruin of his town. To him she told as much of her story as she thought wise and gave him a gold piece, which, she told them, was one of the ten she had. He was now penniless, and so accepted it gladly, promising to her lodging, protection, and the service of his wife as nurse to the child for a month at least. So there Nehushta stayed, keeping herself hidden, and at the end of the month gave another gold piece to her hosts, for they were kindly folk that never dreamed of working her evil or injustice. Seeing this, Nehushta found yet more money, wherewith the man, blessing her, bought two oxen and a plough, and hired labor to help him gather what remained of his harvest.

The shore where the infant was born upon the wrecked ship was at a distance of about a league from Joppa and two days' journey from Jerusalem. From there the Dead Sea could be reached in another two days. When Nehushta had dwelt there for some six months, as the babe grew and proved strong, she offered to pay the man and his wife three more pieces of gold if they would travel with her to the neighborhood of Jericho. She also intended to purchase a mule and an ass for the journey, which she said they should keep once the journey was accomplished. The eyes of these simple folk glistened at the prospect of so much wealth, and they agreed readily, promising also to stay three months by Jericho, if need be, until the child could be weaned. So a man was hired to guard the house and vineyard, and they started out in the late autumn, when the air was cool and pleasant.

Their journey was accomplished without trouble, for they were too humble in appearance to attract the notice of the bandits that swarmed upon the highways, or of the soldiers who were set to catch the bandits.

Skirting Jerusalem, which they did not enter, on the sixth day they descended into the valley of the Jordan, through the desolate hills by which it was bordered. They camped that night outside the city and continued at daybreak of the seventh morning. By two hours after noon, they had come to the village of the Essenes. They halted at its outskirts while Nehushta and the nurse, bearing with them the child that by now could wave its arms and cry out in delight, advanced boldly into the village. It appeared that only men dwelt here—at least no women were to be seen. They found one member of the community and asked to be directed to Brother Ithiel.

The man to whom they spoke, who was robed in white and engaged in cooking outside a large building, averted his eyes in answering, as though it were not lawful for him to look upon the face of a woman. He said, very civilly, however, that Brother Ithiel was working in the fields, and he would not return until suppertime.

Nehushta asked where these fields were, as she desired to speak with him at once. The man answered that if they walked towards the green trees that lined the banks of Jordan, they could not fail to find Ithiel, for he was ploughing in the irrigated land with two white oxen, the only ones they had. Accordingly they set out again, having the Dead Sea on their right, and traveled half a league through the thorn scrub growing in the desert. They passed the scrub and came to well-cultivated lands supplied with water, hand-drawn and carried from the Jordan.

In one of these fields, they saw the two white oxen at their toil and behind them the laborer, a tall man of about fifty years of age, bearded, with a calm face and eyes that were deep and quiet. He was clad in a rough robe of camel's hair, fastened about his middle with a leather girdle, and wore sandals on his feet. They went to him, asking leave to speak with him, upon which he halted the oxen and greeted them courteously but, like the

man in the village, turned his eyes away from the faces of the
women. Nehushta bade the nurse stand back out of hearing and,
bearing the child in her arms, said, "Sir, tell me, I pray you, if I
speak to Ithiel, a priest of high rank among this people of the
Essenes, and brother to the dead lady Miriam, wife of Benoni
the Jew, merchant of Tyre?"

At the mention of these names Ithiel's face saddened, then
grew calm again.

"I am so called," he answered. "The lady Miriam was my sister, who now dwells in the happy and eternal country beyond
the ocean with all the blessed"—for so the Essenes imagined the
heaven to which they went when the soul was freed from the
vile body.

"The lady Miriam," continued Nehushta, "had a daughter
Rachel, and I was her servant."

"Was?" he interrupted, startled from his calm. "Has she then
been put to death by those wicked men and their king, as was
her husband Demas?"

"Nay, sir. She died in childbirth, and this is the babe she
bore." She held the sleeping little one towards him, he gazed at
the babe earnestly, moved even to bend down and kiss it.

"Tell me that sad story," he said.

"Sir, I will both tell and prove it true." And Nehushta told
him all from beginning to end, producing for him the tokens
she had taken from the breast of her mistress and repeating her
last message to him, word for word. When she had finished,
Ithiel turned away in silent mourning for his niece. Then, speaking aloud, he put up a prayer to God for guidance—for without
prayer these people would not enter upon any agreement, however simple—and came back to Nehushta, who was standing by
the oxen.

"Good and faithful woman," he said. "It would seem you
are not fickle and lighthearted, or worse, like the multitude of
women—perhaps because your dark skin shields you from their
temptations. But you have caught me in a dilemma, and there I
am held fast. You must know that the law of my order is that we
should have naught to do with females, young or old. So how

can I receive you or the child?"

"Of the law of your order, sir, I know nothing," answered Nehushta sharply, since the words about the color of her skin had not pleased her. "But of the law of nature I do know, and something of the law of God also for, like my mistress and this infant, I am a Christian. These laws tell me that to cast out an orphan child who is of your own blood, whom a cruel fortune has thus brought to your door, would be an evil act. One for which you must answer to Him who is above the law of any order."

"I am not permitted to wrangle with a woman," replied Ithiel, who seemed ill at ease. "But if my first words are true, this is true also: that those same laws enjoin upon us hospitality, and above all, that we must not turn away the helpless or the destitute."

"Clearly, then, least of any must you turn away this child whose blood is your blood, and whose dead mother sent her to

you, that she might not fall into the power of a grandfather who
has dealt cruelly with those he should have cherished. You must
not abandon her to be brought up among Zealots as a Jew and
taught to make offering to a God who no longer hears."

"No, no, the thought is horrible," answered Ithiel, holding up
his hands. "It is better, far better that she should be a Christian
than one of that obstinate faith." This he said, because among
the Essenes the priesthood of the Temple in Jerusalem was
deemed to be invalid, and they had made an interruption to
blood sacrifice in anticipation of the messiah, an anointed one
whom they believed would be a warrior that would cleanse the
Temple and drive the Romans from the face of the earth.

"The matter is too hard for me," he went on. "I must lay
it before a full Court of the hundred curators, and what they
decide, that will be done. Still, this is our rule: to assist those
who need and to show mercy, to accord aid to such as require
it, and to give food to those in distress. Therefore, whatever the
Court, which it will take three days to summon, may decide, in
the meantime I have the right to give you, and those with you,
shelter and provision in the guesthouse. It stands in the part of
the village where dwell the lowest of our brethren, who are permitted to marry, so there you will find company of women."

"I shall be glad of it," answered Nehushta dryly. "And I
should call them the highest of the brethren, since marriage is
of God, which God the Father has instituted, and God the Son
has blessed."

"I may not wrangle, I may not wrangle," replied Ithiel, declin-
ing the encounter, "but certainly, that is a lovely babe. Look. Her
eyes open and they as are beautiful as flowers." Again he bent
down and kissed the child, then added with a groan of remorse,
"Alas! Sinner that I am, I am defiled. I must purify myself and
do penance."

"Why?" asked Nehushta shortly.

"Because I have touched your dress, and I have given way to
earthly passion and embraced a child—twice! According to our
law, I am defiled."

Nehushta could bear no more.

"Defiled! You puppet of a foolish rule! It is the sweet babe that is defiled! Look, you have fouled its garments with your grimy hand and made it weep by pricking it with your beard. Would that your holy rule taught you how to handle children and to respect honest women who are their mothers, without whom there would be no Essenes."

"I may not wrangle," repeated Ithiel nervously, for now this woman was appearing before him in a new light. Not as artful and fickle, but as an angry creature, reckless of tongue and not easy to be answered. "These matters are for the decision of the curators. Have I not told you so? Come, let us be going. I will drive the oxen. You and your companion walk at a distance behind me. No, not behind—in front, so I may see to it that you do not drop the babe or let it to come to any harm. Truly she is sweet to look at and, may God forgive me, I do not like to lose sight of its face. She is much like my sister when she was also in arms."

"Drop the babe!" began Nehushta with a tone of indignation. Then she understood that this victim of a rule already loved the child dearly and would suffer much before he parted with it. Pitying his weakness, she said only, "Be careful that you do not frighten it with your great oxen, for you men who scorn women have much to learn."

Then, accompanied by the nurse, she stalked ahead in silence while Ithiel followed after at a distance, leading the cattle by the hide loops about their horns lest in their curiosity or eagerness to get home, they should do some mischief to the infant or wake it from its slumber. They proceeded thus to the lower part of the village until they came to a well-furnished house—empty at that season—where guests were accommodated in the best fashion this kind and homely folk could afford. Here a woman was summoned, the wife of one of the lower order of the Essenes, to whom Ithiel spoke, holding his hand before his eyes, as though she were not good to look at. From a distance so modest that he had to raise his voice, he explained to her the case, bidding her to provide all things needful, and to send a man to bring in the husband of the nurse with the beasts of burden and attend to his wants and theirs. Then, warning Nehushta to be very careful of the infant and not to expose it to the sun, he departed to report the matter to the curators and summon the great Court.

"Are all of them like this?" Nehushta asked the woman in frustration.

"Yes, sister," she answered, "fools, every one. I see my own husband very rarely, and although he ranks lowly among them because he is married, the man is forever telling me of the faults of women, and how they are a snare set for the feet of the righteous, leading the righteous astray, especially if they be not their own husbands. At times I am tempted indeed to prove his words true. Oh! It would not be difficult for all their high talk. I have learned enough of that, for God's creation is apt to make a mock of those who deny it. But they mean well, so laugh at them and let them be, I say. And now come into the house. It is good enough for house guests, though if they allowed women to manage it, it would be better."

So Nehushta entered the house with the nurse and her husband, and for several days dwelt there in reasonable comfort. Indeed, there was nothing that she or the child, or those with them, could want that was not provided in plenty. Messages even reached her by the woman to ask if she would wish the rooms altered in any way. When she said that there was not light enough in the room where the child slept, some of the elders of the Essenes arrived and knocked a new window in the wall, working very hard to finish the task before sunset. Even the husband of the nurse was not allowed to attend to his own beasts, which were groomed and fed for him until at length he grew so weary of doing nothing that he went out to plough with the Essenes and work in the fields.

The full Court was gathered on the fourth morning in the great meetinghouse, and Nehushta was summoned to appear before it and to bring the babe with her. She entered the meetinghouse to find the place filled with a hundred grave and devout men, all clad in robes of the purest white. She sat alone on a chair in the lower part of the great chamber, while upon benches ranged before her, one above the other so that all could see, were gathered the hundred curators.

It seemed that Ithiel had already presented the case, for the Overseer at once began to question her on various points of her story, all of which she patiently explained to the satisfaction of the Court. Then they debated the matter among themselves, some of them arguing that as the child and its nurse were both female, neither of them could properly be admitted to the care of the community, especially as both were of the Christian faith, and it was stipulated that in this faith they must remain. Others answered that hospitality was their first duty, and that one would be weak indeed to be led aside from their rule by a Libyan woman of middle age and an infant of a few months. They contended further that the Christians were a good people, and that there was much in the Christian doctrines that agreed with their own. Next, one made a strange objection—namely, that if they adopted this child they would learn to love it too much, when they should love God and their order only. To this another answered, nay, they should love all mankind, and especially the helpless.

"Mankind, not womankind," was the reply. "And this infant will grow into a woman."

Now they desired Nehushta to retire that they might take the vote. Before she went, however, holding up the child that all could see it as it lay smiling in her arms, she implored them not to reject the prayer of a dead woman and so deprive this infant both of the care of the relative whom the departed lady had appointed to be its guardian and the guidance of their Order. Lastly, she reminded them that if they thrust her out, she would have no choice but to bear the infant to its grandfather, who, if he received the child at all, would certainly bring it up in the Jewish faith and thereby, perhaps, cause it to lose its soul, and the weight of the sin would be upon their heads.

After this, Nehushta was led away to another chamber and remained there a long while, until at length she was brought back again by one of the curators. Upon entering the great hall her eyes sought the face of Ithiel, who had not been allowed to speak since it was determined that his judgment might be impaired in a matter concerning his own grandniece. Seeing that he smiled and evidently was well pleased, she knew her cause was won.

"Woman," said the Overseer, "by a great majority of this Court we have come to an irrevocable decision upon the matter that has been laid before us by our brother Ithiel. The decision of the Court is, for reasons I need not explain, that on this point our rule may be stretched so far as to admit the child Miriam to our care, even though it be of the female sex. The care of the Order is to endure until she comes to a full age of eighteen years, when she must depart from among us. During this time, no attempt will be made to turn her from her parents' faith into which she has been baptized. A house will be given you to live in, and both you and our ward, Miriam, will be supplied with the best we have. Twice a week a deputation of the curators will visit the house and stay there for an hour to see that the health of the infant is good, and that you are doing your duty by it, in which, if you fail, you will be removed. It is asked that you do not talk to these curators on matters that do not concern the child. When she grows old enough, the maid Miriam will be admitted to our gatherings and instructed by the most learned amongst us in all proper matters of letters and philosophy, on which occasions you will sit at a distance and not interfere unless your care is required.

"Now, that every one may know our decision, we will escort you back to your house, and to show that we have taken the infant under our care, our brother Ithiel will carry it while you walk behind and give him such instruction in this matter as may be needful."

Accordingly a great procession of grand somberness was assembled as the entire Court paraded to the appointed house, headed by the Overseer with the priestly members trailing behind. In the center of the line marched Ithiel bearing the babe Miriam, to his evident delight, and Nehushta, who instructed him so vigorously that at length he grew confused and nearly let it fall. Thereon, defying this detail of the Court's judgment, Nehushta snatched Miriam from his arms, calling him a clumsy and ignorant clown only fit to handle an ox. To this Ithiel made no answer, nor was he at all angry, but finished the journey walking behind her and smiling foolishly.

Thus was the child Miriam royally escorted to her home. But little did these good men know that it was not a house which they would give her, but a throne, built of the pure gold of their own gentle hearts. For as she grew from an infant into womanhood, she came to be called by them all: the Queen of the Essenes.

Chapter VI
Caleb

It may be wondered whether any girl ever born into this world could boast a stranger or a happier upbringing than Miriam. She was motherless, but by way of compensation, Providence had endowed her with several hundred fathers, each of whom loved her as the apple of his eye. She did not call them "Father," a term that under the circumstances they thought inappropriate. To her, one and all, they went by the designation of "Uncle," with their name added if she happened to know it. It cannot be said, however, that Miriam brought peace to the community of the Essenes. Indeed, before her sojourn with them was complete, she had rent it with deep and abiding jealousies, to the intense but secret delight of Nehushta, who, although she became a person of great importance among them as the one who had immediate charge of their jewel, could never forgive them certain of their doctrines or their habit of persistent interference.

The domiciliary visits that took place twice a week and, by special subsequent resolution passed in full Court, on the Sabbath also, were the first subject of such veiled bitterness. At first a standing committee was appointed to make these visits, of which Ithiel was one. But before two years had gone by, much grumbling had arisen in the community regarding this matter. The dissenters pointed out in increasingly vehement language— for an Essene—that so much power should not be left in the hands of one fixed set of individuals that might become careless or prejudiced, or worst of all, neglectful of the child's welfare. For Miriam was the guest not only of the individuals of the committee, but of the whole Order. It was demanded, therefore, that this committee should alternate every month, so that all might serve upon it in turn, Ithiel, as the blood relation of

Miriam, remaining its only permanent member. The committee opposed this proposal with equally heated speech, but no one else would vote in their favor, so the desired alteration was made. Further, the temporary or permanent exclusion from this roster was from that point recognized as one of the punishments of the Order.

The absurdities to which its existence gave rise, especially as the girl grew in years, sweetness and beauty, are innumerable. It was judged that every visiting member must wash his whole person and clothe himself in clean garments before he was allowed to approach the child, "lest he should convey to her any sickness or impure substance or odor."

When Miriam was five years old, there was much trouble when some members were discovered to be ingratiating themselves with her by secretly presenting her with gifts of playthings, some of them of great beauty, which they fashioned from wood, shells, or even hard stones. Moreover, they found that the child had a taste for sweets, and it was this that led to their discovery. For once, when they had given too much and she had eaten all, she became ill. Nehushta, enraged, disclosed the whole plot, using the most violent language and, amidst the collective murmurs of fatherly indignation, designated the offenders by name. They were removed from their office, and it was decreed that henceforth any gifts made to the child must be offered to her by the committee as a whole, not by a single individual, and they would be handed over in their name only by Ithiel, her uncle.

When Miriam was seven years old and the darling of every brother among the Essenes, she fell ill with a dangerous fever. Among the brethren were several skilled physicians, who attended her night and day. But still the fever could not be abated, and at last, with tears, they announced that they feared for the child's life. Then indeed there was lamentation among the Essenes. For three days and three nights they wrestled in constant prayer to God that she might be spared, many of them touching nothing but water during all that time. They sat about at a distance from her house, praying and seeking tidings. If it was bad, they beat their breasts; if good, they gave thanks.

Never was the sickbed of a monarch watched with more care or devotion than that of Miriam, and never was a recovery—for at length she did recover—received with greater thankfulness and joy.

This was the truth of it: These simple men, in obedience to the strict rule they had adopted, were cut off from all the affections of life. Yet the foundation of their doctrine being love, they who were human must love something, so they loved this child whom they looked upon as their ward, and who, as there was none other of her age and sex in their community, had no rival in their hearts. She was the one joy of their laborious and ascetic hours. She represented all the sweetness and youth of rejuvenation in the world, which to them was so gray and dismal. And she was a lovely maid who, wherever she had dwelt, would have bound all to her.

The years went by, and the time came when, in obedience to the first decree, Miriam must be educated. Long were the discussions that ensued among the curators of the Essenes. At length three of the most learned of their body were appointed to this task, and the teaching began. Miriam proved an apt pupil, for her memory was good, and she had a great desire to learn many things, most especially history and languages, and all things relating to the wonders of creation. One of her tutors was an Egyptian who had been brought up in the priests' college at Thebes, and on a journey to Judea had fallen sick near Jericho. He had been nursed by the Essenes and converted to their doctrine. From him Miriam learnt much of their ancient civilization, and even of the inner mysteries of the Egyptian religion, and of its high and secret interpretations, which were known only to the priests. The second, Theophilus by name, was a Greek who had visited Rome, and he taught her the tongues and literature of those countries. The third, all his life long had studied beasts, birds, insects, the workings of nature, the stars and their movements, in which things he instructed her day by day, taking her abroad with him so she might see these things with her own eyes.

Lastly, when she grew older, she was given a fourth master, an artist. He taught Miriam how to fashion animals and the human form from the clay of the Jordan, how to chisel them in marble, and how to paint them on wooden boards and goatskins. This man, whose gifts were ill-used in this ascetic community, also had some skill of singing and the playing of the cithara, which he taught her in her odd hours. Thus it came about that Miriam grew learned and well-acquainted with many matters that most women had never even imagined.

Nor did she lack knowledge of her own faith, though in these the Essenes did not instruct her further than its doctrines agreed with their own. Of the rest, Nehushta told her something, and on several occasions Christian travelers or preachers visited this country to address the Essenes. When they learned of Miriam, they showed themselves eager to teach her the Christian doctrine. Among them was one old man who had heard the teachings of Jesus Christ, and had been present at His Crucifixion. The girl listened eagerly to all of his stories, remembering them to the last hour of her life.

She lived daily in the company of nature. The Dead Sea lay but a mile or two away, and along its melancholy and lifeless shores, fringed with the white trunks of trees that had been brought down by Jordan, she would often walk. Before her, day by day, loomed the mountains of Moab, while behind her were the fantastic and mysterious sand hills of the desert, backed again by towering mountains and the gray tormented country stretching between Jericho and Jerusalem. The broad and muddy Jordan ran near at hand, whose fertile banks were clothed in spring with the most delicious greenery and haunted by kingfishers, cranes, and wildfowl. About these banks, stretching into the desert land beyond, the flowers of the field grew by myriads, at different periods of the year carpeting the whole earth with various colors, brilliant as the spectrum of the rainbow. She delighted in gathering these and even cultivated them in the garden of her house.

Thus wisdom, earthly and divine, was gathered in Miriam's heart until its light began to shine through her eyes, making them ever more tender and beautiful. And she had no lack of charm or grace. She had always been possessed of a slight figure, with a pale complexion that seemed to glow in the desert sun. Her hair hung dark about her shoulders in thick curls, and her eyes were large and of a deep and tender blue. Her hands and feet were slender, and her every gesture quick and agile as a bird. Thus she passed her girlhood loving all things and beloved by all, for even the flowers she tended and the creatures she fed seemed to find a friend in her.

Nehushta did not approve of so much learning and all this system of solemn ordered hours. For a while she bore with it, but when Miriam was about eleven years of age, she spoke her mind to the Committee and through them to the governing Court of Curators.

Was it right that a child should be brought up thus, she asked, and turned into a grave old woman while, others of her age were occupied with youthful games? The end of it might be that her mind would give way and she would die or become crazy. And then what good would so much knowledge do her? It was necessary that she should have more leisure and other children with whom she could associate.

"White-bearded hermits," she added pointedly, "are not suitable as sole companions to a little maid."

There followed much debate and consultation with the doctors, who agreed that friends of her own years should be found for the child. This, however, proved difficult, for no other girls dwelt among the Essenes. Therefore her friends must all be boys. Even this presented difficulties, as among the boys adopted by the community there was but one of equal birth with Miriam. As far as concerned their own order, the Essenes thought little of social distinctions. But Miriam was not of their order. She was their guest to whom they stood in the place of her parents, and who would go from them out into the great world. Despite their stern views, many of them were men experienced in life, and they did not think it right that she should mix with those of lower station.

The one lad, Caleb, was born in the same year as Miriam when Cuspius Fadus became governor upon the death of Agrippa. His father, Hilliel, was a Jew of high rank who, although he had sided occasionally with the Romans, had been killed by them, or had perished among the twenty thousand who were trampled to death at the Feast of the Passover at Jerusalem when the Procurator Cumanus ordered his soldiers to attack the people. The Zealots, who considered him a traitor because of his alliances with Rome, took possession of all his property, and his son Caleb, whose mother was dead, was brought to Jericho destitute. There, because there was no other way to dispose of him, he was given over to the Essenes to be educated in their doctrine, and, should he wish it, to enter their order when he reached full age. This lad, it was now decreed, should become the playmate of Miriam, a decision that pleased both children very well.

Caleb was a handsome child with flashing dark eyes that watched everything without seeming to watch, and black hair that curled down just below his ears. He was clever as well as brave, but though he did his best to control his temper, he was by nature very passionate and unforgiving. That which he desired he would have, by any means it could be obtained, and he was as faithful in his hates as in his loves. Of his hates, Nehushta was one. With all the skill of a Libyan, whose only guide is that of nature and men's faces, she read the boy's heart at once and said openly that he might come to be the first in any cause— if he did not betray it—and that God had mixed his blood of the best, but lest Caesar should find a rival, He left out the salt of honesty and filled up Caleb's cup with the wine of passion. When Miriam, who thought this a jest fit to tease her playmate, repeated it to him, he did not fly into one of his tempers, as she had hoped, but only screwed up his eyelids after his fashion in certain moods and looked black as the rainstorm above Mount Nebo.

"Did you hear, Caleb?" asked Miriam, somewhat puzzled at his strange reaction.

"Oh, yes, Lady Miriam!" he answered, as he had been ordered to call her. "I heard. Do tell that old black woman that I will lead more causes than she ever dreamed of, for I mean to be the first everywhere. And whatever God left out of my cup, at least He mixed it with a good memory."

When Nehushta heard of this, she laughed and said that it was true enough, but he that tried to climb several ladders at once generally fell to the ground, and when a head had said goodbye to its shoulders, the best of memories got lost between the two.

Miriam liked Caleb, but she never loved him as she did the old men, her uncles, or Nehushta, who to her was more than all. Perhaps this may have been because he never grew angry with her whatever she said or did, never even spoke to her roughly, but always waited on her pleasure and watched for her wish. But of all companions, he was the best. If Miriam desired to walk by the Dead Sea, he would desire the same. If she wanted to go fishing in the Jordan, he would make ready the baits or net and take the fishes off the hook—the only part of fishing she hated. If she sought a rare flower, Caleb would hunt it out for days, though she knew well that in himself he did not care for flowers, and when he had found it, he would mark the spot and lead her there in triumph. There was one thing about him that she was soon perceptive enough to learn: he worshipped her. Whatever else might be false, that note in his nature rang true. If one child could love another, then Caleb loved Miriam, first with the love of children, then as a man loves a woman. But Miriam never loved Caleb. Had she done so, both their stories might have been very different. But to her, he was never more than a pleasant companion.

What made the thing stranger was that he loved no one else except, perhaps, himself. In one way or another, the lad soon came to discover his own history, which was sad enough, with the result that if he hated the Romans who had invaded the country and trampled it beneath their heel, still more did he hate those of the Jews who looked upon his father as their enemy and had stolen all the lands and goods that were his by right. As for the Essenes who reared and protected him, as soon as he came to an age when he could weigh such matters, he held them in contempt, and because of their habitual bathing he called them a company of washerwomen. Their doctrines left on him but a shallow mark. He thought, as he explained to Miriam, that people who were in the world should take the world as they found it, without dreaming ceaselessly of another world to which, as yet, they did not belong.

Wishing, with the zeal of the young, to make a convert, Miriam preached to him the doctrine of Christianity, but without success. By blood, Caleb was a Jew of the Jews, and would not understand or admire a God who would consent to be trodden underfoot and crucified. The Messiah he desired to follow must be a great conqueror, one who would overthrow Rome and take the throne of Caesar. The idea of the humble creature with his mouth full of maxims did not impress him. Like the majority of his own and, indeed, of every generation, Caleb did not perceive that mind is equal to matter, while spirit directs them both, so that in the end, by many slow advances and after many seemingly irremediable disasters, spirit will overcome. He looked to a sword flashing from thrones, not to the word of truth spoken by lowly lips in humble streets or upon the flanks of deserts, trusting to the winds of Grace to bear it into the hearts of men and thus regenerate their souls.

The years went swiftly by. Tumults arose in Judea, and massacres in Jerusalem. False prophets like Theudas, who pretended that he could divide Jordan, attracted thousands to their tinsel standards, to be hewn down by the Roman legions. Caesars rose and fell. The great Temple was almost completed in its full glory, and many events that have never fully been forgotten took place.

But in the little village of the Essenes by the gray shores of the Dead Sea, nothing seemed to change, except that now and then an aged brother died, and now and then a new brother was admitted. They rose before daylight and offered their invocation to God. They went out to toil in the fields and sowed their crops, to reap them in due season, thankful if they were good, still thankful if they were bad. They washed, they prayed, they interceded in prayer for the wickedness of the world and wove themselves white garments emblematic of a better. Although of this Miriam knew nothing, they held higher and more secret gatherings wherein they invoked the presence of the angels and by arts of divination foretold the future, an exercise that brought them little joy. But as yet, however evil might be the omens, none came to molest their peaceful life, which ran quietly towards the looming catastrophe as deep waters swirl to the lip of a precipice.

When Miriam was eighteen years of age, the first shadow of trouble fell upon them.

Once every year the high priests of Jerusalem, who considered the Essenes heretics, had made demands upon them that they should pay tithe for the support of the sacrifices in the Temple. This they refused to do, for they would not acknowledge the legitimacy of the Temple sacrifice, waiting instead for the Day of the Lord. So things went on until the appointment of the high priest Ananus, who sent armed men to the village of the Essenes to take the tithe. When they were refused, they broke open the granary and helped themselves, destroying a great deal that they could not carry away. On that day Miriam, accompanied by Nehushta, had visited Jericho. When they returned in the afternoon, they passed through a riverbed scattered about with many rocks, with thickets of thorn trees among them. There they were met by Caleb, now a noble-looking youth, very strong and active. He was carrying a bow in his hand, and on his back was a quiver of six arrows.

"Lady Miriam," he bowed, "well met. I have come to seek you, and to warn you not to return by the road today, else you may be met by those thieves sent by the high priest to plunder the stores of the Order. They may offer you insult or mischief. Last I saw them, they were drunk with wine. Look. One of them struck me," and he pointed to a bruise upon his jaw and scowled.

"What shall we do?" asked Miriam. "Go back to Jericho?"

"No, they will go there too. Follow this gully until you reach the footpath a mile away, and walk from there to the village. You will avoid these robbers that way."

"It is a good plan," said Nehushta. "Come, lady."

"Where are you going, Caleb?" asked Miriam, lingering, for she saw that he did not mean to accompany them.

"I? Oh, I plan to hide among the rocks nearby until they've passed, and then go to seek that hyena which has been worrying the sheep. I have tracked him down and may catch him as he comes from his hole at sunset. That is why I have brought my bow."

"Come," broke in Nehushta impatiently. "Come. The lad well knows how to guard himself."

"Be careful, Caleb, that you come to no harm from the hyena," said Miriam, doubtfully, as Nehushta seized her by the wrist and dragged her away. "It is strange," she added as they went, "that Caleb should choose this evening to go hunting."

"Unless I am mistaken, it is a human hyena he hunts," answered Nehushta shortly. "One of those men struck him, and he desires to wash the wound with the man's blood."

"Oh, Nou, surely not! That would be taking vengeance, and revenge is evil."

Nehushta shrugged her shoulders. "Caleb may think otherwise, as I do at times. Wait, and we shall see."

As it chanced, they did see something. The footpath by which they returned to the village ran over a high ridge of ground, and from its crest, though they were far away, in the clear desert air they could easily discern the line of the high priest's servants straggling along, driving before them a score or so of mules laden with wine and other produce they had stolen from the stores. Presently the company descended into the gully along the road; and, a minute or two later, there arose a sound of distant shouting. Then they appeared on the far side, or riding their horses up and down as though in search of someone while four of them carried between them a man who seemed to be hurt or dead.

"I think that Caleb has shot his hyena," said Nehushta meaningfully, "but I have seen nothing, and if you are wise, you will say nothing. I do not like Caleb, but I hate these Jewish thieves, and it is not for you to bring your friend into trouble."

Miriam looked frightened but nodded her head, and no more was said of the matter.

That evening as Miriam and Nehushta stood by the doorway

of their garden, in the light of the full moon, they saw Caleb advancing towards them down the road, a sight that made Miriam glad at heart, for she feared lest he might have come into trouble. He caught sight of them and asked them leave to enter through the door, which he closed behind them so that they stood in the little garden within the wall.

"Well," said Nehushta. "I see you have had a shot at your hyena. Did you kill it?"

"How do you know that?" he asked, looking at her suspiciously.

"A stupid question to ask a Libyan woman who was brought up among archers," she replied. "You had six arrows in your quiver when we met you, and now I count but five. Your bow was newly waxed then, and the wax has been rubbed off where the shaft lay."

He grunted in assent. "I shot at the beast, and I believe I hit it. At least, I could not find the arrow again, though I searched long."

"Doubtless. You do not often miss. You have a good eye and a steady hand. Well, the loss of a shaft will not matter. I noticed this one was differently barbed from the others, and double feathered. A true Roman warshaft, such as they do not make here. If any find your wounded beast, you will not get its hide, for everyone knows you do not use such arrows." Then, with a knowing smile, Nehushta turned and entered the house, leaving him staring after her, half in wrath and half in wonder at her wit.

"What does she mean?" he asked Miriam, but in the voice of one who speaks to himself.

"She thinks that you shot at a man, and not a beast," replied Miriam. "But you would not have done that! It would not be right."

"Even the rule of the Essenes permits a man to protect himself and his property from thieves," he answered sulkily.

"Yes, to protect himself if he is attacked, and his property— if he has any. But neither that faith nor mine permits him to avenge a blow."

"I was one against many," he answered boldly. "My life was at risk. It was no coward's act."

"Were there, then, a troop of these hyenas?" asked Miriam, innocently raising her eyebrows. "I thought you said it was a solitary beast that took the sheep."

"It was a whole company of beasts who took the wine and smote those in charge of it like dogs on the street."

"Hyenas that took wine like the tame ape whom the boys make drunk over yonder—"

"Why do you mock me," broke in Caleb. "You must know the truth. Or if you do not know it, here it is. That thief beat me with his staff and called me the son of a dog. I swore that I would pay him back. Pay him back I did, for the head of the shaft that Nehushta noted now stands out a span beyond his neck. They never saw who shot it. They never saw me at all, and they thought at first that the man had only fallen from his horse. By the time they knew the truth, I was well away. Now go and tell the story if you will, or let Nehushta tell it, and give me over to be tortured by the servants of the high priest or crucified as a murderer by the Romans."

"Neither Nehushta nor I saw this deed done, nor shall we bear witness against you, Caleb. But Caleb, you told me that you came out to warn us, and it grieves me to learn the true wish of your heart was to take the life of a man."

"It is a lie," he answered angrily. "I said that I came to warn you, and afterwards to kill a hyena. To make you safe—that was my first thought, and until you were safe, my enemy was safe also. Miriam, you know that well."

"How should I know it, Caleb? To you I think revenge is more than friendship."

"Perhaps, for I am but a penniless orphan brought up by charity, and I have few friends. But, Miriam, to me revenge is not more than . . . love."

"Love," she stammered, turning crimson to her hair and stepping back a pace. "What do you mean, Caleb?"

"I mean what I say, no more, no less," he answered sullenly. "As I have worked one crime today, I may as well work another and dare to tell the Lady Miriam, Queen of the Essenes, that I love her. Even if she does not love me—yet."

"That is madness," faltered Miriam.

"Perhaps, but it is a madness that began when I first saw you—that was soon after we learned to speak—a madness which will continue until I cease to see you, and that shall be when I grow silent forever. Listen, Miriam, and do not think my words only those of a foolish boy, for all my life shall prove them. My love is a thing you must have guessed. You love me not, and even had I the power I would not force myself upon you against your will. But I warn you, learn to love no other man, for then it shall go ill either with him or with me. By this I swear it." And snatching her to him, Caleb kissed her on the forehead. Then he let her go and said, "Fear not. It is the first and last time, unless by your own will. Or if you are afraid, tell the story to the Court of the Essenes, and to Nehushta. I am sure they will right your wrongs."

"Caleb," she gasped, stamping her foot upon the ground in anger, "Caleb, you are more wicked than I dreamed, and," she added, as though to herself, "and greater!"

"Yes," he answered, as he turned to go, "I think you are right. I am more wicked than you dreamed and greater. But I love you as you will never be loved again. Farewell!"

CHAPTER VII
MARCUS

That night the curators engaged in prayer and fasting were disturbed by the return of an officer of the Jews that had robbed them, who complained violently that a man of his company had been murdered by one of the Essenes. They asked how and when and were told that the man had been shot down with an arrow by an unknown person in a gully upon the road to Jericho. They replied that robbers sometimes met with robbers, and asked to see the arrow, which proved to be of a Roman make, such as these men carried in their own quivers. The Essenes pointed this out, and at length, growing angry at the unreasonableness of a complaint made by persons of the worst character, drove him and his escort from their doors, bidding them take their story to the high priest Ananus, with the goods they had stolen or, if they preferred it, to a still greater thief, the Roman procurator, Albinus.

The Jews did not neglect to do this, and presently the Essenes were commanded to send some of their leaders to appear before Albinus in answer to charges laid against them. Accordingly, they dispatched Ithiel and two others, who were kept waiting three months in Jerusalem before they could even obtain a hearing. At length the cause was brought to the floor, and after some few minutes of talk it was adjourned, being but a petty matter. That same evening, Ithiel was informed by an intermediary that if the Order would pay a large sum of money to Albinus, nothing more would be heard of the question. The Essenes refused to do this, for it was against their principles, and they demanded nothing less than justice, which they were not prepared to buy. So they spoke, being ignorant that one of their community had loosed the fatal arrow.

Albinus, wearying of the business and finding that there was no profit to be made out of the Essenes, commanded them to be gone, saying that he would send an officer to make inquiry.

Another two months passed, and at length this officer arrived, attended by an escort of twenty soldiers.

On a certain morning in the winter season, Miriam with Nehushta was walking again on the Jericho road when suddenly they saw approaching them a small body of armed men. Seeing that they were Romans, they turned out of the path to hide themselves among the thorns of the desert. But the commander spotted them and spurred his horse forward to intercept.

"Do not run—stand still," Nehushta warned Miriam. "And show no sign of fear."

So Miriam halted and began to gather a few autumn flowers that still bloomed among the bushes, until the shadow of the officer fell upon her—that shadow in which she was destined to walk all her life's days.

"Lady," said a pleasant voice in Greek, spoken with a somewhat foreign accent. "Pardon, and I pray you, do not be alarmed. I am a stranger to this part of the country, which I visit on official business. Will you of your kindness direct me to the village of a people called Essenes, who live somewhere in this desert?"

"Oh, sir!" answered Miriam, "do you, come with Roman soldiers, mean them any harm?"

"Not I. Why do you ask?"

"Because, sir, I am of their community."

The officer stared at her—this fair, blue-eyed, delicate creature, whose high blood proclaimed itself in every tone and gesture.

"You, lady, of the community of the Essenes! Surely then those priests in Jerusalem lie more deeply than I thought. They told me that the Essenes were old ascetics who worshipped Apollo, and could not bear so much as the sight of a woman. And now you say you are an Essene—you, by Bacchus! You!" And he looked at her with an admiration that was neither brutal nor rude, but undisguisedly amused.

"I am their guest," she said.

"Their guest? Why, that is stranger still. If these spiritual outlaws—the name is of that old high priest's making, not of mine—share their bread and water with such guests, my sojourn among them will be happier than I thought."

"They brought me up, I am their ward," Miriam explained again.

"My estimation of the Essenes rises more and more. You have convinced me that those priests have slandered them. If they can shape so sweet a lady, then surely they must themselves be good and gentle." He bowed gravely to accentuate the compliment.

"Sir, they are both good and gentle," answered Miriam, ignoring his praise. "But of this you will be able to judge for yourself very shortly, seeing that they live near at hand. If you will follow us over that rise we will show you to their village."

"By your leave, I will accompany you," he said, dismounting before she could answer, then added, "Pardon me for one moment. I must give orders to my men," and he called to a soldier.

The man saluted and advanced. Then, turning aside, the young officer began to talk with him, so that now, for the first time, Miriam could study his face. He was young—no more than twenty years of age—of middle height and somewhat slender, but active in movement and athletic in build. Upon his head, which was round and not large, in place of the helmet that hung on his saddle, he wore a little steel lined and padded cap as protection against the sun, and beneath it she could see that his short, dark brown hair curled closely. Under the tan caused by exposure to the heat, his skin was fair, and his gray eyes, set rather wide apart, were quick and observant. For the rest, his mouth was well shaped, though somewhat large, and his chin clean-shaven, prominent and determined. His air was that of a soldier accustomed to command, but friendly enough, and when he smiled, showing his white teeth, even merry—the air of one with a kind and generous heart.

Miriam looked at him, and in an instant was aware that she thought him more handsome than any man of youth she had ever seen. That simple fact was no great compliment to the Roman, since of such acquaintances she had but few. Indeed, Caleb was the only one. But of this she was sure, she liked him better than Caleb because, even then and there, comparing them in her thoughts, she realized the truth if it. And she felt a certain sense of shame that a newcomer should be preferred to the friend of her childhood, though of late that friend had displeased her by showing too ardent an affection.

Having given his instructions, the commander dismissed the orderly, directing him to follow at a distance with the men. Then saying, "Lady, I am ready," he began to walk forward, leading his horse by the bridle.

"You will forgive me," he added, "if I introduce myself more formally. I am Marcus Carius, son of Emilius Carius—a name which was known in its day," he sighed, "as I hope before I have done with it, mine will be. At present I cannot boast that this is so. And unless it should please my uncle Caius to expire and leave me the great fortune he has been squeezing out of the Spaniards—and he shows no present intention of doing either— I am but a soldier of fortune, a tribune under the command of the excellent and most noble procurator Albinus," he added sarcastically.

"For the rest," he went on, "I have spent a year in this interesting and turbulent, but somewhat arid land of yours, coming here from Egypt, and am now honored with a commission to investigate and make report on a charge laid at the door of your virtuous guardians, the Essenes, of having murdered, or been privy to the murder of, a certain rascally Jew, who, as I understand, was sent with others to steal their goods. That, lady, is my style and history. By way of exchange, would you be so pleased to tell me yours?"

Miriam hesitated, not being sure whether she should enter into such confidence on so short a notice. When she did not speak, Nehushta, who was untroubled by such doubts and thought it prudent to be open with this Roman, a man in authority, answered for her.

"Lord, this maiden is my mistress, as was her grandmother

and mother before her—"

"Surely you cannot be so old," interrupted Marcus. He made it a rule to be polite to all women, whatever their color, having noticed that life went more easily with men who were courteous to them.

Nehushta smiled a little as she answered, for at what age does a woman learn to despise a compliment? "Lord, they both died young." Then resumed, "This maiden is the only child of the highborn Greco-Syrian of Tyre, Demas, and his noble wife, Rachel—"

"I know Tyre," he interrupted again. "I was quartered there until two months ago." Then adding in a different tone, "I understand that her parents no longer live."

"They died," said Nehushta sadly, "Demas in the amphitheatre at Berytus by command of the first Agrippa, and Rachel when her child was born."

"In the amphitheatre at Berytus? Was he then a malefactor?"

"No, sir," Miriam declared proudly. "He was a Christian."

"Oh! I understand. Well, they are ill-spoken of as enemies of the human race, but for my part I have had contact with several Christians and found them very good people, though visionary in their views." Here a doubt struck him and he said, "But, lady, I thought you said that you were an Essene."

"Nay, sir," Miriam replied in the same steady voice, "I too am a Christian, and I have been protected by the Essenes."

He looked at her with pity and replied, "That is a dangerous profession for one so young and fair."

"Dangerous as it is," she said, "at least it is mine from the beginning to the end."

Marcus bowed, perceiving that the subject was not to be pursued, and said to Nehushta, "Continue the story, my friend."

"Lord, the father of my lady's mother is a very wealthy Jewish merchant of Tyre, named Benoni."

"Benoni," he echoed to himself. "I know him well, too well for a poor man! A Jew of Jews—a Zealot, they say. At least he hates Rome enough to be one, although I have feasted many times in his palace. He is the most successful trader in all Tyre, beside his rival Amram, the Phoenician. A hard man, and as able as he is hard. Now that I think of it, he has no living children, so why does not your lady, his grandchild, dwell with him rather than in this desert?"

"Lord, you have answered your own question. Benoni is a Jew of Jews. His granddaughter is a Christian, even as I am. When her mother died, I brought her here to be cared for by her uncle Ithiel the Essene, and I do not think Benoni even knows that she lives. Lord, perhaps I have said too much. But you must soon have heard the story from the Essenes, and we must trust to you to keep our secret."

"You do not trust in vain. But it seems sad that all the wealth and station that are hers by right should be so wasted."

"Lord, rank and station are not everything. Faith and freedom of person are more than these. My lady lacks for nothing, and this is all her story."

"No, it is not," he replied immediately. "You have forgotten to tell me her name."

"Her name is Miriam."

"Miriam, Miriam," he repeated, his slightly foreign accent dwelling softly on the syllables. "It is a very pretty name, befitting such a—" and he checked himself.

By now they were on the crest of the rise and, stopping between two clumps of thorn trees, Miriam broke in hastily, "See, sir, there lies the village of the Essenes. Those palms to the left mark the banks of the Jordan, from which we irrigate our fields, and that gray stretch of water there is the Dead Sea."

"Is it so? Well, the green is pleasant in this desert, and those fields look well cultivated. I hope to visit them some day, for I was brought up in the country, and although I am a soldier, I can still manage a farm. As for the Dead Sea, it is even duller than I've been told. Tell me, lady, what is that large building?"

"That," she answered, "is the gathering hall of the Essenes."

"And that?" he asked, pointing to a house which stood by itself.

"That is my home, where Nehushta and I dwell."

"I guessed as much by the pretty garden." Then he asked her other questions, which she answered freely enough, for Miriam, although she was half Jewish, had been brought up among men, and felt neither fear nor shame in talking with them in a friendly and open way, as a Roman or a Grecian lady might have done.

While they were still conversing thus, the bushes on their path were pushed suddenly aside, and from between them emerged Caleb, whom she had seen little for the past weeks. He halted and looked at them.

"Caleb," said Miriam, "this is the Roman tribune Marcus, who comes to visit the curators of the Order. Will you lead him and his soldiers to the council hall and advise my uncle Ithiel and the others of his coming, since it is time for us to go home?"

Caleb glared at her, or rather at the stranger, with sullen fury. Then he answered, "Romans always make their own road. They do not need a Jew to guide them," and once more he vanished into the scrub on the further side of the path.

"Your friend is hardly civil," said Marcus, as he watched him go. "He has a most inhospitable air. Now, if an Essene could do such a thing, I should think that here is a man who might have drawn an arrow upon a Jewish tax gatherer," and he looked inquiringly at Miriam.

"That lad!" put in Nehushta. "Why, I never saw him shoot anything larger than a bird of prey."

"Caleb," added Miriam in excuse, "does not like strangers."

"So I have just seen," answered Marcus. "To be entirely frank, lady, I do not like Caleb. He has an eye like a knifepoint."

"Come, Nehushta," said Miriam, "this is our road, and there runs that of the tribune and his company. Sir, farewell, and thank you for your escort."

"Lady, for this while, farewell and thank you for your guidance."

Thus for that day they parted.

The dwelling that had been built many years before by the Essenes for the use of their ward and her nurse stood in the very shadow of the large guesthouse. Indeed, both occupied the same plot of ground, although now the land was divided into two gardens by an irrigation ditch and a live pomegranate fence that was covered at this season of the year with its golden globes of fruit. That evening, as Miriam and Nehushta walked in the garden, they heard the familiar voice of Ithiel calling to them from the other side of this fence and, presently, above it saw his kindly face and venerable white head.

"What is it, Uncle?" asked Miriam running to him.

"The noble Roman tribune, Marcus, is to stay in the guest-house during his visit with us. I only wanted to tell you not to be frightened if you hear or see men moving about in this garden—If, indeed, Romans care to walk in gardens. I am to stay here with him as host to see that he lacks nothing. I do not think that he will give you any trouble. He seems both courteous and kind." He added with a grin, "For a Roman."

"I am not afraid of him, Uncle," said Miriam. "Nehushta and I have already met the tribune," she added, blushing a little in spite of herself. And she told him of their meeting beyond the village.

"Nehushta, Nehushta," said Ithiel reprovingly, "have I not warned you not to walk so far afield without some of the brethren to escort? You might, perhaps, have met thieves, or drunken brawlers."

"My lady wished to gather some flowers she sought," answered Nehushta, "as she has done without harm for many years. I did not fear thieves, if such men are to be found where all are poor, for I am well-armed."

"Well, no harm has come of it, but do not go out unattended again, lest the soldiers be not so courteous as their commander. But they will not trouble you here. There was not enough room in the guesthouse, so they camp there by the streamlet. Farewell for this night, child. We will meet tomorrow."

Miriam went then to rest and, in her sleep, dreamed of the Roman tribune, that he, she, and Nehushta made a journey together and met with many great adventures in which Caleb played some strange part. In her dream the tribune Marcus protected them from all dangers until at length they came to a calm sea on which floated a single white ship whereon they embarked, and the sign of the cross was woven in its sails. She awoke presently and found that it was morning.

Of all the arts she had been taught, Miriam was fondest of shaping clay, for which her master declared she had a natural gift. So great had her skill become, that the models she made, after they had been baked with fire, were sold by the Essenes to any who took a fancy to them. As to the money they fetched, she desired it should be paid into the fund to be distributed among the poor.

Miriam labored at her art in a reed-thatched shed in the garden. Water ran there through an earthen pipe into a stone basin, in which she would dampen her clay and cloths. Sometimes, with the help of masons and the old master who had taught her, she copied her earthenware models in the marble the Essenes brought to her from the ruins of a palace near Jericho. She was presently finishing a work more ambitious than any she had yet undertaken: a life-sized bust in the likeness of her great uncle, Ithiel, chiseled from the fragment of an ancient column. On the afternoon following the day she had met Marcus, clad in her white working robe, she was occupied in polishing this bust, with the assistance of Nehushta, who handed her the cloths and grinding powder. A shadow fell upon her unexpectedly, and turning, she beheld Ithiel and the Roman.

"Daughter," said Ithiel, smiling at her confusion, "I have brought the tribune Marcus to see your work."

"Oh, Uncle!" she exclaimed indignantly, "am I in any state to receive an officer?" And she extended her wet hands and indicated her garments encrusted with clay and powder. "Look at me!"

"I look," said Ithiel innocently, "and see naught amiss."

"And *I* look, lady," added Marcus in his merry voice, "and see much to admire. Would that more women could be found so delightfully employed."

"Alas, sir," she replied, adroitly misunderstanding him, for Miriam did not lack readiness of wit, "in my poor work there is little to admire. I am ashamed that you should look on the rude fashionings of a half-trained girl. I am sure you have seen far better work in splendid statues of Rome."

"By the throne of Caesar, lady," he said in a voice that carried a conviction of his earnestness, staring hard at the bust of Ithiel before him, "as it is, although I am not an artist, I do know something of sculpture. I have a friend who is held to be the best of our day, and often in payment of debts have sat as model to him. Well, I tell you this—never did the great Glaucus produce a bust like this."

"I daresay not," said Miriam smiling. "I daresay the great Glaucus would go mad if he saw it."

"He would—with envy. He would say that it was the work of one of the glorious Greeks, and of no modern."

"Sir," said Ithiel reprovingly, "do not make jest of the maid. She does the best she can. You are perplexing her, and it is not fitting."

"Friend Ithiel," replied Marcus, turning quite crimson, "you must think that I lack manners, indeed, to say I would come to the home of any artist to mock his work. I say what I mean, neither more nor less. If this bust were shown in Rome, together with yourself who sat for it, the lady Miriam would find herself famous within a week." He ran his eye quickly over the various statuettes, some of them baked and some in the raw clay, most of them models of animals or birds. "Yes, and it is the same with all the rest. These are works of genius."

At this praise, to her so seemingly exaggerated, Miriam, though she could not help feeling pleased, broke into clear laugher, which both Ithiel and Nehushta echoed. The face of Marcus grew quite pale and stern.

"It seems," he growled, "that it is not I who mock. Tell me, lady, what do you with these things?" he asked, pointing to the statuettes.

"I, sir? I sell them. Or at least my uncles do."

"The money is given to the poor," added Ithiel.

"Would it be rude to ask at what price?"

"Sometimes," replied Ithiel with pride, "travelers have given me as much as a silver shekel. Once indeed, for a group of clay camels with their Arabian drivers, I received four shekels, but that took my niece three months to do."

"A shekel! Four shekels!" cried Marcus in a voice of despair. "I will buy them all—no, I will not! It would be robbery. And this bust?"

"That, sir, is not for sale. It is a gift to my uncle, or rather to my uncles, to be set up in their courtroom."

An idea struck Marcus. "I am here for a few weeks," he said. "Tell me, lady, if your uncle Ithiel will permit it, at what price will you execute a bust of myself of the same size and quality?"

"It would be costly," replied Miriam, smiling at the notion, "for the marble costs something, and the tools, which wear out. Oh, it would be very costly!" This she repeated, wondering what she could ask in her charitable avarice. "It would be . . ." yes, she would venture it. "Fifty shekels!"

"I am poor enough," said Marcus quietly, "but I will give you two hundred."

"Two hundred!" gasped Miriam. "That is absurd. I could never accept two hundred shekels for a piece of carved rock. Then indeed you might say that you had fallen among thieves on the banks of Jordan. No, if my uncles will permit it and there is time, I will do my poor best for fifty—only, sir, I advise you against it, since to win that imperfect portrait you must sit for many weary hours."

"If the portrait is imperfect, it will be my own face that is to blame," said Marcus. "So be it. As soon as I get to any civilized place I will send you enough payment to make the beggars in these parts rich for life, and at a very different figure. Let us begin at once."

"Sir, I have no leave."

"The matter," explained Ithiel, "must be laid before the Court of Curators, which will decide upon it tomorrow. Meanwhile, as we are talking here, I see no harm if my niece chooses to work a lump of clay, which can be broken up later should the Court in its wisdom refuse your request."

"I hope for its own sake that the Court in its wisdom will not be such a fool," muttered Marcus to himself, then added aloud, "lady, where shall I place myself?"

"If you will, sir, be seated on that stool and look towards me."

"You will find me the best of sitters," Marcus assured her amiably as he arranged his tunic. "Have I not the great Glaucus for a friend? Hah! Until I show him this work of yours!"

"Hush!" chided Miriam as she set aside the bust of Ithiel and began to wet the clay. "The model is not permitted to speak, lest lips that were meant to be closed be shaped open."

"I am your servant," said Marcus, in his cheerful voice. And the sitting began.

Chapter VIII
Marcus and Caleb

The next day, as he had promised, Ithiel brought this question of whether or not Miriam was to be allowed to execute a bust of the tribune, Marcus, before the Court of the Curators of the Essenes. There was a division of opinion. Some of them saw no harm. Others, more cautious, held that it was scarcely correct that a Roman whose principles, doubtless, were lax, should be allowed to sit for the lady whom they fondly called their child. Indeed, it seemed doubtful that the leave would be given until a curator with more worldly wisdom than the rest suggested that as the tribune seemed desirous of having his picture taken in stone, under the circumstances of his visit, which included a commission to make a general report upon their society to the authorities, it might scarcely be wise to deny his wish. Finally, a compromise was reached. It was agreed that Miriam should be permitted to do the work, but only in the presence of Ithiel and two other curators, one of them her own instructor in art.

Thus it came about that when Marcus presented himself for the second time, at an hour appointed by Ithiel, he found three white-bearded and white-robed old gentlemen seated in a row in the workshop, and behind them, a smile on her dusky face, Nehushta. As he entered they rose and bowed to him, a compliment that he returned. Now Miriam appeared, to whom he made his salutation.

"Are these," he said, indicating the elders, "waiting their turn to be modeled, or are they critics?"

"They are critics," said Miriam dryly, as she lifted the damp cloths from the rude lump of clay.

So the work began. As the three curators were seated in a line at the end of the shed and did not seem to think it right to leave

their chairs, they could see little of its details, and as they were
early risers and the afternoon was hot, they were soon asleep,
every one of them.

"Look at them," Marcus whispered. "There is a subject for
any artist."

Miriam nodded, and taking three lumps of clay, worked
deftly and silently, presently producing to his delighted sight
rough but excellent portraits of these admirable men who, when
they woke up, laughed at them heartily.

Thus things went on from day to day. Each afternoon the
elders attended, and each afternoon they sank to slumber in
their comfortable chairs, an example that Nehushta followed,
or seemed to follow, leaving Miriam and her model practically
alone. The model, who enjoyed conversation, did not neglect
these opportunities, and there were few subjects that the two
of them failed to discuss. He told her of all his life, which had
been varied and exciting, omitting certain risqué details. He
recounted also the wars in which he had served and the countries he had visited. She in turn told him the simple story of her
existence among the Essenes, which he seemed to find of interest. When these subjects were exhausted they discussed other
things—the matter of religion, among them. Miriam ventured
to expound to him the principles of her faith, to which he listened respectfully and with attention.

"It sounds well," he said at length with a sigh, "but how do
such maxims fit in with this world of ours? See now, lady, I
am not old, but already I have studied so many religions. First,
there are the gods of Greece and Rome, my own gods, you
understand—well, the less said of them the better. They serve
a purpose, that is all. Then there are the gods of Egypt. I once
made inquiry of them, and I will say this: beneath the grotesque
cloak of their worship seems to shine some spark of holy fire.
Next come the gods of the Phoenicians, the fathers of a hideous
creed. After them, the flame worshippers and other kindred religions of the East. There remain the Jews, whose doctrine seems
to me a savage and intolerant one. And they are divided, these
Jews, for some are Pharisees, some Sadducees, some Essenes.

Lastly, there are you Christians with your fresh and naïve devotion, whose faith is pure enough in theory, but against whom all unite in hate. What is the worth of a belief in a crucified preacher who promises that he will raise from the dead those who trust in Him?"

"That, you will find out when everything else has failed you," answered Miriam.

"Yes, it is a religion for those who have found all else to fail. When that happens to the rest of us, we commit suicide and sink from sight."

"And we," she said proudly, "rise to life eternal."

"It may be so, lady, it may be so. But let us talk of something more cheerful," and he sighed. "At present, I hold that nothing is eternal—except perhaps such art as yours."

"Which will be forgotten in the first change of taste, or crumbled in the first fire. But see, he is awake. Come here, my master, and work this nostril, for it is beyond me."

The old artist advanced and looked at the bust with admiration.

"Maid Miriam," he said, "I used to have some skill in this art, and I have taught you its rudiments, but now, child, I am not fit to temper your clay. Deal with the nostril as you will. I am but a workman who bears the bricks; you are the heaven-born architect. I will not meddle, I will not meddle. Yet perhaps—" and he squinted from beneath his wispy brows and pressed a finger to the figure. "Perhaps if you should remove a little clay from this point . . ."

"Like so?" said Miriam, touching the clay with her tool. "Oh, look! It is right now. Well done, my master."

"It was always right. I may be practiced, but you have the genius and would have found the fault without any help from me."

"Did I not say so?" broke in Marcus triumphantly.

"Sir," replied Miriam, "you say a great deal, and much of it, I think, you do not mean. Please be silent. At this moment I wish to study your lips, and not your words."

So the work went on. They did not always speak, for soon

they found that speech is not necessary for companionship. Once, Miriam began to sing idly as she worked, and when she discovered that her voice pleased Marcus and soothed the slumbers of the elders, she sang often. From the quaint, sad songs of the desert to the lively chanting of the Jordan fishermen. When she had exhausted her knowledge of songs, she told him tales and legends. When she was finished with these, Nehushta told others—wild stories of Libya, some of them very dark and bloody, others of magic, black and white. Thus these afternoons passed happily enough, and when the clay model was finally finished, the masons among the brethren rough-hewed it for her, and Miriam began to fashion it in marble.

There was one, however, for whom these days did not pass happily. Caleb.

From the time that he had seen Miriam walking side by side with Marcus, he hated the brilliant-looking Roman in whom, his instinct warned him, he had found a dangerous rival. Oh, how he hated him! So much, indeed, that even in the moment of first meeting, he could not keep his rage and envy in his heart but had allowed them to be written on his face and to shine like danger signals in his eyes, which Marcus had not neglected to note.

Of Miriam, Caleb had seen but little lately. She was not angry with him, since his offence was of a nature that a woman can forgive, but in her heart she feared him. In the instant he had confessed his desire, it was as if a curtain had been drawn, and she had seen this man's secret spirit and learned that it was a consuming fire. It had struck her that every word he spoke was true, that he, who was orphaned and unliked even by the gentle elders of the Essenes, loved but one being in all the earth—herself, whereas already his bosom seethed with many hates. She was certain that any man for whom she grew to care would, as Caleb had promised, be in danger at his hands, and the thought frightened her. It frightened her most of all when she saw him glower at Marcus, though in truth the Roman meant nothing to her. But she knew Caleb had judged otherwise.

Though she saw little of him, of this Miriam was sure enough—

he was seldom far from her, and that he found means to learn from day to day how she spent her hours. Indeed, Marcus told her that wherever he went, he met that handsome young man with revengeful eyes, the one named Caleb. So Miriam grew frightened, and not without cause.

One afternoon, while Miriam was at work upon the marble and the three elders were as usual sunk in slumber, Marcus said suddenly, "I'd forgotten. I have news for you, lady. I have found out who murdered that Jewish thief whose end, amongst other things, I was sent to investigate. It was your friend Caleb."

Miriam started so violently that her chisel gave an unexpected effect to one of Marcus's curls.

"Hush!" she said, glancing towards the sleepers, one of whom had just snored so loudly that he began to awake at the sound; then added in a whisper, "They do not know, do they?"

He shook his head, looking puzzled.

"I must speak to you further of this matter," she went on with some agitation, whispering in the same breath, "But not now or here. Alone."

"When and where you will," answered Marcus, smiling, as if the prospect of a solitary conversation with Miriam did not displease him, even if this evildoing Caleb was to be its subject. "Name the time and place, lady."

By now the snoring elder was awake, rising from his chair with a great noise, which in turn roused the others. Nehushta also rose from her seat, and in doing so, as though by accident, overset a copper tray of artisan's implements.

"In the garden, an hour after sunset. Nehushta will leave the little lower door unlocked."

"Good," answered Marcus, then added in a loud voice, "Ye gods, lady! What a noise! Sirs, why do you disturb yourselves? I fear that this long waiting must be as tedious to you as it seems unnecessary to me." Then he saw Miriam's apparent distress as she ruefully inspected the point where the chisel had made an unintended mark. "Don't trouble yourself over that. I think that curl of my hair there improved by the slip. It looks less as though it had been waxed after Egyptian fashion."

The sun had sunk below the desert horizon, the last red glow had faded from the western sky, and the quiet village of the Essenes was now lit only by the soft light of a crescent moon. All the world lay bathed in peace and beauty; even the stern outlines of the surrounding mountains seemed softened, the pale waters of the Dead Sea and the ashen face of the desert gleamed like silver, new cast from the mold. From the oleanders and lilies that bloomed along the edge of the irrigation channels, and from the white flowers of the glossy, golden-fruited orange trees, floated a perfume delicious to the sense, while the silence was broken only from time to time by the bark of a wandering dog or the howl of a jackal in the wilderness.

"A very pleasant night," Marcus reflected, "to talk about Caleb." He had reached the appointed spot ten minutes before the time, and he strolled in anticipation from the narrow belt of trees that were planted along the high, outer wall, into the more open part of the garden. Had Marcus noticed that this same Caleb, walking softly as a cat and keeping with great care in the shadow, had followed him through the little door, which he had forgotten to lock, and was now hidden among those very trees, he might have remembered a proverb spoken by the wisdom of Greek minds: *snakes hide in the greenest grass and the prettiest flowers have thorny stems.* But he thought of no such thing, for he was lost in cheerful hopefulness of a moonlight interview with a lovely and cultured young lady, who in truth had taken so deep a hold upon his thoughts, that sometimes he wondered how he would be able to banish her from his mind.

Presently Marcus caught the gleam of a white robe followed by a dark one, flitting towards him through the dim and dewy garden. And for a moment, he forgot to breathe.

"Ah, I wish she had left the old lady behind," muttered Marcus, but amended, "No, I don't, for there are brutes that would blame her if they knew." Then, fortunately for himself, he walked forward a few paces to meet the figure in the white robe, leaving the little belt of trees almost out of hearing.

Now Miriam stood before him, the moonlight shining on her

delicate face and in her tranquil eyes, which always reminded him of the blue depths of the skies. The first sight of her drove all else from his mind and made him forget the dark form of Nehushta lurking only several steps behind.

"Sir," she began.

"Oh, I pray you," he broke in, "cease from formality and call me Marcus!"

"Tribune Marcus," she repeated, dwelling a little on the unfamiliar name, "I beg that you will forgive me for disturbing you at so unseasonable an hour."

"Certainly I forgive you, Lady Miriam," he replied, also dwelling on her name and copying her accent in a fashion that made even the grim-faced Nehushta smile.

She waved her hand in self-deprecation. "The truth is, that this matter of Caleb—"

"May all the infernal gods take Caleb!" Marcus interrupted angrily. "As I have reason to believe they shortly will."

"But that is just what I wish to prevent. We have met here to talk of Caleb, have we not?"

"Well, if we must, talk and let us be done with him. What about Caleb?"

Miriam clasped her hands. "What do you know of him, Tribune Marcus?"

"What do I know? Only this. A spy from my troop found a country fellow who was hunting for mushrooms or something—I forget what—in a gully a mile away, and saw this interesting youth hide himself there and shoot that Jewish plunderer with a bow and arrow. Moreover—he has found another man who saw Caleb help himself an hour or two before to an arrow out of a Jewish quiver, which appears to be identical to the one found in the poor fellow's throat. Therefore, it seems that Caleb is guilty, and that it will be my duty tomorrow to place him under arrest and, in due course, to convey him to Jerusalem, where the priests will attend to his business. Now, Lady Miriam, is your curiosity satisfied about Caleb?"

"Oh," she said, "that cannot be, it must not be! The man had struck him and he did but return a blow for a blow."

"An arrow for a blow, you mean. The point of a spear for the knock of its handle." He paused to study her closely, for once seeking to look past her beauty. "Lady Miriam, you seem to be very deep in the confidence of Caleb. How do you come to know all this?"

"I do not know," she confessed. "I only guess. I daresay—no, I am sure, that Caleb is quite innocent."

"Why do you take such an interest in Caleb?" Marcus asked suspiciously.

"Because he was my friend and playmate from childhood."

At this he gave an ungracious grunt. "A strange couple you make—a dove and a raven. Well, I am glad that you have not caught his temper, or you would be even more dangerous than you are. Now, what would you have me do?"

"I want you to spare Caleb. You . . . need not believe those witnesses."

"To think of it!" cried Marcus, in mock horror. "To think that one whom I thought so good can prove so immoral. Do you then wish to tempt me from my duty?"

"Yes, I suppose I do. At least the peasants round here can be great liars."

"Lady," he said with stern conviction, "Caleb has improved upon his opportunities as a playmate. He has been seeking your hand, as well as your heart. I thought so from the first."

"Oh," she answered, "how can you know that? Besides, he promised that he would never do it again."

"How do I know?" he exclaimed as if the answer should have been obvious. "I know because Caleb would be a bigger fool than I take him for if he had not. And if it rested with me, he would never do it again. Now be as honest with me as a woman can be on such a matter. Are you in love with Caleb?"

"I? Love Caleb?" she said in surprise. "Of course not. If you do not believe me, ask Nehushta."

"Thank you, I am content with your own word. You deny that you are in love with him, and I am inclined to believe you, but I know you would naturally say this if you thought any other answer would prejudice Caleb's with me."

"With you! What can it matter to you, sir, whether or not I am in love with Caleb? If anything, I fear him."

"And that, I suppose, is why you plead so hard for him?"

"No," she answered with a sudden sternness, "I plead hard for him as, in like case, I would plead hard for you—because he has been my friend; and, if he did this deed, he must have been provoked to it."

"Well spoken," said Marcus, gazing at her steadily. Indeed, his attempt to look past her loveliness was at last futile, for she was more than worth looking at as she stood there before him, her hands clasped, breathing heavily, her usually pale face flushed with emotion and her lovely eyes swimming with tears. Suddenly as he gazed, Marcus lost control of himself. Passion for this maiden and bitter jealousy of Caleb arose like twin giants in his heart and possessed him.

"You say you are not in love with Caleb," he said. "Well, kiss me and I will believe you."

"How could such a thing prove my words?" she cried indignantly.

"I do not know and I no longer care. Kiss me once and I will even believe that the peasants of these parts are all liars. I feel myself beginning to believe it already."

"And if I will not?" she whispered, the glint of madness in his eyes making her shiver in alarm.

"Then I fear I must refer the matter to the court at Jerusalem."

"Nou, you have heard," she said to the woman, who stood within hearing distance. "What shall I do?"

"What shall you do?" said Nehushta dryly. "Well, if you wish to give the noble Marcus a kiss, I shall not blame you overmuch or tell on you. But if you do not wish it, then I think you would be a fool to put yourself to shame to save Caleb."

Miriam's eyes went from Nehushta, who was not being any help at all, back to Marcus who watched her for her answer. At last she gave it. "I will do it—but to save Caleb only," she said with a sob, and she bent towards him with closed eyes, as if in fear of looking on what she was about to do.

But to her surprise Marcus drew back, placing his hand before his face.

"Forgive me," he said. "I was a brute for wishing to buy your kiss in such a fashion. I forgot myself. Your beauty is to blame, and your sweetness and everything that is yours. I pray," he added humbly, "that you will not think the worse of me, for men are frail at times. Do not fear for your friend. I have no right, but because you ask it, I grant your request. Perhaps the witnesses lied. At least, the man's crime, if there be any, can be excused. He has naught to fear from me."

"No," Nehushta interjected, "but I think you have much to fear from him. And I am sorry for that, my lord Marcus, for I see you have a noble heart."

"Yes," he replied bitterly. "So noble as to seek tokens of love from my lady through extortion. It may be so, and Caleb may be a danger. The future is on the knees of the gods, and that which is fated will befall. My Lady Miriam, I, your humble servant and friend, wish you farewell."

"Farewell," she answered. "And Marcus . . . I too believe you do have a noble heart." As she said this she looked at him with such feeling that it occurred to him that were he to ask her again for her kiss, he might not be refused. But Marcus would not do it. He had tasted of the joy of self-control, and after the manner of his age and race, he had denied himself little enough of that in the past. A strange new power was stirring in his heart— something purer, higher, nobler, than he had known before. He would cherish it a while.

Three there were in the garden clearing, but four there were in the garden, and one observed all unseen: Caleb. Of all that was spoken, he could catch no word. The speakers did not raise their voices high enough for the sound to carry, and they stood at a distance. Although he craned his head forward as far as he dared in the shadow of the trees, sharp and trained as they were, naught save a confused murmur reached his ears. But if these failed him, his eyes fed full upon the scene, so that he missed no move or gesture. It was a meeting of passionate love—this was clear—for Nehushta stood at a little distance with her back turned, while the lovers poured out their impassioned speeches to one another. Then at length, as he had dreaded, came the climax. Yes, oh shameless girl! They were embracing. A mist like a red cloud fell upon Caleb's eyes, and the blood drummed in his ears as though his raging, jealous heart would burst. He would kill that Roman now on the spot. Miriam would never kiss him again—*alive.*

Already Caleb had drawn his short sword from its hiding place in the ample folds of his robe, already he had stepped out from the shadow of the trees, when his reason suddenly righted itself like a ship laid over and abandoned by a furious squall, and caution came back to him. If he dared to show himself, that faithless guardian, Nehushta, undoubtedly bought with Roman gold, would come to the aid of her patron and thrust her dagger through his back, as she well could do. Should he chance to escape the dagger, one or the other of them would raise the Essenes on him, and he would be given over to the Court. Caleb wished to slay, not to be slain. It would be sweet to kill the Roman, but if he himself were laid dead across his body, leaving Miriam alive to pass to some other man, what would he gain by it? Presently they must cease from their endearments. Presently his enemy would return the way he had come, and then might poor Caleb find his chance. He would wait, he would wait.

They had parted now. Miriam was gliding back to the house, and Marcus came towards him, walking like a man in his sleep. Only Nehushta stood where she was, her eyes fixed upon the ground as though she were reasoning with herself. Still like a man in a dream, Marcus passed within reach of an outstretched hand. Caleb followed. Marcus opened the door and went out of it. Caleb caught the door in his hand as Marcus moved on, slipped through, and closed it. A few paces down stood another door, by which Marcus had entered the garden of the guesthouse. As he turned to shut this, Caleb pushed in after him, and they were face to face.

"Who are you?" demanded the Roman, springing back out of striking distance.

Caleb, who by now was cool enough, closed the door and

shot the bolt. Then he answered, "Caleb, the son of Hilliel, who wishes a word with you."

"Ah!" said Marcus, "the man himself! And, as usual, unless the light deceives me, in an evil humor. Well, Caleb the son of Hilliel, what is your business with me?"

"One of life and death, Marcus Carius," he answered, in such a tone that the Roman drew his sword and stood watching him warily.

"Be plain and brief, young man," he said.

"The matter is both plain and brief. I love the lady from whom you have just parted, and you also love her, or pretend to love her. Do not deny it. I have seen all, even to your kisses. She cannot belong to both of us, and I intend that in some future day she shall belong to me if my arm does not fail me now. Therefore one of us must die tonight."

Marcus stepped back, overcome not with fear, but with astonishment.

"Insolent dog," he said. "You are grievously mistaken! There were no kisses. All our talk was of your neck, forfeit for the murder of the Jew. And that I gave to her because she asked it."

"Indeed," sneered Caleb. "Now, who would have thought that the noble Tribune Marcus would shelter thus behind a woman's robe? As for me, my life is my own and no other's to give or to receive. Guard yourself, Roman, for I would kill you in fair combat. Had I another mind, you would be dead by now, never knowing the hand that struck you. Have no fear for your piteous honor. I am your equal in station. My forefathers were nobles when yours were savages."

"Are you mad, boy?" said Marcus. "Do you imagine that I, who have fought in three wars, have anything to fear from a beardless youth? Why I have but to blow upon this whistle and my guards would carry you away to a murderer's death. For your own sake, I pray you, reconsider. Setting aside my rank and yours, I will fight you if you insist, and now. But think. If I kill you, that is the end of the matter, but if by chance you should kill me, you will be hunted down as a double murderer. As it is, I forgive you because I know how bitter is the jealousy of youth,

and because you struck no assassin's blow when you might have done so safely. Therefore, I say, go in peace, knowing that I shall not break my word."

"Cease talking," Caleb bit impatiently, "and come out into the moonlight."

"I am glad that is your wish," replied Marcus. "Having done all I can to save you, I will add that I think you a dangerous cub, and the world, the Lady Miriam, and I alike will be well rid of you. Now, what weapon have you? A short sword and no mail? Well, so have I. We are well matched enough. Wait, I have my head cap, and you have none." He removed it quickly and tossed it onto the ground, out of reach. "To make our chances equal. Now wind your cloak about your left arm as I do. I have known worse shields. Ready yourself now . . . engage!"

Caleb needed no encouragement. For one second they stood facing each other, the very embodiments of the Eastern and Western world. The Roman, sturdy, clear-eyed, watchful and fearless, his head erect, his feet apart, his shield arm forward, his sword hand protecting his side. Opposite him was the Jew, crouched like a tiger about to spring, his eyes half closed as though to concentrate the light, his face working with rage, and every muscle quivering until his whole flesh seemed to move upon his bones, like to that of a snake. Suddenly, uttering a low cry, he sprang, and with that savage onslaught the fight began and ended.

Marcus was ready for him. As the man came, he stepped swiftly to one side caught the thrust of Caleb's sword in the folded cloak. Loyalty to Miriam won over battle instinct, and he struck at his opponent's hand rather than his neck. The blow fell upon Caleb's first finger and severed it, so that it dropped to the ground with the sword it had held. Marcus put his foot upon the blade and wheeled round.

"Young man," he said sternly, "you have learnt your lesson and will bear the mark of it until your death day. Now begone."

The wretched Caleb ground his teeth. "The fight was to the death," he snarled. "To the death! You have conquered. Kill me," and with his bloody hand he tore open his robe to make a path for the sword.

"Leave such talk to play actors," answered Marcus. "Begone, and be sure of this—that if ever you try to bring treachery on me or trouble on the lady Miriam, I will kill you sure enough."

Then with a sound that was half curse and half sob, Caleb turned and slunk away. With a shrug of his shoulder Marcus also turned to go, when he felt a shadow fall upon him. He swung round, sword at ready, to find Nehushta at his side.

"And pray where did you come from, my Libyan friend?" he asked.

"Out of that pomegranate fence, my Roman lord. I have seen and heard all."

"Indeed. Then I hope that you give me credit for good swordplay and good temper."

"The swordplay was good enough, though nothing to boast of with such a madman for a foe. As for the temper, it was that of a fool."

Marcus threw his hands up as if in appeal to the gods. "Such is the reward of virtue. But I am curious. Why do you say so?"

"Because, my lord Marcus, this Caleb will grow into the most dangerous man in Judea, and to none more dangerous than to my lady Miriam and yourself. You should have killed him while you had the chance, before his turn comes to kill you."

"Perhaps," answered Marcus with a yawn. "The Roman in me agrees with you. But I have been associating with a Christian and have caught something of her doctrines. This seems a fine sword," he commented as he retrieved Caleb's discarded blade, handing it to Nehushta. "You had better keep it. Goodnight."

CHAPTER IX
THE JUSTICE OF FLORUS

The following morning, when the roll of the neophytes of the Essenes was called, Caleb did not appear. Nor did he answer to his name on the next day, or indeed ever again. None knew what had become of him until a while after a letter was received addressed to the Curators of the Court, in which he announced that, finding he had no vocation for an Essenic career, he had taken refuge with friends of his late father in some place not stated. There, so far as the Essenes were concerned, the matter ended. Indeed, as the peasant who had been concealed in the gully when the Jew was murdered had borne witness of what he had seen, even the most simpleminded of the Essenes could suggest a reason for this sudden departure. Nor did they altogether regret it, as in many ways Caleb had proved himself an unsatisfactory disciple, and already they had been discussing the expediency of rejecting him from the fellowship of their peaceful order. Had they known that when he vanished he had left behind a drawn sword and one of his forefingers, their opinion on this point might have been strengthened. But this they did not know, although Miriam knew it through Nehushta.

Miriam and Marcus did not meet throughout the entire next week, as no further sittings were arranged for the completion of the bust. In fact, they were not needed, for she could work from the clay model, which she did until, laboring at it continually, she had finished the marble and polished it with care. One morning, as the artist was putting the last touches to her labors, the door of the workshop was darkened and she looked up to see Marcus, who, except for his helmet, was clad in full metal plate as though about to start out on a journey. Miriam was alone in the shed; Nehushta had gone to attend to house-

hold affairs. Thus for the first time they met with no other eyes to watch them.

At the sight of him, she colored, letting the cloth fall from her hand, which remained about the neck of the marble.

"I ask your pardon, Lady Miriam," said Marcus, bowing gravely, "for intruding upon your privacy like this. But I am pressed for time, so I neglected to notify your guardians of my visit."

"Are you leaving us?" she faltered.

"Yes, I am leaving you."

Miriam turned aside and picked up the cloth, then answered, "Well, the work is done, or will be in a few minutes. So if you think it worth the trouble, take it."

"I will take it with me. The price I will settle with your uncles."

She nodded. "Yes, yes, but if you will permit me, I should

like to pack it myself, so that it comes to no harm on the journey. Also with your consent I will keep the clay model, though by right it belongs to you. I am not satisfied with this marble. I wish to make another."

"The marble is perfect. But keep the model if you will. I am very glad that you should keep it."

She glanced at him, a question in her eyes, but looked away before he could ascertain what she had been about to say.

"When do you go?" she asked, though that was not the question she had been considering.

"Three hours after noon. My task here is finished. My report—which is to the effect that the Essenes are a most worthy and harmless people who deserve to be encouraged, not molested—is written. And I am called in haste by a messenger who arrived from Jerusalem but an hour ago. Would you like to know why?"

"If it pleases you to tell me."

"I think that I told you of my uncle Caius, who was proconsul under the late emperor for the richest province of Spain."

"Yes."

"Well, he certainly made use of his opportunities. But now the old man has been smitten with a mortal disease. For all I know, he may be already dead, although the physicians seemed to think he would live for another ten months, or perhaps a year. In his condition, he has suddenly grown fond of his relations, or rather *relation,* for I am the only one, and he expressed a desire to see me, who for many years he has never given a single penny. He has even announced his intention—by letter—of making me his heir 'should he find me worthy to carry on his legacy,' which, to be truthful, I hope I am not. For whatever faults *I* possess, I have already told him in the past that of all men, I consider him the worst. Still, he has forwarded a sum of money to enable me to journey to him in haste and, with it, a letter from Nero Caesar to the procurator Albinus, commanding him to give me instant leave to go. So, lady, it seems wise that I should go."

"Yes," answered Miriam. "I know little of such things, but I think that it is wise. Within two hours the bust shall be finished and packed," and she stretched out her hand in farewell.

Marcus took the hand and held it. "I am loath to part with you thus," he said.

"There is only one fashion of parting," answered Miriam, striving to withdraw her hand.

"Nay, there are many. And I hate them all—from you."

"Sir," she asked with mild vexation, "is it worth your while to squander these pretty words upon me? We have met for an hour, we separate now for a lifetime."

"I see no need of that. Oh, the truth may as well be known. I wish it least of all things."

"Yet it is so. Come, let go of my hand. The marble must be finished and packed."

The young tribune's face became troubled, as though he were reasoning with himself; as though he wished to take her at her word and go, yet could not.

"Are you quite finished?" asked Miriam presently. She had stopped trying to wrest her hand from his firm but gentle grasp and was now considering him with her quiet eyes.

"I think not. I think I am only begun. I love you, Miriam."

"Marcus," she answered, fighting to hold her voice steady, "I do not think I should be asked to listen to such words."

"And why should you not? They have been spoken of man to woman since time began, and they have ever been in earnest."

"Perhaps, when they were meant in earnest. But in this case they scarcely can be."

He grew hot and red. "What do you mean? Do you suppose—"

"I suppose nothing, Tribune Marcus."

"Do you suppose," he repeated, "that I would offer you any place less than that of wife?"

"Certainly not," she replied. "I would not insult your honor so. But I never supposed that you ever really meant to offer me that place."

"Yet that is in my mind, Miriam."

Her eyes grew soft, but she answered, "Then, Marcus, I ask

you to put it out of your mind. Between you and me rolls a great sea."

"Is this sea named Caleb?" he asked bitterly.

She smiled and shook her head. "You know well that it has no such name."

"Then tell me of this sea, and I shall sail it if I can."

"You are a Roman worshipping the Roman gods. I am a Christian worshipping the one true God. We are forever separate, and there can be no meeting between us."

"Why? If you and I were married you might come to believe as I do, or I might come to believe as you. It is a matter of the spirit and the beyond, not of the body and the present."

"That is where you are mistaken," she reproved him gently. "The spirit is as ever present as the body. And the body will be found in the beyond beside the sprit."

That idea was too high for him. He felt more at ease dealing only with the present world. "I have heard that Christians often wed those who are not Christians. I have even heard that they sometimes convert them."

"Yes, I know. But it should not be so. And in my case it cannot be, even if I wished it could be." She tried again, half-heartedly to extract her hand from his. He held resolutely on.

"Why not?"

"The reason is two-fold. You are not in covenant with my God. How, then, should I be joined to you? It must not be. And I have the further command of my martyred father and my mother, who with her dying breath laid upon me that I should not be unequally yoked with any man who was not of our faith. How can I defy my parents and my God?"

Marcus's face fell. "I know nothing of this covenant of yours, but the other, I understand. So you hold yourself to be bound by the command of your dead parents?"

"I do, without doubt and to the end. I must and will obey."

"However much you might love a man who is not a Christian?"

"However much I might happen to love such a man," she answered, so decisively and with so resolute a gaze that Marcus wondered if the possibility in question was as likely as he had at first thought. He did not see the effort she had needed to affect such a face.

He let her hand fall. "I think I had best go," he said.

"Yes," she murmured as she withdrew from him.

There was a pause while he seemed to be struggling with himself.

"Miriam, I cannot go."

"And yet you must."

"Miriam, I must ask. Do you love me?"

She stared at him for long moments, as if astonished he should ask. Then the coldness of her face vanished suddenly, like the winter's frost at the dawning of spring, revealing the anguish beneath. "Christ forgive me, Marcus, I do."

"How much?"

"As much as a woman may love a man."

"And still," his voice broke bitterly, "you bid me begone because I am not a Christian."

"Because my faith must command my love. I must offer my love upon the altar of my faith." She added hurriedly, "I am bound by chains that cannot be cut or broken. To break it would bring down upon your head and mine the curse of Heaven and of my parents, who dwell there."

"And if I became of your faith?"

For a moment her face lit like the sun, but its light died just as quickly.

"It is too much to hope. This is not a question of casting incense on an altar. It is a matter of a changed spirit and a new life. Oh, have done! Why do you toy with me?"

"A changed spirit and a new life. That would take time," he said, wondering that he spoke of such things this way. How could he hope to achieve something he did not understand?

"Yes, it takes time, and more. These are gifts, and must be freely given of God—they cannot be gained by your effort."

"Well, it does not seem that these . . . gifts you speak of are to be given me just now."

Her eyes turned downcast. "No, it does not seem so."

"Would you wait for me? Would you wait for these gifts to be given me, even as I wait? With such beauty and sweetness you will not lack for suitors."

"I shall wait. I have told you I love you. No other man will be anything to me. I shall wed no other."

"You give all and take nothing. It is not right."

"It is as God has willed. If it pleases God to quicken your heart and to preserve us both alive, then in days to come our lives may be one life. Otherwise, they must run apart until one day we may meet again in the eternal morning."

"Oh, Miriam, I cannot leave you thus! Teach me your faith as you will. How shall I learn of it otherwise?"

"Nay, go, Marcus! You must learn of it apart from me, through the Scriptures and by the Spirit. When the heart is made willing, the path need not be long, though it may be fraught with difficulty. But my Lord has said that he who seeks will find. Therefore, seek, Marcus! Now fare you well."

"May I write to you from Rome?" he asked, when it was clear she could not be dissuaded.

"Yes, why not, if by that time you should care to write. But I'm sure by then you will have recovered from this folly of the desert and an idle moon."

"I shall write and I shall return, and we will talk of these matters. So, most sweet, if we must part, farewell."

"Farewell, Marcus, and may the love of God go with you."

"God's love?" he said with some frustration. "What of your love?"

"My love is ever with him who has won my heart."

"If that is so, then at least I have not lived in vain. Forget not what you have said today, for I will not. And one day, I may call you to account for it." He knelt before her and, taking her hand in his once again, he kissed it. Then he released her and pressed his lips to the hem of her robe with the deepest reverence. Without another word, he turned and went.

That night, watching from the roof of her house by the light of the full moon, Miriam saw Marcus ride away at the head of his band of soldiers. On the crest of a little ridge of ground outside the village, he halted, sending them on ahead of him. And turning his horse's head, he looked back the way he had come. Thus he stood awhile, the silver rays of the moon shining on his bright armor and making him a point of light set between two vales of shadow. Miriam could guess where his eyes were turned and what was in his heart. It seemed to her that she could feel his loving thought play upon her and that with the ear of his spirit he could catch the answer of her own. Then suddenly he turned and was lost in the gloom of the night.

Now that he was quite gone, Miriam's courage seemed to leave her; she leaned her head upon the parapet and wept tears, soft but bitter. She felt a hand laid upon her shoulder and a voice, that of old Nehushta, speaking in her ear.

"Do not mourn," it said, "for he whom you lose in the night, you may find again in the morning."

"In no morning that dawns from an earthly sun, I fear me, Nou. Oh, Nou! He has gone and taken my heart with him, leaving in its place a throbbing pain that is more than I can bear."

"He will come back. I tell you that he will come back," she answered, almost fiercely, "for your life and his are intertwined—yes, to the end—a single cord bearing a double destiny. Ask me not how I know it, but be comforted, for it is the truth. And though it be sharp, your pain is no more than you can bear, else it would never be laid upon you."

"But, Nou, if he does come back, how will it help me? To break the command of my mother would be double the sin, against both God and man."

"I do not know. I only know this, that in that wall, as in others, a door will be found. Trouble not for the future, but leave it in the hands of Him who shapes all futures. *Sufficient to the day is the evil thereof.* So He said. Accept the saying and be grateful. It is something to have gained the love of such a one as this Roman, for unless the wisdom I have gained through many years is at fault, he is true and honorable. It is by God's grace only that a man reared in Rome and in the worship of its gods might yet retain such honest dignity. Remember these things and be grateful, for there are many who go through their lives never knowing such joy, even for an hour."

"I will try, Nou," said Miriam miserably, still staring at the ridge where Marcus had vanished.

"You will try, and you will succeed. Now there is another matter of which I must speak to you. When the Essenes received us, it was solemnly decreed that if you lived to reach the full age of eighteen years you must depart from among them. That hour struck for you nearly a year ago, and although you heard nothing of it, this decree was debated by the Court. Such decrees may not be broken, but it was argued that the words 'full age of eighteen years,' meant and were intended to mean until you reached your nineteenth birthday. That is only a month from now."

"Then must we go, Nou?" asked Miriam in dismay, for she knew no other world but this village in the desert, and no other friends than these venerable men whom she called her uncles.

"It seems so, especially as it is now guessed that Caleb fought the Tribune Marcus upon your account. Oh, that tale is talked of—for one thing, the gardener found the severed claw the young wildcat left behind."

"I trust then it is known also that the fault was none of mine. But, Nou, where shall we go? We have no friends, nor home, nor money."

"I know not. But doubtless in this wall also there is a door. When the worst comes to the worst, a Christian has many brothers. And with your skill as an artisan, you need never lack for a living in any great city of the world."

"That may be true," said Miriam, brightening, "if I may believe the word of Marcus and my old master."

Nehushta continued, "And I still have almost all the gold the Phoenician Amram gave us when I fled with your mother. Added to that, what I took from the strong box of the captain of the galley on the night when you were born. So have no fear, we shall not want, nor indeed would the Essenes allow such a thing. Now, child, you are weary. Go to rest and hope that Marcus might one day be to you a Christian husband."

It was with a heavy heart that Caleb, defeated and shamed, shook the dust of the Essene village off his feet. At the first dawn after the night that he had fought the duel with Marcus, he was observed by provincial shepherds, a staff in his bandaged hand and a bag of provisions over his shoulder, standing upon the little ridge and gazing towards the house that sheltered Miriam. In love and war, things had gone ill with him. So ill that at the thought of his discomfiture, he ground his teeth. Miriam cared nothing for him. Marcus had defeated him almost without thought and had given him his life. And worst of all, these two from whom he had endured so much loved each other.

While Caleb looked, the red rim of the sun rose above the horizon, flooding the world with light and life. Now birds began to chirp, and beasts to move; now the shadows fled away. Caleb's impressionable nature answered to this change. Hope stirred in his breast, while even the pain of his maimed hand was forgotten.

"I will win yet," he shouted to the silent sky. "My troubles are done with. I will shine like the sun. I will rule like the sun, and my enemies shall whither beneath my power. It is a good omen. I am glad the Roman spared my life, so in a day to come, I may take his. And in that day shall I have Miriam for my own."

Then he turned and trudged onward through the glorious sunlight, watching his own shadow as it stretched away before him.

"It goes far," he observed. "This is also a very good omen."

Caleb thought much on his way to Jerusalem; and he talked with all whom he met, even with bandits and thieves whom his poverty could not tempt, for he desired to learn how matters stood in the land. When he arrived in Jerusalem, he sought out the home of the lady who had been his mother's friend and had given him as a helpless orphan to the care of the Essenes. He found that she was dead, but her son lived, a man of kind heart and given to hospitality, who had heard his story and sheltered him for his mother's sake. When his hand was healed and he had procured some good clothes and a little money from his friend, without saying anything of his purpose, Caleb traveled to Caesarea to attend the court of Gessius Florus, the Roman procurator, at his palace, seeking an opportunity to speak with him.

Thrice did he wait there for hours at a time, on each occasion to be driven away at last by the guards. On his fourth visit he was more fortunate, for Florus, who had noted him before, asked why he stood there so patiently. An officer replied that the man had a petition to make.

"Let me hear it then," said the governor. "I sit in this place to administer justice by the grace and in the name of Caesar."

Accordingly, Caleb was summoned and found himself in the presence of a small, dark-eyed, beetle-browed Roman with cropped hair, who appeared just as he was—one of the most evil rulers that ever held power in Judea.

"What do you seek, Jew?" he asked, his voice little more than a bark.

"What I am confident I shall find at your hands, O most noble Florus. Justice against the Jews—pure justice." The courtiers and guards laughed at these words behind their hands, and even Florus smiled.

"Justice is to be had at a price," he replied.

"I am prepared to pay the price."

"Then set out your case," he encouraged with growing interest.

So Caleb set it out. He told how many years before his father had been accidentally slain in a tumult, and how when he was but an infant, certain Jews of the Zealots had seized and divided his estate on the ground that his father was a partisan of the Romans, leaving him, the son, to be brought up by charity. The estate, consisting of tracts of rich lands and certain house property in Jerusalem and Tyre, was still in their possession or in that of their descendants.

The black eyes of Florus glistened as he heard.

"Their names," he said, holding up his tablets. But Caleb was not yet inclined to give the names. First, he intimated that he desired to arrive at a formal agreement as to what proportion of the property, if recovered, would be handed over to him, the heir. Then followed much haggling, but in the end it was agreed that as he had been robbed because his father was supposed to favor the Romans, the lands in Tyre and a large dwelling with a warehouse attached, together with half the back rents, if recoverable, should be given to the plaintiff. The governor—or Caesar, as Florus put it—for his share was to retain the property in Jerusalem and the other half of the rents. In this arrangement Caleb proved himself, as usual, perceptive. Houses, as he explained afterwards, could be burned or pulled down, but beyond the crops on it, no man could injure the land. After the agreement had been duly signed and witnessed, he gave the names, bringing forward clear evidence to prove all that he had said.

Within a week, the Jews who had committed the theft were imprisoned, and they were not released until they had been stripped, not only of the stolen property, but of everything else they had possessed. Either because he was pleased at so great and unexpected a harvest, or perhaps because he saw in Caleb an able fellow who might be useful in the future, Florus fulfilled his bargain with him to the letter.

Thus it came about that by a strange turn of destiny, within a month of his flight from the colony of the Essenes, Caleb, the outcast orphan, his neck in danger of the sword, had become a man of influence, having great possessions. His sun had risen indeed.

CHAPTER X
BENONI

One month later, Caleb, no longer a solitary wanderer with only his feet to carry him, his staff to protect him, and a bow and arrow to supply him with food, departed Jerusalem. He was now a young and gallant gentleman, well armed, clad in furs and a purple cloak, accompanied by servants, and riding a splendid horse. On the rising ground beyond the Damascus Gate, he halted and looked back at the glorious city with her crowded streets, her mighty towers, her luxurious palaces, and her world-famed temple that dominated all. The view of the Temple from this point seemed as a mountain covered with snow and crowned with glittering gold.

"I will rule there when the Romans have been driven out," he said to himself, for already Caleb had grown ambitious. Indeed, the wealth and the place that had come to him so suddenly, with which many men would have been satisfied, did but serve to increase his appetite for power and fame. To him this money was but a stepping stone to greater fortunes.

Caleb was journeying to Tyre to take possession of his house there, which the Roman commander of the district had been bidden to hand over to him. But he also had another purpose. At Tyre dwelt the old Jew, Benoni, Miriam's grandfather, as he had discovered years before. For when they were still children together she had told him all her story. This Benoni, he desired to see.

On a certain afternoon in a palace of Tyre, a man sat in a long veranda overlooking the Mediterranean. The blue waters of the Mediterranean lapped the straight-scarped rock below—for this house was in the island city, not on the mainland where most of the rich Syrians dwelt.

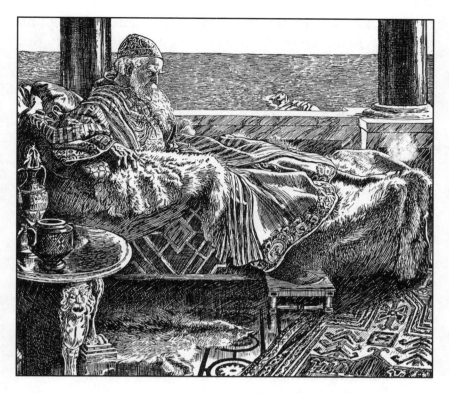

The man was old but still very handsome. His dark eyes were quick and full of fire, his nose was hooked like the beak of an eagle, his hair and beard were long and snowy white. His robes were rich and splendid, and he wore a cloak of costly northern furs over them, to shield against the cold that reached even Tyre in this season. The house was worthy of its owner. Built throughout of the purest marble, the rooms were roofed and paneled with the sweet-smelling cedar of Lebanon, hung about with many silver lamps and decorated by various abstract mosaics and frescoes. On the marble floors, rugs were spread, beautifully wrought in colors, while here and there stood couches, tables and stools, fashioned of ebony from Libya, inlaid with ivory and pearl.

Benoni, the owner of all this wealth, having finished his business for the day, having taken count of a shipload of merchandise that had reached him from Egypt, had eaten his midday meal and now sought his couch under the portico to rest a while in the sun. Reclining on the cushions, he was soon asleep, but his dreams were unhappy—he turned from side to side muttering and clenching his hands. At last he sat up with a start.

"Rachel, Rachel!" he moaned. "Why do you haunt my sleep? Oh, my child, my child, have I not suffered enough? Must you bring my sin before me? Might I not shut my eyes even here in the sunlight and be at peace a while? What have you to tell me that you come thus often to stand here so silent and so still? Nay, it is not you. It is my sin that wears your shape!" Benoni hid his face in his hands, rocking himself to and fro and moaning aloud.

Presently he sprang up. "It was no sin," he said. "It was a righteous act. I offered her to the outraged majesty of Jehovah, as Abraham, our father, would have offered Isaac, but the curse of that false prophet is upon me and mine. The sin belongs to Demas, the half-bred hound who crept into my kennel. She loved him, and so I gave her to him as wife. Thus did he repay me, the traitor, and I—I repaid him. Aye! But the sword fell upon two necks. He should have suffered, and he alone. Oh, Rachel, my lost daughter Rachel, forgive me! I cannot bear those eyes of yours. I am old, Rachel, I am old."

Thus Benoni muttered to himself, as he walked swiftly to and fro. Then, worn out with his burst of solitary, dream-bred passion, he sank back upon the couch.

As he sat thus, an Arab doorkeeper, gorgeously appareled and armed with a great sword, appeared in the portico, and after looking carefully to see that his master was not asleep, made a low bow.

"What is it?" asked Benoni shortly.

"Master, a young lord named Caleb wishes speech with you."

"Caleb? I know not the name," replied Benoni. "Wait, it must be the son of Hilliel, whom the Roman governor"—he turned to spit upon the ground—"has brought to his own again. I heard that he had come to take possession of the great house on the wharf. Bring him in."

The Arab saluted and went. Presently he returned and ushered in Caleb, now a noble-looking young man clad in fine raiment. Benoni bowed to him and prayed him to be seated. Caleb bowed in return, touching his forehead in Eastern fashion with his hand, from which, as his host noticed, the forefinger was missing.

"I am your servant, sir," said Benoni with grave courtesy.

"Master, I am your slave," answered Caleb. "I have been told that you knew my father. Therefore, on this, my first visit to Tyre, I come to pay you my respects. I am the son of Hilliel, who perished many years ago in Jerusalem. You may have heard his story and mine."

"Yes," answered Benoni scanning his visitor, "I knew Hilliel. A shrewd man, but one who fell into a trap at last. And I see that you are his son. Your face proves it. Indeed, it might be Hilliel who stands before me."

"I am proud that you should say so," answered Caleb, though already he guessed that between Benoni and his father no love had been lost. "You know," he added, "that certain of our people seized my inheritance, which has now been restored to me—in part."

"By Gessius Florus the procurator, I think, who on this account, has cast many Jews—some of them innocent—into prison."

"Indeed! Is that so? Well, it was concerning this Florus that I came chiefly to ask your advice. The Roman has kept a full half of my property," and Caleb sighed and looked indignant.

"You are indeed fortunate that he has not kept it all."

"I have been brought up in the desert far from cities," pleaded Caleb. "Is there no law by which I may have justice of this man? Cannot you help me who are great among our people?"

"None," answered Benoni. "Roman citizens have rights, Jews have what they can get. You may appeal to Caesar if you wish, as the lamb may appeal to the lion when a jackal assails. But if you are wise you will be content with half the carcass. I can do nothing to help you. I am but an old merchant, and I have no authority."

Caleb looked crestfallen "It seems that the days are hard for

Jews," he said. "Well, I will be content and strive to forgive my enemies."

"Better to be content and yet strive to smite your enemies," answered Benoni. "You who were poor are rich. For this much, thank God."

"Night and morning, I do thank Him," replied Caleb earnestly.

Then there was silence for a while.

"Is it your intention to reside in Hezron's—I mean in *your* house—in Tyre?" asked Benoni, breaking it.

"For a time, perhaps, until I find a tenant. I am not accustomed to towns, and at present they seem to stifle me."

"Where were you brought up, sir?"

"Among the Essenes by Jericho. But I am not an Essene—their creed disgusted me. I belong to that of my fathers."

"There are worse men," replied Benoni. "A brother of my late wife is an Essene, a kind-hearted fool named Ithiel. You may have known him."

"Oh, yes, I know him. He is one of their curators and the guardian of the lady Miriam, his grandniece."

The old man started violently, then, recovering himself, said, "Forgive me, but Miriam was the name of my lost wife—one that disturbs me to hear. But how can this girl be Ithiel's grandniece? He had no relations except his sister."

"I do not know," answered Caleb carelessly. "The story is that the lady Miriam, whom they call the Queen of the Essenes, was brought to them nineteen or twenty years ago by a Libyan woman named Nehushta,"— here again Benoni started—"who said that the child's mother, Ithiel's niece, had been shipwrecked and died after giving birth to the infant, commanding that it should be brought to him to be reared. The Essenes consented, he accepted the charge, and there she is still."

"Then is this lady Miriam an Essene?" Benoni barked a laugh, full of disbelief.

"No, she is of the sect of the Christians, the faith in which she has been brought up, as her mother desired."

The old man rose from his couch and walked up and down

the portico.

"Tell me of the lady Miriam, sir," he said presently, "for the tale interests me. What is she like?"

"She is, as I believe, the most beautiful maiden in the whole world, though small and slight. And she is the most sweet and learned."

"That is high praise, sir," said Benoni.

"Yes, master, and perhaps I exaggerate her charms, as is but natural."

"Why is it natural?"

"Because we were brought up together, and I hope that one day she will be my wife."

"Are you then betrothed to this maid?"

"No, not betrothed—as yet," replied Caleb, with a little smile. "But I will not trouble you with a history of my love affairs. I have already trespassed too long upon your kindness. It is a great deal to ask of one who may not desire my acquaintance, but if you will do me the honor to sup with me tomorrow night, your servant will be grateful."

"I thank you, young sir. I will come, I will come," he added hastily, "for in truth, I am anxious to hear news of all that passes at Jerusalem, which, I understand, you left but a few days since, and I perceive that you are one whose eyes and ears are always open."

"I try both to see and to hear," said Caleb modestly. "But I am very inexperienced, and I am not sure which cause a man who hopes to become both wise and good ought to espouse in these troubled days. I need guidance such as you could give me, if you wished. For this while, farewell."

Benoni watched his visitor depart, then once more began to wander up and down the portico.

"I do not trust that man," he declared to the marble walls, "for I have heard something of his doings. But he is rich and able, and may be of service to our cause. This Miriam of whom he speaks. Who can she be? Unless, indeed, Rachel bore a daughter before she died. Why not? She would not have left it to my care if she desired that it should be reared in her own accursed faith.

She did, after all, look upon me as the murderer of her husband. If so, I who thought myself childless, yet have issue upon the earth—at least there is one in whom my blood runs. Beautiful, gifted—but a Christian! The sin of the parents has descended upon the child—yes, the curse is on her also. I must seek her out. I must know the truth. Man, what is it now? Can you not see that I would be alone?"

"Master, your pardon," said the Arab servant, bowing, "but the Roman tribune, Marcus, desires speech with you."

"Marcus? Oh, I remember. The officer who was stationed here. I am not well. I cannot see him. Bid him come tomorrow."

"Master, he bid me say that he sails for Rome tonight."

"Well, well, admit him then," answered Benoni. "Perhaps he comes to pay his debt," he added, though without much hope.

The Arab departed, and presently the Roman was ushered in.

"Greetings, Benoni," he said, with his pleasant smile. "Here am I, yet alive, for all your fears. So you see your money is still safe."

"I am glad to hear it, my lord Marcus," answered the Jew, bowing low. "But if it will please you to produce it, with the interest, I think," he added dryly, "it may be even safer in my strongbox."

Marcus laughed pleasantly. "Produce it?" he said. "What jest is this? Why, I come to borrow more to defray my costs to Rome."

Benoni's mouth shut like a trap.

"Nay," said Marcus, holding up his hand, "don't begin. I know it all. The times are full of trouble and danger. Such little ready cash as you have at command is out at interest in safer countries—Egypt, Rome . . . perhaps even Britannia. Your correspondent at Alexandria has failed to make you the expected remittance, and you have reason to believe that every ship in which you are concerned is now at the bottom of the ocean. So would you be so good as to lend me half a talent of silver—a thousand shekels in cash and the rest in bills of exchange on your agents at Brundisium?"

"No," said Benoni, sternly.

"Yes," countered Marcus with conviction. "Look you, friend Benoni, the security is excellent. If I don't get drowned, or have my throat slit between here and Italy, I am about to become one of the richest men in Rome. So this is your last chance of lending me a trifle. You don't believe it? Then read this letter from my uncle and this prescript signed by Nero Caesar."

Benoni perused the documents and returned them.

"I offer you my congratulations," he said. "If God permits it and you walk steadily, your future should be brilliant, since you are of a pleasant countenance, and when you choose to use it, behind that countenance lies a mind. But here I see no security for my money, since even if all things go right, Italy is a long way off."

"Man, do you think that I should cheat you?" asked Marcus hotly.

"No, no, but accidents might happen."

"Well, I will make it worth your while to risk them. For the half-talent write a talent charged upon my estate, whether I live or die. And be swift, I pray you, for I have matters to speak of, more important than this miserable money. While I was commissioner among the Essenes on the banks of Jordan—"

"The Essenes! What of the Essenes?" broke in Benoni.

Marcus considered him with his gray eyes, then answered, "Let us settle this little matter of business and I will tell you."

"Good. It is settled. You shall have the acknowledgment to sign and the consideration in cash and bills before you leave my house. Now what of these Essenes?"

"Only this," said Marcus. "They are a strange people who foretell the future, I know not how. One of them, with whom I became friends, foretold that mighty troubles were about to fall upon this land of yours—slaughter, pestilence, and famine, such as the world has never seen."

"That is the prophecy of those accursed Nazarenes," broke in Benoni.

"Call them not accursed, friend," said Marcus, in an odd voice, "for you should do so least of all men. Nay, hear me out. It may be a prophecy of the Nazarenes, but it is also believed among the Essenes, and I believe it, for I watch the signs of the times. Now the elder told me this, that there will be a great uprising of the Jews against the strength of Caesar, and that most of those who join in it shall perish. He even gave names, and among them was yours, friend Benoni. Therefore, because you have lent me money, although I am a Roman, I have come to Tyre to warn you to keep clear of rebellions and other tumults."

The old man listened quietly, but not as one who disbelieves.

"All this may be so," he said, "but if my name is written in that book of the dead, the angel of Jehovah has chosen me, and I cannot escape his sword. Moreover, I am aged, and"—here his eyes flashed—"it is a good end to die fighting one's country's enemies."

"How you Jews do love us to be sure!" said Marcus with a little laugh.

"The nation that sends a Gessius Florus, or even an Albinus, to rule its alien subjects demands much love," replied Benoni with bitter sarcasm. "But let us be done with politics lest we grow angry. It is strange, but a visitor has just left me who was brought up among these Essenes."

"Indeed," said Marcus, staring vacantly into the sea.

"He told me that a young and beautiful woman resides with them who is named the Queen of the Essenes. Did you chance to see her, my lord?"

Instantly Marcus became very wide awake. "Oh, yes, I saw her. And what else did he tell you?"

"He told me that this lady was both beautiful and learned."

"That is true," said Marcus with enthusiasm. "To my mind, although she is small, I never saw one lovelier, nor do I know a sculptor who is her equal. If you will come with me to the ship I will open the case and show you the bust she made of me. But tell me, did this visitor of yours lack the forefinger on one hand—his right?"

"He did."

"Then I suppose that he is named Caleb."

"Yes, but how do you know that?"

"Because I cut off his forefinger," said Marcus, "in a fair fight." He added casually, "He is a young rascal, as murderous as he is able. I think I did ill to spare his life."

"Ah," said Benoni, "it seems that I have still some discernment, for I judged him likewise. Well, what more do you know of the lady?"

"Something, for in a strange way I am betrothed to her."

"Indeed! Well, this is strange, for so is Caleb, or so he claimed."

"He told you that?" said Marcus springing from his chair. "Then he lies, and would that I had time to prove it on his body! She rejected him. I have it from Nehushta, also I know it in other ways."

"Then she did accept you, my lord Marcus?"

"No," he replied sadly. "But that was only because I am not a Christian. She loves me all the same," he added, recovering. "Upon that point I have no doubt."

"Caleb seemed to doubt it," suggested Benoni.

"Caleb is a liar," repeated Marcus with emphasis, "and one of whom you will do well to beware."

"Why should I beware of him?"

Marcus paused a moment, then answered boldly, "Because the lady Miriam is your granddaughter and the heiress of your wealth. I say it, since if I did not Caleb would. He has probably done so already."

For a moment Benoni hid his face in his hands. Then he lifted it and said, "I thought as much, and now I am sure. But, my lord Marcus, if my blood is hers my wealth is my own."

"Just so. Keep it if you will, or leave it where you will. It is Miriam I seek, not your money."

"I think that Caleb seeks both Miriam and my money—like a prudent man. Why should he not have them? He is a Jew of good blood. I think he will rise high."

"And I am a Roman of better blood who intends to rise higher."

"Yes, a Roman. And I, her grandfather, am a Jew who has no love for Romans."

"And Miriam is neither Jew by faith nor Roman by birth, but a Christian, brought up not by you, but by the Essenes. And she loves me, though she will not accept me for the sake of her faith."

Benoni shrugged his shoulders as he answered, "All of this is a problem which I must ponder on and solve."

Marcus sprang from his seat and stood before the old man with menace in his air.

"Look you, Benoni," he said, "this is a problem not to be solved by you or by Caleb, but by Miriam herself, and none other. Do you understand?"

"I understand that you threaten me."

"Aye, I do. Miriam is of full age. Her sojourn with the Essenes must soon come to an end. Doubtless you will seek to take her to dwell with you. Well, beware how you deal by her," he intoned. "If she wishes to marry Caleb of her own free will, let her do so. But if you force her to it, or suffer him to force her, then by your God, and by my gods, and by her God, I tell you that I will come back and take such a vengeance upon him and you, and upon all your people, that it shall be a story for generations. Do you believe me?"

Benoni looked up at the man who stood before him in his youth and splendor, his face as cold as chiseled marble, but his eyes on fire. He shrank back a little at the sight. He had not judged that this carefree Roman had such strength and purpose at command. Now he understood for the first time that he was the true son of a terrible race of conquerors, and if he were crossed, he could be as merciless as the worst of them. His very honesty and openness made him more worthy of fear.

"I understand that you believe what you say. Whether, when you are back at Rome where there are women as fair as the Queen of the Essenes, you will *continue* to believe it, is another matter."

"That is a matter for me to settle."

"Quite so—for you to settle. Have you anything to add to the commands you are pleased to lay upon Benoni the merchant, your humble creditor?"

"Yes, two things. First, that when I leave this house you will no longer be my creditor. I have brought money to pay you off in full, principal and interest. My talk of borrowing was but an excuse to learn what you knew of Miriam. It may seem strange to you that I also can be subtle. Foolish man, did you think that I with my prospects should lack for a miserable half-talent? Why, there at Jerusalem I could have borrowed ten or twenty if I promised my patronage by way of interest. My servants wait outside your door with the gold. Call them in presently and pay yourself, principal, interest, and something for a bonus.

"Now for the second, Miriam is a Christian. Beware how you tamper with her faith. It is not mine, but I say—beware how you tamper with it. You gave her father and her mother, your own daughter, to be slaughtered by gladiators and to be torn by lions because they did not believe as you do. Lift one finger against her and I will speed you on your way to the amphitheatre at Rome, where you will be slaughtered by gladiators or torn by lions. Even when I am absent I shall know all that you do, for I have friends who are good and spies that are better. And I will return here shortly. Now I ask you, will you give me your solemn word, swearing it by the God you worship, first, that you will not attempt to force your granddaughter Miriam into marriage with Caleb the Jew, and second, that you will shelter her, treating her with all honor and suffering her to follow her own faith in freedom?"

Benoni sprang from his couch.

"No, Roman, I will not. Who are you to dare dictate to me in my own house how I shall deal with my own grandchild? Pay what you owe and get you gone. Darken my doors no more. I have done with you."

"Ah!" said Marcus. "Well, perhaps it is time that you should travel. Those who travel to see strange countries and peoples, grow open-minded, which you are not. Be pleased to read this paper," and he laid a parchment before him.

Benoni took it and read. It was worded thus:

Gessius Florus, Procurator of the Roman province of Judea, to Marcus Carius, the tribune, in the name of Caesar, greetings. Hereby we command you, should you in your discretion think fit, to seize the person of Benoni, the Jewish merchant, a dweller in Tyre, and to convey him as a prisoner to Rome, there to answer charges which have been laid against him, with the particulars of which you are acquainted, which said particulars you will find awaiting you in Rome, of having conspired with certain other Jews, to overthrow the authority of Caesar in Judea.

Having read this, Benoni sank back upon his couch, gasping, his white face livid with surprise and fear. Then a thought seemed to strike him. Tearing the parchment he strode to a great brazier in the corner of the veranda and tossed it onto the burning coals.

"Now, Roman," he said, "where is your warrant?"

"In my pocket," answered Marcus. "The one I showed you was but a transcript. See this," he drew a silver whistle from his robe. "Outside your gate stand fifty soldiers. Shall I sound for them?"

"No," answered Benoni. "I will swear your oath, though indeed it is needless. Why should you suppose that I would wish to force this maid into any marriage or to work her evil on account of matters of her faith?"

"Because you are a Jew and a zealot. You gave her father and her mother to a cruel death, why should you spare her? And hate me and all my people. Why should you not favor my rival, even if he is a murderer whose life I have twice spared at the prayer of Miriam? Swear now."

So Benoni lifted his hand and spoke through clenched teeth. "I swear before God and man, I shall not force my granddaughter, Miriam, to marry Caleb or any other. I swear I shall not betray the secret of her faith or persecute her because of it.

"It is not enough," said Marcus, handing the Jew a wooden tablet. "Write it in wax and give it your seal."

So Benoni took the tablet, wrote out his undertaking and impressed the signet of his ring upon the wax. Marcus did likewise in witness.

"Now, Benoni," he said, as he took the tablet. "Listen to me. That warrant leaves your arrest to my discretion, after I have made search into the facts. I have made such search and it seems that I am not satisfied. But remember that the warrant is still in effect and can be executed at any moment. Remember also that you are watched, and if you lift a finger against the girl, it will be put in force. For the rest—if you desire that the prophecy of the Essenes should not come true, it is my advice that you cease from making plots against the majesty of Caesar. Now bid your servant summon him who waits in the antechamber, that he may discharge my debt. And so farewell. When and where we shall meet again, I do not know, but be sure that we shall." Without so much as waiting for an answer, Marcus left the portico.

Benoni watched him go, and as he watched, a dark look clouded his face.

"Threatened. Trodden to the dirt. Outwitted by a Roman boy," he murmured. "Is there any cup of shame left for me to drink? Who is the traitor and how much does he know? Something, but not all, else my arrest could scarcely have been left to the fancy of this patrician, favorite though he be. Yes, my lord Marcus, I too am sure that we shall meet again, but the fashion of that meeting may be little to your taste. You have had your hour, mine is to come. For the rest, I must keep my oath, since to break it would be too dangerous and might cut the hair that holds the sword. Why should I wish to harm the girl or to wed her to this braggart Caleb? Perhaps even the Roman would be better! At least he is a man who does not cheat or lie. Indeed, I long to see the maid. I will go at once to Jordan."

He sounded his bell and commanded that the servant of the lord Marcus should be admitted.

CHAPTER XI
THE ESSENES LOSE THEIR QUEEN

The Court of the Essenes was gathered in council to debate the subject of Miriam's departure. It was evident that she must go, for their ancient, sacred rule could not be broken even for her, whom each member of the community loved as a daughter. But where was she to go and how should she be supported? These were the questions that troubled them and they debated them earnestly. At length, her great uncle Ithiel suggested that she should be summoned before them, that they might hear her wishes. To this his brethren agreed, and he was sent to fetch her.

A while later, Miriam arrived, clad in a robe of pure white and attended by Nehushta. The maid wore on her head a shawl of white, edged with purple, and about her waist a purple sash. So greatly did the Essenes love and reverence her that as she entered, all the hundred of the Court rose and remained standing until she was seated. The Overseer, sorrowfully and even shamefaced, addressed her, telling her their trouble and praying her pardon for the ordinance of their order. Then he asked her what were her wishes regarding her own future, adding that for her provision she need have no fear, since out of their revenues a modest sum would be set aside annually, which would be enough to keep her from poverty.

In answer, Miriam, also speaking sadly, thanked them from her heart for all their goodness, telling them she had long known this hour of separation to be at hand. As to where she should dwell, Jerusalem was out of the question, for it had become a hotbed of unrest. She suggested she might find a home in one of the coastal cities, where some friend or relative of the brethren might shelter her.

Eight of those present immediately said they knew such trust-worthy folk in one place or another, and the various offers were submitted to the Court for discussion. While the talk was still underway there came a knock upon the door. After the usual precautions, a brother was admitted to inform them that there had arrived in the village, at the head of a considerable retinue, Benoni, the Jewish merchant of Tyre, and he desired speech with them.

"Here may be an answer to our quandary," said the Overseer. "We know of this Benoni, and that he purposed to demand his granddaughter of us. But until he did so, it was not for us to speak." Then he put it to the Court that Benoni should be admitted.

To this they agreed, and presently the Jew came, splendidly attired, his long white beard flowing down a robe that glittered with embroideries of gold and silver. Entering the dim, cool hall, he stared in amazement at the long half-circles of vener-able, white-robed men gathered there. His eyes quickly found the lovely maiden who, attended by the dark-visaged Nehushta, sat before them on a seat of honor. He knew that she could be none other than Miriam.

"Little wonder," reflected Benoni to himself, "that all men seem to love this girl. At the sight of her, even my heart soft-ens."

He bowed to the Overseer of the Court and received like respect in answer. But not one of the rest so much as moved his head, for already every man of them hated this stranger who was about to carry away the one they called their Queen.

"Sirs," said Benoni breaking the silence, "I come here upon a strange errand—to ask of you a maid whom I believe to be my granddaughter, of whose existence I learned not long ago and whom, as it seems, you have sheltered from her birth. Is she among you here?" he asked, looking directly at Miriam.

"The lady Miriam sits here," said the Overseer. "She is your granddaughter," he confirmed, "as we have known her to be from the beginning."

"Then why," said Benoni, "did I not know it also?"

"Because," answered the Overseer quietly, "we did not deem it fitting to deliver a child committed to our charge into the care of one who had brought her father and tried to bring her mother, his own seed, to a most horrible death."

As he spoke, he fixed his eyes grimly upon Benoni, as did every man of all that great company, until the bold faced Jew dropped his head in shame.

"I am not here," he said, recovering his composure, "to make defense of what I have or have not done in the past. I am here to demand that my grandchild, now a grown woman, be handed over to me, her natural guardian."

"Before this can be considered," answered the Overseer, "we who have been her guardians for so many years should require guarantees and sureties."

"What guarantees and what sureties?" asked Benoni.

"These among others: that money sufficient for her support

after your death should be left to her in your legacy. That she shall be given reasonable liberty in the matter of her daily life and of her marriage, if it should please her to marry. Lastly, that as we have undertaken not to meddle with her faith, or to persuade her into changing it, so must you undertake as well."

"And if I refuse these things?" asked Benoni.

"Then you see the lady Miriam for the first and last time," answered the Overseer boldly, while the others murmured their approval. "We are men of peace, but you must not think us men without power. We must part with the lady Miriam, who is as a daughter to every one of us, because the rule of our order ordains that she may no longer remain among us. But wherever she dwells, to the last day of her life, our love shall go with her and the whole strength of our Order shall protect her. If any harm is attempted against her, we shall be swift to hear and swifter to avenge. If you refuse our conditions, she will vanish from your sight. And then, you may search the world, the coasts of Syria, the banks of Egypt, and the cities of Italy—and find her if you can. We have spoken."

Benoni stroked his white beard before he answered. "You speak proudly," he said. "If I shut my eyes, I might think that this voice was that of a Roman procurator speaking the decrees of Caesar. Still, I am ready to believe that what you promise you can perform, since I for one am sure that the Essenes are not mere harmless heretics who worship angels and demons, see visions, prophesy things to come by the aid of familiars, and adore the sun in desert huts."

He paused, but the Overseer, without taking the slightest notice of his insults or sarcasms, repeated merely, "We have spoken." And as with one voice, like some great echo, the whole hundred of them cried, "We have spoken!"

"Do you hear them, master?" said Nehushta in the quiet that followed. "They mean what they say, and you are right—that which they threaten they can perform."

"Let my grandchild speak," said Benoni. "Daughter, is it your wish that such dishonoring bonds should be laid upon me?"

"Grandsire," replied Miriam, in her pure, clear voice, "I may not quarrel with that which is done for my own good. For the wealth I care little, but I would not become a slave in all but name, nor do I desire to set my feet on the same path my parents trod. What my uncles say—all of these," she said with a wave of her hand, "speaking in the name of the thousands that are without—I will do, for they love me and I love them, and their mind is my mind and their words my words."

"Proud-spirited, and well spoken," muttered Benoni. "Like all her race."

Still he hesitated.

"Be pleased to give your answer," said the Overseer, "that we may finish our discussion before the hour of evening prayer. To help you to it, we may remind you—we ask no new conditions." Benoni glanced up quickly and the Overseer added, "Those that you swore to and signed in the presence of Tribune Marcus Carius are sufficient for us."

Miriam's breath caught in her throat, and she looked up in surprise before again casting her eyes down in modesty, lest she betray her thought. As for her grandfather, he turned white with anger and broke into a bitter laugh.

"Now I understand—"

"—that the arm of the Essenes is longer than you thought, since it can reach from here to Rome," said the Overseer.

"Aye! And that you can plot with Romans. Be careful lest the sword of these Romans prove longer than *you* thought and reach even to your hearts, O you peaceful dwellers in the desert!" Then, as though he feared some answer, he added quickly, "I am minded to return and leave this maiden with you to dispose of as you think fit. Yet I will not do so, for she is very fair and gracious, and with the wealth that I can give her, may yet fill some high place in this world. Also—and this is more to me—I am old and draw near my end, and she alone has my blood in her veins. I will agree to all your terms. I shall take her home with me to Tyre, trusting that she may learn to love me."

"Good," said the Overseer. "Tomorrow the documents shall be prepared and signed. Meanwhile we pray you to be our guest."

Next evening they were signed accordingly, Benoni agree-

ing without demur to all that the Essenes had asked on behalf
of their ward, and even assigning to her an additional revenue
during his lifetime. Indeed, now that he had seen her, so loath
was he to part with this newfound daughter that he would have
done still more had it been asked of him, lest she should be spirited from his sight.

Three days later, Miriam bade farewell to her protectors, who
accompanied her by hundreds to the ridge above the village.
Here they stopped, and seeing that the moment of parting was
at hand, Miriam could not stop her tears.

"Weep not, beloved child," said Ithiel, "for though we part
with you in body, yet shall we always be with you in spirit.
Moreover, by night and day, we shall watch over you, and if any
seek to harm you—" he glanced at Benoni, that brother-in-law
to whom he bore little love—"the very winds will bear us tidings, and in this way or that, help will come."

"Have no fear, Ithiel," broke in Benoni, "my bond is good,
and it will be backed by love."

"If that is so, grandsire," said Miriam, "then I will repay love
for love." Then she turned to the Essenes and thanked them in
a voice broken with tears.

"Be not sorrowful," said Ithiel in a thick voice, "for I hope
that even in this life we shall meet again."

"May it be so," answered Miriam, and they parted, the
Essenes returning sadly to their home and Benoni taking the
road through Jericho to Jerusalem.

They traveled slowly; at the evening of the second day they
set their camp on open ground not far from the Damascus Gate
of the Holy City, within the new north wall that had been built
by Agrippa. Benoni would not enter into the city itself, fearing
that the Roman soldiers should plunder them. As the moon rose
over the arid slopes, Nehushta took Miriam by the hand and
led her past the resting camels to a spot a few yards from the
camp.

There, standing with her back to the second wall, she pointed
out a cliff, steep but of no great height, in which appeared little
caves and ridges of rock that gave to its face a rude resemblance

to a human skull.

"See," she said solemnly. "On that hill the Lord was cruci-fied."

Miriam heard and sank to her knees in prayer. As she knelt there, the grave voice of her grandfather spoke behind her, bidding her rise.

"Child," he said, "it is true. There were signs and wonders after the death of that false Messiah. For me and mine, he left a curse behind him that has not yet run its course. I know your faith, and I have promised to let you follow it in peace. But do not make prayers to your God here in public, lest others less tolerant should see you and drag you to your father's death."

Miriam bowed her head briefly and returned to the camp, and for a time, no further words pass between them on this matter of her religion. But she was careful from then on to do nothing that could bring suspicion on her grandfather.

Four days later they came to the rich and beautiful city of Tyre, and Miriam saw the sea upon which she had been born. She had imagined that its waters were much like those of the Dead Sea, upon whose shores she had dwelt so many years, but when she gazed upon the billows rushing onwards, white-crested, to break in thunder against the walls of island Tyre, she clapped her hands with joy. Indeed, from that day to the end of her life she loved the sea in all its moods, and for hours at a time would find it sufficient company. Perhaps this was because the seethe of its waves was the first sound that her ears had heard, while her first breath had been salted with its spray.

From Jerusalem, Benoni had sent messengers mounted on swift horses bidding his servants make ready to receive a guest. When she entered his palace in Tyre for the first time, Miriam found it decked as though for a bride. She wandered from room to room in amazement, these halls that for generations had been the home of kings and governors, for she had never known anything but the mud houses of the Essenes. Benoni followed her steps, watching her with grave eyes, until at length all was visited save his gardens on the mainland.

"Are you pleased with your new home, daughter?" he asked

presently.

"It's beautiful," she answered. "Never have I dreamed of such a place. Might I work my art in one of these great rooms?"

"Miriam," he answered, "you are the mistress of this house, as in due time you will be its owner. Believe me, child, it was not necessary that so many and such different men should demand from me sureties for your comfort and safety. All I have is yours, and all you have, including your faith and your friends, of whom there seem to be many, remains your own. Yet, should it please you to give me in return some small share of your love, you shall have the gratitude of a childless and friendless man."

"That is my desire," answered Miriam without hesitation, but a look of apprehension stole across her face. "But between you and me—"

"Speak it not," he said, with a gesture almost of despair. "Rather, I will speak it first—between you and me runs the river of your parents' blood. It is so, Miriam. But I repent of that deed. Age makes one judge more kindly. To me your faith is nothing, and your god a sham, but now I think that to worship him is not worthy of death. Not for that cause would I bring any to their death today, or even to stripes and bonds. I will go further. I will stoop even to borrow from his creed. Do not his teachings bid you to forgive those who have done you wrong?"

"They do," she answered gravely. "And that is why Christians show love for all mankind."

"Then bring that law into this home, Miriam, and love even me, for I sorrow for what I did in the blind rage of my zeal, and in my old age I am haunted by its memory."

Then for the first time Miriam threw herself into the old man's arms and kissed him on the brow.

So it came about that they made their peace and were happy together.

Day by day Benoni loved her more, until at length she was everything to him, and he grew jealous of all who sought her company, especially of Nehushta.

CHAPTER XII
THE RING, THE NECKLACE, AND THE LETTER

So Miriam came to Tyre, where, for many months, her life was peaceful and happy. At first she had feared meeting Caleb, for her grandfather had told her he was dwelling there. But she soon learned he had left the city upon business of his own, so for the while, she was free of him. In Tyre there were many Christians with whom she made friends and worshipped, and Benoni pretended to know nothing of the matter. Indeed, at this time and place, it was the Jews and not the Christians who were in danger at the hands of the Syrians and Greeks, who hated them for their wealth and faith, threatening them continually with robbery and murder. But that storm had not yet burst, and while its dark clouds gathered, the relatively few Christians, humble, and of all races, escaped notice.

Thus Miriam dwelt in quiet, occupying herself much with her art of sculpture and going abroad but little. It was scarcely safe for her, the grandchild of a rich Jewish merchant, to show her face in the streets. Though she was surrounded by every luxury—far more than she needed—this lack of liberty troubled her. She had been reared in the desert, and was not accustomed to the limits of walls. At times when she grew most melancholy, she would sit for hours looking on the sea and thinking. She thought of her mother who had sat thus before her, of her father who had perished beneath the gladiators' swords, of the kindly old men who had nurtured her, and of the sufferings of her brothers and sisters in the faith in Rome and Jerusalem.

But mostly she thought of Marcus, and for all her striving, she could not forget him for a single hour. She loved him—that was the truth of it—and between them lay a great gulf, not of the sea only, which ships could sail, but of faith and law. It was likely he had forgotten her by now, a girl who had taken his fancy in the desert. At Rome there were many noble and lovely women. She could scarcely bear to think of it. Yet each night she prayed for him, and morning by morning his face arose before her half-awakened eyes. Where was he? What was he doing? For all she knew, he might be dead. But surely, if that were so, her heart would have warned her. Still, she craved for tidings, and for too long, there were none.

At length, tidings did come—the best of tidings. One day, when she had grown weary of the house, Miriam took Nehushta and went to walk in her grandfather's gardens of Palaetyrus, north of the main district of Tyre. They were lovely gardens, well-watered and running down to the seashore; majestic palms and other trees grew there, beside fruitful shrubs and flowers. Here, when they had roamed a while, Miriam and Nehushta sat down upon the fallen column of some old temple to rest. There was a sudden stirring of a footstep behind them, and Miriam looked up to see before her a Roman officer, clad in a sea-salt encrusted cloak and guided by one of Benoni's servants.

The officer, a rough but kindly looking man of middle age, bowed to her, asking in Greek if he spoke to the lady Miriam, the granddaughter of Benoni the Jew, who had been brought up among the Essenes.

"Sir, I am she," answered Miriam.

"Then lady, I, Gallus, have an errand to perform." As he said this, he drew from his robe a parchment tied with silk and sealed with wax, together with a package, and handed them to her.

"Who sends these?" she asked, hope shining in her eyes, "and from where do they come?"

"From Rome, lady, as fast as the wind could waft them. They are sent by the hand of the noble Marcus, called Fortunatus."

"Is he well?" Miriam went on eagerly, blushing to her eyes.

"He is not so unwell that such a look as that, lady, would not better him were he here to see it," answered the Roman, gazing at her with open admiration.

"Did you then leave him ill?" she asked in mild distress. "I do not understand."

"No, his health seemed sound, and as his uncle is dead, they say his wealth can scarce be counted, for the old fool made him his heir. Perhaps that is why the divine Nero has taken such a fancy to him that he can scarce leave the palace. I cannot say whether Marcus is well today, for Nero's friends are sometimes short-lived. Nay, be not frightened. I did but jest. Your Marcus is safe enough."

"My Marcus . . ." she repeated to herself, having quite forgotten the messenger.

"Read the letter, lady, and waste no time. As for me, my mission is fulfilled. Thank me not. It is reward enough to have looked upon your sweet face. Fortunate indeed is the star of Marcus. I am jealous of the man, but for your sake, I pray that it may lead him back to you. Farewell, Lady."

"Cut the silk, Nou," said Miriam when the officer Gallus had gone. "Quick. I have no knife."

Nehushta obeyed with a knowing smile and the letter was unrolled. It ran thus:

> To the lady Miriam, Queen of the Essenes, from Marcus, her friend, tribune by the will of the Senate and of the People, by the hand of the centurion Gallus.
>
> Dear friend and lady, greetings. Already since I came here I have sent you one letter, but today news has reached me that the ship that bore it foundered off the coast of Sicily. So, as Neptune has that letter, and with it many good men, although I write more ill than I do most things, I send you another by this occasion, hoping as a vain youth that you have not forgotten me, and that the reading of it may even give you pleasure. Dearest Miriam, know that I accomplished my voyage to Rome in safety, visiting your grandsire on the way to pay him a debt I owed. But that story you will perhaps have heard.
>
> From Tyre I sailed for Italy, but was cast away upon the coasts of Melita, where many of us drowned. By the favor of some god, however—ah, what god I wonder—I escaped, and taking another ship came safely to Brundisium, and from there I traveled to Rome as fast as horses would carry me. I arrived here just in time, for I found my uncle very ill. Believing, moreover, that I had been drowned in the shipwreck at Melita, he was

about to make a will bequeathing his property to Nero Caesar, but by good fortune, he had said nothing of this. Had he done so, I think I should be as poor today as when I left you, dear. And perhaps poorer still, for I might have lost my head with my inheritance.

As it was I found favor in the sight of my uncle Caius, who a week after my arrival executed a formal testament leaving to me all his land, goods, and money, which on his death three months later I inherited. Thus I have become rich—so rich that now, having much money to spend, by some perversity that I cannot explain, I have grown careful and spend as little as possible. After I had entered into my inheritance, I made plans to return to Judea, for one reason alone—to be near to you, sweetest Miriam. At the last moment I was stayed by a very evil chance. That bust you made of me I had managed to save from the shipwreck and bring safe to Rome. Now I wish it was at the bottom of the sea.

When I came into possession of this house in the Via Agrippa, which is large and beautiful, I set it in a place of honor in the antechamber and summoned that sculptor, Glaucus, of whom I told you, and others who follow the art, to come and pass judgment upon the work. They came, they wondered, and they were silent, for each of them feared lest in praising it he should exalt some rival. When, however, I told them that it was the work of a lady in Judea, although they did not believe me—for they all declared that no woman had shaped that marble—knowing that they had nothing to fear from so distant an artist whoever he might be, they began to praise the work with one voice, and all that evening until the wine overcame them, they talked of nothing else. Also they continued talking into the morrow until at length the fame of the thing came to the ears of Nero, who is also an artist of music and other things. The end of it was that one day, without warning, the Emperor visited my house and demanded to see the bust, which I showed him. For many minutes he examined it through the emerald with which he aids his sight, then asked, 'What land had the honor to bear the genius who wrought this work?'

I answered, 'Judea,' a country of which he seemed to know little, except that some fanatics who refused to worship him

dwelt there. He said that he would make that artist ruler of
Judea. I replied that the artist was a woman, whereon he
answered that he cared not—she should still rule Judea, or
if this could not be managed he would send and bring her to
Rome to make a statue of him to be set up in the Temple at
Jerusalem for the Jews to worship.

Now I saw that I had been foolish, and knowing well what
your fate would have been, my Miriam, had he once set eyes
on you, I sighed and answered that alas, it was impossible,
since you were dead—a fact I attested to him by a long story
with which I will not bore you. Moreover, now that he was
sure that you were dead, I showed him the little statuette you
gave me of yourself looking into water. Whereon he burst into
tears at the thought that such a one had departed from the
earth, while it was still cursed with so many who are wicked,
old, and ugly.

Still he did not go, but remained admiring the bust, until at
length one of his favorites who accompanied him whispered
in my ear that I must present it to the Emperor. I refused,
whereon he whispered back that if I did not, assuredly before
long it would be taken together with all my other goods and,
perhaps, my life. So, since I must, I changed my mind and
prayed him to accept it, whereon he embraced, first the marble
and then me, and caused it to be borne away then and there,
leaving me mad with rage.

Now I tell you this silly story for a reason, for it has hindered and still hinders me from leaving Rome. Two days later
I received an Imperial decree, in which it was stated that
the incomparable work of art brought from Judea by Marcus
Carius, had been set up in a certain temple where those who
would please their Emperor were desired to present themselves
and worship it and the soul of her by whom it was fashioned.
Moreover, it was commanded that I, Marcus, whose features
had served as a model for the work, should be its guardian
and attend twice weekly in the temple that all might see how
the genius of a great artist is able to make a thing of immortal
beauty from a coarse original of flesh and blood. Oh, Miriam!
I have no patience to write of this folly, yet the end of it is,
that except at the cost of my fortune and the risk of my life,
it is impossible for me to leave Rome. Twice every week I must

attend in that accursed temple where my own likeness stands upon a pedestal of marble, and before it a marble altar, on which are cut the words, 'Sacrifice, O passerby, to the spirit of the departed genius who wrought this divine work.'

Yes, there I sit, a soldier, while fools come in and gaze first at the marble and then at me, saying things for which I often long to kill them and casting grains of incense into the little fire on the altar in sacrifice to your spirit, whereby I hope it may somehow be benefited. Thus, Miriam, are we ruled in Rome today.

Meanwhile, I am in great favor with Nero, so that men call me 'Fortunatus,' and my house the 'Fortunate House,' a title of ill omen.

Yet out of this evil comes some good, for because of his present affection for me, or for my bust, I have now and again for your sake, Miriam, been able to do service, even to saving the lives of those of your faith. Here there are many Christians who Nero amuses himself by hunting, torturing, and killing, sometimes by soaking them in tar and making of them living torches to illuminate his gardens, and sometimes in other even more monstrous methods. The lives of a few of these poor people he gave to me, when I begged them of him. Indeed, he has done more. Yesterday Nero came himself to the temple and suggested that certain of the Christians should be sacrificed here in a very cruel fashion as an offering to your spirit. I answered that this could give your spirit little pleasure, seeing that in your lifetime you also were a Christian. At this, he wrung his hands, crying out, 'Oh! What a crime have I committed!' And instantly he gave orders that no more Christians should be killed. So for a little while, thanks to your handiwork, and to me who am called 'the Model,' they are safe—those that are left of them.

I hear that there are wars and tumults in Judea, and that Vespasian, a great general, is sent to quell them. If I can, I will come with him, but at present—such is the madness of my master—this is too much to hope for unless, indeed, he wearies suddenly of the 'Divine Work' and its attendant 'Model.'

Meanwhile I also cast incense upon your altar, and pray that in these troubles you may come to no harm.

Miriam, I am most unhappy. I think of you always and yet

I cannot come to you. I picture you in many dangers, and I am not there to save you. I even dare to hope that you wish to see me again. But it is the Jew Caleb, and other men, who will see you and make offerings to your beauty while I must make them to your spirit. I beseech you, Miriam, do not accept their offerings, lest in some day to come, when I am once more a soldier and have ceased to be a custodian of busts, it should be the worse for those worshippers, and especially for Caleb.

What else have I to tell you? I have sought out some of the great preachers of your faith, hoping that by the magic of which they are said to be masters, they would be able to assure me of your welfare. But to my sorrow they gave me no magic—in which it seems they do not deal after all—only maxims. Also, from them I bought certain manuscripts written by them containing the doctrines of your law, which I intend to study when I have time. Indeed, this is a task that I wish to postpone, since did I read I might believe and turn Christian, to serve in due course as a nightlight in Nero's gardens.

I send you a present, praying that you will accept it. The emerald in the ring was cut by my friend, Glaucus, the sculptor. The pearls are fine and have a history that I hope to tell you some day. Wear them always, beloved Miriam, for my sake. I do not forget your words—nay, I ponder them day and night. But at least you said you loved me, and in wearing these trinkets you break no duty to heaven or to the dead. Write to me, I pray you, if you can find a messenger. Or, if you cannot write, think of me always as I do of you. Oh, that we were back together in that happy village of the Essenes, to whom, as to yourself, be all good fortune! I remain forever your faithful friend and love, Marcus Carius Fortunatus. Farewell.

Miriam finished her letter, kissed it, and hid it in her bosom. Then she opened the packet and unlocked the ivory box within by the key that hung to it. Out of the casket she took a roll of soft leather. This she undid and uttered a little cry of delight, for there lay a necklace of the loveliest pearls she had ever seen. Nor was this all, for threaded on the pearls was a ring, and cut upon its emerald bezel the head of Marcus, and her own likeness taken from the clay figure she had given him.

"Look! Nou, look!" said Miriam, showing her the magnificent ornaments.

"A sight to make old eyes glisten," answered Nehushta handling them. "I know something of pearls, and these are worth a fortune. Happy maid, to whom such love is given."

"Unhappy maid who can never be a happy wife," sighed Miriam, her blue eyes filling with tears.

"Grieve not. That still may come," answered Nehushta, as she fastened the pearls about Miriam's neck. "At least you have heard from him and he still loves you, which is much. Now for the ring . . . the marriage finger—look how well it fits," she said, taking Miriam's hand and slipping the ring onto it.

"Nay, I have no right," murmured Miriam. But she did not draw it off.

"Come, let us be going," said Nehushta, hiding the casket in her walking robe. "The sun sinks, and tonight there are guests to supper."

"What guests?" asked Miriam absently.

"Plotters, every one," said Nehushta, shrugging her shoulders. "The great scheme to drive the Romans from the Holy City ripens fast, and your grandsire waters its root. I pray that we may not all of us gather bitter grapes from that vine. Did you hear that Caleb is back in Tyre?"

"Caleb!" faltered Miriam, "No, I did not."

"He arrived yesterday and will be among the guests tonight. He has been fighting up in the desert there, and bravely, for I am told that he was one of those who seized the fortress of Masada and put its Roman garrison to the sword."

"Then he is against the Romans?"

"Yes, because he hopes to rule the Jews and risks much to gain more."

"I do not wish to meet him," said Miriam.

"Nay, but you must, and the sooner the better. Why do you fear the man?"

"I know not, but I do fear him, now and always."

When Miriam entered the supper chamber that night, the twelve guests were already seated on their couches, waiting for the feast to begin. By her grandfather's command, she was arrayed in her richest robes, fashioned and broidered after the Grecian fashion, and her hair was gathered into coils upon her head and held in place by a golden net. Round her waist was a girdle of gold set with gems, about her throat Marcus's necklace of pearls, and on her hand a single ring—that with his likeness and her own.

As she entered the great chamber, looking most lovely, her grandfather came forward to meet her and present her to the guests, who rose in greeting. One by one they bowed to her, and one by one she searched their faces with her eyes—stern faces and fierce. Now all had passed and she sighed with relief, for the one she feared was not among them. But even as she did so, a curtain swung aside and Caleb entered.

It was he; of that there could be no doubt. But oh, how changed he was since last she had seen him two years since! Then he had been but a raw, passionate youth. Now he was a tall and splendid young man, very handsome in his dark fashion, powerful of frame and quick of limb. His attire, that of an Eastern warrior noble, matched his person, and his bearing was proud and conquering. The guests bowed to him in respect as he advanced, as to a man of great and assured position who may become greater still. Even Benoni showed him this respect, stepping forward to greet him. All these greetings Caleb acknowledged haughtily, even lightly, until he saw Miriam watching from the shadow. Heedless of the other guests, he pushed his way towards her.

"Thus we meet again, Miriam," he said, his proud face softening as he spoke and his eyes gazing on her with a sort of rapture. "Are you pleased to see me?"

"Naturally, Caleb," she answered. "Who would not be pleased to meet the playmate of her childhood?"

He frowned, for childhood and its play were not in his thoughts. Before he could speak again Benoni commanded the company to be seated, whereon Miriam took her accustomed place as mistress of the house.

To her surprise, Caleb seated himself beside her on the couch that should have been reserved for the oldest guest, who for some moments was left to wander in silent wrath until Benoni, seeing what had passed, called him to his side. Then, golden vessels of scented water having been handed by slaves to each guest in turn, the feast began. As Miriam was about to dip her fingers in the water, she remembered the ring upon her left hand and turned the bezel inwards. Caleb noted the action, but said nothing.

"Where have you been, Caleb?" she asked.

"I've been in the wars, Miriam. We have thrown down the gate to Rome, and she has picked it up."

She looked at him inquiringly and asked, "Was it wise?"

"Who can tell?" he answered. "But it is done. For my own part I hesitated long, but your grandfather won me over. So now I must follow my fate."

Then he began to tell her of the taking of Masada and of the bloody struggles of the factions in Jerusalem.

After this he spoke of the Essenes, who still occupied their village, though in fear, since war was all about them. He did not forget to talk of their childhood days together—talk that pleased her greatly. While they spoke thus, a messenger entered the room and whispered something into Benoni's ear. The old Jew immediately raised his hands to Heaven as though in gratitude.

"What tidings?" asked one.

"This, my friends. Cestius Gallus the Roman has been routed from the walls of Jerusalem and his army is destroyed in the pass of Beth-horon."

"God be praised!" said the company as though with one voice.

"God be praised," repeated Caleb, "for so great and glorious a victory! The accursed Romans are fallen indeed."

Only Miriam said nothing.

"What is in your mind?" he asked her apart from the others.

"That they will spring up again stronger than before," she

replied. Then at a signal from Benoni, she rose and left the feast.

From the supper chamber Miriam passed down a passage to the portico and there seated herself, resting her arms upon the marble balustrade and listening to the waves as they lapped against the walls below.

The day had been disturbed. Different, indeed, from all the peaceful days to which she had grown accustomed. First had come the messenger bearing her Marcus's gifts and the letter she already longed to read again. Then hard upon his heels, like storm upon the sunshine, came Caleb who, unless she was mistaken, still wished her to be his wife. How curious was the lot of all three of them! How strangely they had been exalted! She, the orphan ward of the Essenes, was now a great and wealthy lady with everything her heart could desire. Except the one thing she desired most of all. And Marcus, the debt-saddled Roman soldier of fortune had also become suddenly great and wealthy. Pomp that he held at the price of playing some fool's part in a temple to satisfy the whimsy of an Imperial madman.

Caleb, too, had found fortune and had suddenly risen in these tumultuous times to place and power. All three of them were seated upon pinnacles, but Miriam felt they were pinnacles of snow that might be melted by the very sun of their prosperity. She was young, and of little experience, yet as she sat there watching the ever-shifting sea, there came upon her a great sense of the instability of things and an instinctive knowledge of their vanity. The men who were great one day, whose names sounded in the mouths of all, in the next could vanish, disgraced or dead. Factions rose and fell, high priest succeeded high priest, general supplanted general. Yet upon each of them at last, like the following waves that rolled beneath her, came dark night and oblivion. A little dancing in the sunshine, a little sighing in the shade, then death, and after death . . .

"What are you thinking of, Miriam?" said a rich deep voice at her elbow, the voice of Caleb.

She started, for she had believed herself alone, but she recovered herself quickly and answered, "What I think does not matter. Why are you here? You should be with your fellow—"

"Conspirators—why not just say the word? I am not with them, because sometimes one wearies even of conspiracy. Now we have triumphed and can take our ease. I wish to make the most of it. What ring do you wear on your finger?"

Miriam straightened herself and grew bold.

"Marcus's ring, which he sent me but today," she answered.

"I guessed as much. I have heard news of him. He has become a creature of the mad Nero. The laughingstock of Rome."

"I do not laugh at him, Caleb," she said solemnly.

"No," he dismissed her words brusquely. "You were ever faithful. But do you laugh at me?"

"Indeed not. How can I, when you seem to fill so great and dangerous a part with such dignity?"

He was silent a moment, struggling to decide whether or not she was mocking him. He finally elected to take her at her word. "Yes, Miriam, my part is both great and dangerous. I have risen high and I mean to rise higher."

"How high?"

"To the heavens, Miriam," he responded, his eyes glinting. "To the throne of Judea."

"A cottage stool would be safer, Caleb."

"Perhaps, but I have no taste for such seats. Listen, Miriam, I will be great or I will die. I have thrown in my lot with the Zealots, and when we have cast out the Romans I shall rule."

"*If* you cast out the Romans, and *if* you live. Caleb, I have no faith in your venture. We are old friends, and I ask you to escape from it while there is yet time."

"Why, Miriam?"

"Because He whom your people crucified and whom I serve prophesied its end. The Romans will crush you, Caleb. His blood lies heavy upon the head of this generation, and the hour of payment is at hand."

Caleb thought a while, and when he spoke again, the note of confidence had left his voice.

"It may be so, Miriam," he said, "though I put no faith in the sayings of your prophet. But at least I have taken my part and

will see the matter through. Now for the second time I ask you
to share its fortunes. I have not changed my mind. As I loved
you in childhood and as a youth, so I love you as a man. I offer
to you a great future. In the end I may fall or I may triumph,
but either the fall or the triumph will be worth your sharing. A
throne or a glorious grave—both are good. Who can say which
is better? Seek them with me, Miriam."

"Caleb, I cannot," she answered immediately, not meeting
his eyes, but looking at his right hand where his forefinger was
missing.

"Why?"

"Because it is both my duty and my birthright that I should
wed no man who is not of the faith. You know the story."

"If there were no such duty would you wed me, Miriam?"

"No," she said faintly.

"Why not?"

"Because I love another man that I am also forbidden to wed,
and until death I am pledged to him."

"Marcus the Roman?"

"Aye, Marcus the Roman. I wear his ring," she lifted her hand,
"and his gift is about my neck," and she touched the necklet of
pearls. "In this life until death I am his and his alone. This I say,
because it is best for all of us that you should know the truth."

Caleb ground his teeth in bitter jealousy. "Then may death
soon find him!"

"That would not help you, Caleb. Oh, why can we not be
friends as we were in the old times?"

"Because I seek more than friendship, and soon or late, somehow I swear that I will have it."

As the words left his lips, footsteps were heard, and Benoni
appeared.

"Friend Caleb," he said, "we await you. Why, Miriam, what
are you doing here? To your chamber, girl. Affairs are afoot in
which women should have no part."

"Yet as I fear, grandfather, women will have to bear the burden," answered Miriam. Then, bowing slightly to Caleb, she
turned and left them.

CHAPTER XIII
WOE, WOE TO JERUSALEM

Two more years flew by. Two dreadful, bloody years. Factions in Jerusalem tore each other. The Jewish leader Josephus, under whom Caleb was fighting, did all he could in Galilee, but Vespasian and his generals stormed city after city, massacring their inhabitants by the thousands. In the coast towns and elsewhere, Syrians and Jews made war. The Jews assaulted Gadara and Gaulonitis, Sebaste and Ascalon, Anthedon and Gaza, putting many to the sword. Then came their own turn, for the Syrians and Greeks rose upon them and slaughtered them without mercy.

There had not yet been any bloodshed in Tyre, though all knew that it must come. The Essenes, driven from their home by the Dead Sea, had taken refuge in Jerusalem. From this place, they sent messengers to Miriam warning her to flee from Tyre, where a massacre was being planned; warning her also not to come to Jerusalem, which they believed to be doomed, but to escape, if possible across sea. Nor was this all, for her own people, the Christians, besought her to flee for her life's sake with them to the city of Pella, where they were gathering from Jerusalem and all Judea. To both Miriam answered that what her grandfather did, that she would do also. If he fled, she would flee; if he stayed at Tyre, she would stay; if he went to Jerusalem, she would go; for he had been good to her and she had sworn that while he lived she would not desert him. So the Essene messengers went back to Jerusalem, and then a group of Christian leaders visited Miriam. The Christian elders prayed with her, and having blessed her and consigned her to the care of the Most High and His Son, their Lord, departed to Pella, where, as it had been ordained, through all those dreadful times not a hair of their heads was touched.

When she had parted from them, Miriam sought out her grandfather, whom she found pacing his chamber with a troubled air.

"Why do you look so sad, Miriam?" he asked. "Have some of your friends warned you that new sorrows are afoot?"

"Yes, grandfather," and she told him all.

"I do not believe them," he said passionately. "Why should you? Where is their authority? I tell you that we shall triumph. Vespasian is now Emperor in Rome, and they will forget this little land. The enemies who are of our own race we will conquer and kill, together with the Gentile dog. The Messiah will come, the true Messiah! Many signs and wonders declare that he is at hand. Aye! I myself have had a vision concerning him. He will come, and he will conquer, and Jerusalem shall be great and free and see her desire upon her enemies. I ask—where is your authority for these croakings?"

Miriam drew a scroll from her robe and read, "But when you see Jerusalem encompassed by armies, then you shall know that her desolation is at hand. Then let them which are in Judea flee into the mountains, and let them which are in the midst of her depart. And let not them that are in the country enter therein. For these are days of vengeance, that all things that are written may be fulfilled. Woe to them that are with child and to them that give suck in those days! For there shall be tribulation upon the land and wrath upon this people. And they shall fall by the edge of the sword and shall be led captive into all the nations, and Jerusalem shall be trodden down of the Gentiles until the time of the Gentiles be fulfilled."

Benoni listened in silence until she had finished. But when he answered he made no effort to hide his contempt. "So says the book of *your* law, but mine tells me otherwise. Well, child, if you believe it and are afraid, begone with your friends, the Christians, and leave me to meet this storm alone."

"I do believe it," she answered quietly, "but I am not afraid."

"That is strange, indeed," he said, "for you must believe also that you will come to a cruel death, terrible for the young and fair."

"Not so, grandfather, for this same writing promises that in these troubles not one Christian shall perish. It is for you that I fear, not for myself. I will go where you go, and bide where you bide. But, once more, and for the last time, I pray you to be wise and flee this wrath for otherwise you will perish." And as Miriam said the words her blue eyes filled with tears.

Benoni looked at her and for a moment his courage was shaken.

"Of your book I take no account," he said, "but in the vision of your pure spirit I am tempted to believe. Perhaps the things that you foresee will happen. So, child, I would have you flee. You will not lack an escort and I can give you money."

She shook her head. "I have said that I will not go without you."

"Then I fear that you here must bide, for I will not leave my wealth and home, even to save my life, and still less will I desert my people in their holy war. But if things fall ill for us, remember that I entreated you to depart, and do not reproach me."

"That I shall never do," she answered, smiling, and coming to the old man kissed him tenderly.

So they abode on in Tyre, and a week later the storm burst.

For many days it was not safe for Jews to show themselves in the streets of the city. Several who crept out about their business, or to fetch water or provisions, had been set upon and beaten to death by the mob, stirred up to the work by Roman emissaries. Benoni set to putting his house, which was part of an ancient fortress that had withstood many a siege, into a state of defense, and in supplying it with an ample store of victuals. He sent messengers to Caleb, rumored to be in command of the Jewish force at Joppa, telling him of their peril. Over a hundred noble Jews of Tyre had flocked into Benoni's palace-fortress, together with their wives and children, seeking refuge behind its walls, for there was no other place for them that could be so easily defended. Finally, in the outer courts and galleries were stationed fifty or more faithful servants and slaves who understood the use of arms.

Thus things remained for a while, the Syrians threatening

them through the gates or from the windows of high houses, and no more, until one night Miriam was awakened by a dreadful sound of screaming. She sprang from her bed and instantly Nehushta was at her side.

"What's happening?" she gasped as she dressed herself hastily.

"The Syrian dogs are attacking the Jews," answered Nehushta, "on the mainland and in the lower city. Come to the roof. We shall watch." Hand in hand, they ran to the sea portico and up its steep steps.

The dawn was just breaking, but looking from the walled roof they had no need of its light, since everywhere in the dim city below and in Palaetyrus on the mainland, houses flared like gigantic torches. In their red glare they could see the thousands of attackers dragging out their inmates to death, or thrusting them back into the flames, while the night was made horrible with the shouts of the maddened mob, the cries of the victims and the crackling roar of burning houses.

"Oh! Christ have mercy on them," sobbed Miriam.

"Why should He?" murmured Nehushta. "They rejected and slew Him. Now they pay the price He foretold. May He have mercy on us, His servants."

"He would not have spoken thus," said Miriam indignantly.

"Nay, it is His justice that speaks now. Those who take up the sword shall perish by the sword. Even so have these Jews done to the Greeks and Syrians in many of the cities—they who are blind and mad. Now it is their hour, and perhaps ours. Come, lady, this is no sight for you. But you might do well to learn to bear them, for if you escape tonight you may see many of the like. Come, and if you wish we will pray for these Jews, for their children, and for our own safety."

By noon that day, most of the poor and unprotected Jews of the city were slain, and the Syrians began their attack upon the fortified palace of Benoni. The defenders now learned that they were dealing with no mere rabble, but with savage hordes, many thousands strong, directed by officers of war. Armored men might be seen moving among the mob, and from their appearance it was easy to guess that they were Romans.

First an attack was made against the main gates, but when it was found that these were too strong to be easily taken, the assailants retreated with a loss of a score of men shot down by the defenders on the wall. Other tactics were then adopted, and the Syrians, now occupying the neighboring houses, began to vex the garrison with arrows from the rooftops. Thus they drove them under cover, but did little more, for the palace was built of marble with reinforced roofs and was not ignited by the burning shafts sped down upon it.

So the first day passed, and during the night no attack was made upon them. When dawn came they learned the reason, for there opposite the gates was reared a great battering-ram, and in the harbor a huge galley was being rowed in as close to their walls as the depth of water would allow, and from the decks the sailors prepared to hurl stones and siege arrows to break down their defenses and destroy them.

Then the real fight began. The Jews posted on the roof of the house poured arrows onto the men striving to work the ram, killing many of them, but the Syrians were finally able to push the ram so close that it could no longer be commanded. Now it went to work and with three blows of the great baulk of timber, the gates burst inward. The defenders, led by old Benoni himself, rushed out and put to sword those manning the ram. Then before they could be overcome, they retreated across the ditch to the inner wall, breaking down the wooden bridge behind them. The ram was of no further use, as it could not be dragged through the ditch, and the galley, now anchored within a hundred paces, began to catapult huge stones and arrows at them, knocking down the walls and killing both combatants and bystanders.

Thus matters went on until noon, the besiegers wearing them down with arrows from the land and the galley battering them from the sea. The defenders could do little to answer against the siege weapons. Benoni called a council and presented their desperate case. It was evident that they could not hold out another day, for at nightfall the Syrians would cross the narrow protecting ditch and set up the battering ram against the inner wall. They must either set out now and attempt to cut their way through and gain open ground, or fight on until the end, and at the last kill the women and children and rush out to be hacked down by the besieging thousands. The first plan was hopeless. Encumbered as they were by their families, they could not expect to escape the city. In their despair they decided on the second. All must die; therefore they would perish by each other's hands. When this decision was announced, a wail went up from the women and the children began to scream with fright.

Nehushta caught Miriam by the arm.

"Come to the highest roof," she said. "It is safe from stones and arrows. We shall see how this scene plays out."

So they went and crouched there praying, for their case was desperate. Suddenly Nehushta touched Miriam and pointed to the sea. She looked and saw another galley approaching fast as oars and sails could bring her.

"What of it?" she asked heavily. "It will but hasten the end."

But as the ship approached the shore the light of fire revealed what Nehushta had already suspected. The vessel was flying upon its mast neither the Roman Eagles nor the Phoenician banner, but the golden Menorah.

"Miriam," said Nehushta, gripping her arm. "The ship is Jewish. Look! The Syrian galley is raising anchor and preparing for a fight."

It was true enough, for now the oars of the Syrian shot out and she forged ahead towards the newcomer. But just then the current caught her, laying her broadside on, whereon the Jewish ship, driven by the gusting wind, shifted her helm and, amidst a mighty shouting from sea and shore, drove down upon her, striking her amidships with its beak so that she keeled over. Then there was more tumult, and Miriam closed her eyes to shut out the horrid sight.

When she opened them again, the Syrian galley had vanished, but the water was dotted with the heads of men in the throes of panic.

"Gallantly done!" Nehushta exclaimed. "See, she anchors

and puts out her boats; they will save us yet. Down to the water gate!"

On their way they met Benoni coming to seek them, and with him won the steps that were already crowded with fugitives. The two boats of the galley drew near, and in the bow of the first of them stood a tall and noble looking figure.

"It is Caleb," said Miriam. "Caleb who has come to save us."

Caleb it was indeed. At a distance of ten paces from the steps, he halted his boat and called aloud, "Benoni, Lady Miriam, and Nehushta, if you live, stand forward."

They stood forward.

"Wade into the sea," he cried again. They waded out until the water reached their necks; strong hands seized them one by one and dragged them into the boat. Many followed them and were also dragged in. When both boats were quite full, they turned and were rowed to the galley. Having transferred their passengers, the two boats went back and were again filled with fugitives, for the most part women and children.

Again they went, but as they set out for the third time, the ends of ladders appeared above the encircling walls of the steps, and the Syrians rushed out upon the portico, lowering themselves with ropes. The end of that scene was dreadful. The boats were filled until the water began to overflow their gunwales, but many still remained upon the steps or rushed into the water, women screaming and holding their children above their heads, and men thrusting them aside in the mad rush for life. The boats rowed off, some who could swim following them. For the rest, their end was the sword. In all, seventy souls were rescued.

Miriam flung herself downwards upon the deck of the galley and burst into tears, crying out, "Save them! Can no one save them?"

Benoni, seated at her side, the water running from his blood-stained garment, groaned, "My house sacked, my wealth taken, my people slain by the Gentiles!"

"Thank the God who has saved us," broke in old Nehushta, "God and Caleb. And as for you, master, blame yourself. Did not we Christians warn you of what was to come? Well, as it has been in the beginning, so it shall be in the end."

Just then Caleb appeared before them, proud and flushed with triumph, as he well might be who had done great things and saved Miriam from the sword. Benoni rose and, casting his arms about his neck, embraced him.

"Behold your deliverer!" he said to Miriam, and stooping down, he drew her to her feet.

"I thank you, Caleb. I can say no more," she murmured. But in her heart she knew that God had delivered her and that Caleb was but His instrument.

"I am well repaid," answered Caleb gravely. "For me this has been a fortunate day, for upon this day I have sunk the great Syrian galley and rescued the woman I love from the very jaws of death."

"Oath or no oath," broke in Benoni, abandoning the promise he had made, "the life you saved is yours, and if I have my will, you shall take her and whatever heritage remains to her."

"Is this a time to speak of such things?" said Miriam, looking up. "Look," she pointed to the seashore. "They drive our friends and servants into the sea and drown them," and once more she began to weep.

Caleb sighed. "Cease from useless tears, Miriam. We have done our best and it is the fortune of war. I dare not send out the boats again even if the mariners would listen to my command. Nehushta, lead your lady to the cabin and strip her of these wet garments lest she take cold in this bitter wind. Benoni, what is your will?"

"To go to my cousin Mathias, the high priest in Jerusalem," answered the old man, "who has promised to give me shelter, if in these days any can be found."

"Nay," broke in Nehushta, "sail for Egypt."

"Where also they massacre the Jews by thousands until the streets of Alexandria run with their blood," replied Caleb with sarcasm, adding, "Well, I cannot take you to Egypt. I must bring this ship to those who await her on this side of Joppa. From there I am summoned to Jerusalem."

"It is well, for there and nowhere else I will go," said Benoni, "to share in my nation's death or triumph. If Miriam wills it, I have told her she may leave me."

"What I have said before I say again," replied Miriam, "that I will never do."

Then Nehushta took her to the cabin, and presently the oars began to beat and the great galley stood out of the harbor, until in the silence of the sea, the screams of the victims and the shouts of the victors faded into memory. As night fell, naught could be seen of Tyre but the flare from the burning houses of the slaughtered Jews.

But for the weeping of the fugitives who had lost their friends and goods, the night passed in quiet, and although it was winter, the sea was calm and none pursued their ship. At daybreak she anchored, and coming from the cabin with Nehushta, in the light of the rising sun, Miriam saw before her a ridge of rocks over which the water poured, and beyond it a little bay backed by a desolate coast. Nehushta also saw and sighed.

"What is this place?" asked Miriam.

"Lady, it is where you were born. On that flat rock lay the vessel, and there I burned her many years ago. See those blackened timbers half buried in the sand upon the beach; they are her ribs."

"It is strange that I should return here, and in this condition, Nou," said Miriam sighing.

"Strange, indeed, but perhaps there is a meaning in it. You came in a storm to grow to womanhood in peace. Now, perchance, you come on a peaceful sea to pass through womanhood in a storm."

"Both journeys began with death, Nou."

"As all journeys end. Darkness behind and darkness in front, and between them a space of sunshine and shadow—that is the law. Yet have no fear. Anna, who had the gift of prophecy, foretold that you should live out your life. But my days are almost done, and it may be otherwise with me."

Miriam's face grew troubled.

"I fear neither life nor death, Nou, and I am willing to meet either as God wills. But to part with you—that thought brings me fear."

"I think that it will be yet awhile," said Nehushta, "for although I am old, I still have work to do before I lay myself down to sleep. Come, Caleb calls us. We are to disembark while the weather holds."

So Miriam entered the boat with her grandfather and others who had escaped, for the faces of all of them were set towards Jerusalem. They were rowed to the shore over the very rock where she first drew breath. Here they found Jews who had been watching for the coming of the galley. These men gave them a kind reception and what they needed even more—food, fire, and beasts of burden for their journey.

When all were gathered on the beach, Caleb joined them, having handed over the galley to another who was to depart immediately upon some secret mission of intercepting Roman corn ships. When the galley owners heard what he had done at Tyre, they were at first inclined to be angry, for they said that he had no right to risk the vessel thus, but afterwards, seeing that he had succeeded, and with no loss of men, praised him and said that it was a very great deed.

So the galley put about and sailed away, and those remaining began their journey to Jerusalem. A little while later, they came to the same village where Nehushta had found the peasant and his wife. The inhabitants, fled at the sight of them, thinking they were one of the companies of robbers that hunted the land in packs like wolves, plundering or murdering all they met. But when they learned the truth, the people returned and heard their story in silence, for in those days such tales were common enough. As it came to an end, a withered, sunburned woman advanced to Nehushta, and, laying one hand upon her arm, pointed with the other at Miriam, saying, "Tell me, friend, is that the babe I suckled?"

Then Nehushta, recognizing the nurse who had traveled with them to the village of the Essenes, greeted her, and answered, "She is." The woman rushed forward and cast her arms about Miriam, embracing her.

"Every day," she said, "I have thought of you, little one. My husband is gone and I have no children. But now that my eyes have seen you grown so sweet and fair, I care not how soon they close upon the world." Then she blessed her and called upon her angel to protect her yonder in Jerusalem, and the woman found her food and an ass to ride. So they parted, to meet no more.

They journeyed in relative security. With the armed guard of twenty men who accompanied Caleb, they were too strong a party to be attacked by the wandering bands of thieves, and although it was reported that Titus and his army had already reached Caesarea from Egypt, they met no Romans. Their only enemy was the cold, which proved so bitter that when, on the second night, they camped upon the heights over Jerusalem, having no tents and fearing to light fires, they were obliged to walk about until daylight to keep their blood moving. With the rising of the sun, they saw strange and terrible things.

In the clear sky over Jerusalem blazed a great comet, in appearance like a sword of fire. They had seen it before at Tyre, but never before had it shown so bright. And in Tyre, it had not had the appearance of a sword. Benoni sought to ease the fear they all felt at the sight, declaring that the point of the sword stretched out over Caesarea, presaging the destruction of the Romans by the hand of God. Towards dawn, the pale, unnatural luster of the comet faded, and the sky grew overcast and stormy. At length when the sun came up, to their marveling eyes, the fiery clouds took strange shapes.

"Look, look!" said Miriam, grasping her grandfather by the arm, "there are armies in the heavens, and they fight together."

They looked, and as they gazed skyward it seemed as though two great hosts were there embattled. The clouds, lit by the rising sun, took the form of legions, the wind-blown standards, the charging chariots, and the squadrons of impetuous horse. The firmament had become a battleground, and lo! It was red as with the blood of the fallen, while the air was full of strange and dreadful sounds, bred, perhaps, of wind and distant thunder that came to them like the wail of the vanquished and the dull roar of triumphant armies. So terrified were they at the sight, that they crouched upon the ground and hid their faces in their hands. But Benoni stood tall, his white beard and robes stained red by the ominous light, crying out that this celestial scene foretold the destruction of God's enemies.

"Aye!" said Nehushta, "but which enemies?"

The tall Caleb, marching on his round of the camp, echoed, "Yes, which enemies?"

Suddenly as the light grew, all these fantastic shapes melted into a red haze and sank down until Jerusalem before them seemed as though she floated in an ocean of blood and fire. Then a dark cloud came up, and for a while the holy Hill of Zion vanished utterly away. It passed, the blue sky stretched above the city, and the clear light of dawn streamed upon her marble palaces and clustered houses, reflecting off the golden crown of the Temple. So calm and peaceful did the glorious city now look that none would have guessed that she was already nothing but a house of slaughter, where factions fought furiously and hundreds of Jews perished day by day beneath the swords of their own brethren.

Caleb gave the word to break camp, and with bodies shivering in the cold and spirits terrified by fear, they marched across the rugged hills towards the Joppa gate, noting as they passed into the valley that the country had been desolated, for but little grain grew in the fields, and even that was trodden down; of flocks and herds they saw none. They found the city gate shut and were challenged there by soldiers, wild-looking men with cruel faces of the army of Simon of Gerasa who held the Lower City.

"Who are you and what is your business?" these asked.

Caleb set out his rank and titles, and as these did not seem to satisfy them, Benoni explained that the rest of them were fugitives from Tyre, where there had been a great slaughter of the Jews.

"Fugitives always have money," said the captain of the gate. "Best kill them. Doubtless they are traitors and deserve to die."

Caleb grew angry and commanded them to open, asking by what right they dared to exclude him, a high officer who had done great service in the wars.

"By the right of the strong," they answered. "Those who let in Simon have to deal with Simon. If you are of the party of John or of Eleazar go to the Temple and knock upon its doors," and they pointed mockingly to the gleaming gates above.

"Has it come to this, then," asked Benoni, "that Jew eats Jew in Jerusalem, while the Roman wolves raven round the walls? Man, we are of no party, although, as I think, my name is known and honored by all parties—the name of Benoni of Tyre. I demand to be led, not to Simon, or to John, or to Eleazar, but to my cousin, Mathias, the high priest, who bids us here."

"Mathias, the high priest," said the captain, "that is another matter. Well, this Mathias let us into the city, where we have found good quarters and good plunder, so we may as well let his friends in. Pass, cousin of Mathias the high priest, with all your company," and he opened the gate.

They entered and marched up the narrow streets towards the Temple. It was the hour of the day when all men should be stirring and busy with their work, but the place was desolate. The crowds that met them were not of trade and commerce, but of desolation. On the pavement lay bodies of men and women slain in some midnight outrage. From behind the lattices of the windows they caught sight of the eyes of hundreds peeping at them, but none gave them greeting or said one single word.

The silence of death brooding upon the empty streets was presently broken by a single wailing voice that reached their ears from so far away that they could not catch its meaning. Nearer and nearer it came, until at length in the dark and narrow street, they caught sight of a thin, white-bearded figure, naked to the waist as if to display the hideous scars and rod-weals with which its back and breast were scored, some of them still festering. This was the man who uttered the cries, and these were the words he spoke, "A voice from the East! A voice from the West! A voice from the four Winds! A voice against Jerusalem and against the Temple! A voice against the bridegroom and the bride! A voice against the whole people! Woe, woe to Jerusalem!"

Now he was upon them, and marching through them as though he saw them not, although they shrank to either side of the narrow street to avoid the touch of this ominous, unclean creature who scarcely seemed to be a man.

"Sir, what do you mean by these words?" cried Benoni in angry fear.

But, taking no heed, his pale eyes fixed upon the heavens, the wanderer answered only, "Woe, woe to Jerusalem! Woe to you who come up to Jerusalem!"

So he passed on, still uttering those awful words, until at length they lost sight of his naked form and the sound of his crying grew faint and died away.

"What a fearful greeting!" said Miriam, wringing her hands.

"Aye!" answered Nehushta, "but the farewell will be worse. The place is doomed and all in it."

But Caleb, striving to look unconcerned, said, "Have no fear, Miriam. I know the man. He is mad."

"Where does wisdom end and madness begin?" asked Nehushta.

Then they went on towards the gates of the Temple, through a maze of empty, bloodstained streets.

CHAPTER XIV
THE ESSENES FIND
THEIR QUEEN AGAIN

They went on towards the gates of the Temple, but many long days were destined to pass before Miriam would enter through them. They were directed to the two Huldah Gates on the south side of the Royal Cloister, and there they crossed the valley of Tyropaeon. As they drew near to them, the eastern Huldah gate was suddenly flung wide, and out of it emerged a thousand or more armed men, like ants from a broken nest, who rushed toward their company, shouting and brandishing swords. At that moment they were in the center of open ground that once had been covered with houses but was now strewn with hundreds of blackened and tottering walls devoured by fire.

"It is John's men," cried a voice. At this, moved by a common impulse, the little band turned and fled for shelter among the ruined houses, Caleb and Benoni heading the group.

Before they could reach shelter, out rushed another body of savage warriors, the men of Simon who held the Lower City.

In the confusion, Miriam knew little of what happened. Swords and spears flashed round about her, the factions met with a mighty crash, and fell to slaughtering one other. She saw Caleb cut down one of John's soldiers, only to be instantly assaulted in turn by one of Simon's, for all desired to kill, but none cared whom they slew. She saw her grandfather rolling over and over on the ground in the grip of a man who looked like a priest; she saw women and children pierced with spears. Then Nehushta seized her by the hand to drag her away, plunging a knife into the arm of a man that tried to lay hold of them. They fled, an arrow sang past her ear; something struck her foot. Still they fled, where she knew not, until at length the sound of the tumult died away. But Nehushta would not yet stop, for she feared they might be followed. So on they went, and on, meeting few and heeded by none. At length, Miriam sank to the ground, worn out with fear and flight.

"Up," said Nehushta.

"I cannot," she answered. "Something has hurt my foot. See, it bleeds!"

Nehushta looked about her, and saw that they were outside the second wall in the new city of Bezetha, not far from the old Damascus Gate, for there, to their right and a little behind them, rose the great tower of Antonia. Beneath this wall were rubbish-heaps, foul smelling and covered over with rough grasses and some spring flowers, which grew upon the slopes of the ancient ditch. Here seemed a place where they might lie hid awhile, since there were no houses and it was unsavory. She dragged Miriam to her feet and, ignoring her complaints and swollen ankle, forced her on until they came to a spot where the wall was built upon foundations of living rock, roughly shaped, and lined with crevices covered by tall weeds. Nehushta brought Miriam to one of these crevices and, seating her on a bed of grass, examined her foot, which seemed to have been injured by a stone from a sling. Having no water with which to wash the bleeding wound, she made a poultice of crushed herbs and tied it about the ankle with a strip of linen. So exhausted was Miriam that she fell fast asleep even before Nehushta had finished her task. She watched Miriam a while, wondering what they should do next, and in that lonely place bathed by the warm spring sun, she also began to doze.

She awoke with a start, having dreamed that she saw a man with a white face and beard peering at them from behind a rough angle of rock. She stared . . . there was the rock just as she had dreamed, but no man. She looked upward. Above them rose the city wall, piled block upon gigantic block, towering and impregnable. No man could have gone that way. Nor was he anywhere else, for there was no cover. She decided that he must have been some searcher of the rubbish-heap, who had fled away when he saw them hidden in the tall grasses. Miriam was still sound asleep, and in her weariness presently Nehushta again began to

doze, until at length—it may have been one hour later, or two or three, she knew not—some sound disturbed her. Opening her eyes, once more behind that ridge of rock she saw, not one white-bearded face, but two, staring at her and Miriam. As she sat up they vanished. She remained still, pretending to sleep, and again they appeared, scanning her closely and whispering to each other in eager tones. Suddenly one of the faces turned a little so that the light fell on it. Now Nehushta knew why in her dream it had seemed familiar, and in her heart thanked God.

"Brother Ithiel," she said in a voice hardly louder than a whisper, "why do you hide like a coney in these rocks?"

Both heads disappeared, but the sound of whispering continued. Then one of them rose again among the green grasses as a man might rise out of water. It was Ithiel's aged face that stared at them.

"It is indeed you, Nehushta?" said his well-remembered voice.

"Who else?" she asked.

"And that lady who sleeps at your side?"

"Once they called her Queen of the Essenes. Now she is a hunted fugitive, waiting to be massacred by Simon, or John, or Eleazar, or Zealots, or Sicarii, or any other of the holy cut-throats who inhabit this Holy City," answered Nehushta bitterly.

Ithiel raised his hands as though in thankfulness, then said, "Hush! Hush! Here the very birds are spies. Brother, go to that rock and look if any men are moving."

The Essene obeyed, and answered, "None. And they cannot see us from the wall."

Ithiel motioned to him to return.

"Does she sleep sound?" he asked of Nehushta, pointing to Miriam.

"Like the dead."

Then, after another whispered conference, the pair of them crept round the angle of the rock. Bidding Nehushta follow them, they lifted the sleeping Miriam, and carried her between them through a dense growth of shrubs to another rock. Here they moved some grass and pushed aside a stone, revealing a hole not much larger than a jackal would make. Into this, the brother entered, heels first. Then Nehushta, by his direction, taking the feet of the sleeping Miriam, with her help he bore her into the hole, which opened presently into a wide passage. Last of all Ithiel, having lifted the grass where their feet had trod, followed them, pulling the stone back to its place, and cutting off the light. Once more they were in darkness, but this did not seem to trouble the brethren, for again lifting Miriam, they went forward a distance of thirty or forty paces, Nehushta holding on to Ithiel's robe. At length, the cold air of this cave, or perhaps its deep gloom and the motion, awoke Miriam from her swoon-like sleep. She struggled in their hands, and would have cried out, had not Nehushta bade her to be silent.

"Where am I?" she said. "Is this the hall of death?"

"Nay, lady. Wait a while, all shall be explained."

While she spoke and Miriam clung to her uneasily, Ithiel struck iron and flint together. Catching the spark upon tinder, he blew it to a flame and lighted a taper which burnt up slowly, causing his white beard and face to appear by degrees out of the darkness, like that of a ghost rising from the tomb.

"Surely I am dead," said Miriam, "for before me stands the spirit of my uncle Ithiel."

"Not the spirit, Miriam, but the flesh," answered the old man in a voice that trembled with joy. Then, since he could restrain himself no longer, he gave the taper to the brother, and, taking her in his arms, kissed her again and again.

"Welcome, dearest child," he said. "Yes, even to this den of darkness, welcome, thrice welcome, and blessed be the eternal God who has led our feet forth to find you. Nay, do not stop to talk, we are still too near the wall. Give me your hand and come."

Miriam glanced up as she obeyed, and by the feeble light of the taper she saw a vast rocky roof arching above them. On either side of her were walls of rough-hewn rock, dripping with water, and piled upon the floor or still hanging half-cut from the roof were boulders large enough to fashion a temple column.

"What awful place is this, Uncle?" she asked.

"The cavern where Solomon, the great king, drew stone for the building of the Temple. Look, here are his mason's marks upon the wall. Here he fashioned the blocks, and thus no sound of saw or hammer was heard within the building. Doubtless also other kings before and since his day have used this quarry, for no man knows its age."

While he spoke thus, he was leading her onwards over the rough, stone-hewn floor, where the damp gathered in little pools. Following the windings of the cave, they turned once, then again and yet again, so that soon Miriam was utterly bewildered and could not have found her way back to the entrance for her life's sake. And the air was becoming so hot and stifling that she could scarcely breathe.

"It will be better presently," said Ithiel, noting her distress, as he drew her limping after him into what seemed to be a natural crevice of rock, hardly large enough to allow the passage of his body. They scrambled along this crevace for eight or ten paces, to find themselves suddenly in a tunnel lined with masonry, and so large that they could stand upright.

"It was once a watercourse," explained Ithiel, "that filled the great tank, but it has been dry for centuries."

Down this darksome shaft hobbled Miriam, until presently it ended in a wall, or what seemed to be a wall—when Ithiel pressed upon a stone, it turned. Beyond it the tunnel continued for twenty or thirty paces, leading them at length into a vast chamber with vaulted roof and cemented sides and floor. Lights were burning here, and even a charcoal fire, at which a brother sat cooking. The air was pure and sweet, perhaps because of the winding water channels that ran upwards. Nor did the place lack inhabitants, for there, seated in groups round the tapers or watching the cooking over the charcoal fire, were forty or fifty men, most of them still clad in the robes of the Essenes.

"Brethren," cried Ithiel, in answer to the challenge of one who was set to watch the entry, "I bring back to you her whom we lost a while ago, the lady Miriam."

Upon hearing this news, they siezed their tapers and ran forward to see for themselves.

"It is she!" they cried, "our queen and none other, and with her Nehushta the Libyan! Welcome, welcome, a thousand times, dear lady!"

Miriam greeted them one and all, and before these greetings were finished they brought her food to eat, rough but wholesome, together with good wine and sweet water. While she ate, she heard all their story. More than a year ago, the Romans, marching on Jericho, had fallen upon their village and put a number of them to death, seizing others as slaves. The remnant fled to Jerusalem, where many more perished, for, being peaceable folk, all the factions robbed and slew them. Seeing, at last, that to live at large in the city would be to doom themselves to extinction, and yet not daring to leave it, they sought a refuge in this underground place, of which one of their brethren knew the secret. He had inherited the knowledge from his father, and so far as they knew, it was known to no other living man.

Slowly they laid up a great store of provisions of all sorts, of charcoal for burning, and other necessaries, also amassing clothes, bedding, cooking utensils, and even some rough furniture in the place. When these preparations had been made, the fifty of them who remained moved to the vaults where now they had already dwelt three months, and here, as much as was possible, continued to practice the rules of their order. Miriam asked how they kept their health in this darkness, to which they replied that sometimes they went out by that path which she had just followed, and mingled with the people in the city, returning to their hole at night. Ithiel and his companion were on such a journey when they found her. Also they had another passage to the upper air, which they would show her later.

When Miriam had finished eating, dressed her wound, and rested a while, they took her to explore the wonders of the place. Beyond this great cistern, which was their common room, lay six or seven more, the smallest of which they gave to Nehushta and herself to dwell in. Others were filled with stores enough to last them all for months. Last of all was a cave, not very large, but deep, through which always flowed sweet water. Doubtless there was a spring at the bottom of it that, when the other rainfed tanks grew dry, kept it full. From this cistern a little stair ran upwards, worn smooth by the feet of folk long gone who had come to draw water.

"Where does it lead?" asked Miriam.

"To the ruined tower above," answered Ithiel. "Nay, another time I will show you. Now your place is made ready for you. Go, let Nehushta bathe your foot, and sleep, for you must be tired."

So Miriam went and laid herself down to rest in the little cemented vault which was to be her home for four long months, and being worn out, despite the sufferings she had endured and her fears for her grandfather, slept there as soundly as ever she had done in her windswept chamber at the palace of Tyre or in her house at the village of the Essenes.

When she awoke and saw the darkness all about her, she thought that it must be night. Then she remembered that in this place it was always night. She called to Nehushta, who uncovered the little lamp that burned in a corner of the vault and went out, to return presently with the news that according to the Essenes, it was day. So she rose and put on her robes, and they passed together into the great chamber. Here they found the Essenes at prayer and making their reverences, after which they ate their morning meal. Now Miriam spoke to Ithiel, telling him of her trouble about her grandfather, who, if he still lived, would think that she was dead.

"One thing is certain," replied her great uncle. "You must not go out to seek him, nor tell him of your hiding place, for sooner or later this might lead to our destruction, if only for the sake of the food which we have hoarded."

Miriam asked, "Can we at least send word?"

He answered, "No, for none would dare take it." In the end, however, after she had pleaded with him long and earnestly, it was agreed that she should write the words, "I am safe and well, but in a place that I must not tell you of," and sign her name upon a piece of parchment. Ithiel, who planned to creep into the city that evening disguised as a beggar to seek tidings, said he would take this letter, and if necessary, bribe some soldier to deliver it to Benoni at the house of the high priest.

So Miriam wrote the letter, and at nightfall Ithiel and another brother departed, taking it with them.

The following morning they returned safely, but with a dreadful tale of the slaughter in the city and in the Temple courts, where the mad factions still fought furiously.

"Your tidings, my uncle?" said Miriam, rising to meet him. "Does he still live?"

"Be at ease," he answered. "Benoni reached the house of Mathias in safety, and Caleb also, and now they are sheltering within the Temple walls. This much I had from one of the high priest's guards, who, for the price of a piece of gold I gave him, swore that he would deliver the letter without fail. But I will take no more, for that soldier eyed me curiously and said it was scarcely safe for beggars to carry gold."

Miriam thanked him for his goodness and his news, saying that they lifted a weight from her heart.

"I have other tidings that may perhaps make it lighter still," went on the old man, looking at her sideways. "Titus draws near to Jerusalem from Caesarea at the head of a mighty host."

"There is no joy in that tale," replied Miriam. "The Holy City will be besieged and taken."

"Nay, but among that host is one who, if all the stories are true," and again he glanced at her face, "would rather take you than the city."

"Who?" she said, pressing her hands against her heart and turning redder than the lamplight.

"Titus's prefect of horse, the noble Roman, Fortunatus, whom you knew by the banks of the Jordan."

Now the blood fled back to Miriam's heart, and she turned so faint that she would have fallen had not the wall been near at hand.

"Marcus?" she said. "Indeed, he swore he would come, yet it will hardly bring him nearer to me." She left in silence to seek her chamber.

So Marcus had come. Since he sent the letter and the ring that was upon her hand, and the pearls that were about her neck, she had heard no more of him. Twice she had written and sent word by the most trustworthy messenger she could find, but whether they reached him, she did not know. For more than two years the silence between them had been that of death until, indeed, at times she thought that he must be dead. And now he was come back, a commander in the army of Titus, who marched to punish the rebellious Jews. Would she ever see him again? Miriam could not tell. Yet she knelt and prayed from her pure heart that if it were once only, she might speak with him face to face. Indeed, it was this hope of meeting that, more than any other, supported her through all those dreadful days.

A week went by, and although the injury to her foot had healed, like some flower in the dark, Miriam drooped and languished in those gloomy vaults. Twice she prayed her uncle to be allowed to creep to the mouth of the hole behind the ridge of rock, there to breathe the fresh air and see the blessed sky. But this he would not permit. It was too dangerous, he said, for although none knew the secret of their hiding place, already two or three fugitives had found their way into the quarries by other entrances, and these made it very difficult to pass unseen.

"So be it," answered Miriam, and crept back to her cell.

Nehushta looked after her anxiously, then said, "If she cannot have air I think that she will soon die. Is there no way?"

"One," answered Ithiel, "but I fear to take it. The staircase from the spring leads to an ancient tower that, I am told, once was a palace of the kings. But it has been deserted for many years, and its entrance is bricked up lest thieves should make it their home. None can come into that tower, nor is it used for purposes of war, not standing upon any wall. There she might sit at peace and see the sun, but I fear to let her do so."

"It must be risked," answered Nehushta. "Take me to visit this place."

So Ithiel led her to the cistern, and from there they ascended a flight of steps to a small vaulted storeroom, which they entered through a stone trapdoor. It was made of the same rock as the paving of the chamber so that when it was closed none would guess there was a passage beneath. From this old chamber ran more steps, which appeared to lead directly into a bare wall. Coming to it, Ithiel thrust a piece of flat iron, a foot or more in length, into a crack in this wall, lifted some stone latch within, and pushed, whereon a block of masonry of something more than the height and width of a man, and quite a yard in thickness, swung outwards. Nehushta passed through the aperture, followed by Ithiel.

"See," he said, loosing his hold of the stone, which without noise instantly closed, so that behind them there appeared to be nothing but a wall, "it is well hidden, is it not? To come here without this iron would be dangerous. Here is the crack where it must be set to lift the latch within."

"Whoever lived here guarded their food and water well," answered Nehushta.

Then Ithiel showed her the place. It was a massive tower about forty feet square, and the only entrance, as he told her, had been bricked up many years before to keep the thieves and vagabonds from sheltering there. In height it must have measured nearly a hundred feet, and its roof had long ago rotted away. The staircase cut into the stone of the cave still remained, leading to four galleries. Perhaps once there had been floors as well, but if so they had vanished, and only the stone galleries and their balustrades remained. Ithiel led Nehushta up the stair, which, though narrow, was safe and easy. Resting at each story, at length they came to that gallery, which projected from its sides within ten feet of the top of the tower. From this point, they saw Jerusalem and the countryside nearby spread like a map before them. Then, as it was sunset, they returned. At the foot of the stair Ithiel gave Nehushta the iron key and showed her how to lift the secret latch and pull upon the block of hewn stone that was a door, so that it opened to swing closed behind them.

Next morning, before it was dawn in the world above, Miriam aroused Nehushta. She had been promised that this day she should be taken up the Old Tower, and so great was her longing for the scent of the free air and the sight of the blue sky that she had scarcely closed her eyes the whole night.

"Have patience, lady," said Nehushta. "Have patience. We cannot start until the Essenes have finished their prayers. Down in this black hole, they worship more earnestly than ever."

So Miriam waited, though she would eat nothing, until at length Ithiel came and led them past the cistern up the stairs to the store or treasure chamber, where the trapdoor stood wide, since, except in case of some danger, they had no need to shut it. Next, they reached the door of solid stone, which Ithiel showed her how to open, and entered the base of the massive building. There, far above her, Miriam saw the sky again, red from the light of morning, and at the sight of it she clapped her hands and called aloud for happiness.

"Hush!" Ithiel warned. "The walls are thick, but it is not safe to raise a voice of joy in Jerusalem, for it has become the home of a thousand miseries. If some should hear it through a cleft in the masonry, they might search for the singer. Now, if you will, follow me."

So they went up and up, until at last they reached the topmost gallery, where the wall was pierced with loopholes and overhanging platforms, where stones and other missiles could be hurled upon an attacking force. Miriam looked out eagerly, walking round the gallery from aperture to aperture.

To the south lay the marble courts and glittering buildings of the Temple, where the smoke of sacrifice still curled up to heaven, even as men fought daily in them. Behind these were the Upper and the Lower City, crowded with thousands of houses, packed, every one of them, with human beings who had come here for refuge or, in spite of the dangers of the time, to celebrate the Passover. To the east was the rugged valley of Jehoshaphat, and beyond it the Mount of Olives, green with trees soon to be laid low by the Romans. To the north the new city of Bezetha, bordered by the third wall and the rocky land beyond. Not far away, but somewhat in front of them and to the left, rose the mighty tower of Antonia, now one of the strongholds of John of Gischala and the Zealots, while to the west, across the width of the city, stood the towers of Hippicus, Phasael, and Mariamme, backed by the splendid palace of Herod. Besides these were walls, fortresses, gates, and palaces without number, so intricate and many that the eye could scarcely follow or count them, and between them, the numberless streets of Jerusalem. These and many other things Ithiel pointed out to Miriam, who listened eagerly until he wearied of the task. Then they looked forward through the overhanging platforms of stone to the marketplace directly below, and then to the roofs of the houses, mostly of humbler build, situated behind them almost up to the walls of the Old Tower, where people were gathered as though for safety, eating their morning meal, talking anxiously together, and even praying.

While they were thus engaged, Nehushta touched Miriam and pointed to the road running from the Valley of Thorns on the northeast. She looked, and saw a great cloud of dust and smoke advancing swiftly and ominously, through the glint of spears and armor.

"The legions," said Nehushta quietly.

She was not the only one who had caught sight of them, for

suddenly the battlement of every wall and tower, the roof of every lofty house, the upper courts of the Temple, and all high places became crowded with thousands and tens of thousands of heads, each of them staring towards the advancing dust. In silence they stared as though their multitudes were stricken dumb, until presently, from far below out of the maze of winding streets, floated the wail of a single voice.

"Woe, woe to Jerusalem!" the voice echoed. "Woe, woe to the City and the Temple!"

They shuddered, and as it seemed to them, all the listening thousands within reach of that mournful cry shuddered also.

"Aye!" repeated Ithiel, "woe to Jerusalem, for yonder comes her doom."

Now on the more rocky ground, the dust grew thinner, and through it they could distinguish the divisions of the mighty army of destroyers. First came thousands of Syrian auxiliaries and clouds of scouts and archers, who searched the country far and wide. Next appeared the road makers and the camp setters, the beasts of burden with the general's baggage and its great escort, followed by Titus himself, his bodyguard and officers, by pikemen and horsemen. Then were seen strange and terrible engines of war beyond count, and with them the tribunes, and the commanders of cohorts and their guards who preceded the engines, and that "abomination of desolation," the Roman Eagles. The gilded standards were surrounded by bands of trumpeters, who from time to time uttered a loud, defiant note. After them marched the vast army in ranks six deep, divided into legions and followed by their camp bearers and squadrons of horse. Last were seen the packs of baggage and mercenaries by thousands and tens of thousands. On the Hill of Saul, the great host halted and prepared to encamp. An hour later, a band of horsemen, five or six hundred strong, emerged out of this camp and marched along the straight road to Jerusalem.

"It is Titus himself," said Ithiel. "See, the Imperial Standard goes before him."

On they came until, from their lofty perch, Miriam, who was keen-sighted, could see the details of their armor and distinguish the color of their horses. Eagerly she searched them with her eyes, for well she guessed that Marcus would be one of those who accompanied his general upon this service. That plumed warrior might be him, or that with the purple cloak, or that who galloped out from near by the Standard on an errand. He was there; she was sure he was there, and yet they were as far apart as when the great sea had rolled between them.

Now, as they marched onward past the Tower of Women, the gate burst open, and from alleys and houses where they had lain in ambush, thousands of Jews poured out. They pierced through the thin line of horsemen, uttering savage cries, then doubled back upon the severed flanks. Many Romans were cut down; Miriam could see them falling from their horses. The Imperial Standard sank, then rose and sank again, only to rise once more. Now dust hid the combat, and she thought that all the Romans must be slain. But no, for presently they began to appear beyond the dust, riding back by the way they had come, though fewer than they had been. They had charged through the multitude of Jews and escaped. But who had escaped and who had been left behind? That she could not tell, and it was with a sick and anxious heart that Miriam descended the steps of the tower, returning to the darkness of the caves.

Chapter XV
What Passed in the Tower

Nearly four months went by. Never during the whole history of the world has there been more cruel suffering than was endured by the inhabitants of Jerusalem during those years, or by the survivors of the Jewish nation who were crowded together within its walls. Forgetting their quarrels in the face of overwhelming danger, too late the factions united and fought against the common foe with a ferocity that has been seldom equalled. Nothing that desperate men could do they left undone. Again and again they advanced against the Romans, slaughtering hundreds of them. They captured their battering rams and catapults. They undermined the great wooden towers Titus erected against their walls and burnt them. With varying success they made assault after assault, but the legions made slow, steady progress. Titus took the third wall and the new city of Bezetha. He took the second wall and pulled it down. Then he sent Josephus, the Jewish historian, to persuade the defenders to surrender, but his countrymen cursed him and the war went on.

At last, when it seemed to be impossible to capture the place by assault, Titus adopted a surer and more terrible plan. Enclosing the first unconquered wall, the Temple, and the fortress by a siege wall of his own making, he sat back and waited for starvation to do its work. Then came the famine. At the beginning, before the maddened, devil-inspired factions began to destroy each other and to prey upon the peaceful people, Jerusalem was amply provisioned. But each party squandered the stores that were within its reach, and whenever they could do so, burnt those of their rivals, so that the food that might have supplied the whole city for months vanished quickly in orgies of wanton waste and destruction. Now nearly all was gone, and thousands of people starved.

The horrors of the siege and the depths of depravity to which the people sunk in their time of adversity are too terrible to be repeated. History does not record, and the mind of man cannot invent a cruelty that was not practiced by the famished Jews upon their brethren suspected of having hidden food to feed themselves or their families. Mothers devoured their own infants, and children snatched the last morsel of bread from the lips of their dying parents. If these things were done between those who were of one blood, what dreadful torment can there be that was not practiced upon stranger by stranger? The city went mad beneath the weight of its abominable and obscene misery. Thousands perished every day, and every night thousands more escaped, or attempted to escape, to the Romans, who caught the poor wretches and crucified them beneath the walls until there was no more wood to make the crosses, and no more ground on which to raise them.

All these things Miriam saw from her place of outlook in the gallery of the deserted tower. She saw the people lying dead by the hundreds in the streets beneath. She saw robbers drag them from their houses and torture them to discover the hiding place of the food they were supposed to have hidden, and when they would not confess, they were put to the sword. Miriam saw the Valley of the Kidron and the lower slopes of the Mount of Olives covered with captive Jews writhing on their crosses, there to die as the Messiah whom they rejected had died. She saw the furious attacks, the yet more furious assaults and the dreadful daily slaughter, until at length her heart grew so sick within her that although she still took refuge in the ruined tower to escape the gloom beneath, she would spend whole hours with her back pressed against the tower wall, her hands covering her ears to shut out the sights and sounds of this unutterable woe.

Meanwhile, the Essenes, who still had stores of food, ventured forth but rarely, lest the good condition of their bodies, although their faces were white as death from dwelling in the darkness, should tempt the starving hordes to seize and torture them in the hope of discovering the hiding place of their nutriment. Indeed, to several of the brethren this happened, but in obedience to their oaths, they endured all and died without a murmur, having betrayed nothing. Still, notwithstanding the danger, driven to it by utter weariness of their confinement in the dark and by the desire of obtaining news, from time to time one of them would creep forth at night to return again before daybreak. The past Overseer Theophilus went out and was heard of no more.

From those that returned, Miriam heard that after the murder of the high priest Mathias and his sons, together with sixteen of the Sanhedrin, on a charge of correspondence with the Romans, her grandfather had been elected to that body, in which he exercised much influence and caused many to be put to death who were accused of treason or of favoring the Roman cause. Caleb also was in the Temple and foremost in every fight. He was said to have sworn an oath that he would slay the prefect of horse, Fortunatus, with whom he had an ancient quarrel, or himself be slain by him. It was said, indeed, that they had met once already and had exchange blows before being separated by the surge of battle.

The beginning of August came at length, and the wretched city, in addition to its other miseries, panted in the heat of a scorching summer sun and was poisoned by the stench of dead bodies filling the streets and hurled by the thousands from the walls. The Romans had captured the great fortress Antonia on the north wall of the Temple mount and had set up their battering engines at the very gates of the Temple. Slowly but surely, they were winning their way into its outer courts.

One night, about an hour before the dawn, Miriam woke Nehushta, telling her that she was stifling there in those vaults and must ascend the tower. Nehushta said that it was folly, so Miriam answered that she would go alone. Nehushta would have none of that, so together they passed up the stairs according to custom, and having reached the base of the tower through the swinging door of stone, climbed the steps that ran in the thickness of the wall until they reached the topmost gallery. Here they sat, fanned by the slight evening breeze, and watched the Roman fires stretching far and wide around the walls and even among the ruins of the houses almost beneath them, for that part of the city had been taken weeks before.

Presently the dawn broke, a splendid, fearful dawn. It was as though the angel of daybreak had dipped his wing into a sea of blood and dashed it against the brow of Night, still crowned with her fading stars. Suddenly the heavens were filled with blots and threads of flaming color latticed against the pale background of the twilight sky. Miriam watched it with a kind of rapture, letting its glory and peace sink into her troubled soul, while from below arose the sound of awakening camps making ready for the daily battle. Soon a ray of burning light, cast like a spear from the crest of the Mount of Olives across the Valley of Jehoshaphat, struck full upon the gold-roofed Temple and its courts. At its coming, as though at a signal, the northern gates were thrown wide, and through them poured a flood of gaunt and savage warriors. They came on in thousands, uttering fierce war cries. Some pickets of Romans tried to stay their rush, but in a minute they were overcome and destroyed. Now they were surging round the feet of a great wooden tower filled with archers. The fight turned desperate, for the soldiers of Titus rushed up by companies to defend their siege engine. But they could not drive back that onset, and presently the tower was in flames, and in a last mad effort to save their lives, its defenders were casting themselves headlong from the lofty platform. With shouts of triumph, the Jews rushed through the breaches in the second wall, and leaving what remained of the castle of Antonia on the left, they poured down into the maze of streets and ruined houses that lay immediately behind the Old Tower where Miriam stood watching.

In front of this building, which the Romans had judged useless for military purposes, lay the open space, once part of its garden, but of late years used as a cattle market and a training ground for young men in arms. Bordering the waste on its further side were strong fortifications, the camping ground of the twelfth and fifteenth legions. Across this open space, those who remained of the Romans fled back towards their outer line, followed by swarms of furious Jews. Those who were not overtaken reached the line, but the Jews who pursued were met with a charge so fierce, delivered by fresh troops behind the defenses, that they were in turn swept back and took refuge among the ruined houses. Suddenly Miriam's attention became concentrated upon the mounted officer who led this charge, a gallant-looking man clad in splendid armor, whose clear, ringing voice, as he uttered the words of command, had caught her ear even through the tumult and the shouting. The Roman onslaught had reached its limit and began to fall back again like the water from an exhausted wave upon a slope of sand. At the moment, the Jews were in no condition to press the enemy's retreat, and the mounted officer, withdrawing last of all, turned his horse, heedless of the arrows that sang about him, to study the ground now strewn with the wounded and the dead. Presently he looked up at the deserted tower as though wondering whether he could make use of it, and Miriam saw his face. It was Marcus, grown older, more careworn, and altered somewhat by a short curling beard, but still Marcus and no other.

"Look! Look!" she exclaimed.

Nehushta nodded. "Yes, it is he. I thought so from the first. And now, having seen him, lady, shall we be going?"

"Going?" said Miriam. "Why?"

"Because one army or the other may think that this building would be useful to them, and break open the walled-up door. Or they might explore this staircase, and then—"

"And then," answered Miriam quietly, "we should be taken. What of it? If the Jews find us we are of their party. If the Romans—well, I do not greatly fear the Romans."

"You mean you do not fear one Roman. But who knows, he may presently lie dead—"

"Oh! Say it not," cried Miriam, pressing her hand to her heart. "Nay, safe or unsafe, I will see this fight through. Look, there is Caleb—yes, Caleb himself—shouting to the Jews. How fierce he looks, like a hyena in a snare. Nay, I will not go now—go you and leave me in peace to watch the end."

"Since you are too heavy and strong for my old arms to carry down those steep steps, so be it," answered Nehushta calmly.

"After all, we have food with us, and our angels can guard us as well on the top of a tower as in those black cisterns. Perhaps this fray will be worth the watching."

As she spoke, the Romans, led by Marcus and his fellow officers, reformed their line and advanced from their entrenchment to be met halfway by the Jews, Caleb among them, now reinforced from the Temple. There in the open space, they fought hand to hand, for neither force would yield an inch. Miriam, watching through the stone bars from above, watched for only two of all that multitude of men—Marcus, whom she loved, and Caleb, whom she feared. A Jew attacked Marcus, felling him from his horse, and was instantly stabbed by a legionary coming to the rescue of his commander. After this the prefect fought on foot. Caleb killed first one soldier then another. Watching him, Miriam grew aware that he was cutting his way towards a single point, and that the point was Marcus. Marcus seemed to know this; at least, he also strove to cut his way towards Caleb. Nearer and nearer they came, until at length they met and began to rain blows upon each other. But not for long, for just then a charge of some Roman horsemen separated them. After this both parties retired to their lines, taking their wounded with them.

Thus, with pauses, sometimes of two or three hours, the fight went on from morning to noon, and from noon to sunset. From midday to evening the Romans made no more attacks, but were contented with defending themselves while they awaited reinforcements from outside the city.

Thus the advantage rested, or seemed to rest, with the Jews, who held all the ruined houses and swept the open space with their arrows. Now it was that Nehushta's fears were justified, for having a little leisure, the Jews took a beam of wood and battered in the walled-up doorway of the tower.

"Look!" said Nehushta, pointing down.

"Oh, Nou!" Miriam answered, "I was wrong. I have run you into danger. But indeed I could not go. What shall we do now?"

"Sit quiet until they come to take us," said Nehushta grimly. "And then, if they give us time, we shall explain as best we may."

But the Jews did not come, for they feared that if they mounted the stair some sudden rush of Romans might trap them within before they had time to descend again. They made use only of the base of the tower to shelter those of their wounded whose injuries were so desperate that they dared not move them.

The fighting ceased for a while, and the soldiers of both sides amused themselves with shouting taunts and insults at each other, or issuing challenges to single combat that were neither sincerely meant nor accepted.

Taking advantage of the pause in battle, Caleb stepped forward from the shelter of a wall and called out, "If the Prefect Fortunatus has a mind to meet me alone between our battle lines, I have a word to say that he would be glad to hear."

Thereupon Marcus, stepping out from his defenses, where several of his officers seemed to be striving to detain him, answered, "I will come." So he walked to the center of the market, and was met by Caleb.

The two of them spoke together alone, but they spoke in low voices, and neither Miriam nor Nehushta, watching them from above, could discern what they said.

"Will they fight?" said Miriam in a hushed voice.

"It seems likely, since each of them has sworn to slay the other," answered Nehushta.

While she spoke, Marcus shook his head as though to decline some proposal, and pointing to the men of his command who stood watching him, turned to walk back to his own lines.

Caleb pursued him. "There goes the coward Marcus!" he cried loudly enough for both lines to hear. "He hastens back to hide behind Roman shields, for he dares not stand alone against a single Jew!"

At this, Marcus winced and paused mid-stride, but went on again, because the personal grudges had no part in the Roman legions. Seeing that even his taunts could not draw the Roman out, Caleb drew his sword and struck Marcus across the back with the flat of the blade. The Jews laughed at the Roman prefect's humiliation while the Romans uttered a shout of rage at the intolerable affront offered to their commander. In the midst of the uproar, Marcus wheeled round, sword in hand, and flew straight at Caleb's throat.

But this was what the Jew had been waiting for, for he knew that no Roman, and least of all Marcus, would submit to the indignity of such a blow. As his adversary came on, made almost blind with fury, he leapt lightly to one side as a lion leaps, and with all the force of his long sinewy arm brought down his heavy sword upon Marcus's head. The Roman helmet was good, or the skull beneath would have been split in two by the blow, but it was not enough to deflect the blow entirely. The blade shore through it and bit deeply into bone. Marcus staggered beneath the shock; his arms swung wide, and his sword clattered to the ground.

With a shout, Caleb sprang to make an end of him, but before he could strike, Marcus seemed to recover and without his weapon did the only thing he could—charged straight at his foe. Caleb's sword rang on the tempered plates guarding his shoulder, and in the next instant Marcus had the Jew gripped in his arms. Together they crashed to the earth, rolling one over the other, the Jew struggling to stab the Roman, the Roman to choke the Jew with his bare hands. From the Roman lines rose a cry of "Rescue!" and immediately after, the order, "Impetus!" The legionaries rushed forward. From the Jews, a cry of "Kill him!" put their fighters into motion.

Out poured the combatants from either side of the marketplace by hundreds and by thousands, and there in its center, round the struggling forms of Caleb and of Marcus, began the fiercest fight of all that day. Where men stood, there they fell, for none would give way. The Romans, outnumbered though they were, preferred to die rather than leave a wounded and beloved commander prisoner in the hands of cruel enemies, and the Jews knew too well the value of such a prize to let it escape them easily. So great was the slaughter that presently Marcus and Caleb were hidden beneath the bodies of the fallen. More and more Jews rushed into the fray, but still the Romans pushed onwards with steady valor, fighting shoulder to shoulder and shield to shield.

Then at the west end of the marketplace, a fresh body of Jews, three or four hundred strong, appeared with a savage yell and charged upon the Romans, taking them in flank. The senior officer saw the danger, and knowing that it was better that his commander die than that the whole company be destroyed and the arms of Caesar suffer a grave defeat, he gave the order for retreat. Steadily, as though on parade, and dragging with them those of their wounded comrades who could not walk, the legionaries fell back, heedless of the storm of spears and arrows, reaching their own lines before the outflanking body of Jews could rush between them.

The Jews, having won a momentary victory, retreated when they saw there was nothing more to be gained; to attempt a charge against the Roman battle line itself was foolishness. This time they withdrew not to the houses behind the tower, but only to the old market wall thirty or forty paces in front of it, which they proceeded to hold and fortify in the fading light. Seeing that they were lost, the wounded Romans that remained upon the field fell upon their own swords, preferring to die at their own hands than to fall into the hands of the Jews to be tortured and crucified. There was little choice for them in that matter, for it was the decree of Titus that any soldier taken alive should be publicly disgraced by name and expelled from the ranks of his legion, and if recaptured, that he should suffer death or banishment.

Gladly would Marcus have followed their example and saved himself much misery and shame in the future, but he had neither occasion nor weapon, and so weak was he with struggling and loss of blood that even as he and Caleb were dragged from among the fallen by Jewish combatants, he fell unconscious. At first they thought he was dead, but one of the Jews, a physician by trade, declared that this was not so, and that if he were left alone for a while, he would come to himself again. They desired to preserve this prefect alive, either to be held as a hostage or to be executed in sight of the army of Titus, so they brought him into the Old Tower, clearing it of their own wounded but leaving the slain. Here they set a guard over him, though there seemed to be little need of it, and went under the command of the victorious Caleb to assist in strengthening the market wall.

All of these things Miriam observed from above in such an agony of fear and doubt that at times she thought she would die. She had seen Marcus and Caleb fall, locked in each other's arms, and had seen the hideous fray that raged around them. She had seen them dragged from the heap of slain, and at the end of it all, by the last light of day, saw Marcus—living or dead, she knew not which—borne into the tower, and there laid upon the ground.

"Take comfort," whispered Nehushta, pitying her dreadful grief. "The lord Marcus lives. If he were dead, they would have stripped him and left his body with the others. He lives, and they intend to hold him captive, else they would have let Caleb put his sword through him as you saw he wished to do as soon as he found his feet."

"Captive," answered Miriam, "is little better. They will crucify him like the others we saw yesterday on the Temple wall."

Nehushta shrugged her shoulders. "That may be so," she said, "unless he finds means to kill himself or—is saved."

"Saved! How can he be saved?" Then in her woe the poor girl fell upon her knees clasping her hands and murmuring, "Oh, Jesus Christ whom I serve, teach me how to save Marcus. Jesus, I love him, though he is yet blind to your truth. Pity him if for no reason but that I love him, and teach me how to save him. Or if one must die, take my life for his!"

"Cease," said Nehushta, "for I think I hear an answer to your prayer. Look, he is laid at the foot of the stair and but six feet from the stone door that leads down into the cistern. Except for the dead, the tower is empty. The two sentries stand outside the breach in the brickwork, for they think that their prisoner, unarmed and wounded as he is, cannot attempt escape. If the Roman lives and can stand, we can open the stone door and pull him through it."

"But the Jews might see us and discover the secret of the hiding place of the Essenes. They will kill them when they find they have hidden food."

"Once we are on the other side of the door, they will never get to them, even if they have time to try," answered Nehushta. "Before they break down the door the stone trap beneath can be closed and the roof of the stair let down by knocking away the props and flooding the place in such a fashion that a week of labor would not clear it. Oh, have no fear, the Essenes know and have guarded against any discovery."

Miriam threw her arms about the neck of Nehushta and kissed her.

"We will try, Nou, we will try," she whispered, "and if we fail, then we shall die with him."

"You may find that prospect pleasing, but I have no desire to die with the lord Marcus," Nehushta answered dryly. "I like him well enough, but were it not for your sake I would leave him to his chance. Nay, do not answer or give way to too much hope. Remember, he may be as dead as he appears."

"We must find out," said Miriam wildly. "Shall we go now?"

"Aye, while there is still a little light, for these steps are treacherous in the dark. Follow me."

So on they glided down the ancient, darksome stairway, where the bats darted at the disturbance and flittered in their faces. Now they were at the last flight, which descended to a little recess set at right angles to the steps and flush with the floor of the basement, for once the door of the stairway had opened here. Thus a person standing on the last stair could not be seen by any in the tower. They reached the step and halted. Then very stealthily, Nehushta went on to her hands and knees and thrust her head forward so that she could look into the base of the tower. It was dark as a grave, only a faint gleam of starlight reflecting from his armor showed where Marcus lay, so close that she could touch him with her hand. Almost opposite to her the gloom was relieved by a patch of faint gray light. That was where the wall had been broken in, for Nehushta could see the shadows of the sentries crossing back and forth before the ragged opening.

She leant yet lower towards Marcus and listened. He was not dead, for he breathed, and she heard him stir his hand and thought that she could see it move upwards towards his wounded head. Then she drew back.

"He lives," she whispered, "and I think he is awake. Now you must do the rest as your wits may guide you. If I speak to him he will be frightened, but your voice he may remember."

All doubt and fear seemed to vanish from Miriam's heart at these words. Her hand grew steady and her mind clear, for her heart told her that if she wished to save Marcus she would need both a clear mind and steady hand. The timid, lovesick girl was transformed into a woman of iron will and purpose. In her turn, she knelt and crept a short ways from the stair, so that her face drifted over his. Then she spoke to him in a soft whisper.

"Marcus, awake and listen. Do not stir or make noise. It is Miriam, whom once you knew."

At this name, the dim form beneath her seemed to quiver, and his lips muttered, "I was not certain, but now I know I'm dead. Had I known Hades wore so lovely a face I'd have died long ago. Speak on, sweet vision of Miriam."

"Nay, Marcus, you are only wounded and I am no vision. I am flesh and blood, the same woman you knew by the banks of Jordan. I've come to save you. Listen quickly. If you have the strength to stand we can guide you into a secret place where the Essenes are hidden. They will care for you until you are able to return to the Romans. If you do not escape you will be crucified."

"By Bacchus, I know it," said the ragged whisper beneath, "and that will be worse than being beaten by Caleb. But if I am not dead then surely I dream. Only a dream of Miriam. Let me dream on." And he turned his head.

Miriam frowned in thought. Time was short and it was necessary to make him understand. Well, that was not difficult. Slowly she bent lower, turning his head back to face her, and pressed her lips to his.

"To show you that I am no dream," she murmured. "For you must be awakened. Had I light I could prove to you that I am Miriam by the ring on my finger and the pearls about my neck."

"Cease," he answered. "It is enough for me, Most Beloved.

You are real. Strange, that I must be so wounded to win your kiss. And many thanks to Caleb who has brought us together again! Against his will, I think," he added. "What must I do?"

"Can you stand?" asked Miriam.

"Perhaps. I am not sure. I will try."

"Nay, wait. Nehushta, come here. You are stronger than I. I'll unlatch the door; you lift him up. Quickly, I hear the guard stirring."

Nehushta glided forward and knelt by the wounded man, placing her arms beneath him.

"Ready," she said. "Here is the iron."

Miriam took it, stepping to the wall, and felt with her fingers for the crack, invisible in the darkness. At length she found it, and inserting the thin hooked iron, lifted the hidden latch and pulled. The stone door was heavy and she pressed all her weight against it before it moved. At last it began to swing.

"Now!" she said to Nehushta. The older woman straightened herself and dragged the wounded Marcus to his feet.

"Quick, quick!" said Miriam, "the guards are coming!"

Supported by Nehushta, Marcus took three tottering steps and reached the open door. But on its very threshold his strength failed him, for his knee as well as his head had been wounded.

He groaned weakly and fell to the ground, dragging the old Libyan with him, his breastplate crashing loudly against the stone threshold. The sentry outside heard the sound and called to a companion to give him the lantern. In an instant, Nehushta was up again and, seizing Marcus by his right arm, began to drag him through the opening while Miriam, setting her back against the swinging stone to keep it from closing, kicked his feet through the doorway.

The lantern appeared round the angle of the broken masonry.

"For your life's sake, move!" said Miriam, and Nehushta dragged her hardest at the heavy, helpless body of the fallen man, gaining little ground. It was too late. If the light fell on him all was lost. In an instant, Miriam gathered her resolve. With an effort, she swung the door wide, and as Nehushta pulled again she sprang

forward, the iron key in hand, keeping to the shadow of the wall.
The Jew holding the lantern, alarmed by the sounds within,
entered hastily and, catching his foot against the body of a dead
man who lay there, stumbled to his knees. The guard regained
his feet, and the lantern shone brightly in her face. Before he
could recover from his astonishment, she swung the key with all
her might, shattering the lamp and extinguishing it.

She turned to flee, for the stone would now be swinging on
its pivot to close.

Alas! Her chance had gone, for the man caught her about the
waist and held her fast, crying out for help. Miriam struggled,
battering him with the iron key and pushing at him with her
left hand in vain, for in that grip she was as helpless as a child
fighting against its nurse. While she fought thus, she heard the
dull thud of the closing stone, rejoicing even in her despair, for
she knew that until Marcus was beyond its threshold it could
not be shut. She ceased from her useless struggle and gathered
her thoughts. Marcus was safe; the door was shut and could not
be opened from the other side until another key was made, and
the guard had seen nothing. But her escape was impossible. Her
part was played; only one thing remained for her to do—remain
silent and keep his secret.

Men rushed into the tower, bearing lights. Her right hand,
which held the key, was free of the guard's grip, and lest it
should reveal all she cast it into a corner of the room buried
deep in fallen stones, fragments of rotted timber and dirt from
the nests of birds. Then she stood still. They were upon her now,
Caleb at their head.

"What is it?" he cried.

"I know not," answered the guard. "I heard a sound of clank-
ing armor and ran in, when this one here struck the lantern
from my hand. Strong rascal! I have struggled sorely with him,
despite the blows he rained upon me with his sword."

They held up their lights and when they saw her beautiful,
disheveled form, small and frail of stature, they laughed aloud.

"A strong thief, truly," said one. "Why, it's a girl! Do you summon the watch every time a maid catches hold of you?"

Before the words died upon the speaker's lips, another man called out, "The Roman! The prefect is gone! Where is the prisoner?" With a roar of wrath they began to search the place, as a cat searches for a mouse that has escaped her. Only Caleb stood still and stared at the girl.

"Miriam!" he said, a grim look on his face.

"Yes, Caleb," she answered quietly. "Strange meeting, is it not? Why do you break in thus upon my hiding place?"

"Woman," he shouted, mad with anger, "where have you hidden the Prefect Fortunatus?"

"Marcus?" she answered. "Is he here? I did not know it. Well, I did see a man run from the tower, perhaps that was he. Be swift and you may catch him."

"No man left the tower," answered the other sentry. "Seize that woman, she has hidden the Roman in some secret place. Seize her and search."

So they laid hold of Miriam, bound her, and began following the wall round the room. "There is a staircase here," called a man. "He must have gone up. Come, friends."

Then taking lights with them, they mounted the stairs to the very top, but they found no one. Even as they came down again a trumpet blew and from outside the chamber rose the sound of a mighty shouting.

"What now?" said one.

As he spoke an officer appeared in the opening of the tower.

"Begone," he cried. "Back to the Temple, and take your prisoner with you. Titus himself is upon us at the head of two fresh cohorts, mad at the loss of his prefect and so many of his soldiers. Where is the wounded Roman, Fortunatus?"

"He has vanished," answered Caleb sullenly. "Vanished," he glanced at Miriam with jealous and vindictive hate, "and in his place has left to us this woman, the granddaughter of Benoni, who strangely enough was once his lover."

"Is it so?" said the officer. "Girl, tell us what you have done with the Roman, or die. Come, we have no time to lose."

"I have done nothing," she answered demurely. "I saw a man walk past the sentries. That is all."

"She lies," said the officer contemptuously. "Here, kill this traitress."

A man advanced lifting his sword, and Miriam, thinking that all was over, closed her eyes while she waited for the blow. Before it fell, however, Caleb whispered something to the officer that caused him to change his mind.

"So be it," he said. "Hold your hand and take this woman with you to the Temple, there to be tried by her grandfather, Benoni, and the other judges of the Sanhedrin. They have means to cause the most obstinate to speak, but death seals the lips forever. Swift, now, swift. Already they are fighting on the marketplace."

So they seized Miriam and dragged her away from the Old Tower, which an hour later was taken possession of by the Romans, who destroyed it with the other buildings.

Chapter XVI
The Sanhedrin

The Jewish soldiers escorted Miriam roughly through dark and tortuous streets, bordered by burnt-out houses, and up steep stone slopes deep with the debris of the siege. Indeed, they had need to hasten, for lit with the lamp of flaming dwellings, behind them flowed the tide of war. The Romans, driven back from this part of the city by that day's furious battle, under cover of the night were reoccupying in overwhelming strength the ground they had lost, forcing the Jews before them and striving to cut them off from their stronghold in the Temple and the quarter of the Upper City that they still held.

The party of Jews with Miriam in their charge was returning to the Temple enclosure, but they could not reach it from the north or east because the outer courts and cloisters of the Holy House were already in possession of the Romans. So it happened that they were obliged to make their way round by the Upper City, a long and tedious journey. Once during that night they were forced to hide until a great company of Romans had marched past. Caleb wished to attack them, but the other captains said they were too few and weary, so they lay hid for nearly three hours before going on again. After this there were other delays at gates still in the hands of their own people, which one by one were unbolted to them. Thus it was not far from daylight when at length, they passed over a narrow bridge that spanned some ravine and through massive doors into a vast dim place that, as Miriam gathered from the talk of her captors, was the inner enclosure of the Temple. Here, at the command of the captain that had ordered her to be slain, she was thrust into a small cell in one of the cloisters. The doors of the cell were locked, and she was left alone.

Sinking exhausted to the floor, Miriam tried to sleep, but could not, for her brain seemed to be on fire. Whenever she shut her eyes, there sprang up before her visions of some dreadful scene that she had witnessed. In her ears echoed the shouts of the victors and the pitiful cries of the dying and, finally again, the voice of the wounded Marcus calling her "Most Beloved."

Was this so, she wondered? Was it possible that he had not forgotten her during those years of separation, when there must have been so many lovely ladies striving to win him, the rich, high-placed Roman lord, to be their lover or husband? She did not know; she could not tell. Perhaps, in such a plight, he would have called any woman who came to save him his Most Beloved. Perhaps, she thought with a curious smile, even old Nehushta. Yet his voice had rung true, and he had sent her his ring, the pearls, and the letter. The letter that, although she knew every word of it, she still carried hidden in the bosom of her robe. Oh, she believed that he did love her, and believing, rejoiced with all her heart that it had pleased God to allow her to save his life, even at the cost of her own. She remembered suddenly. There was still his wound—he might die of it. Nay, surely he would not die. For her sake, the Essenes who knew him would treat him well, and they were skillful healers. And what better nurse than Nehushta could be found? Poor Nou, how she would grieve over her. What sorrow must have taken hold of her when she heard the rock door shut and found that Miriam was cut off and captured by the Jews?

Happy, indeed, it was for Miriam that she did not witness what had taken place on the other side of that block of stone; that she could not see Nehushta beating at it with her hands and striving to thrust her thin fingers to the latch which she had no instrument to lift, until the bones were stripped of skin and flesh. That she could not hear Marcus, awake but unable to rise from off his knees, cursing and raving with agony that the tender lady whom he loved had, for his sake, fallen into the hands of the Zealots. That she could not hear him crying out in his utter helplessness, until at length he succumbed to his wounds and fell into a fevered madness, that for many weeks was unpierced by any light of reason or memory. All this, at least, was spared to her.

Well, the deed was done and she must pay the price, for without a doubt they would kill her for saving a Roman commander from their clutches. Or if they did not, Caleb would, for it seemed his bitter jealousy had turned his love to hate. Never would he let her live to fall, perchance, as his share of the Temple spoil, into the hands of the Roman rival who had escaped him.

It was not too great a price. She knew she could never be a wife to Marcus. And she was weary, sick with the sight and sound of slaughter and with the misery that in these latter days, as her Lord had prophesied, was come upon the city that rejected Him and the people that had slain Him, their Messiah. Miriam wished to die, to pass to her home of perfect and eternal peace. Perhaps, there it might be given to her, in reward of her sufferings, to watch over the soul of Marcus from afar and to make ready an abode for him to dwell in through all the ages of eternity. The thought pleased her, and lifting his ring, she pressed it to her lips. The same lips that had kissed his lips that very night. She drew the ring off her finger and hid it in her hair. She wished to keep that ring until the end if she could. As for the pearls, she could not hide them, and though she loved them as his gift—well, they must go to the hand of the spoiler, and to the necks of other women, who would never know their tale.

Then she rose to her knees and began to pray with the pure, simple faith that was given to the first children of the Church. She prayed for Marcus, that he might recover and not forget her, and that the light of truth might shine upon him. For Nehushta, that her sorrow might be soothed. For herself, that her end might be merciful and her awakening happy. For Caleb, that his heart might be turned, and for the dead and dying, that their sins might be forgiven. For the little ones of Jerusalem, that the Lord might have pity on their sufferings. For the Jews, that He would lift the rod of His wrath from their backs. And even for the Romans, though for them, she knew not what petition to make.

When her prayer was finished, Miriam tried again to sleep

and dozed a little, only to be aroused by a curious sound of
feeble sighing, which seemed to come from the far side of the
cell. By now, the dawn was streaming through the stone lattice
work above the doorway, and in its faint light, Miriam saw the
outlines of a figure with snowy hair and beard, wrapped in a
filthy robe that had once been white. At first she thought that
this figure must be a corpse thrust here out of the way of the living, it was so still. But corpses do not sigh as this man seemed
to do. Who could he be, she wondered? A prisoner like herself,
left to die as she, perhaps, would be left to die? The light grew
a little. Surely there was something familiar about the shape of
that white head. She crept closer, thinking that she might be
able to help this old man who was sick and suffering. Now she
could see his face and the hand that lay upon his breast. They
were like those of a living skeleton, for the bones stood out, and
over them the yellow skin was drawn like shriveled parchment.
But the deep sunk eyes still shone round and bright. She knew
the face. It was Theophilus the Essene, a past Overseer of the
Order! Indeed, he had been her friend from earliest childhood
and the master who had taught her languages in the distant
happy years she had spent in the village by the Dead Sea. She
had found Theophilus dwelling with the Essenes in their cavern
home, and none of them had welcomed her more warmly. But
some thirty days earlier, against the advice of Ithiel and others,
he had insisted on creeping out to take the air and gather news
in the city. He had been a stout and hale old man, although
pale-faced from dwelling in the darkness. He had never returned
from that journey. Some said he had fled to the country. Others
thought he had gone over to the Romans, and yet others that he
had been slain by Simon's men. Now she found him thus!

Miriam came and bent over him.

"Master," she said, "what ails you? How came you here?"

He turned his hollow, vacant eyes upon her face.

"Who are you that speaks to me so gently?" he asked in a
feeble voice.

"I, your ward. Miriam."

"Miriam! Miriam! What is Miriam doing in this torture den?"

"Master, I am a prisoner. But tell me of yourself."

"There is little to say, Miriam. They caught me, those devils, and seeing that I was still well fed and strong, though sunk in years, demanded to know where I had my food in this city of starvation. To tell them would have been to give up our secret and to bring doom upon the brethren, and upon you, our guest and lady. I refused to answer, so they tortured me, to no avail, and cast me in here to starve, thinking that hunger would make me speak. But I have not spoken. How could I, who have taken the oath of the Essenes, and been their ruler? And now, I die."

"No! Do not say so," cried Miriam, wringing her hands.

"I do say it and I am thankful. Have you any food?"

"Yes, a piece of dried meat and barley bread. They were in my robe when I was captured. Take them and eat."

"Nay, Miriam, that desire has gone from me, nor do I wish to live, whose days are done. But save the food, for doubtless they will starve you also. And look, there is water in that jar. They gave it to me to make me live longer. Drink, drink while you can, for tomorrow you may go thirsty."

For a time there was silence, while the tears that gathered in Miriam's eyes fell upon the old man's face.

"Weep not for me," he said presently. "I go to my rest. But how came you here?"

She told him as briefly as she might.

"You are a brave woman," he said when she had finished, "and that Roman owes you much. Now I, Theophilus, who am about to die, call down the blessing of God upon you, and upon him also for your sake, for your sake. The shield of God be over you in the slaughter and the sorrow."

Then he shut his eyes and did not speak again, though his breathing continued in a brittle rasp.

Miriam drank from the pitcher of water, for her thirst was great. Crouched at the side of the old Essene, she watched him until at length the door opened, and two gaunt, savage-looking men entered, who went to where Theophilus lay and kicked him brutally.

"What do you want now?" he said, opening his eyes.

"Wake up, old man," cried one of them. "See, here is meat," and he thrust a lump of some filthy carrion to his lips. "Smell it, taste it," he went on. "Is it not good? Well, tell us where is that store of food which made you so fat who now are so thin, and you shall have it all, yes, all, all."

Theophilus shook his head.

"Reconsider you," cried the man, "if you do not eat, by sunrise tomorrow you will be dead. Speak then and eat, obstinate dog, it is your last chance."

"I eat not and I tell not," answered the aged figure in a voice like a hollow groan. "By tomorrow's sunrise I shall be dead, and soon you and all this people will be dead, and God will have judged each of us according to his works. Repent *you*, for the hour is at hand."

Then they cursed him and smote him because of his words of ill omen, and so went away, taking no notice of Miriam in the corner. When they had gone she came forward and looked. His jaw had fallen slack. The spirit of Theophilus the Essene had flown.

Another hour went by. Once more the door was opened, and there appeared that captain who had ordered her to be killed. With him were two Jews.

"Come, woman," he said, "to stand trial."

"Who is to try me?" Miriam asked.

"The Sanhedrin. As much as is left of it," he answered. "Come now, we have no time for talking."

So Miriam rose and accompanied them across the corner of the vast court that surrounded the Temple, which towered over them in all its glittering majesty. As she walked, she noticed that the pavement was dotted with corpses, and from beyond the cloisters rose flames and smoke. They seemed to be fighting there, for the air was full of the sound of shouting, above which echoed the dull, continuous thud of battering rams striking against the massive walls.

They took her into a great chamber supported by pillars of white marble, where many starving folk, some of them women who carried or led hollow-cheeked children, sat silent on the floor or wandered to and fro, their eyes fixed upon the ground as though in aimless search for something that had left their memory. Seventy chairs stretched across the dais at the end of the chamber, but only fourteen men occupied the carved chairs; the others stood empty to their left and right. The men were clad in magnificent robes, which seemed to hang ill upon their gaunt forms, and like the people in the hall, their eyes looked scared and their faces were white and shrunken. These were all who were left of the Sanhedrin of the Jews.

As Miriam entered, one of their number was delivering judgment upon a wretched starving man. Miriam looked at the judge. It was her grandfather, Benoni, but oh, how changed! He who had been tall and upright was now hunched down almost to half his former height, his teeth showed yellow between his lips, his long white beard was ragged and had come out in patches, his hand shook, his gorgeous headdress sat upon his brow awry. Nothing was the same about him except his eyes, which still shone bright, but with a fiercer fire than of old. They looked like the eyes of a famished wolf.

"Man, have you anything to say?" he was asking of the prisoner.

"Only this," the prisoner answered. "I hid some food, my own food, which I bought with all that remained of my fortune. Your hyena-men caught my wife and tormented her until she showed it to them. They fell upon it, and with their comrades, ate nearly all. My wife is dead of her wounds, my children of starvation, all except one, a child of six. I fed her with what remained. But starvation began to take her too, so I bargained with the Roman, giving him jewels and promising to show him a weak place in the wall if he would take the child to his camp and feed her. I showed him the place, and he fed her in my presence and took her away. But, as you know, I was caught, and the wall was strengthened, so no harm came of my betrayal. I would do it again to save the life of my child—twenty times over, if need be. You murdered my wife and my children. Murder me also if you will. I no longer care."

"Wretch," spat Benoni. "What are your miserable wife and

children compared to the safety of this holy place, which we defend against the enemies of Jehovah? Lead him away, and let him be slain upon the wall, in the sight of his friends, the Romans."

"I go," said the victim, rising and stretching out his hands to the guards, "but may you also all be slain in the sight of the Romans, you mad murderers. In your lust for power, you have brought doom and agony upon the people of the Jews."

Then they dragged him out, and a voice called, "Bring in the next traitor."

Miriam was brought forward. Benoni looked up and knew her.

"Miriam?" he gasped, rising, to fall back again into his seat. "You, Miriam? Here?"

"It seems so, grandfather," she answered quietly.

"There is some mistake," said Benoni. "This girl can have harmed none. Let her be dismissed."

The other judges looked up.

"Best hear the charge against her first?" said one suspiciously, while another added, "Is not this the woman who dwelt with you at Tyre, and who is said to be a Christian?"

"We do not sit to try questions of faith, at least not now," answered Benoni evasively.

"Woman, is it true that you are a Christian?" queried one of the judges.

"Sir, I am," replied Miriam, and at her words the faces of the Sanhedrin grew hard as marble, while someone watching in the crowd hurled a stone at her.

"Let it be for this time," said the judge, "as the Rabbi Benoni says, we are trying questions of treason, not of faith. Who accuses this woman, and of what?"

A man stepped forward, the captain who had wished to put Miriam to death, and she saw that behind him were Caleb, who looked ill at ease, and the Jew who had guarded Marcus.

"I accuse her," he said, "of having released the Roman prefect, Fortunatus, whom Caleb here wounded and took prisoner in the fighting yesterday, and brought into the Old Tower, where he was laid until we knew whether he would live or die."

"The Roman Prefect Fortunatus?" said one. "Why, he is the friend of Titus and would have been worth more to us than a hundred common soldiers. Throughout this war, none has done us greater injury. Woman, if indeed, you let him go, no death can repay your wickedness. Did you help him escape?"

"That is for you to discover," answered Miriam, for now that Marcus was safe she would tell no more lies.

"This renegade is insolent, like all her accursed sect," said the judge, spitting on the ground. "Captain, tell your story, and be brief."

He obeyed. After him, the soldier from whose hand Miriam had struck the lantern was examined. Then Caleb was called and asked what he knew of the matter.

"Nothing," he answered, "except that I took the Roman and saw him laid in the tower, for he was senseless. When I returned, the Roman had gone, and this lady Miriam was there, who said that he had escaped by the doorway. I did not see them together and know no more."

"That is a lie," said one of the judges roughly. "You told the captain that Fortunatus had been her lover. Why did you say this?"

"Because years ago by the Jordan she, who is a sculptor, carved a likeness of him in stone," answered Caleb.

"Are artists always the lovers of those whom they picture, Caleb?" asked Benoni, speaking for the first time.

Caleb made no answer, but one of the Sanhedrin, a sharp-faced man, named Simeon, the friend of Simon bar Gioras, the Zealot, who sat next to him, cried, "Cease this foolishness. The daughter of Satan is beautiful—doubtless Caleb desires her for himself. What has that to do with us?" But he added vindictively, "It should be remembered against him that he is striving to hide the truth."

"There is no evidence against this woman, let her be set free," exclaimed Benoni.

"So we might expect her grandfather to think," said Simeon, his voice thick with scorn. "Little wonder that we are smitten with the sword of God when Rabbis shelter Christians because they chance to be of their house, and when warriors bear false witness concerning them because they chance to be fair. For my part, I say that she is guilty and has hidden the man away in some secret place. Otherwise why did she dash the light from the soldier's hand?"

"Perhaps to hide herself lest she should be attacked," answered another, "though how she got into the tower, I cannot guess."

"I lived there," said Miriam. "It was bricked up until yesterday and safe from robbers."

"So!" commented that judge, "you lived alone in a deserted tower like a bat or an owl, and without food or water. Then these must have been brought to you from without the walls, perhaps by some secret passage that was known to none, down which you loosed the prefect, but had no time to follow him. Woman, you are a Roman spy, as a Christian well might be. I say that she is worthy of death."

Then Benoni rose and rent his robes.

"Does not enough blood run through these holy courts?" he asked, "that you must seek that of the innocent also? What is your oath? To do justice and to convict only upon clear unshaken testimony. Where is this testimony? What is there to show that the girl Miriam had any dealings with this Fortunatus, whom she has not seen for years? In the Holy Name, I protest against this iniquity."

"It is natural that you should protest," said one of his brethren.

Then they fell into discussion, for the question perplexed them sorely, for although they were savage, they still wished to appear honest.

Suddenly Simeon looked up, for a thought struck him.

"Search her," he said, "she is in good health, she may have food, or the secret of food, about her, or," he added, "other things."

Now two hungry-looking officers of the court seized Miriam and rent her robe open at the breast with their rough hands, since they would not be bothered with courtesy.

"See," cried one of them, "here are pearls, fit wear for so fine a lady. Shall we take them?"

"Fool, let the trinkets be," answered Simeon angrily. "Are we common thieves?"

"Here is something else," said the officer, drawing the roll of Marcus's cherished letter from her breast.

"Not that, not that," the poor girl gasped.

"Give it here," said Simeon, stretching out his lean hand.

Then he undid the silk ribbon and, opening the letter, read its first lines aloud. *"To the lady Miriam, Queen of the Essenes, from Marcus, her friend, tribune by the will of the Senate and of the People, by the hand of the centurion Gallus.* What do you say to that, Benoni and brethren? Why, there are pages of it, but here is the end: *I remain forever your faithful friend and love, Marcus Carius Fortunatus. Farewell.* Read it if you will. For my part, I am satisfied. This woman is a traitress. I give my vote for death."

"It was written from Rome two years ago," pleaded Miriam,

but no one seemed to heed her, for all were talking at once.

"I demand that the whole letter be read," shouted Benoni.

"We have no time, no time," answered Simeon. "Other pris-
oners await their trial, and the Romans are battering our gates.
Can we waste more precious minutes over this Nazarene spy?
Away with her."

"Away with her," said Simon bar Gioras, and the others nodded their heads in assent.

Then they gathered together, discussing the manner of her
end while Benoni stormed at them in vain. Not entirely in vain,
however, for they yielded something to his pleading.

"So be it," said their spokesman, Simon. "This is our sentence
on the traitress—that she suffer the common fate of traitors and
be taken to the upper gate, called the Gate Nicanor, that divides
the Court of Israel from the Court of Women, and bound with
the chain to the central column that is over the gate, where she
may be seen both of her friends the Romans and of the people of
Israel whom she has betrayed, there to perish of hunger and of
thirst, or in such fashion as God may appoint, for so shall we be
clean of a woman's blood. Yet, because of the prayer of Benoni,
our brother, of whose race she is, we decree that this sentence
shall not be carried out before the setting of the sun, and that
if the traitress meanwhile elects to give information that shall
lead to the recapture of the Roman prefect, Fortunatus, she shall
be set at liberty without the gates of the Temple. The case is finished. Guards, take her to the prison from which she came."

So they seized Miriam and led her back through the crowd of
onlookers, who paused from their wanderings and weary searching of the ground to spit at or curse her, and thrust her back into
her cell and to the company of the cold corpse of Theophilus
the Essene.

Here Miriam sat down; partly to pass the time and partly
because she needed it, she ate the bread and dried meat she had
left hidden in the cell. Sleep came to her then, for she was weary
and the worst being at hand, had nothing more to fear. For four
or five hours she rested sweetly, dreaming that she was a child
again, gathering flowers on the banks of Jordan in the spring

season until, at length, a sound awoke her. She looked up to see Benoni.

"What is it, grandfather?" she asked.

"Oh! My daughter," groaned the wretched old man, "I am come here at some risk to bid you farewell and to ask your pardon, for because of you and for other reasons those wolf-hearted men suspect me."

"Why should you ask my pardon, grandfather? Seeing things as they see them, the sentence is just enough. I am a Christian, and—if you would know it—I did, as I hope, save the life of Marcus, a deed for which my own is forfeit."

"How?" he asked.

"That, grandfather, I will not tell you."

"Tell me, and save yourself. There is little chance that they will take him, for the Jews have been driven from the Old Tower."

"The Jews might recapture the tower. I will not tell you. And the lives of others are at stake, my friends who have sheltered me, and who, as I trust, will now shelter him."

"Then you must die, and by this death of shame, for I am powerless to save you. Tied to a pinnacle of the gateway, a mockery to friend and foe. Why, if it had not been that I still have some authority among them, and that you are of my blood, girl though you be, they would have crucified you upon the wall, serving you as the Romans serve our people."

"If it pleases God that I should die, I shall die. What is one life among so many tens of thousands? Let us talk of other things while we have time."

"What is there to talk of, Miriam, save misery?" and again he groaned. "You were right, and I have been wrong. That Messiah of yours whom I rejected, and still reject, had at least the gift of prophecy, for the words that you read me yonder in Tyre will be fulfilled upon this people and city to the last letter. The Romans hold even the outer courts of the Temple. There is no food left. In the upper town the inhabitants devour each other and die until none can bury the dead. In a day or two, or ten—what does it matter—we who are left shall perish also by hunger and

the sword. The nation of the Jews is trodden out, the smoke of
their sacrifices goes up no more, and the Holy House that they
have built will be pulled stone from stone, or serve as a temple
for the worship of heathen gods."

"Will Titus show no mercy? Can you not surrender?" asked
Miriam.

"Surrender? To be sold as slaves or dragged a spectacle at the
wheels of Caesar's triumphal car, through the shouting streets
of Rome? No, girl, best to fight it out. We will seek mercy of
Jehovah and not of Titus. Oh! I would that it were done with,
for my heart is broken, and this judgment is fallen on me—that
I, who of my own will brought my daughter to her death must
bring her daughter to death against my will. If I had listened
to you, you would have been in Pella, or in Egypt. I lost you,
and thinking you dead, what I have suffered no man can know.
Now I find you, and because of the office that was thrust upon
me, I from whom your life has sprung, must bring you to your
doom."

"Grandfather," Miriam broke in, wringing her hands, for the
grief of this old man was awful to witness, "cease, I beseech you,
cease. Perhaps, after all, I shall not die."

He looked up eagerly. "Have you hope of escape?" he asked.
"Perchance Caleb—"

"No, I know nothing of Caleb, except that at the last he tried
to save me—for which I thank him. But I would sooner perish
here alone than escape in his company, for I do not fear death
in my spirit, whatever my flesh may fear."

"What then, Miriam? Why should you think—" He paused.

"I do not think, I only trust in God—and hope. One of our
faith, now long departed, foretold that I should be born, and
foretold also that I should live out my life. It may be so, for that
woman was holy, and a prophetess."

As she spoke, there came a rolling sound like that of distant
thunder, and a voice called from the cloister, "Rabbi Benoni,
the wall is down. Waste not time here, Rabbi Benoni. They seek
you."

"Alas! I must leave you," he said, "for some new horror is fallen upon us, and they summon me to the council. Farewell, most beloved Miriam, may my God and your God protect you, for I cannot. Farewell, and if by any chance you live, forgive me and try to forget the evil that, in my blindness and my pride, I have brought upon you and yours, but most of all upon myself!"

Then he embraced her passionately and was gone, leaving Miriam weeping.

CHAPTER XVII
THE GATE OF NICANOR

Another two hours went by, and the lengthening shadows cast through the stonework of the lattice told Miriam that the day was drawing to its end. Suddenly the bolts were turned and the door opened.

"The time is at hand," she said to herself, and at the thought her heart beat fast and her knees trembled, while a mist came before her eyes, so that she could not see. When it passed, she looked up, and there before her, very handsome and stately, though worn with war and hunger, stood Caleb, sword in hand and clad in a breast plate dinted with many blows. At the sight, Miriam's courage came back to her; at least before him she would show no fear.

"Are you sent to carry out my sentence?" she asked.

He bowed his head. "Yes, shortly, when the sun sinks," he answered bitterly. "The judge, Simeon, is a man with a savage heart. He accused me of trying to save you from the wrath of the Sanhedrin. He thought that I—"

"Let be what he thought," interrupted Miriam, "and do your office, friend Caleb. Do you remember when we were children, you often tied my hands and feet with flowers? Well, tie them now with cords, and make an end of it."

"You are cruel," he said, wincing.

"Indeed! Some might think it is you who are cruel. If only they had heard your words in the tower last night when you gave up my name to the Jews and linked it with another's."

"Oh, Miriam!" he broke into a pleading voice. "If I did that— and in truth I scarcely know what I did—it was because love and jealousy maddened me."

"Love? The love of the lion for the lamb! Jealousy? Why were you jealous? Because, having striven to murder Marcus—oh, I saw the fight and it was little better, for you struck him in the back, being fully prepared when he was not—you feared I might have saved him from your fangs. Well, thanks be to God! I did save him, as you feared. And now, officer of the most merciful and learned Sanhedrin, do your duty."

"At least, Miriam," Caleb went on humbly, for her bitter words, unjust as they seemed to him, weighed heavily on his heart, "at least, I strove my best for you today—after I had found time to think."

"Yes," she answered, "to think that other lions would get the lamb you desire for yourself."

"There is more," he continued, taking no note. "I have a plan."

"A plan to do what?"

"To escape. If I give the signal on your way to the gate where I am to lead you, you will be rescued by friends of mine who will hide you in a place of safety, while I, the officer, shall appear to be cut down. I will join you afterwards, and we can flee together under cover of night."

"Flee? Where to?"

"To the Romans, who will spare you because of what you did yesterday—and me also."

"Because of what *you* did yesterday?" she said dubiously.

"No. Because you will say that I am your husband. It will not be true, but what of it?"

"What of it, indeed," asked Miriam, "since it can always become true? But how is it that one of the chief Jewish warriors is prepared to fly and ask the mercy of your foes? Is it only because—"

"Spare your insults, Miriam. You know well why it is. You know well that I am no traitor, and that I do not flee for fear."

"Yes," she answered, in a changed tone, for his words had touched her, "I know that."

"It is for you that I fly, for your sake I will eat this dirt and crown myself with shame. I fly that for the second time I may save you."

"And in return you demand what?"

"Only yourself."

"I will not give you that, Caleb," she replied shortly. "I reject your offer."

"I feared that," he answered huskily. "I am accustomed to such denials. Then I demand this, for I know that if you give your word I may trust it: that you will not marry the Roman Fortunatus."

"I cannot marry Marcus any more than I can marry you, because neither of you are of my faith, and you know well that it is laid upon me to give myself to no such man."

"For your sake, Miriam," he answered slowly, "I am prepared to be baptized into your faith. Let this show you how much I love you."

"It does not show that you love the faith, Caleb, nor if you did love it could I love you as you wished me to. Jew or Christian, I will not be your wife."

He turned his face to the wall and for a while was silent. Then he spoke again.

"So be it, Miriam. But I would still save you. Go, and marry your Marcus if you can, though if I live, I will kill him if I can. But you need scarcely fear that, for I do not think that I shall live."

She shook her head. "I will not go, Caleb. I am weary of flight and hiding. Let God deal with me and Marcus and you as He pleases. But I thank you, and I am sorry for the unkind words I spoke. Oh, Caleb! Cannot you put me out of your mind? Are there not many fairer women who would be glad to love you? Why do you waste your life upon me? Take your path and let me take mine. Both are likely to be short enough."

"Your path, my path, and that of Fortunatus are all one path, Miriam, and I seek no other. As a boy, I swore that I would never take you against your will, and to that oath I hold. But I also swore that I would kill my rival if I could, and to that oath I hold. If he kills me, you may wed him. If I kill him, you need not wed me unless you so desire. But this fight is to the death, and whether you live or die, it is still to the death between me and him. Do you understand?"

"Your words are quite plain, Caleb, but this is a strange hour to speak them. For all I know, Marcus may already be dead, and within a short time, I with him. And the same death threatens you and all within this Temple."

"Yet we do live, Miriam, and I believe that for us three, the end is not yet at hand. Well, you will not fly, either with me or without me?"

"I will not fly."

"Then the time is come. I must do my duty, and leave the rest to fate. If, perchance, I can rescue you afterwards, I will, but do not hope for such a thing."

"Caleb, I neither hope nor fear. I will struggle no more. I am in other hands than yours or those of the Jews, and as those hands fashion the clay, so shall it be shaped. Now, will you bind me?"

"I have been given no such command. Come if it pleases you, the officers are waiting. Had you wished to be rescued, I should have taken the path on which my friends await us. Now we must go another."

"So be it," said Miriam with finality.

Then they went. Four men waited outside the cloister, two of them the doorkeepers who had searched her in the morning, the others, soldiers.

"You have been a long time with the pretty maid, master," said one of them to Caleb with a leer. "I hope you have been making good use of her."

Caleb ignored the quip. "I have been trying to discover the hiding place of the Roman, but the witch is obstinate," he answered, glaring at Miriam.

"She will soon change her tune on the Nicanor. The nights are cold and the days are hot for those who have neither cloak for their back nor water for their lips. Come on, Blue-Eyes, but first let's have those pearls. They may serve to buy a bit of bread or a drink of wine," and he grasped wildly at her chest.

In an instant, a sword flashed in the red light of the evening and hacked through the ruffian's skull; he fell to the pavement with a choked grunt.

"Swine," said Caleb with an angry snarl, "go seek your bread and wine in Gehenna. The maid is doomed to death, not to be plundered by lechers. Are there any others who would despoil the condemned?" he challenged, his eyes flashing to the other soldiers.

The companions of the fallen man stared at him. Then one laughed, for death was too common a sight to excite pity or surprise, and said, "He was ever a grasping fellow. Let us hope that he has gone where there is more to go around."

Then, led by Caleb, they marched through the long cloisters, past an inner door, turning down more cloisters on the right, and, following the base of the great wall, they came to its beautiful center gate, Nicanor, adorned with gold and silver, which separated the Court of Women and the Court of Israel. Over this gateway stood a square building, fifty feet or more in height, containing store chambers and rooms where the priests kept their instruments of music. On the flat roof towered three columns of marble, crowned by gilded spikes. One of the Sanhedrin was waiting for them by the gate, the same judge, Simeon, who had ordered Miriam to be searched.

"Has the woman disclosed the hiding place of the Roman?" he asked of Caleb.

"No," he answered, "she says she knows nothing of any Roman."

"Then bring her up," he intoned sternly, and they passed through some stone chambers to a staircase with a cedar door. The judge unlocked it, locking it again behind them, and they climbed the stairs until they came to another little door of stone. When it was opened, Miriam found herself on the roof of the gateway. They led her to the center pillar, to which was fastened an iron chain about ten feet in length. Here Simeon commanded that her hands should be bound behind her. Then he drew from his robe a scroll written in large letters, and tied it about her neck.

This was the writing on the scroll: *Miriam, Nazarene and Traitress, doomed here to die as God shall appoint, before the face of her friends, the Romans*. After this lettering followed the signatures of the Sanhedrin members, including that of her grandfather, Benoni, who had thus been forced to show the triumph of patriotism over kinship.

When this was done, the end of the chain was clamped fast round her waist and riveted with a hammer so that she could not possibly escape its grip. Then all being finished, the men prepared to leave.

But first, Simeon addressed her, "Remain here, traitress, until your bones drop from that chain," he said. "Stay through storm and shine, through light and darkness, while Roman and Jew alike make merry of your sufferings, which, if my voice had been listened to, would have been shorter, but more cruel. Daughter of the Devil, go back to the Devil and let the son of the carpenter save you if he can."

"Spare your words, Simeon," broke in Caleb with a cautious voice, "for curses are spears that fall on the heads of those that throw them."

"Had I my will," answered the judge, "a spear should fall upon your head, insolent, for daring to rebuke your elders. Begone before me, and be sure of this. If you attempt to return here, it will be for the last time. More is known about you than you think, Caleb, and perhaps you also would make friends with the Romans."

Caleb made no answer, for he knew the venom and power of the Zealot Simeon, who was the chosen friend and instrument of the savage John of Gischala. He looked at Miriam with sad eyes and muttered, "You would have it so; I can do no more. Farewell." And he left her to her fate.

So there in the red light of the sunset, with her hands bound, a placard setting out her shame upon her breast, and chained like a wild beast to a column of marble, Miriam was left alone. Walking as near to the little battlement as the length of her chain would allow, she looked down into the Court of Israel, where many of the Zealots had gathered to see her. When she appeared, they yelled and hooted and cast a shower of stones, one of which struck her on the shoulder. With a little cry of pain she ran back as far as she could reach on the farther side of the pillar. From here she could see the great Court of Women, where fifteen steps forming the half circle and fashioned of white marble led up to the Gate Nicanor. The court had been made into a camp, for the outer Court of Gentiles had been taken by the Romans, and their battering rams were working at its walls.

Then the night fell, and the rams continued to thunder. But as they were not strong enough to break through the huge stones of the mighty wall, the Romans renewed their attempt to take them by storm in the hours of darkness. But indeed, the evening brought no darkness, for the Jews lit fires upon the top of the wall, and by their light drove off the attacking Romans. Again and again, from her towering perch, Miriam saw the scaling ladders appear above the crest of the wall. Then lines of men, each holding a shield above his head, would climb them. As the foremost of these scrambled on to the wall, the waiting Jews rushed at them and cut them down with savage shouts while other Jews, seizing the rungs of the ladder, thrust it from the edge to fall with its living load back into the ditch beneath. Once there was a shout of triumph, for two standard bearers had come up the ladders carrying their ensigns with them. The men were overpowered and the ensigns captured, to be waved in derision at the Romans beneath, who answered the insult with sullen roars of rage.

So things went on until at length the legionaries, weary of this desperate fighting, took other counsel. Until now, Titus had desired to preserve the entire Temple, even to the outer courts and cloisters, but now he commanded that the gates, built of great cedar beams and overlaid with silver plates, should be burnt. Through a storm of spears and arrows the soldiers rushed up to them and thrust lighted brands into every joint and hinge. They caught flame, and presently the silver plates ran down their blazing surface in molten streams of metal. Nor was this all, for from the gates the fire spread to the cloisters on either side, and the exhausted Jews did not attempt to stay its ravages. They drew back sullenly and seated themselves in groups upon the pavement of the Court of Women, watching the circle of devouring flame creep slowly on. At length, the sun rose. Now the Romans were laboring to extinguish the fire at the gateway and make a path over the ruins for their advance. Shouts of triumph signaled their success, and the legionaries advanced into the Court of Women, commanded by Titus himself and accompanied by a body of horsemen. The Jews fled before them, surging up the steps of the Gate Nicanor beneath the pinnacle where Miriam watched. But they took no note of her. None had time to think, or even to look at the single girl bound there on high in punishment for some offence of which most of them knew nothing. They manned the walls to the right and left and held the gateway, but they did not climb to the roof where Miriam was, because its parapet was too low to shelter them from the arrows of their assailants.

The Romans saw her, however, and she saw some of the officers pointing her out to a man on horseback, clad in shining plate, a purple cloak draped over his shoulders. It was Titus himself. One of the soldiers took aim and loosed an arrow at her, which struck the spiked column above her head, rebounded, and fell at her feet. Titus evidently noted this, for she saw the man brought before him, and by his gestures she gathered that the general was issuing an angry reprimand. After this, no more arrows were shot at her, and she understood that they did not wish to do her harm, for their curiosity had been stirred by the sight of a woman chained upon the gateway.

The August sun shone out from a cloudless sky until the hot air danced above the roofs of the Temple and flowed thick over the paving of the courts. The thousands shut within their walls were glad to crowd into the shadow to shelter from its fiery beams, but Miriam could not escape them thus. In the morning and again in the afternoon she was able to take some shelter by creeping round to take refuge in the narrow line of shade thrown by the marble column to which she was chained. But at midday it flung no shadow, so for those dreadful hours she panted in the burning heat without a drop of water to relieve her thirst. She bore it until at length came evening and its cool.

That day, the Romans made no attack, nor did the Jews attempt a foray. Some of the lighter of the engines were brought

into the Court of Women, where they hurled their great stones
and heavy darts into the Court of Israel beyond. Miriam watched
these missiles as they rushed by her, once or twice so close that
the draft they made stirred her hair. The sight fascinated her
and took her mind from her own sufferings. She could see the
soldiers working at the levers and pulleys until the strings of the
catapult or the boards of the ballista were drawn to their places.
Then the darts or the stones were set in a groove, a cord was
pulled and the missile sped on its way, making an angry hum
as it clove the air. At first it looked small, then it grew large as it
approached, and then became small again to her sight as its arc
ended in a crash. Sometimes the stones, which did more dam-
age than the darts, fell upon the pavement and bounded along,
marking their course by fragments of shattered marble and
clouds of dust. Others crashed into huddled Jews, destroying all
they touched. Wandering among these people was that crazed
man Yeshua, the son of Annas, who had met them with his
wild prophetic cry when they had entered into Jerusalem, and
whose ill-omened voice Miriam had heard again before Marcus
was taken at the fight near the Old Tower. None hindered him,
though many thrust their fingers in their ears and looked aside
as he passed back and forth, wailing, "Woe, woe to Jerusalem!
Woe to the city and the Temple!" Suddenly, as Miriam watched,
he was still for a moment, then throwing up his arms, cried in
a piercing voice, "Woe, woe to me also!" Before the echo of his
words died against the Temple walls, a great stone, cast from the
Court of Women, rushed through the air and felled him to the
earth. On it went with great bounds, but the son of Annas lay
still. Now, in the hour of the accomplishment of his prophecy,
his pilgrimage had finally ended.

All day, the cloisters that surrounded the Court of Women
burned fiercely, but the Jews, having lost all heart, did not
rush forth to fight, and the Romans made no attack upon the
inner Court of Israel. At length, the last rays of the setting sun
struck upon the slopes of the Mount of Olives, the white tents
of the Roman camps, and the hundreds of crosses, each bearing its ghastly burden, that filled the Valley of Jehoshaphat and

climbed up the mountain sides wherever space could be found for them to stand. Then over the tortured, famished city fell the welcome night. To none was it more welcome than to Miriam, for with it came a copious dew that condensed upon the gilded spike of her marble pillar and trickled down, so that by licking a little groove in the marble, she was able to briefly ease the worst pangs of her thirst. The dew gathered also upon her hair, bare neck, and garments, so that through them she might take in moisture and renew her life. After this she slept a while, expecting always to be awakened by some fresh conflict. But on that night, none took place—the fight was for tomorrow. For now, there was peace.

Miriam dreamed in her uneasy sleep, and many visions came to her. She saw this sacred hill of Moriah, where the Temple stood, as it had been in the beginning, a rugged spot clothed with untended carob trees and olives, and inhabited not by men, but by wild boars and hyenas that preyed upon their own young. Almost at its center lay a huge black stone. To this stone came a man clad in the garb of the Arabs of the desert, and with him a boy whom he bound upon the stone as though to offer him in sacrifice. Then, as he was about to plunge a knife into the boy's heart, a glory shone round the place, and a voice cried to him to hold his hand. It was a vision of the offering of Isaac. It passed, and there came another.

Again she saw the sacred height of Moriah, and lo, a Temple stood upon it! A splendid building, but not that which she knew. And in front of this Temple lay the same black rock. On the rock, where once the boy had been bound, was an altar, and before the altar a glorious man clad in priestly robes, offering sacrifice of lambs and oxen and, in a resonant voice, giving praise to Jehovah in the presence of a countless host of people. This she knew was the vision of Solomon the King.

It passed, and lo, by this same black rock stood another man, pale and earnest, with piercing eyes. He reproached the worshippers in the Temple because of the wickedness of their hearts and drove them from before him with a scourge of cords. This was a vision of Jesus, the Son of Mary, the Messiah she worshipped, for as He drove out the people He prophesied the desolation that should fall upon them, but as they fled they mocked Him. And she saw him stand upon the Mount of Olives, weeping for the city.

The vision passed, and again she saw the black rock, but now it lay beneath a gilded dome and light fell upon it through painted windows. About it moved many priests whose worship was strange to her, and so they seemed to move for ages. At length, the doors of that dome burst open, and upon the priests rushed pale-faced, noble-looking men, clad in white mail and bearing upon their shields and tunics the emblem of a scarlet cross. They slaughtered the votaries of the strange worship, and once more the rock was red with blood. But they were gone in turn and other priests moved beneath the dome. The scarlet cross had vanished, and its pinnacles were crowned with crescents.

That vision passed, and there came another of dim, undistinguishable hordes, riding great machines of war that tore down the crescents, slaughtering the ministers of the strange faith, and giving the domed temple to the flames.

That vision passed, and once more the summit of Mount Moriah was as it had been in the beginning. The wild olive and the wild fig flourished among its desolate terraces, the wild boar roamed beneath their shade, and there were none to hunt him. Only the sunlight and the moonlight still beat upon the ancient rock of sacrifice.

That vision passed, and lo, around the rock, filling the Valley of Jehoshaphat and the valleys beyond, and the Mount of Olives and the mountains above, in the empty air between earth and sky, further than the eye could reach, stood, rank upon rank, all the countless millions of mankind, all the millions that had been and were yet to be, gazing, every one of them, awestruck and in utter silence upon the scarred and naked rock. For above the rock there grew a glory so bright that at the sight of it all the millions averted their eyes. And from the glory pealed forth a voice of a trumpet saying, "This is the end and the beginning, all things are accomplished in their order. The day of judgment has come."

Then upon the winds, voices murmured in the air, and upon the rock, stretching east and west, stood a cross of fire; above the cross, filling the heavens, was gathered legion upon legion of angels. This last vision of judgment passed also and Miriam awoke again from her haunted sleep to see the watch fires of the Romans burning in the Court of Women before her, and from the Court of Israel behind her, herded like cattle in the slaughterer's yard, the groans of the starving Jews who were destined to the sword tomorrow.

Chapter XVIII
The Death Struggle
of Israel

The light began to grow, but no sun rose that morning over the thousands who waited for its coming. The whole heaven was dark with a gray mist that seemed to drift up in billows from the sea, bringing with it a salty dampness. For this mist Miriam was thankful, for had the sun shone hotly she knew not how she could have lived through another day. Already she grew very weak, for she had suffered so much and eaten so little. Her only drink had been the dew, but she felt that while the mist hid the sun her life would yet remain.

The mist was a welcome sight to others as well. Under its cover, Caleb approached the gateway, and although he could not ascend it, as the doors were locked and guarded, he hurled onto its roof a linen bag containing a leather bottle of wine mixed with water, and with it a moldy crust of bread—all that he could find, or buy, or steal. The bag fell almost at Miriam's feet. Kneeling down, Miriam loosed the string of the bag with her teeth and devoured the crust of bread, again giving thanks that Caleb had been moved to this thought. But she could not drink from the bottle, for her hands were bound behind her, and she was unable to lift it or untie the thong that held fast its neck. She determined to try to free her hands, for she sorely needed drink and longed to protect herself from the tormenting attacks of stinging gnats and carrion flies.

The gilt spike that crowned her pillar was held fast with irons set into the marble at an angle, and the rough edge of one of these protruded somewhat from the pillar. Looking at it, the thought came into Miriam's mind that it might serve to rub through the cord with which her hands were bound. So standing with her back to the pillar she began her task, finding that it must be done little by little, since the awkward movement wearied her, and her swollen arms chafing against the marble of the column became intolerably sore. Yet, although the pain made her weep, she persevered, returning from time to time with new effort. But by nightfall the frayed cord had not yet parted.

In the mist, the Romans also came near to the gate, their curiosity overcoming caution, and called to her asking why she was bound there. She replied in Latin, a language understood by few Jews, that she had been accused of rescuing a Roman from death. Before her questioners could speak again, they were driven back by a shower of arrows loosed from the wall. But in the distance she thought she saw one of them make report to an officer, who on its delivery appeared to give some order.

Meanwhile, also under cover of the mist, the Jews were preparing themselves for battle. Over four thousand men strong, they gathered silently in the Court of Israel. Then in an instant, the gates were thrown open, among them the Nicanor. The *shofar* trumpeted the signal and they poured into the Court of Women, driving back the Roman guards and outposts like sticks and straws driven by a sudden flood.

But the legionaries were ready for them, and locking their shields together, they stood firm, so that the Jews fell back from their iron line like a flood receding from the shore. Yet they would not retreat, but fought furiously, killing many of the Romans, until at length Titus charged on them at the head of a squadron of horse and drove them back headlong through the gates. Then the Romans pressed forward and put those whom they had captured to the sword, but as yet they did not attempt the storming of the gates. Officers advanced as near to the wall as they dared and called to the Jews to surrender, saying that Titus desired to preserve their Temple and to spare their lives. But the Jews answered them with insults, taunts, and mockery, and Miriam, listening, wondered what spirit of madness had entered into these people that they should choose death and destruction rather than peace and mercy. Then she remembered her strange visions of the night, and in them she seemed to find an answer.

Having repulsed this desperate attack, the Roman officers set thousands of men to work in an attempt to extinguish the flaming cloisters, for regardless of the answer of the Jews, Titus still desired to save the Temple. As for its defenders, beyond guarding the walls of the Court of Israel, they did no more. Gathering in places most protected from the darts and stones thrown by the engines, they crouched upon the ground, some in sullen silence, some beating their breasts and rending their robes, while the women and children wailed in their misery and hunger, throwing dust upon their heads. The Gate of Nicanor, however, was still held by a strong guard, and they allowed none to approach it, nor did any attempt to ascend to its roof. Miriam knew Caleb still lived, for she had seen him, covered with dust and blood, driven back by the charge of Roman horse up the steps of the gateway. He was one of the last to pass through before it was closed and barred to keep out the pursuing Romans. It was the last time she would see him in Jerusalem.

So that day also ebbed away into history. At nightfall the thick mist cleared, and for one day more the rich rays of sunset shone upon the gleaming roof and were reflected from the dazzling whiteness of its walls. Never had the Temple looked more beautiful than it did in that twilight as it towered, still perfect, above the black ruins of the desolated city. The clamor and shouting had died away; even the mourners had ceased their pitiful cries. The Romans had withdrawn and were eating their evening meal, while those who worked the terrible engines ceased from their destroying toil. A dismal tranquility brooded on the place. But for the flames that crackled among the cedar beams in the roofs of the cloisters, everywhere was deep silence, like the calm that settles before the bursting of a cyclone.

To Miriam it seemed as though in the midst of this unnatural quiet, Jehovah was withdrawing Himself from the house where His Spirit dwelt and from the people who worshipped Him with their lips, but rejected Him in their hearts. Her tormented nerves shuddered with a fear that was not of the body as she stared upwards at the immense arch of the azure evening sky, half expecting that her mortal eyes would catch some vision of the departing wings of the Angel of the Lord. But she saw nothing but the shapes of the hundred eagles poised high over the city walls.

"Where the carcass is, there shall the eagles be gathered together," she murmured to herself. Then she remembered that these birds were come to feast upon the bones of the Jews and upon her own, and she shut her eyes and groaned.

Then the light died on the Temple towers and faded from the pale slopes of the mountains, and in place of the wheeling carrion birds, bright stars shone one by one upon the black mantle of the night.

Once again, setting her teeth against the agony of the marble chafing her raw and swollen flesh, Miriam began to work at the cords binding her wrists against the rough edge of the iron. She was sure that it was nearly worn through, but the bonds biting into her flesh made her dizzy with pain. Still she endured, for the bottle lay at her feet, and burning thirst drove her on. Her reward came at last, and she felt her arms break free. Numbed, swollen, and bleeding, they fell against her sides, wrenching the stiffened muscles of her shoulders back to their place so sharply that she nearly fainted with the pain. But they were free, and presently she was able to lift them and loosen the ends of the cord with her teeth, so that the blood could run once more through her blackened wrists and hands. Again she waited until some feeling had come back into her numbed fingers. Then she knelt down, and drawing the leather bottle to her, held it between her palms, while, with her teeth, she undid its thong. The task was hard, for it was well tied, but at length the knots gave, and Miriam drank. So fearful was her thirst that she could have emptied the bottle in a single gulp, but she had lived in the desert and was too wise to do that, for she knew that it might kill her. And when that was gone there would be no more. So she drank half of it in slow sips, then tied the string as well as she was able and set it down again.

The wine, although it was mixed with water, took hold of her who for so long had eaten nothing but a moldy crust. Strange sounds drummed in her ears, and sinking down against the column, she became senseless for a while. She awoke again, feeling somewhat refreshed, and though her head felt as though it did not belong to her, she was well able to think clearly. Her arms were less sore, and her fingers did not feel so dead. If only she could loose that chafing chain, she might escape, for now death was very near and unlovely. To die and pass quickly to Heaven—that would be well, but to perish slowly of starvation, heat, cold, and cramped limbs, suffering pain within and without, was hard to bear. She knew that even were she free, she could not hope to descend the gateway by its staircase, for the doors were locked and barred, and if she passed them it would be only to find herself among the Jews in the vaulted chambers beneath. But perhaps she could drop from the roof, which was not very high, onto the pavement in front of the first stair, and if she was unhurt she could run or crawl to the Romans, who might give her shelter.

So Miriam tried to undo the chain, only to find that she might sooner hope to pull down the Gate Nicanor with her bare hands. While she sat helpless against the marble, Miriam heard a stir in the Court of Israel, and by the dim starlight saw that men were gathering for some unknown purpose. Presently the great gates were opened very softly and out poured the Jews upon their last attack. Miriam was witnessing the death struggle of the nation of Israel. At the foot of the marble steps they split into two groups, half of them rushing towards the cloister on the right, and the other to that upon the left. Their object, as it seemed to her, was to slay those Roman soldiers who, by the command of Titus, were still engaged in fighting the flames that devoured these beautiful buildings, and then to surprise the camp beyond. The scheme was such as a madman might have made, for the Romans, warned by the sortie of the morning, had thrown up a wall across the lower part of the Court of Women, and beyond that were protected by every safeguard known to the science of war. The moment the first Jew set foot upon the staircase, the sentries cried out in warning and trumpets gave the call to arms.

Still, they reached the cloisters and killed a few Romans who had not retreated quickly enough. Following those who fled,

they came to the wall and began to try to force it, when suddenly on its crest and to the rear appeared thousands of the
men they had hoped to destroy, every one of them wakeful,
armed, and marshaled. The Jews hesitated, and like a stream of
living steel, the Roman ranks poured over the wall. Terror seized
the Temple soldiers, and with a melancholy cry of utter despair,
they turned to flee back to the Court of Israel. But this time
the Romans were not content with driving them away; they
pressed close behind the fleeing Jews, and some of them even
reached the gate before them. Up the marble steps poured friend
and foe together. Together they passed the open gate, in their
mad rush sweeping away those who had stayed to guard it, and
burst into the Court of Israel. Then leaving some to hold the
gate, reinforced continually by fresh companies from the camps
within and without the Temple courts, the Romans marched on
towards the doors of the Holy House, cutting down the defenders as they went. Now none attempted to stand. There was no
fight made; even the bravest of the Jewish warriors, feeling that
their hour was come and that Jehovah had deserted His people,
flung down their weapons and fled, some to escape to the Upper
City, more to perish on the Roman spears.

A few attempted to take refuge in the Holy House itself, pursued by Roman soldiers bearing torches. Miriam watched in
a terrified alarm from the roof of the Gate Nicanor; she saw
them dash toward the great golden entrance, torches floating
above their heads on the dusky air like points of wind-tossed
fire, and suddenly from a certain window on the north side of
the Temple sprang out a flame so bright that from where she
stood upon the gate, Miriam could see every detail of the golden
tracery. A soldier mounted on the shoulders of his comrade, not
knowing in his madness that he was a destroying angel, had
cast a torch into one of the Temple windows. Up ran the bright,
devouring flame, spreading outwards like a fan so that within
minutes the whole side of the Temple had become a roaring furnace. Meanwhile, the Romans were pressing through the Gate
Nicanor in an unending stream, until presently there was a cry.
"Make way! Make way!"

Miriam looked down to see a man, bareheaded and with close-cropped hair, white-robed also and unarmored, as though he had risen from his couch, riding on a great warhorse, an ivory rod in his hand and preceded by an officer who bore the standard of the Roman Eagles. It was Titus himself, who came shouting orders to the centurions to beat back the legionaries and extinguish the fire. But who could beat them back now? Easier to restrain the hosts of Gehenna than to reason with men in such a state. They were mad with the lust of blood and the lust of plunder, and even to the voice of their lord they paid no heed.

New flames sprang up in other parts of the vast Temple. It was doomed. The golden doors were burst open and, attended by his officers, Titus passed through them to view for the first and last time the house of Jehovah, God of the Jews. From chamber to chamber he passed, even into the Holy of Holies itself. He emerged from the vacant chamber and gave the command for the Holy Place to be emptied of the golden seven-branched candlestick and the golden table of shrewbread.

In but an hour, the Temple that for over a thousand years had stood upon the sacred summit of Mount Moriah was engulfed in a sheet of flame, while soldiers stripped it of its gold and ornaments, tossing the sacred vessels to each other and tearing down the silken curtains of the shrine. In their fury the Romans fell upon even the people crowded in the Court of Israel and slew more than ten thousand of their number, warrior and priest, citizen, woman and child together, until the court swam with blood and the polished marble floor was covered with the dead who had taken refuge there.

From the Court of Israel went up one mighty wail of those who sank beneath the sword. From the thousands of the Romans went up a savage shout of triumph, the shout of those who put them to the sword. From the multitude of the Jews who watched the ruin from the Upper City went up a ceaseless scream of utter agony, and overshadowing all, like the accompaniment of some fearful music, rose the fierce, triumphant roar of fire. In straight lines and jagged pinnacles, the flames soared hundreds of feet into the still air, leaping higher and ever higher as the white walls and gilded roofs collapsed, until all the Temple was but one gigantic furnace, where none but the dead could abide, whose very garments took fire as they lay upon the ground. Never was such a sight seen before; never, perhaps, will such a sight be seen again.

Every living being the Romans could find was slain, and then they drew back, bearing their spoil with them. The thousands of Jews that remained sought to escape across the valley into the Upper City by the bridges, breaking them behind them. Miriam watched until she could bear the sight no longer. The glare blinded her, the heat of the radiant furnace shriveled her up; her white dress was scorched and turned brown. She crouched behind the shelter of her pinnacle gasping for breath. She prayed that she might die, but could not. Now she remembered the drink that remained in the leather bottle, and swallowed it to the last drop. Then she crouched down again against the pillar, and as she lay thus, her senses left her.

When the Romans returned to the grounds it was daylight, and from the heap of ashes that had been the Temple of Herod, the most glorious building in the whole world, rose a thick cloud of black smoke, pierced here and there by little angry tongues of fire. The Court of Israel was strewn so thick with the dead that the soldiers walked upon them as on a carpet, or to be rid of them, they hurled them into the smoldering ruins. Upon the altar that stood on the rock of sacrifice, a strange sight was to be seen, for set up there was an object like the shaft of a lance wreathed with what seemed to be twining snakes, crowned by a globe on which stood a golden eagle with outspread wings. Gathered in front of it were a vast number of legionaries who did obeisance to this object, offering worship to the Roman standards as they stood upon the ancient altar of the God of Israel. Presently a figure rode before them attended by a glittering staff of officers, to be greeted with a mighty shout of, *"Titus Imperator! Titus Imperator!"* There in their triumph the victorious legions named their general Caesar.

But fighting was not altogether ended, for on the roofs of some of the burning cloisters were gathered a few of the most desperate survivors, who retreated slowly towards the Gate

Nicanor as the cloisters crumbled beneath them. The Romans, weary with slaughter, called to them to come down and surrender, but they would not, and as Miriam watched, to her horror she saw that one of these men was none other than her grandfather, Benoni. When they would not yield, the Romans shot at them with arrows, so that presently every one of them had fallen except Benoni, whom no dart seemed to touch.

"Cease shooting," cried a voice, "and bring a ladder. That man is brave and one of the Sanhedrin. Let him be taken alive."

A ladder was brought and reared against the wall near the Gate Nicanor and the Romans quickly ascended. Benoni retreated before them until he stood upon the edge of the gulf of advancing fire. Then he rounded to face them. As he turned, he caught sight of Miriam huddled at the base of her column upon the roof of the gate, and thinking that she was dead, wrung his hands and tore his beard. She guessed his grief, but she was so weak and parched that she could call no word of comfort to him.

The soldiers advanced along the top of the wall until they feared to approach nearer to the fire, lest they should fall through the burning rafters.

"Yield!" they cried. "Yield, fool, before you perish! Titus gives you your life."

"That he may drag me, an elder of Israel, in chains through the streets of Rome?" answered the old Jew scornfully. "Nay, I will not yield, and I pray God that the same end that you have brought upon this city and its children may fall upon your city and its children at the hands of men even more cruel."

Then stooping down he lifted a spear lying upon the wall and hurled it at them so fiercely that as it struck the buckler of a soldier it pierced even through the arm behind the buckler.

"Would that it had been your heart, heathen, and the heart of all your race!" he screamed, and lifting his hands as though in invocation, leaned backward and plunged into the flames beneath.

Thus, fierce and brave to the last, died Benoni the Jew.

The door that led from the gate chambers to its roof burst open and through it sped a bareheaded and disheveled figure,

his torn raiment black with blood and smoke. Staring at him, Miriam knew the man. It was Simeon, her cruel judge, who had doomed her to this dreadful end. After him, gripping his robe, came a Roman centurion, a stout man of middle age, with a weather-beaten but kindly face, which in some dim way seemed to be familiar to her; after him followed six soldiers.

"Hold him!" he panted. "We must have one of them to show, if only that the people may know what a live Jew looks like." The centurion tugged so fiercely at the robe that in his struggles to free himself to die by casting himself from the gateway tower, Simeon fell down.

In the next instant, the soldiers were on him and held him fast. Then it was for the first time that the centurion caught sight of Miriam crouched at the foot of her pillar.

"Why," he said, "I had forgotten. That's the girl we saw yesterday from the Court of Women whom we have orders to save. Is the poor thing dead?"

Miriam lifted her pale face and looked at him.

"By Bacchus!" he said, "I have seen that face before; it is not one that a man would forget." Then he stooped and eagerly read the writing that was tied upon her breast: *Miriam, Nazarene and Traitress, doomed here to die as God shall appoint, before the face of her friends, the Romans.*

"Miriam," he muttered to himself in thought. He was stirred by a sudden memory and checked himself.

"The girl wears pearls," declared one of the soldiers, "and good ones." He drew forth his knife, moving to cut them from her throat.

"Let them be," the centurion ordered. "Neither she nor her pearls are for any of us. Loose her chain, not her necklet."

So with much trouble they broke the rivets of the chain.

"Can you stand, lady?" said the centurion to Miriam.

She made an attempt but stumbled faintly.

"Then I shall carry you," and stooping down he lifted her in his strong arms as though she were but a child, and ordering the soldiers to bring the Jew Simeon with them, slowly and with great care descended the staircase Miriam had climbed more than sixty hours before.

The centurion passed through the outer doors into the archway, where the great gate by which the Romans had gained access to the Temple stood wide, then he turned into the Court of Israel, where some soldiers were engaged in dividing spoil. They looked up laughing and asked him whose baby he had captured. He paid them no heed as he walked across the court, picking his way through the heaps of dead to a range of the southern cloisters still standing, where officers could be seen coming and going. Under one of these cloisters was Titus, seated on a stool and occupied in examining the vessels and other treasures of the Temple being brought before him one by one. He looked up, saw this strange procession and commanded that they should be brought before him.

"Who is it that you carry in your arms, centurion?" he asked.

"Caesar," he answered, "it is the girl who was bound upon

the Nicanor. You gave orders that she should not be harmed."

"Is she alive?"

"Alive," he confirmed. "Little more. Thirst and heat have withered her."

"Why was she there?"

"This writing tells the story, Caesar."

Titus read. "Ah!" he said, "Nazarene. An evil sect, worse even than these Jews, or so thought the divine Nero. Traitress also. The girl must have deserved her fate. But what is this? 'Doomed to die as God shall appoint before the face of her friends, the Romans.' In what way are the Romans her friends, I wonder? Girl, if you can speak, tell me who condemned you."

Miriam lifted her head from the shoulder of the centurion on which it lay and pointed with her finger at the Jew, Simeon.

"Is that so, man?" asked Caesar. "Now tell the truth, for I shall learn it, and if you lie you die."

"She was condemned by the Sanhedrin, and her own grand-father, Benoni, was among them. There is his signature with the rest upon the scroll," Simeon answered sullenly.

"For what crime?"

"Because she helped a Roman prisoner to escape," and he added furiously, "may her soul burn in Gehenna for ever and aye!"

"What was the name of the prisoner?" asked Titus.

"I do not remember," answered Simeon with a sideways glance.

"Well," said Caesar, "it does not greatly matter, for either he is safe or he is dead. Your robes, what are left of them, show that you also are one of the Sanhedrin. Is it not so?"

"Yes. I am Simeon, a name that you may have heard."

"Ah! Simeon, here it is, written on this scroll first of all. Well, Simeon, you doomed a highborn lady to a cruel death because she saved a Roman soldier, and it is but just that you should drink of your own wine. Take him and fasten him to the column on the gateway and leave him there to perish. Your Holy House is destroyed, Simeon, and as you are a faithful priest, I am sure you have no wish to survive your religion."

"Well enough, Roman," he answered, "though I should have been better pleased with a quicker end, such as I pray may overtake you."

They led him off, and presently Simeon appeared upon the gateway with Miriam's chain about his waist and Miriam's rope freshly knotted about his wrists.

"Now for this poor girl," went on Titus Caesar. "It seems that she is a Nazarene, a sect of which all men speak ill, for they try to subvert authority and preach doctrines that would bring the world to ruin. And she was false to her own people, which is a crime, though one for which we Romans cannot complain. Therefore, if only for the sake of example it would be wrong to set her free. Besides, to do so would be to give her to death. My command is, then, that she shall be taken good care of, and if she recovers, be sent to Rome to adorn my Triumph, should the gods grant me such a thing, and afterwards be sold as a slave for the benefit of the wounded soldiers and the poor. Meanwhile, who will take charge of her?"

"I shall," said that centurion who had freed Miriam. "There is an old woman who tends my tent. She can nurse her in her sickness."

"Understand, friend," answered Titus, "that no harm is to be done to this girl. She is my property."

"I understand, O Caesar," said the centurion. "She shall be treated as though she were my daughter."

"Good. You who are present, remember his words and my decree. In Rome, if we live to reach it, you shall give account to me of the captive lady, Miriam. Now take her away, for there are greater matters to be dealt with than the fortunes of this girl."

CHAPTER XIX
PEARL MAIDEN

Many days passed, but the fighting was not ended, for the Jews continued to hold the Upper City. In one of the assaults upon the remaining Jewish forces, the centurion who had rescued Miriam was badly wounded in the leg by a spear. He could be of no more service in this war, so because he was a man whom Titus trusted, he was ordered to sail for Rome with the other wounded soldiers, taking in his charge much of the spoils that had been captured. With this purpose, he traveled down to Tyre, where his vessel was to put to sea. In obedience to the command of Caesar, he had carried the captive Miriam to the camp of the tenth legion upon the Mount of Olives, and there placed her in a tent, where an old slave-woman tended her. For several days, it was not certain whether the girl would live or die, for her sufferings and all that she had seen had brought her so near to death that it was hard to keep her from passing its half-opened gates. But with good food and care, strength returned to her body. But the strain of the siege had proven too much for Miriam's ailing mind; during all these weeks, her speech wandered, and no word of reason passed her lips.

Many would have wearied of her and thrust her out to take her chance with the hundreds of other poor creatures who roamed about the land, but this Roman did not act thus. As he had promised, so it was. Had Miriam been his daughter, she could not have been better tended. Whenever his duties gave him time he would sit with her, trying to draw her out of her madness. During most of the daylight hours, in spite of his wounded condition, Gallus remained attentive. Over time, the poor girl grew to love him in a crazy fashion and would throw her arms about his neck and call him "Uncle," as in the old days she had called the Essenes. As the days passed, she learned to know the soldiers of the legion, who became fond of her and brought her gifts of fruit and winter flowers, or of anything else they thought would please her. When the centurion received his orders to proceed to Tyre with the spoils and take ship there, he and his guard took Miriam with them and, journeying easily, reached the city on the eighth day.

Their ship was not ready, so they camped on the outskirts of Paleotyrus, by strange coincidence in the very garden that had been the property of Benoni. They reached the place after sunset and set up their tents, that of Miriam and the old slave-woman being placed on the seashore next to the tent of her protector. She slept well that night, and when she was awakened at the dawn by the murmur of the sea upon the rocks, she went to the door of the tent and looked out. All the camp was sleeping, for here they had no enemy to fear, and a great calm lay upon the sea and land. Presently the mist lifted and the rays of the rising sun poured across the blue ocean and its gray, bordering coast.

With that returning light, the light returned also into Miriam's darkened mind. She became aware that this scene was familiar; she recognized the outlines of the proud and ancient island town. And she remembered the garden. Yes, there was the palm tree beneath which she had often sat, and there the rock under whose shadow grew white lilies. There she had rested with Nehushta when the Roman centurion brought her the letter and the gifts from Marcus. Instinctively Miriam put her hand to her neck. About it still hung the string of pearls, and on the pearls the ring, which the slave-woman had found in her hair and tied there for safety. She took off the ring and placed it back on her finger. Then she walked to the rock, sat down and tried to think. But her mind was not yet clear enough to remember all, for there rose up vision after vision of blood and fire, heavy and overwhelming. All that had happened before the siege was clear, but the rest was a great red confusion.

While she sat thus, the Roman centurion hobbled from his pavilion, resting on a crutch, for his leg was still lame and pained. First he went to Miriam's tent to inquire about her of the old slave woman, as was his custom at the daybreak. When he learned that Miriam had left her tent, he went looking for her. He found her sitting in the shade of the rock, gazing at the sea, and went to join her.

"Good morning to you, daughter," he said. "How have you slept after your long journey?" He paused, expecting to be answered with some babbling, gentle nonsense. But instead of this she rose and stood before him looking confused.

Then she replied, "Sir, I thank you, I have slept well. But tell me, is that Tyre? And is this not the garden of my grandfather, Benoni, where I used to wander? How can it be? So long has passed since I walked in this garden, and so many things have happened—terrible, terrible things that I cannot remember," and she hid her eyes in her hands.

"Don't try to remember them," he said cheerfully. "There is so much in life that it is better to forget. Yes, this is Tyre, sure enough. You could not recognize it last night because it was too dark, and this garden, I am told, did belong to Benoni. Who it belongs to now, I do not know. To you, I suppose, and through you to Caesar."

While he spoke thus somewhat at random, Miriam kept her eyes fixed upon his face, as though searching there for something that she could but half recall. Suddenly an inspiration entered into them and she said, "I remember! You are the Roman centurion, Gallus, who brought me the letter from—" and she paused, thrusting her hand into the bosom of her robe, then went on with something like a sob, "Oh! It is gone. How have I lost it? Let me think."

"Don't think," said Gallus. "There are so many things in the world that are better unthought of. Yes, as it happens, I am that man, and some years ago I did bring you the letter from Marcus, called Fortunatus. Also, as it chanced, I never forgot your sweet face and knew it again at a time when it was well that you should find a friend. No, we won't talk about it now. Look, the old slave calls you. It is time that you should break your fast, and I also must eat and have my wound dressed. Afterwards we will talk."

All that morning Miriam saw nothing more of Gallus. Indeed, he did not mean that she should, for he was sure that her newfound sense ought not to be overstrained at first, lest it should break down again, never to recover. So she went out and sat alone by the garden beach gazing at the sea, for the soldiers had orders to respect her privacy.

As she sat thus in quiet, the terrible past came back to her, event by event. She remembered it all now—their flight from Tyre, the march into Jerusalem, the sojourn in the dark with the Essenes, the Old Tower and what befell there, the escape of Marcus, her trial before the Sanhedrin, the execution of her sentence upon the gateway, and then that fearful night when the flames of the burning Temple scorched the memories from her mind. The sights and sounds of slaughter withered her heart. After this she could recall but one more thing—the vision of the majestic figure of Benoni standing against a background of black smoke upon the lofty cloister-roof, defying the Romans before he plunged backward into the flames beneath. Of her rescue on the roof of the Gate Nicanor, of her being carried before Titus Caesar in the arms of Gallus, and of his judgment concerning her she could recall nothing. The time between that day and the recovery of her mind by the seashore in the garden of Tyre remained a blank, troubled fragment of her life sunk into a black sea of oblivion.

At length, the old woman came to summon Miriam to her midday meal and led her, not to her own tent, but to that which was pitched to serve as an eating place for the centurion, Gallus. As they walked, she saw bands of soldiers gathered across her path as though to intercept her. She turned to flee, for the sight of them brought back the terrors of the siege.

"Have no fear of them," said the old woman, smiling. "It would go ill here with him who dared to lift a finger against their Pearl Maiden."

"Pearl Maiden! Why? What do you mean?" asked Miriam.

"That is what they call you, because of the necklace that was upon your breast when you were captured, which you wear still. As for why—well, I suppose because they love you, the poor sick thing they nursed. They have heard that you are better and gather to give you joy of it. That is all."

Sure enough, the words were true, for as Miriam approached, these rough legionaries cheered and clapped their hands. One of them, an evil-looking fellow with a broken nose, who was said to have committed great cruelties during the siege, came forward, bowed, and presented her with a handful of wildflowers, which he must have collected with some trouble, since at that season of the year they were uncommon. She took them, overcome with feeling, while tears streamed down her cheeks.

"Why should you treat me thus," she asked. "I am but a poor captive."

"Nay, nay," answered a sergeant, with an uncouth oath. "It is we who are your captives, Pearl Maiden, and we are glad that your mind has come to you . . . though, seeing how sweet you were without it, we do not know how it can better you very much."

"Oh! Friends, friends," began Miriam, but once more faltered.

Meanwhile, hearing the disturbance, Gallus came out of his tent and began to hobble towards them. Suddenly, he caught sight of the tears upon Miriam's face and broke out into such foul language as could only be used by a Roman officer of experience.

"What have you been doing to her, you cowardly hounds?" he shouted. "By Caesar and the standards, if one of you has even said a word that she should not hear, he shall be flogged until the bones break through his skin!" His very beard bristling with wrath, Gallus uttered a series of the most fearful maledictions upon the head of that supposed offender, his female ancestry, and his descendants.

"Your pardon, centurion," said the sergeant, "but *you* are uttering many words that no maiden should hear."

"Do you dare to argue with me, you foul tongued camp scavenger?" shouted Gallus. "Here, guard, lash him to that tree! Fear not, daughter. The insult shall be avenged. We shall teach his dirty tongue to sing another tune," and again he cursed him, naming him by new names.

"Oh, Sir! Sir," broke in Miriam, "what are you doing? This

man offered me no insult. None of them offered me anything but kind words and flowers."

"Then why do you weep?" asked Gallus suspiciously.

"I weep because they who are conquerors were so kind to a slave and an outcast."

"Oh!" said Gallus. "Well, guard, you need not tie him up this time, but I still take back nothing I have said, for they *did* make you weep. What business had they to insult you with their kindness? Men, from now on you will be so good as to remember that this maiden is the property of Titus Caesar, and after Caesar, of myself, in whose charge he placed her. If you have any offerings to make to her, and I do not dissuade you from that practice, they must be made through me. Meanwhile, there is a cask of wine, that good old stuff from Lebanon that I had bought for the voyage. If you should wish to drink to the health of our—our captive, it is at your disposal."

Then taking Miriam by the hand he led her into the tent, still grumbling at the soldiers, who for their part laughed and sent for the wine. They knew their commander's temper, for they had served with him through many battles, and they knew also that this crazed Pearl Maiden whom he saved had twined herself into his heart, as was her fortune with most men with whom she was forced to seek shelter.

In the tent, Miriam found two places set, one for herself and one for Gallus.

"You needn't talk now," he said, "but sit down and eat, for you have swallowed little enough all the time you were sick, and we sail tomorrow evening at the latest. After that, unless you differ from most women, you'll swallow little enough on these winter seas until it pleases whatever god you worship to bring us to the coasts of Italy. Now here are oysters brought by runner from Sidon, and I command that you eat six of them before you say a word."

So Miriam ate the oysters obediently, and after the oysters, fish, and after the fish the breast of a woodcock. But her filled belly forced her to decline the autumn lamb, roasted whole, which followed.

"Send it to the soldiers," she suggested, and it was sent as her gift.

"Now, my captive," said Gallus, drawing his stool near to her, "I want you to tell me what you can remember of your story. Ah! I see you don't remember that for many days past we have dined together and it has been your custom to sit with your arm round my old neck and call me your uncle. You need not blush, child, for I am more than old enough to be your father, let alone your uncle, and nothing but a father shall I ever be to you."

"Why are you so good to me?" asked Miriam.

"Why? Oh, for several reasons. First, you were the friend of a comrade of mine who often talked of you, but who is now dead. Secondly, you were a sick and helpless thing whom I chanced to rescue in the great slaughter, and who has ever since been my companion. And thirdly—yes, I will say it, though I do not love to talk of that matter, I had a daughter, who died, and who, had she lived, would have been about your age. Your eyes remind me of hers . . . there, is that not enough?

"But now for your story. I will tell you first what I know of it. Marcus, he whom they called Fortunatus, but whose fortune has deserted him, was in love with you—like the rest of us. Often he talked to me of you in Rome, where we were friends after a fashion, though he was far above me, and by my hand he sent to you that letter which I delivered here in this garden, and the trinket that you wear about your neck, and if I remember right, with it a ring—yes, it is on your finger. Well, I took note of you at the time and went my way to the war, and when I chanced to find you upon the top of the Gate Nicanor, although you were more like a half-burnt cinder than a fair maiden, I knew you again and carried you off to Caesar, who named you his slave and bade me take charge of you and deliver you to him in Rome. Now I want to know how you came to be upon that gateway."

So Miriam began and told him all her tale, while he listened patiently. When she had done he rose and, limping round the little table, bent over and kissed her solemnly upon the brow.

"By all the gods of the Romans, Greeks, Christians, Jews, and barbarian nations, you are a noble hearted woman," he said, "and that kiss is my tribute to you. Little wonder that puppy, Marcus, is called Fortunatus. Even when he deserved to die for allowing himself to be taken alive you appeared to save him—to save him, by Venus, at the cost of your own sweet self. Well, most noble traitress, what now?"

"I ask that question of you, Gallus. What now? Marcus, whom you should call no ill name, who was overwhelmed through no fault of his own, fighting like a hero, has vanished—"

"Across the Styx, I fear. Indeed that would be best for him, since no Roman must be taken prisoner and live."

"No, I think not, or at the least I hope he lives. My servant would nurse him for my sake, and for my sake the Essenes, among whom I dwelt, would guard him, even to the loss of their own lives. Unless his wound killed him, I believe that Marcus is alive today."

"And if that is so, you wish to communicate with him?"

"What else, Gallus? Tell me, what fate will befall me when I reach Rome?"

"You will be kept safe until Titus comes. Then, according to his command, you must walk in his Triumph, and after that, unless he changes his mind, which is not likely, since he prides himself in never having reversed a decree, however hastily it was made, or even added to or taken from a judgment, you must be set up in the Forum and sold as a slave to the highest bidder."

"Sold as a slave to the highest bidder!" repeated Miriam faintly. "That is a poor fate for a woman, is it not? Had it been that daughter of yours who died, for instance, you would have thought it a poor fate for her, would you not?"

"Do not speak of it, do not speak of it," muttered Gallus into his beard. "Well, in this, as in other things, let us hope that fortune will favor you."

"I should like Marcus to learn that I am to march in the Triumph and afterwards to be set up in the Forum and sold as a slave," said Miriam.

"I too should like Marcus to learn—but, in the name of the gods, how is he to learn, even if he still lives? Look you, we sail tomorrow night. What do you wish me to do?"

"I wish you to send a messenger to Marcus bearing a token from me to him."

"A messenger! What messenger? Who can find him? I can dispatch a soldier, but your Marcus is with the Essenes, who for their own sakes will keep him as a hostage, if they have cured him. And according to your story, they live in some hyena burrow, opening out of an underground quarry in Jerusalem. That is if they have not been discovered and killed long ago. How, then, will any soldier find their hiding place?"

"I do not think that such a man would find it," answered Miriam, "but I have friends in this city, and if I could find them I might discover one who would have a better chance. You know that I am a Christian, brought up among the Essenes. Both of them are persecuted people that have their secrets. If I find a Christian or an Essene he would take my message and—unless he is prevented—deliver it."

Now Gallus thought for a while, then said, "If I were to go out into Tyre asking for Christians or Essenes, none would appear. As well might a stork go out and call upon a frog. But that old slave woman who has tended on us is cunning in her way, and if I promised to set her at liberty should she succeed, well, perhaps she might succeed. Wait here, I will summon her," and he left the tent.

Some minutes later he returned, bringing the slave with him.

"I have explained the matter to this woman, Miriam," he said, "and I think that she understands and can prove to any who are willing to visit you that they will have a free pass into and out of the camp, and need fear no harm. Tell her, then, where she is to go and whom she must seek."

So Miriam told the woman, saying, "Tell any Essene you can find that she who is called their Queen, bids his presence, and if he asks more, give him this word—'The sun rises.' Tell any Christian whom you can find that Miriam, their sister, seeks their aid, and if he asks more, give him this word—'The Son is risen.' Do you understand?"

"I understand," answered the woman.

"Then go," said Gallus, "and be back by nightfall. Remember that if you fail, in place of liberty you travel to Rome."

"My lord, I go," answered the woman, beating her forehead with her hand and bowing herself from their presence.

By nightfall she returned with the tidings that no Christians seemed to be left in Tyre. All had fled to an unknown place. However, she had found one of the Essenes, a minor brother by the name of Samuel who, on hearing that Miriam was the captive and receiving the watchword, said he would visit the camp after dark, although he greatly feared that this might be some snare set to catch him.

After dark he came as he had promised, and was led by the old woman to the tent where Miriam sat with Gallus. Samuel was a brother of the lowest order of the Essenes, whom, although he knew of Miriam, had never seen her. He had been absent from the village by the Jordan at the time of the flight of the sect, and had come to Tyre by leave of the Court to bid farewell to his mother, who had been on her deathbed. Hearing that the brethren had fled, he had remained in Tyre instead of seeking to rejoin them at Jerusalem, thus escaping the terrors of the siege. That was all his story. Now, having buried his mother, he desired to rejoin the brotherhood, if any of them were left alive.

After Gallus had left the tent, as it was not lawful that she should speak of their secrets in the presence of any man who was not of the Order, Miriam, having first satisfied herself that he was in truth a brother, told Samuel all she knew of the hiding place of the Essenes beyond the ancient quarry and asked him if he was willing to seek it out. He readily agreed, for he desired to find them, and he was bound to give her any help he could. Should the brethren discover that he had refused it, he would be expelled from their order.

Then, having pledged him to be faithful to her trust, she took from her hand the ring that Marcus had sent her, bidding him find the Essenes, and if their Roman prisoner was yet alive and among them, to deliver it to him with a message telling him of her fate and where she had gone. If he was dead, or not to be found anywhere, then he was to deliver the ring to the Libyan woman named Nehushta, with the same message. If he could not find her either, then to her uncle Ithiel, or, failing him, to whoever was Overseer of the Essenes, with the same message, praying any or all of them to aid her in her troubles, if it were possible. At the least they were to let her have tidings at the house of Gallus, the centurion, in Rome, where he proposed to place her in charge of his wife until the time came for her to be handed over to Titus and to walk in the Triumph.

Moreover, in case Samuel should forget, she wrote a letter that he might deliver to any of those for whom she gave the message. In this letter Miriam set out briefly all that had befallen her since that night of parting in the Old Tower, and by the help of Gallus, whom she now recalled to the tent, the particulars of her rescue and of the judgment of Caesar upon her person. She ended it with these words, "If it be the will of God and your will, O you who may read this letter, hasten to help me, that I may escape the shame more sore than death which awaits me in Rome."

She signed the letter, *Miriam, of the house of Benoni,* but did not write the names of those to whom it was addressed, fearing lest it should fall into other hands and bring trouble upon them.

Then Gallus asked the man Samuel what money he needed for his journey and as a reward for his service. He answered that it was against his rule to take any money, for he was bound to help those under the protection of the Order without reward or fee. Gallus stared in shock after hearing this response and said that there were stranger folk in this land than in any others that he knew.

So Samuel bowed before Miriam and pressed her hand to his forehead in token of brotherhood and fidelity, and was led from the camp again, never again to be seen by the Queen of the Essenes.

The next day, at Miriam's request, Gallus also wrote a letter to a friend of his who was a fellow officer with the army at Jerusalem. He also wrote one to be handed to Marcus if, perchance, he should have rejoined the Standards.

"Now daughter," he said, "we have done all that can be done, and must leave the rest to fate."

"Yes," she answered with a sigh, "we must leave the rest to fate, as you Romans call God."

In the evening they set sail for Italy, and with them much of the captured spoil, many sick and wounded men, and a guard of soldiers. Having taken to sea after the autumn gales and before those of midwinter began, they had a swift and easy voyage, enduring few hardships. Within thirty days, they docked at Rhegium, and from there marched overland to Rome, being received everywhere gladly by people who were eager for tidings of the war.

Chapter xx
The Merchant Demetrius

When on that fateful night in the Old Tower, when Miriam sprang forward to strike the lantern from the hand of the Jew, Nehushta, who was bending over the fallen Marcus and dragging at his body, did not even see that she had left the door.

With an effort, and the help of the sloped rocky passage beyond, she half-drew, half-lifted the Roman through the entrance. As she straightened herself a little to take a breath, she heard the thud of the rock door closing behind her. Still, as it was dark, she did not guess that Miriam was parted from them. "Ah! Into what troubles do not these men lead us poor women. Well, just in time, and I think that none of them saw us."

There was no answer. Sound could not pierce that wall and the place was silent as a tomb.

"Lady! For mercy's sake, where are you, lady?" asked Nehushta in a piercing whisper, and the echoes of the gallery answered, "Where are you, lady?"

Marcus awoke. "What has happened? What place is this, Miriam?" he asked.

"This has happened," answered Nehushta in the same awful voice. "We are in the passage leading to the vaults. Miriam is in the hands of the Jews in the Old Tower, and the door is shut between us. Accursed Roman! To save your life she has sacrificed herself. She must have sprung from the door to delay the guard. Now they will crucify her because she rescued you—a Roman."

"Don't talk, woman," interrupted Marcus savagely. "Open the door. I am still a man. I can still fight, or," he added with a groan, remembering that he had no sword, "at least I can die for her."

"I cannot open it," gasped Nehushta. "She had the iron that lifts the latch. If you had kept your sword, Roman, it might perhaps have served, but that is gone also."

"Break it down," said Marcus. "Come, I will help."

"Yes, yes, Roman," she scoffed bitterly, "you will help to break down three feet of solid stone."

Nehushta strove to reach the latch with her fingers. Marcus, standing upon one foot, strove to shake the stone with his shoulder, but he could not even stir it. Yet they worked madly, their breath coming in great gasps, knowing that the work was in vain, and that even if they could open the door, by now it would be only to find Miriam gone, or at the best to be taken themselves. Marcus ceased from his labor in despair.

"Lost!" he moaned. "And for my sake. O, gods! For my sake." Then down he fell, his harness clattering on the rocky step, and lay there, muttering and laughing foolishly.

Nehushta ceased also, gasping, "The Lord help you, Miriam, for I cannot. Oh, after all these years to lose you thus, and because of this man!" She glared through the darkness towards the fallen Marcus, thinking in her heart that she would kill him. No, she thought to herself. Miriam loved him, and if she knew, she would never approve.

As she sat thus, helpless, hopeless, she saw a light coming up the stair towards them. It was borne by Ithiel. Nehushta rose and faced him.

"Praise be to God! There you are at length," he said. "Thrice have I been up this stair wondering why Miriam did not come."

"Brother Ithiel," answered Nehushta, "Miriam will come no more. She is gone, leaving us in exchange this man Marcus, the Roman prefect of horse."

"What do you mean? What do you mean?" he gasped. "Where is Miriam?"

"In the hands of the Jews," she answered. Then she told him the whole story.

"There is nothing to be done," he moaned when she had finished. "To open the door now would be but to reveal the secret of our hiding place to the Jews or to the Romans, either of whom would put us to the sword, the Jews for food, the Romans because we are Jews. We can only leave her to God and protect ourselves."

"Had I my will," answered Nehushta, "I would leave myself to God and still strive to protect her. Yet you are right. Many lives cannot be risked for the sake of one girl. But what of this man?"

"We will do our best for him," answered Ithiel, "for so she who sacrificed herself for his sake would have wished. Years ago he was our guest and befriended us. Stay here a while and I will bring men to carry him to the vault."

So Ithiel went away to return with several of the brethren, who lifted Marcus and bore him down the stairs and passages to that darksome chamber where Miriam had slept, while other brethren shut the trapdoor and loosened the roof of the passage, blocking it with stone so that none could pass that path ever again.

In the silent, sunless vault, Marcus lay sick with fever for many days, and had it not been for the skillful nursing of Nehushta and the doctors among the Essenes, he would certainly have died. But the surgeons, who were very practiced, mended the deep sword cut in his head, using little iron hooks to remove the fragments of bone pressed against his brain and dressing that wound and another in his knee with salves.

Meanwhile, they learned by their spies that both the Temple and Mount Zion had fallen. They heard also of Miriam's trial and of her exposure on the Gate Nicanor, but of what happened afterwards they could gather nothing. So they mourned her as dead.

At length, their food supply was exhausted, and as the watch of the Romans had relaxed, those of them who were left determined to attempt to escape from the hateful vaults that had sheltered them for all these months. A question arose as to what was to be done with Marcus, now but a shadow of a man, who still wandered somewhat in his mind, but who had passed the worst of his sickness and seemed likely to live. Some were for abandoning him, some for sending him back to the Romans, but Nehushta reasoned that it would be wise to keep him as a hostage. If they were attacked they might produce him and, in return for their care, perhaps buy their lives. In the end, they agreed upon this course, not so much for what they might gain by it, but because they knew that it would have pleased the lost maid whom they called their Queen, who had perished to save this man.

So it came about that upon a night fraught with rain and storm, when none were stirring, a number of men with faces white as lepers, might have been seen traveling down the cavern quarries, now tenanted only by the corpses of those who had perished there from starvation, climbing through the hole beneath the wall into the free air. With them went litters bearing their sick, and among the sick, Marcus and Ithiel, who had fallen very ill. None hindered their flight, for the Romans had deserted this part of the ruined city and were encamped about the towers overlooking Mount Zion, where some few Jews still held out.

Thus it happened that by morning they were well on the road to Jericho, which had always been a desert country, but was now completely devoid of life. On they went, living on roots and the little food that still remained. They came to Jericho itself, where they found nothing but a ruin, haunted by a few starving wretches. From there they traveled to their own village, only to discover that, for the most part, this also had been burnt. But scattered caverns in the hillside behind, which they had used as storehouses, still remained, and undiscovered in them was a secret stock of corn and wine that gave them food.

Here, they camped and set to work to sow the fields which no Romans or robbers had been able to destroy, and so lived arduously but unmolested, until at length the first harvest came and with it plenty.

In this dry and wholesome air, Marcus recovered rapidly, for he was by nature very strong. When first his wits returned to him, he recognized Nehushta and asked her what had taken place. She told him all she knew, and that she believed Miriam to be dead—tidings that caused him to fall into a deep melancholy. Meanwhile, the Essenes treated him with kindness but let him understand that he was their prisoner. Even had he wished it, and had they given him leave to go, he could not have left them at that time, for the slightest of his wounds proved to be the worst. The spear had penetrated to the joint and the wound in his knee would heal very slowly. For many weeks he was left so lame that he could not walk without a crutch. So here he sat by the banks of the Jordan, mourning the past and hopeless for the future.

Thus in solitude, tended by Nehushta, now grown very grim and old, and by the poor remnant of the Essenes, Marcus passed four or five miserable months. As he grew stronger, he would limp down to the village where his hosts were rebuilding some of their dwellings and sit in the garden of the house that had once been occupied by Miriam. Now it was overgrown with wild shrubs, but among the pomegranate bushes still stood the shed she had used as a workshop, and in it, lying here and there as they had fallen, some of her unfinished marbles, among them one of himself which she had begun and cast aside before she had executed the bust that Nero had named divine and set him to guard in the Temple at Rome. To Marcus it was a place of sadness, haunted by a thousand memories, yet he loved it because those memories were all of Miriam.

Titus, said rumor, having accomplished the utter destruction of Jerusalem, had moved his army to Caesarea or Berytus, where he passed the winter season in celebrating games in the amphitheatres. These he made splendid by the slaughter of vast numbers of Jewish prisoners, who were forced to fight against each other or, after the cruel Roman fashion, were exposed to the attacks of ravenous wild beasts. But although he thought of doing so, Marcus had no means of sending word to Titus and was still too lame to attempt escape. Even if he could find any, they might bring destruction upon the Essenes, who had treated him kindly and had saved his life.

Besides, among the Romans it was a disgrace for a soldier, especially for an officer of high rank, to be made prisoner, and he was loath to expose his own shame. As Gallus had told Miriam, no Roman should be taken alive. So Marcus attempted to do nothing, but waited, sick at heart, for whatever fate might send him. Indeed, had he been quite sure that Miriam was dead, he, who was disgraced and a captive, would have slain himself and followed her. But although none doubted her death—except Nehushta—his spirit told him that it must not be so. Thus it came about that Marcus lived on among the Essenes until his health and strength came back to him, as it was appointed that he should do until the time came for him to act. At length, the time came.

When Samuel, the Essene, left Tyre, bearing the letter and the ring of Miriam, he journeyed to Jerusalem to find the Holy City but a heap of ruins, haunted by hyenas and birds of prey that feasted on the innumerable dead. Still, faithful to his trust, he strove to discover the entrance to the caverns of which Miriam had told him, and to this end hovered day by day upon the north side of the city near the old Damascus Gate. He could not find the hole, for there were thousands of stones behind which jackals had burrowed, and there was no way to know which of these led to the caverns, nor were there any left to direct him. Still, Samuel searched and waited in the hope that one day an Essene might appear who would guide him to the hiding place of the brethren. But no Essene appeared, for they had already fled.

In the end, he was seized by a patrol of Roman soldiers who had observed him hovering about the place and questioned him very strictly about his business. He replied that it was to gather herbs for food, whereon their officer said that they would find him food and with it some useful work. So they took him and enlisted him into a gang of captives engaged in pulling down the walls that Jerusalem might never again become a fortified city. In this gang he was forced to labor for over four months, receiving only his daily bread in payment, and with it many blows and hard words, until at last he found an opportunity to make his escape.

Among his fellow slaves was a man whose brother belonged

to the Order of the Essenes, and from him he learned that they had gone back to Jordan. So Samuel started out again, with Miriam's ring still hidden safely about his person. Reaching the place without further accident, he declared himself to the Essenes, who received him with joy, which was not to be wondered at, since he was able to tell them that Miriam, whom they named their Queen and believed to be dead, was still alive. He asked them if they had a Roman prisoner called Marcus hidden away among them, and when they answered that this was so, said that he had a message from Miriam that he was charged to deliver to him. They led him to the garden where her workshop had been, telling him that there he would find the Roman.

Marcus was seated in the garden, basking in the sunshine, and with him Nehushta. They were talking of Miriam—indeed, they spoke of little else.

"Alas! Although I feel she is yet alive, I fear that she must be dead," Marcus was saying. "It is not possible that she could have lived through that night of the burning of the Temple."

"It does not seem possible," answered Nehushta, "yet I believe that she did live—as in your heart you believe also. I do not think it was destined that any Christian should perish in that war, for it has been prophesied otherwise."

"Prove it to me, woman, and I will be inclined to become a Christian, but of prophecies and such vague talk I am weary."

"You will become a Christian when your heart is touched and not before," answered Nehushta sharply. "That light is from above."

As she spoke, the bushes parted and they saw the Essene, Samuel, standing in front of them.

"Whom do you seek, man?" asked Nehushta, who did not know him.

"I seek the noble Roman, Marcus," he answered, "for whom I have a message. Is this he?"

"I am he," said Marcus, "and now, who sent you and what is your message?"

"The Queen of the Essenes, whose name is Miriam, sent me," replied the man.

Now both of them sprang to their feet.

"What token do you bear?" asked Marcus in a slow, restrained voice. "We thought the lady was dead."

"This," he answered, and drawing the ring from his robe he handed it to him, adding, "Do you acknowledge the token?"

"I acknowledge it. There is no such other ring. Have you anything else?"

"I had a letter, but it is lost. The Roman soldiers robbed me of my robe in which it was sewn, and I never saw it again. But the ring I saved by hiding it in my mouth while they searched me."

Marcus groaned, but Nehushta said quickly, "Did she give you no message? Tell us your story and be swift."

So he told them all.

"How long ago was this?" asked Nehushta.

"Nearly five months. For a hundred and twenty days I was kept as a slave at Jerusalem, laboring at the leveling of the walls."

"Five months," said Marcus. "Tell me, do you know whether Titus has sailed?"

"I heard that he had departed from Alexandria on his way to Rome."

"Miriam will walk in his Triumph, and afterwards be sold as a slave! Woman, there is no time to lose," said Marcus.

"None," answered Nehushta. "But there is time to thank this faithful messenger."

"Aye," said Marcus. "Man, what reward do you seek? Whatever it be, it shall be paid to you, for you have endured much. Yes, it shall be paid, though here and now I have no money."

"I seek no reward," replied the Essene. "I have but fulfilled my promise and done my duty."

"Yet Heaven shall reward you," said Nehushta. "And now let us go to Ithiel."

They went swiftly to the caves where the Essenes were residing during the rebuilding of their houses. In a little cabin open to the air lay Ithiel. The old man was on his deathbed, for age, hardship, and anxiety had done their work with him, and he was now unable to stand, but reclined upon a pallet awaiting his release. To him they told their story.

"God is merciful," he said, when he had heard it. "I feared that she might be dead, for in the presence of so much desolation, my faith grows weak."

"It may be so," answered Marcus, "but your merciful God will allow this maiden to be set up in the Forum at Rome and sold to the highest bidder. It would have been better that she perished on the gate Nicanor."

"Perhaps this same God," answered Ithiel with a faint smile, "will deliver her from that fate, as He has delivered her from many others. Now what do you seek, my lord Marcus?"

"I seek liberty, which you have refused me until now, Ithiel. I must travel to Rome as fast as ship and horse can carry me. I desire to be present at that auction of the captives. At least, I am rich and can purchase Miriam—unless I am too late."

"Purchase her to be your slave?"

"No, to be my wife."

"She will not marry you."

"Then, if she asks it, I will set her free. Man, would it not be better that she should fall into my hands than into those of the first passerby who chances to take a fancy to her face?"

"Yes, I think it is better," answered Ithiel, "though who am I that I should judge? Let the Court be summoned. This matter must be laid before them. If you purchase her and she desires it, do you promise to set her free?"

"I promise it."

Ithiel looked at him strangely and said, "Good, but in the hour of temptation, if it should come, see that you do not forget your word."

So the Court was called together, not the full hundred that used to sit in the great hall, but a bare score of the survivors of the Essenes, and Samuel repeated his tale to them. To them Marcus also made his petition for freedom, that he might journey to Rome with Nehushta, and if it were possible, deliver Miriam from her bonds. Some of the more timid of the Essenes spoke against the release of so valuable a hostage upon the chance of his being able to aid Miriam, but Ithiel cried from his litter, "What! Would you allow our own advantage to prevail against the hope that this maiden, who is loved by everyone of us, may be saved? Shame upon the thought. Let the Roman go upon his errand, since we cannot."

So they agreed to let him go and even provided money out of their scanty, secret store for his journey, trusting that he might find opportunity to repay it in the future.

That night Marcus and Nehushta bade farewell to Ithiel.

"I am dying," said the old Essene. "Before ever you can set foot in Rome the breath will be out of my body, and beneath the desert sand I shall lie at peace—who desire peace. Yet, say to Miriam, my niece, that my spirit will watch over her spirit, awaiting its coming in a land where there are no more wars and tribulations, and that, meanwhile, I who love her bid her to be of good cheer and to fear nothing."

So they parted from Ithiel and traveled upon horses to Joppa, Marcus disguising his name and rank lest some officer among the Romans should detain him. There by God's Providence they found a ship sailing for Alexandria, and in the port of Alexandria a merchant vessel bound for Rhegium, in which they took passage, and none asked them who they might be.

Upon the night of the burning of the Temple, Caleb escaped the slaughter and was driven with Simon bar Gioras across the bridge into the Upper City. Once he tried to return in the mad hope that during the confusion he might reach the gate Nicanor and, if she still lived, rescue Miriam. But already the Romans held the head of the bridge, and already the Jews were hacking at its timbers, so in that endeavor he failed and his heart was sure that Miriam had perished. So bitterly did Caleb mourn, who still loved her more than all the world, that for six days he sought death in every desperate adventure that came to hand, and they were many. But death fled him, and on the seventh day he had tidings.

A man hidden among the ruins of the cloisters managed to escape to the Upper City. From him Caleb learned that the woman said to have been found upon the roof of the gate Nicanor

had been brought before Titus, who gave her over to the charge of a Roman centurion, by whom she had been taken without the walls. He knew no more. The story was slight enough, but it sufficed for Caleb, who was certain that this woman must be Miriam. From that moment he determined to abandon the cause of the Jews, which was now hopeless, and to seek out Miriam wherever she might be. Yet, search as he would, another fifteen days went by before he could find his opportunity.

At length, Caleb was placed in charge of a watch upon the wall, and when the other members of his company fell asleep from faintness and fatigue, he let himself down in the dark with a rope, dropping from the end of it into a ditch piled with dead bodies. From one of them, that of a peasant who had died but recently, he took the clothes and a long winter cloak of sheepskins, exchanging them for his own garments. Then, keeping only his sword, which he hid beneath the cloak, he passed the Roman pickets in the gloom and fled into the country. When daylight came, Caleb cut off his beard and trimmed his long hair short. After this, he met a countryman with a load of vegetables and a license to sell in the Roman camp. Caleb bought his store from him for a piece of gold—for he was well furnished with money—and promised the simple man that if he said a word of it he would find him out and kill him. Then mimicking the speech and actions of a peasant, which he, who had been brought up among them down by the banks of Jordan, could well do, Caleb marched boldly to the nearest Roman camp and offered his wares for sale.

The camp was situated outside the gate of Gennat, not far from the tower Hippicus. Therefore, it is not strange that although in the course of his bargaining he made diligent inquiry as to the fate of the girl who had been taken to the gate Nicanor, Caleb could discover nothing of her, for she had been sent to the camp on the Mount of Olives on the other side of Jerusalem. Caleb's attempts were thwarted that day, but he continued his inquiries on the next, taking a fresh supply of vegetables to another cohort of soldiers camping in the Valley of Himnon. So he went on from day to day, searching the troops that surrounded the city and working from the Valley of Himnon northwards along the Valley of the Kedron, until on the tenth day, he came to a little hospital camp pitched on the slope of the hill opposite to the ruin that once had been the Golden Gate. Here, while selling his vegetables, he fell into talk with the cook who was sent to deal with him.

"Ah!" said the cook handling the basket in appraisal of the wares. "It is a pity, friend, that you did not bring these supplies a week ago when they were needed more. Fresh vegetables are hard to come by in this barren, sword-wasted land."

"Why were they more needed before?" asked Caleb casually.

"There was a prisoner here then. A girl whose sufferings had made her sick in mind and body. I never did learn how to tempt her appetite. She refused meat, and kept asking for fish and greens, of which, of course, we had none."

"What was her name? How did she come to be here?" asked Caleb.

"I don't think she even knew her own name. We called her Pearl Maiden because of a collar of pearls she wore and because she was white and beautiful as a pearl. Beautiful indeed, and so gentle and sweet, even in her sickness, that the roughest brute of a legionary with a broken head could not but love her. That old bear Gallus was so besotted, he watched her as though she were his own cub."

"Indeed? And where is this beautiful lady now? I should like to sell her something."

"Gone, gone, and left us all mourning."

"Not dead!" Caleb exclaimed in a voice of eager dismay, "Oh, tell me she did not die!"

The fat cook looked at him through narrow eyes.

"You take a strange interest in our Pearl Maiden, Cabbage-seller," he said. "And, now that I come to think of it, you are a strange looking man for a peasant."

With an effort Caleb recovered his composure.

"Once I was better off than I am now, friend," he answered. "In this country, fortune has turned rather quick of late."

"Yes, yes," the cook agreed, "and left many crushed flat behind it."

"The reason I am interested," Caleb went on, taking no heed, "is that I may have lost a fine market for my goods."

"Well, and so you have, friend. Some days ago the Pearl Maiden departed to Tyre in charge of the centurion, Gallus. Off to Rome. Perhaps you would wish to follow and sell her your onions there."

"Perhaps I would," answered Caleb. "When you Romans have gone, this seems likely to become a bad country for gardeners. Owls and jackals do not buy fruit, and I imagine you will leave no other living thing behind you."

"True," answered the cook. "Caesar knows how to handle a broom and he has made a very clean sweep," he said, waving his hand vaguely to the heaped up ruins of the Temple before them before returning his attention to Caleb's produce. "Well, then. How much for the whole basket?"

"Take them, friend," said Caleb, "and sell them to your mess for the best price that you can get. You need not mention that you paid nothing."

"Oh! No, I won't mention a word of it. Good day, Master Cabbage-grower, good day."

Then he stood still, watching as Caleb vanished among the great grove of olive trees. "What can stir a Jew so much," he reflected to himself, "as to make him give something for nothing. And to a Roman, at that! Perhaps he is Pearl Maiden's brother. No, that can't be. From his eyes—her lover more likely. Well, it is no affair of mine. The vegetables are good and fresh, even if *he* never grew them."

That evening as Caleb, still disguised as a peasant, traveled through the growing twilight across the hills that bordered the road to Tyre, he heard a mighty wailing rise from Jerusalem and knew that it was the death-cry of his people. Above the sections of the beleaguered city yet standing, wreaths of flame spiraled upward into the sky. Titus had forced the walls, and thousands of Jews were perishing beneath the swords of his soldiers or in the fires of their burning homes. Still, almost one hundred thousand were kept alive to be driven like cattle into the Court of Women. More than ten thousand of them died there of starvation, while some were set aside to grace the Triumph, some to be slaughtered in the amphitheatres in Rome, Caesarea, and Berytus. But the most were deported to Egypt to labor in the desert mines until they died.

Thus was the last desolation accomplished and the prophecy fulfilled. *And the Lord shall bring thee into Egypt again with ships, and there ye shall sell yourselves unto your enemies for bondmen and for bondwomen, and no man shall buy you.* Thus did Ephraim return to Egypt, from where he came forth to sojourn in the Promised Land until the cup of his sin was full. Now once more the land was a desert without inhabitants. All its pleasant places were laid waste, all its fenced cities destroyed, and over its ruins and the bones of its children flew Caesar's eagles. The war was ended; there was peace in Judea.

When Caleb reached Tyre, by the last light of the setting sun he saw a white-sailed galley beating her way out to sea. He entered the city and inquired who had gone in the galley and was told that Gallus, a Roman centurion, in charge of a number of sick and wounded men, many of the treasures of the Temple, and a beautiful girl, said to be the grand-daughter of Benoni of that town, sailed thereon.

Then Caleb groaned in bitterness of spirit, for he knew he was too late. Presently, however, he took thought. He was wise among those of his generation, for at the beginning of this long war he had sold all his land and houses for gold and jewels which, to a very great value, he had left hidden in Tyre in the house of a man he trusted, an old servant of his father's. To this store he had added from time to time the proceeds of plunder, of trading, and the ransom of a rich Roman equestrian who had been his captive, so that now his wealth was great. When he had arrived at the man's house, Caleb claimed and packed this treasure in bales of Syrian carpets to resemble merchandise.

Then the peasant who had traveled into Tyre upon business about a mule was seen no more. In place of him stood Demetrius, the Egyptian merchant, who traded mainly, always at night, of the merchandise of Tyre, and sailed with it by the first ship to Alexandria. Here this merchant bought more goods that might find a ready sale in the Roman market, enough to fill half the galley that lay in the harbor near the Pharos, bound for Syracuse and Rhegium.

At length, the galley launched, meaning to sail for Crete, but it was caught by a late autumn storm and driven to Paphos in Cyprus. Fear of the stormy seas overtook the captain and crew, and they determined to winter in the docks, despite all the merchant Demetrius did to urge them onward. So they beached her in the harbor and went up to the great temple, rejoicing to pay their vows and offer gifts to Venus, who had delivered them from the fury of the seas, that they might swell the number of her votaries.

But although he accompanied them, for otherwise they might have suspected that he was a Jew, Demetrius sought another goddess, cursing Venus in his heart and knowing that had it not been for her delights the sailors would have braved the weather.

But there was no help for it and no other ship by which he could sail, so there he remained for more than three months, spending his time in Curium, Amathos, and Salamis, trading among the rich natives of Cyprus, from whom he made a large profit, and adding wine and copper from Tamasus to his other merchandise, as much as there was room for on the ship.

After the great spring festival—the captain insisted that it would not be fortunate to leave until this had been celebrated—they set sail and came to the Island of Crete, and from there sailed to Cythera, and then to Syracuse in Sicily, and at last to Rhegium. There the merchant, Demetrius, loaded his goods onto a vessel sailing to the port of Centum Cellae, and when he reached that place, he hired transport to convey them to Rome, nearly forty miles away.

Chapter XXI
The Caesars and Prince Domitian

Gallus halted at the outskirts of Rome, for he had no wish for Miriam to be led through the streets in daylight, which would certainly raise questions concerning her. He sent a messenger into the city, bidding the man find his wife Julia if she were still living, for he had not seen or heard from her in several years. The messenger was to inform her, if he found her, that the centurion would be with her shortly, bringing with him a maiden who had been placed in his charge by Titus. Before nightfall, the messenger returned, and with him Julia herself, a woman past middle age, but although gray haired, still attractive and stately.

Miriam observed their meeting, which was a touching sight, for this childless couple had been married for almost thirty years, and during their long separation a rumor had reached Julia that her husband was not wounded, but dead. Her joy and thankfulness at his coming were even greater than they would otherwise have been.

One thing, however, Miriam noted, that whereas her friend and benefactor, Gallus, held up his hands and thanked the gods that he found his wife living and well, Julia on her part said, "Aye, I thank God," touching her breast with her fingers as she spoke the words.

Presently the matron seemed to notice her, and, looking at her with a inquisitive eye, asked, "How comes it, husband, that you are in charge of this captive Jewess, who is so fair?"

"By the order of Titus Caesar," he answered, "to whom she must be delivered on his arrival. She was condemned to perish on the gate Nicanor as a traitress to the Jews and as a Nazarene."

Julia's breath seemed to catch, and she now looked at the girl with more interest.

"Are you of that faith, daughter?" she asked in a changed voice, crossing her hands upon her breast as though unconsciously.

"I am, mother," answered Miriam, returning the sign.

"Well, husband," said Julia, "the maid's tale can wait. Whether she was a traitress to the Jews, or a follower of Christus, is not our affair. She is in your charge, and therefore welcome to me." And stepping to where Miriam stood with bowed head she kissed her on the forehead, saying aloud, "I greet you, sweet daughter," adding beneath her breath, "in the Name you know."

Thus Miriam had little doubt that she had been delivered into the hands of a Christian woman, and was thankful in her heart, for while the Caesars sat upon the Roman throne, the Christians of every rank and race were one great family.

That evening, as soon as darkness fell, they entered Rome by the Appian Gate. There they separated, Gallus leading his soldiers to convey the treasure to the safe keeping of the officer appointed to receive it, and afterwards to the camp prepared for them, while Julia, with Miriam and an escort of two men, departed to her own home, a small dwelling in a clean but narrow and crowded street that overhung the River Tiber between the Pons Aelius and the Porta Flamina. At the door of the house, Julia dismissed the soldiers, saying, "Go without fear, and witness that I am bond for the safety of this captive."

So the men went gladly enough, for they desired to rest after the toils of their long journey. The door of the house was opened by a servant and locked again behind them, and Julia led Miriam across a little court to the sitting room that lay beyond. Hanging lamps of bronze burned in the room, and by their light, Miriam saw that it was very clean and well, though not richly, furnished.

"This is my own house, daughter," she explained, "which my father left me, where I have dwelt during all these weary years that my husband has been absent in the wars of the East. It is a humble place, but you will find peace and safety in it, and, I trust, comfort. Poor child," she added in a gentle voice, "I am also a Christian, though my husband knows nothing of it. I welcome you here in the Name of the Lord."

"In the Name of our Lord, I thank you," answered Miriam, "for I am but a friendless slave."

"Such find friends," said Julia, "and if you will allow it, I think that I shall be one of them." Then at a sign from the elder woman they knelt down, and in silence each of them put up her prayer of thanksgiving, the wife because her husband had returned safely to her, the maiden because she had been led to a house ruled by a woman of her own faith.

After this they ate, a plain meal but well cooked and served. When it was done, Julia conducted Miriam to the little white-washed chamber that had been prepared for her. It was well lit from the court by a lattice set high in the wall, and like all the house, very clean and orderly, with a floor of white marble.

"Once another maid slept here," said Julia with a sigh, glancing at the white bed in the corner.

"Flavia?" said Miriam. "She was your only child, was she not? Nay, do not be astonished. I have heard so much of her that I feel as if I know her quite well."

"Did Gallus tell you?" asked Julia. "He rarely used to speak of her."

Miriam nodded. "He told me. He was very good to me, and we became friends. For all that he has done, may Heaven bless him. Although he seems rough, he has so kind a heart."

"May Heaven bless us all," answered Julia.

Then she kissed Miriam and left her to her rest.

When Miriam came out of her bedchamber on the following morning, she found Gallus clad in his armor, now freshly cleaned, though dinted by many blows, standing in the court and watching the water spurt from a leaden pipe to fall into a little basin.

"Greeting, daughter," he said, looking up. "I trust you have rested well beneath my roof, who have sojourned so long in tents."

"Very well," she answered, adding, "If I may ask, why do you wear your mail here in peaceful Rome?"

"I am summoned to have an audience with Caesar, within the hour."

"Is Titus come, then?" she asked hurriedly.

"Nay, not Titus Caesar, but Vespasian Caesar, his father, to whom I must make report of all that had passed in Judea when we left, of the spoils that I brought with me—and of yourself."

"Oh! Gallus," said Miriam, "will he take me away from your charge?"

"I know not. I hope not. But who can say? It is as his whim may move him. But if he listens to me, I swear that you shall stay here forever. Be sure of that."

Then he went, leaning on a spear shaft, for the wound in his leg had caused it to shrink so much that he could never hope to be sound again.

Three hours later he returned to find the two women waiting anxiously for him. Julia glanced at his face as he came through the door of the street wall into the courtyard where they were waiting.

"Have no fear," she said. "When Gallus looks so solemn he brings good tidings, and if they are bad he smiles and makes light of them." She advanced and took him by the hand, leading him past the porter's room into the atrium.

"What news, husband?" she asked when the door was shut behind them so that none might overhear their talk.

"Well," he answered, "first, my fighting days are over. The physicians have declared that my leg will never be well again, so I have been discharged from the army. Wife, why do you not weep for my loss?"

"Because I rejoice," answered Julia calmly. "Thirty years of war and bloodshed are enough for any man. You have done your work. You have been spared long, and it is for you to rest. I have saved while you were away, and there will be food enough to fill our mouths."

"Yes, yes, wife, and as it happens, more than you think. Vespasian was pleased with my report, and in his grace has granted me half-pay for all my life, to say nothing of a gratuity and share of the spoil, whatever that may bring. But I do grieve, for I can never hope to lift spear again."

"Grieve not, for I would have had it thus, Gallus. But what of the maid?" Julia asked.

"Well, I made my report about her, as I was commanded to do, and at first Domitian, Caesar's son, was curious to see her. He prompted Vespasian to order that she should be brought to the palace, almost Caesar gave that order, then a thought seemed to strike him and he was silent. I saw my chance and said that she had been very sick and still needed care and nursing, and that if it was his will, my wife could tend her until such time as Titus Caesar, whose spoil she was, might arrive. Again Domitian interrupted, but Vespasian answered, 'The Jewish maid is not your slave, Domitian, or my slave. She is the slave of your brother, Titus. Let her bide with this worthy officer until Titus comes, he being answerable in his person and his goods that she shall then be produced before him, she or proof of her death.' Then, waving his hand to show that the matter was done with, he went on to speak of other things, demanding details of the capture of the Temple and comparing my list of the vessels and other gear with that which was furnished by the treasurer, into whose charge I handed them yesternight. So, Maid Miriam, until Titus comes you are safe."

"Yes," answered Miriam with a sigh, "until Titus comes. But after that?"

"The gods alone know," he said impatiently. "Meanwhile, while my mind is on it, I must ask you to give your word that you will attempt no flight."

"I give my word, Gallus," she answered smiling, "for I would die rather than bring evil on you or yours. Besides, where would I fly?"

"I know not. But you Christians find many friends. Surely, the rats themselves have fewer hiding places. But I trust you, and for now you are free until Titus comes."

"Aye," repeated Miriam, "Until Titus comes."

So for nearly six months—until midsummer, indeed, Miriam dwelt in the house of Gallus and his wife, Julia. She found little happiness there, though she became to them as a daughter. How could she be happy in the sunshine of a peaceful present, when her world walked between two such banks of shadow? Behind her lay the shadow of the terrible past; in front, black and forbidding, rose the shadow of the future, which might be yet more terrible, a future in which she would be the slave of some man unknown.

Sometimes walking with Julia, mingling with the crowd in her humble dress, her shawl arranged to hide her face as much as possible, she saw the rich lords of Rome go by in chariots, on horseback, in litters. There were all kinds of them in all conditions. Fat, proud men with insolent eyes, hard-faced statesmen or lawyers, war worn and cruel looking officers, dissolute youths with foppish dress and perfumed hair. She would shudder at the sight of them, wondering whether she was appointed to any one of these. Or was it, perhaps, to that rich and greasy tradesman, or to the lowborn freedman with the stomach-turning leer? God alone knew, and in Him must be her trust.

Once, as Miriam was walking in the city, lavishly clad slaves armed with rods of office appeared, forcing their way through the crowded streets to an accompaniment of oaths and blows. Behind them came lictors bearing the *fasces,* the Roman symbol of power, on their shoulders. At the end of this parade thundered a splendid chariot drawn by four white horses and driven by a heavily perfumed charioteer with unnaturally curled hair. Beside the charioteer, standing upon a block so that he might be better seen, rode a young man, tall, ruddy, and clad in the Imperial purple. He looked downward as though in modesty, but all the while scanned the crowd out of the corners of his dim blue eyes shaded by bare lids denuded of its lashes. For a moment Miriam felt those eyes rest upon her, and knew that she was the subject of some jest that their owner addressed to the exquisite charioteer, causing him to laugh. A dreadful horror of the man gripped her, and she bowed her head, not out of respect, but that her face might be hidden from his roving eyes. When he had passed, bowing in answer to the shouts of the people, who seemed to cheer more from fear than with admiration, she asked Julia who he might be.

"Domitian," she answered simply. "The son of one Caesar and the brother of another, who hates both and would like to wear their crown. He is an evil man, and if he should chance to cross your path, beware of him, Miriam."

Miriam shuddered. "As well, mother, might you bid the mouse that is caught abroad to beware of the cat it meets at night."

"Some mice find holes that cats cannot enter," answered Julia with meaning as they turned their faces homeward.

During Miriam's sojourn, although Gallus made diligent inquiry among the soldiers arriving from Judea, Miriam could discover nothing of Marcus, so at last she came to think that he must be dead, and with him the beloved and faithful Nehushta. And if that were so, she earnestly hoped that she might soon join them. Yet amongst all her trouble, she had one great comfort. Under the mild rule of Vespasian, although many of their gathering places were known, the Christians lived in peace for a while.

Therefore, she was able to visit the catacombs on the Appian Way by night, where she and Julia found the company of many others of the congregation of Rome. There, in those dismal, endless tombs, she offered prayer and received the ministrations of the Church. The great apostles, Peter and Paul, had suffered martyrdom, but they had left many teachers behind them, and the chief of these soon grew to know and love the poor Jewish captive that had been doomed to slavery. So here also she found friends and consolation of spirit.

In time, Gallus came to learn that his wife was also of the Faith, and for a while this knowledge seemed to dishearten him. In the end, however, he shrugged his shoulders and said that she was certainly of an age to judge for herself and that he trusted no harm might come of it. Indeed, when the Christian hope was explained to him, he listened to them eagerly enough, who had lost his only child, and until now had never heard this strange story of resurrection and eternal life. But although he listened, and even from time to time was present when the brethren prayed, he would not be baptized, for he said that he was too sunk in years to throw incense on a new altar.

At length, Titus came. The Senate, which long before his arrival had decreed for him a Triumph, met him outside the walls, and there after the ancient way, communicated to him their decision. It was determined that Vespasian, his father, should share in this Triumph because of the great deeds he had done in Egypt, so that it was whispered everywhere that this would be the most splendid procession that Rome had ever seen. After this, Titus moved on to his palace and there lived privately for several weeks, resting while the preparations for the great event went forward.

One morning early, Gallus was summoned to the palace, and he returned rubbing his hands and trying to look pleased. With him, as Julia had said, it was a sure sign of evil tidings.

"What is it, husband?" she asked.

"Oh! Nothing, really," he answered. "Our Pearl Maiden here is to accompany me after the midday meal into the august presences of Vespasian and Titus. The Caesars wish to see her, so that they may decide where she is to walk in the procession. If she is deemed beautiful enough, they will grant to her a place of honor by herself. Do you hear that, wife—by herself, not far in front of the very chariot of Titus? As for the dress that she will wear," he went on nervously, as neither of his listeners seemed delighted with his news, "it is to be splendid, quite splendid, all of the purest white silk with little discs of silver sewn about it, and a representation of the Gate Nicanor worked in gold thread upon the breast of the robe."

At these tidings, Miriam broke down and began to weep.

"Dry your tears, girl," he said roughly, but the thickness of his voice suggested that water and his own eyes were not far apart. "What must be, must be, and now is the time for that God you worship to show you some mark of favor. Surely, He should do so, seeing how long and how often you pray to Him in burrows that a jackal would turn from."

"I think He will," answered Miriam, ceasing her sobs with a bold uplifting of her soul towards the light of perfect faith.

"I am sure He will," added Julia, gently stroking Miriam's dark, curling hair.

"Then," broke in Gallus, driving the point to its logical conclusion, "what have you to fear? A long, hot walk through the shouting populace, who will do no harm to one so lovely, and after that, whatever good fate your God may choose for you.

Come, let us eat, so you may look your best when you appear before the Caesars."

"I would rather look my worst," said Miriam, thinking of Domitian and his monstrous eyes. Still, to please Gallus, she tried to eat, and afterwards, accompanied by him and by Julia, was carried in a closed litter to the palace.

Too soon she was there, arriving a little before them, and was helped from the litter by slaves wearing the Imperial livery. They ushered her past the majestic colonnade of the palace, and she suddenly found herself alone in a great marble court filled with officers and nobles awaiting audience.

"That is the Pearl Maiden," exclaimed one of them, and they all crowded around her, appraising her aloud in their idle curiosity.

"Too short," said one. "Too thin," said another. "Too small in the foot for her ankle," said a third. "Fools," broke in a fourth, a young man with a fine figure and dark rings round his eyes, "what is the use of trying to cheapen this piece of goods thus in the eyes of the experienced? I say that this Pearl Maiden is as perfect as those pearls about her neck. A little small, perhaps, but quite perfect, and you will admit that I ought to know."

"Lucius says that she is perfect," remarked one of them in a tone of acquiescence, as though that verdict settled the matter.

"Yes," went on the critical Lucius, "now, to take one thing only, a point so often overlooked. Observe how fresh and firm her flesh is. When I press it thus,"—he matched the action to the word—"as I thought, my finger scarcely leaves a mark."

"But my arm does," said a gruff voice beside him, and in the next moment this scented judge of human beauty received the point of the elbow of Gallus between the eyes just where the nose is set into the forehead. The blow was directed with such force and skill that next instant the critic was sprawled on his back upon the pavement, blood gushing from his nostrils.

Most of them laughed at the beauteous arbiter's misfortune, but some murmured, while Gallus warned them all, "Back down, friends! I am charged to deliver this lady to the Caesars and to certify that while she was in my care no man has so much as laid a finger on her. As for that whimpering puppy on his back, if he wishes it, he knows where to find Gallus. My sword will mark him deeper than my elbow, if he wants bloodletting—that I swear."

Now with jests and excuses, they fell back as one. There were few of them who did not know that, lame as he might now be, old Gallus was still the fiercest and most dreaded swordsman of his legion. Indeed he was commonly reported to have slain eighteen men in single combat, and when young even to have faced the most celebrated gladiator of the day for sport, and to have given him life as he lay at his mercy.

So they passed on through long halls guarded by soldiers, until at length, they came to a wide passage leading to a room hidden by splendid curtains. There the officer on duty asked them their business. Gallus told him and he vanished through the curtains. He returned presently, beckoning them to advance. They followed him down a corridor lined with busts of departed emperors and empresses, to find themselves in a round marble chamber, very cool and lighted by an opening in the ceiling above. Three men sat in the chamber. Vespasian, whom they knew by his strong, quiet face and grizzled hair; Titus, his son, "the darling of mankind," thin, active, and aesthetic-looking, with eyes that were not unkindly, a sarcastic smile playing about the corners of his mouth; and Domitian, his brother, a man taller than either of them by half a head, and more extravagantly attired. In front of the august three was a master of ceremonies clad in a dark robe, showing them drawings of various sections of the triumphal procession, and taking their orders as to such alterations as they wished.

Also there were present, a treasurer, some officers and two or three of the intimate friends of Titus.

Vespasian looked up.

"Greeting, worthy Gallus," he said in the friendly, open voice of one who has spent his life in camps, "and to your wife, Julia, greeting also. So this is the Pearl Maiden of whom we have heard so much talk. Well, I do not pretend to be a judge of beauty, but I say that this Jewish captive does not belie her name. Titus, do you recognize her?"

"In truth, no, father. When last I saw her, she was a sooty, withered little thing, whom Gallus carried in his great arms as a child might carry a large doll rescued from the fire. Yes, I agree she is beautiful and worthy of a very good place in the procession. And she should fetch a large price afterwards, for that necklace of pearls goes with her—make a note of this, Scribe—and the reversion to considerable property in Tyre and elsewhere. This, by special favor, she will be allowed to inherit from her grandfather, the old rabbi, Benoni, one of the Sanhedrin, who perished in the burning of the Temple."

"How can a slave inherit property, son?" asked Vespasian, raising his eyebrows.

"I don't know," answered Titus with a laugh. "Perhaps Domitian can tell you. He says that he has studied law. But so I have decreed."

"A slave," interrupted Domitian shrewdly, "has no rights and can hold no property, but the Caesar of the East," he sneered, "can declare that certain lands and goods will pass to the highest bidder with the person of the slave, and this, Vespasian Caesar, my father, is what I understand Titus Caesar, my brother, has thought it good to do."

"Yes," said Titus in a quiet voice, though his face flushed. "Indeed, I have thought it good to do so. In such a matter is not my will enough?"

"Conqueror of the East," replied Domitian, "Thrower-down of the mountain stronghold Jerusalem, to which the topless towers of Ilium were as nothing. Oh, Exterminator of misguided fanatics, in what matter is not your will enough? But I ask a boon, O Caesar. Be thou as generous as you are great," and with a mocking gesture he bowed the knee to Titus.

"What boon do you seek of me, brother? You know that all I have is—or," he added slowly, "will . . . be yours?"

"One that is already granted by your precious words, Titus. Of all you have, which is much, I seek only this Pearl Maiden, who has taken my fancy. The girl only, not her property in Tyre, wherever that may be, which you can keep for yourself."

Vespasian looked up, but before he could speak, Titus answered quickly:

"I said, Domitian, 'all I have.' This maid I have not, therefore the words do not apply. I have decreed that the proceeds of the sale of these captives are to be divided equally between the wounded soldiers and the poor of Rome. Therefore she is their property, not mine. I will not rob them."

"Virtuous man! No wonder that the legions love him who cannot withdraw one lot from a sale of thousands, even to please his only brother," soliloquized Domitian.

"If you wish for the maid," went on Titus, taking no heed of the insult, "the markets are open—buy her. It is my last word."

Suddenly Domitian grew angry, the false modesty left his face, and he launched his tall form from his seat, staring round with his blear, evil-looking eyes.

"I appeal!" he cried. "I appeal from Caesar the Small to Caesar the Great, from the murderer of a brave barbarian tribe to the conqueror of the world. O Caesar, Titus here has in your presence declared that all he has is mine. Yet when I ask him for the gift of one captive girl he refuses me. Command, I pray you, that he should keep his word."

Now the officers and the secretaries looked up, for unexpectedly, this small matter had become very important. The quarrel between Titus and his jealous brother had long smoldered, and now over the petty question of a captive, it was breaking into flame.

The face of Titus grew hard and stern as that of some statue of the offended Jove.

"Command, I pray you, father," he said, "that my brother should cease to offer insult to me. Command also that he should cease to question my will and my authority in matters great or small that are within my rule. Since you are appealed to as Caesar, as Caesar judge, not of this thing only but of all, for there is much between him and me that needs to be made plain."

Vespasian looked round him uneasily, but seeing no escape and that beneath the quarrel lay issues that were deep and wide, he spoke out in his brave, simple fashion.

"Sons," he said, "as there are but two of you, who together, or one after the other, must inherit the world, it is an evil omen that you should quarrel thus, for on the chances of your enmity may hang your own fates and the fates of peoples. Be reconciled, I pray you. Is there not enough for both? As for the matter at hand—this is my judgment. With all the spoils of Judea, this fair maid is the property of Titus. Titus, whose boast it is that he does not go back upon his word, has decreed that she shall be sold and her price divided between the wounded and the poor. Therefore she is no longer his to give away, even to his brother. With Titus I say—if you desire the girl, Domitian, bid your agent buy her in the market."

"Aye, I will buy her," snarled Domitian, "but this I swear, that soon or late, Titus shall pay the price and one that he will be loath to give." Then followed by his secretary and an officer, he turned and left the audience hall.

"What does he mean by that?" asked Vespasian, looking after him with wary eyes.

"He means—" and Titus checked himself. "Well, time and my destiny will show the world what he means. So be it. As for you, Pearl Maiden, you have cost Caesar dear, though you know it not. You are fairer than I thought, and shall have the best of places in the pageant. Yet, for your sake, I pray that one may be found who may outbid Domitian when you go to the market-place," and he waved his hand to show that the audience was at an end.

CHAPTER XXII
THE TRIUMPH

Another week went by, and the eve of the Triumph was at hand. On the afternoon before the great day, seamstresses had come to the house of Gallus, bringing with them the robe that Miriam was to wear. As had been promised, it was splendid, of white silk covered with silver discs and having Gate Nicanor woven in gold on the breast, but it was cut so low that it shamed Miriam to put it on.

"It is nothing," said Julia. "The designer has fashioned it so that the multitude may see those pearls from which you take your name." But in her heart she thought, Oh monstrous age, and monstrous men, whose eyes can delight in the disgrace of a poor friendless maiden. Surely the cup of iniquity of my people grows full, and they shall drink it to the dregs!

That same afternoon also came an assistant officer, with orders to Gallus as to when and where he was to deliver his charge upon the morrow. With him he brought a packet, which, when opened, proved to contain a splendid golden girdle, fashioned to the likeness of a fetter. The clasp was an amethyst, and round it were cut these words: *The gift of Domitian to her who shall be his tomorrow.*

When Miriam saw it, she threw the thing across the room as though it were a snake.

"I will not wear it," she said. "I say that I will not wear it. At least today I am my own." Julia groaned and Gallus cursed under his breath.

Knowing her sore plight, that evening there came to visit her one of the elders of the Christian Church in Rome, a bishop named Cyril, who had been the friend and disciple of the Apostle Peter. The poor girl poured out to him all the agony of her heart.

"Oh! My father, my father in Christ," she said, "I swear to you that were I not of our holy faith, rather than endure this shame, I would slay myself tonight! Other dangers have I passed, but they have been of the body alone, whereas this . . . Pity me and tell me, what must I do?"

"Daughter," answered the grave and gentle man, "you must trust in God. Did He not save you in the house at Tyre? Did He not save you in the streets of Jerusalem? Did He not save you on the gate Nicanor?"

"He did," answered Miriam.

"Aye, daughter, and so shall He save you in the slave market of Rome. I will continue to pray that no shame shall come near to you, as will the whole of our congregation. Tread your path, drink your cup, and fear nothing, for the Lord shall send His angel to protect you until such time as it pleases Him to take you to Himself."

Miriam looked at him, and as she looked, peace fell upon her soul and shone in her soft eyes.

"I hear the word of the Lord spoken through the mouth of His messenger," she said, "and from now I will strive to fear nothing. Not even Domitian."

"Least of all Domitian, daughter, that son of Satan, whom Satan shall pay in his own coin."

Then going to the door he summoned Julia, and while Gallus watched without, the two of them prayed long and earnestly with Miriam. When their prayer was finished the bishop rose, blessed her, and bade her farewell.

"I leave you, daughter," he said, "but though you see Him not, another takes my place. Do you believe?"

"I have said that I believe," Miriam answered confidently.

Indeed, in the days when men still lived who had seen the Christ and His voice still echoed through the world, to the strong faith of His followers, it was not hard to trust that His angels did descend to earth to protect and save at their Master's bidding.

So Cyril, the bishop, went, and that night from many a catacomb prayers rose up to Heaven for Miriam in her peril. That night also she slept peacefully.

Two hours before dawn, Julia woke Miriam and arrayed her

in the glittering, repulsive garments. When all was ready, she bid her farewell with tears.

"Child, child," she said, "you have become to me as my own daughter was, and now I know not how and when we shall meet again."

"Perhaps sooner than you think," Miriam answered. "But if not . . . if, indeed, I speak to you for the last time, why, then, my blessings on you who have played a mother's part to a helpless maid that was no kin of yours. Yes, and on you Gallus also, who have kept me safe through so many dangers."

"And who hopes, dear one, to keep you safe through many more. Since I may not swear by the gods before you, I swear it by the Eagles that Domitian will do well to be careful how he deals by you. To him I owe no allegiance, and as has been already proved, the sword of vengeance can reach the heart of princes."

"Aye, Gallus," said Miriam gently, "but let it not be your sword. Nor, I trust, shall you need to think of vengeance."

Then the litter was brought into the courtyard with the guards that were sent to accompany it, and they started for the gathering place beyond the Triumphal Way. Dark though it still was, all of Rome was astir. On every side shone torches, from every house and street rose the murmur of voices, for the mighty city made herself ready to celebrate the greatest festival her populace had seen. Even now, at times, the crowd was so dense that the soldiers had to force a way through the people, who swept the streets in waves to find the choicest places along the line of the Triumph. Others in the crowd moved to take up their station on stands of timber, and in houses they had rented, whose roofs, balconies, and windows overlooked the path of the pageant.

They crossed the River Tiber. Miriam could not see the river from her litter, but she knew by the roar of the water beneath, and because the crush upon the narrow bridge was so great. From there she was borne along through comparatively open country to the gateway of some large building, where she was ordered to dismount the litter. One of the officers waiting there took charge of her, giving to Gallus a written receipt for her person. Then, either because he would not trust himself to bid her farewell, or because he did not think it wise to do so in the presence of the officers, Gallus turned and left her without a word.

"Come on, girl," grunted the officer, but a secretary, looking up from his tablets, called to him.

"Gently there with that lot, or you will hear about it. That is the Pearl Maiden, the captive who started the quarrel between the Caesars and Domitian. Gently, I tell you, gently, for many free princesses are worth less today."

Hearing this, the officer bowed to Miriam, almost with reverence, and begged her to follow him to a place that had been set apart for her. She obeyed, passing through a great number of people, of whom all she could see in the gloom of the breaking dawn was that, like herself, they were captives. They entered a little chamber where she was left alone to watch the light grow through the lattice, listening to the hum of voices that rose steadily outside, mingled now and then with sobs and wails of grief. Presently the door opened and a servant entered with bread on a platter and milk in an earthenware vessel. She took them thankfully, knowing that she would need food to support her during the long day, but she had hardly taken a bite before a slave appeared, clad in the Imperial livery and bearing a tray of luxurious meats served in silver vessels.

"Pearl Maiden," he said, "my master, Domitian, sends you greeting and this present. The vessels are your own, and will be kept for you, but he bids me add that tonight you shall sup off dishes of gold."

Miriam made no answer, though one rose sharply to her lips. But after the man had departed, she lifted her dress and kicked the silver tray, sending the vases clattering to the floor and spilling the savory meats. She went on eating the bread and drinking the milk until her hunger was satisfied.

Scarcely had she finished her meal, when an officer entered the cell and led her out into a great square, where she was assembled amongst many other prisoners. By now, the sun was up and she saw before her a splendid building, and gathered below the building all the Senate of Rome in their robes, and many equestrians on horses, and nobles, and princes from every country with their retinues—a very marvelous and gallant sight.

Behind them, in the cloisters before the building were set two
ivory chairs, while to the right and left of these chairs, as far as
the eye could reach, were drawn up thousand upon thousands
of soldiers. Presently from the cloisters, clad in garments of silk
and wearing crowns of laurel, appeared the Caesars, Vespasian
and Titus, attended by Domitian and their staff. As they came,
the soldiers set up a mighty triumphal shout that sounded like
the roar of the sea, which endured while the Caesars sat themselves upon their thrones. Up and up went the sound of the
continual shouting, until at length Vespasian rose and lifted his
hand.

Then silence fell and, covering his head with his cloak, he
seemed to make some prayer, after which Titus also covered his
head with his cloak and offered a prayer. This done, Vespasian
addressed the soldiers, thanking them for their bravery and
promising them rewards, at which they shouted again until
they were marched off to the feast that had been made ready.
Now the Caesars vanished and the officers began to order the
great procession, of which Miriam could see neither the beginning nor the end. All she knew was that before her in lines,
eight men wide, were marshaled two thousand or more Jewish
prisoners bound together with ropes, among whom, immediately in front of her, were a few women. Next she came, walking
by herself, and behind her, also walking by himself, a dark, sullen man, clad in a white robe and a purple cloak, with a gilded
chain about his neck.

She looked at him, wondering where she had seen his face
before, for it seemed so familiar to her. Then there rose before
her mind a vision of the Court of the Sanhedrin sitting in the
cloisters of the Temple, and of herself standing there before
them. She remembered that this man was seated next to that
Simeon who had been so bitter against her and pronounced
upon her the cruel sentence of death. Someone in the crowd
had addressed him as Simon, the son of Gioras, none other than
the savage general whom the Jews had admitted into the city to
make war upon the Zealot, John of Gischala. From that day to
this, she had heard nothing of him until now they met again,

the judge and the victim, caught in a common net. Presently, in the confusion they were brought together and he knew her.

"Are you Miriam, granddaughter of Benoni?" he asked.

"I am Miriam," she answered, "whom you, Simon, and your fellows doomed to a cruel death, but I have been preserved—"

"—to walk in a Roman Triumph. Better that you had died, maiden, at the hands of your own people."

"Better that you had died, Simon, at your own hands, or at those of the Romans."

"That I am about to do," he replied bitterly. "Fear not, woman, you will be avenged."

"I ask no vengeance," she answered. "As cruel as you were, I grieve that you should come to this."

"I grieve also, maiden. Your grandsire, old Benoni, chose the better end."

Then the soldiers separated them and they spoke no more.

An hour passed, and the procession began its march along the Triumphal Way. Miriam could see little of it. All she knew was that in front there were ranks of fettered prisoners, while men behind them carried upon trays and tables the golden vessels of the Temple, the seven branched Menorah and the ancient sacred book of the Jewish law. They were followed by other men, who bore aloft images of victory in ivory and gold. Then came the Caesars, each of them attended by lictors having their fasces wreathed with laurel. They were to join the Triumph when it had reached the *Porta Triumphalis*. First went Vespasian Caesar, the father. He rode in a splendid golden chariot, to which were harnessed four white horses led by Libyan soldiers. Behind him stood a slave clad in a dull robe, holding a crown above the head of the Imperator, and now and again whispering in his ear the words of warning, *Respice post te, hominem memento te.* "Look back at me and remember that you are but a man."

After Vespasian Caesar, the father, came Titus Caesar, the son, but his chariot was of silver, and graved upon its front was a picture of the Holy House of the Jews melting in the flames. Like his father he was attired in the *toga picta* and *tunica palmata*, the gold-embroidered over-robe and the tunic laced with silver leaves, while in his right hand he held a laurel bough, and in his left a scepter. He also was attended by a slave who whispered in his ear the same message of mortality and fleeting human glory.

Alongside the chariot of Titus, and as little behind as custom would allow, rode Domitian, gloriously arrayed and mounted on a splendid steed. Then came the tribunes and the eques-trians on horseback, and after them five thousand legionaries, every one of them bearing a spear wreathed in laurel.

Now the great procession was across the Tiber, and following its appointed path down broad streets and past palaces and tem-ples, drew slowly towards its destination, the shrine of Jupiter Capitolinus, which stood at the head of the Via Sacra beyond the Forum. The side paths, the windows of houses, the great scaffoldings of timber, and the steps of temples were all crowded with spectators. Miriam had never imagined that so many peo-ple could inhabit a single city. They passed them by thousands and by tens of thousands, and still, far as the eye could reach, stretched the white sea of faces. Ahead that sea would be quiet, then, as the procession pierced it, it began to murmur. Presently the murmur grew to a shout, the shout to a roar, and when the Caesars appeared in their glittering chariots, the roar to a tri-umphant peal that shook the street like thunder. And so it was for miles and miles, until Miriam's eyes were dim with the glare and glitter, and her head swam at the ceaseless sound of shout-ing.

Often the procession would halt for a while, either because of a check to one of the pageants in front, or so that some of its members might refresh themselves with drink. Then the crowd, ceasing from its cheers, would make jokes, and appraise whatever person or thing they chanced to be near. Greatly did they evaluate Miriam in this fashion, and she was made to hear every word of it. Most of them, she found, knew her by her name of Pearl Maiden, and pointed out to each other the neck-lace about her throat. Some had heard something of her story and strained to catch a glimpse of the Gate Nicanor blazoned in gold upon her breast. But most concerned themselves only with her delicate beauty, passing from mouth to mouth the gossip concerning Domitian, his quarrel with the Caesars, and the intention he had announced of buying this captive at the public sale. It was always the same talk, sometimes more cruel and open than others—that was the only difference.

Once they halted thus in the street of palaces through which they passed nearby the Baths of Agrippa. Here the endless comments began again, but Miriam tried to shut her ears to it and looked around her at her surroundings where she had stopped. To her left was a noble house built of white marble, but she noticed that its shutters were closed and it was undecorated by garlands, and idly she wondered why. Others wondered too, for when they had wearied of discussing her features, she heard one plebeian ask another whose house that was and why it had been shut up upon this festal day. The fellow answered that he could not remember the owner's name, but he was a rich noble who had fallen in the Jewish wars, and that the palace was closed because it was not yet certain who was his heir.

At that moment, her attention was distracted by a sound of groans and laughter coming from behind. She looked round to see that the wretched Jewish general, Simon, had sunk fainting to the ground, overcome by heat or the terrors of his mind, or by the sufferings which he was forced to endure at the hands of his cruel guards, who flogged him for the pleasure of the people as he walked. Now they were beating him again to consciousness with their rods. Thus the laughter of the audience and the groans of the victim. Sick at heart, Miriam turned away from this horrid sight, to hear a tall man, whose back was turned to her, but who was clad in the rich robes of an Eastern merchant, asking in thickly accented Latin whether it was true that the captive Pearl Maiden was to be sold that evening in the auction mart of the Forum. The marshal answered yes, such were the orders regarding her and the other women, since there was no convenient place to house them, and it was thought best to be rid of them and let their masters take them home at once.

"Does she please you, sir? Are you going to bid?" he added. "If so, you will find yourself in high company."

"Perhaps, perhaps," answered the man with a shrug of his shoulders.

Then he vanished into the crowd.

For the first time that day, Miriam's spirit failed her. The weariness of her body, the vulgar talk, the fouler cruelty, the cold discussion of the sale of human beings to the first comer as though they were sheep or swine, the fear of her fate that night, pressed upon and overcame her mind, so that she felt inclined, like Simon bar Gioras, to fall to the pavement and lie there until the cruel rods beat her again to her feet. Hope sank low and faith grew dim, while in her heart she wondered vaguely why poor men and women were made to suffer thus for the pleasure of other men and women; she wondered also what escape there could be for her.

While she mused thus, like a ray of light through the clouds, a sense of consolation, sweet as it was sudden, seemed to pierce the darkness of her bitter thoughts. She knew not from where it came, nor what it might portend, but it was there, and the source of it seemed near. She scanned the faces of the crowd, finding pity in a few, curiosity in more, but in most, there was only gross admiration if they were men or scorn of her misfortune and jealousy of her loveliness if they were women. Not from among these did that consolation come. She looked up to the sky, half expecting to see there that angel of the Lord into whose keeping the bishop Cyril had delivered her. But the skies were empty and brazen as the faces of the Roman crowd. Not a cloud could be seen in them, much less an angel.

As her eyes sank earthwards her glance fell upon one of the windows of the marble house to her left. She had thought that some few minutes before the shutters of that window had been closed, now they were open, revealing two heavy curtains of blue embroidered silk. Miriam thought this strange, and kept her eyes fixed upon the curtains. Presently, she saw fingers between them—long, dark fingers. Then very slowly the curtains were parted, and in the opening appeared a face, the face of an old woman, dark and noble and crowned with snow white hair. Even at that distance Miriam knew it in an instant.

Oh, Heaven! It was the face of Nehushta, whom she thought dead or lost forever. For a moment Miriam stood paralyzed, wondering whether this was not some vision born of the turmoil and excitement of that dreadful day. But surely it was no vision. Surely it was Nehushta herself who looked at her with loving eyes. For behold! She made the sign of the cross in the air before her, the symbol of Christian hope and greeting, then laid her finger upon her lips in token of secrecy and silence. The curtain closed and she was gone, whom not five seconds before had so mysteriously appeared.

Miriam's knees gave way beneath her, and while the marshals shouted to the procession to move forward, she felt herself sinking to the ground. Indeed, she would have fallen had not some woman in the crowd stepped forward and pressed a goblet of wine to her lips, saying, "Drink that, Pearl Maiden. It will make your pale cheeks even prettier than they are."

The words were coarse, but Miriam, looking at the woman, knew her as one of the Christian community with whom she had worshipped in the catacombs. So she took the cup, fearing nothing, and drank it. New strength came to her, and she went forward with the others on that toilsome, endless march.

At length, however, it did end, an hour or so before sunset. They had passed miles of streets. They had trodden the Via Sacra bordered by innumerable temples and adorned with statues set on columns, and now they marched up the steep slope that was crowned by the glorious temple of Jupiter Capitolinus. As they began to climb it, guards broke into their lines, and seizing the chain that hung about the neck of Simon, dragged him away.

"Where are they taking you?" asked Miriam as he passed her.

"To what I desire—death," he answered, and was gone.

Now the Caesars, dismounting from their chariots, took up their stations by altars at the head of the steps, while beneath them, rank upon rank, gathered all those who had shared their Triumph, each company in its allotted place. Then followed a long pause, and upon the multitude went a murmur of question at the delay. Presently men were seen running from the Forum up a path that had been left open, one of them carrying in his hand some object wrapped in a napkin. Arriving in face of the Caesars, he threw aside the cloth and held up before them and in sight of all the people the grizzly head of Simon, the son of Gioras. By this public execution of the brave captain of their foes, the Triumph was consummated, and at the sight of its crimson proof, trumpets blew, banners waved, and from half a million throats went up a shout of victory that seemed to rend the very skies, for the multitude was drunk with the glory of its brutal vengeance.

Then silence was called, and there before the Temple of Jove the beasts were slain, and the Caesars offered sacrifice to the gods to which they credited the victory.

Thus ended the Triumph of Vespasian and Titus, and with it, the record of the struggle of the Jews against the iron beak and claws of the Roman Eagle.

Chapter XXIII
The Slave Ring

Had Miriam looked out of her litter as she passed the Temple of Isis, escorted by Gallus and the guards before dawn broke upon that great day of the Triumph, and had there been light enough to see, she might have seen two figures galloping into Rome as fast as their weary horses would carry them. Both were garbed as men, but one of them, wrapped in an Eastern garment that hid the face, was in fact a woman.

"Fortune favors us, Nehushta," said the man in a strained voice. "At least we are in time for the Triumph. We might easily have been too late. Look, they are already gathering by Octavian's Walks." He pointed to the companies of soldiers hurrying past them to the meeting place.

"Yes, my lord Marcus, we are in time. There go the eagles and here comes their prey," and in her turn, Nehushta pointed to a guarded litter—had they but known it, the very one that carried the beloved woman they sought. "But where now? Would you also march in the train of Titus?"

"No, woman, it is too late. And I know not what would be my welcome."

"Your welcome? Why, you were his friend, and Titus is faithful to his friends."

"Aye, but perhaps not to those who have been taken prisoner by the enemy. Towards the commencement of the siege, that happened to a man I knew. He was captured with a companion. His companion the Jews slew, but as he was about to be beheaded upon the wall, this man slipped from the hands of the executioner, and leaping from it escaped with little hurt. Titus gave him his life, but dismissed him from his legion. Why should I fare better?"

"That you were taken was no fault of yours. You were struck senseless and overwhelmed."

"Perhaps, but would that avail me? The rule is that no Roman soldier should yield to an enemy. If he is captured while insensible, then on finding his wits he must slay himself, as I should have striven to do, if I had awakened to find myself in the hands of the Jews. But things happened otherwise. Still, I tell you, Nehushta, that had it not been for Miriam, I should not have turned my face to Rome, at any rate, until I had received pardon and permission from Titus."

"Then what is your plan, lord Marcus?"

"We shall go to my own house near the Baths of Agrippa. The Triumph must pass there, and if Miriam is among the captives we shall see her. If not, then either she is dead or already sold, or perchance given as a present to some friend of Caesar's."

They ceased talking then, for the people were so many that they could hardly force their way through the press, riding one after the other. Thus, Nehushta and Marcus crossed the Tiber and passed through many streets, most of them decorated, for the coming pageant, until at length Marcus drew rein in front of a marble mansion on the Via Agrippa.

"A strange homecoming," he muttered. "Follow me," and he rode round the house to a side entrance.

He dismounted and knocked at the small door for some time without avail. At length, it was opened a little way, and a thin, querulous voice, speaking through the crack, said, "Begone, whoever you are. No one lives here. This is the house of Marcus, who is dead in the Jewish war. Who are you that disturb me?"

"The heir of Marcus."

"Marcus has no heir, unless it be Caesar, who doubtless will take his property."

"Open, Stephanus," said Marcus, in a tone of command, at the same time pushing the door wide and entering. "Fool," he added, "what kind of a steward are you that you do not know your own master's voice?"

Now the doorkeeper, a withered little man in a scribe's brown robe, peered at this visitor with his sharp eyes, then threw his hands up and staggered back. "By the spear of Mars! It is Marcus himself, Marcus returned from the dead! Welcome, my lord, welcome."

Marcus led his horse through the deep archway, and when Nehushta had followed him into the courtyard beyond, he returned to close and lock the door.

"Why did you think me dead, friend?" he asked.

"Oh! My lord," answered the steward, "all who returned from the war declared that you had vanished during the siege of the Jews, and that you must either be dead or taken prisoner. I knew well that you would never disgrace your ancient house, or your own noble name, or the Eagles you serve, by falling alive into the hands of the enemy."

Marcus laughed bitterly, then turning to Nehushta, said, "You hear that, woman? If such is the judgment of my steward and freedman, what will be that of Caesar and my peers?" Then he added, "Stephanus, what you thought impossible—what I myself should have thought impossible—has happened. I was taken prisoner by the Jews, though through no fault of mine."

"Oh! If so," said the old steward, "hide it, my lord, hide it. Why, two such unhappy men who had surrendered to save their lives and were found in some Jewish dungeon have been condemned to walk in the Triumph today. Their hands are to be tied behind them, and in place of their swords they must wear a distaff, and on their breasts a placard with the words written: *I am a Roman who preferred dishonor to death.* You would not wish their company, my lord."

The face of Marcus went first red, then white.

"Man," he said, "cease your ill-omened talk, lest I should fall upon my sword here before your eyes. Bid the slaves make ready the bath and food, for we need both."

"Slaves, my lord? There are none here, save one old woman, who attends to me and the house."

"Where are they then?" asked Marcus angrily.

"The most part of them I have sent into the country, thinking it better that they should work upon your estates rather than live here idle, and others who were not needed I have sold."

"You were ever prudent, Stephanus." Then he added by an afterthought, "Have you any money in the house?"

The old steward looked towards Nehushta suspiciously and seeing that she was engaged with the horses out of earshot, answered in a whisper, "Money? I have so much of it that I know not what to do. The storeroom is almost full of gold and it keeps coming. The rents and profits of your great estates have been collecting here for three years, with no one here to spend it. And the proceeds of the sale of slaves and properties, together with the large outstanding amount that was due to my late master, the Lord Caius is also here. You will not lack for money."

"There are other things that I could spare less readily," said Marcus, with a sigh. "But it may be needed. Now tether the horses by the fountain, and give us food, whatever you have. We have ridden thirty hours without rest. You can talk afterwards."

It was midday. Marcus had bathed, anointed, and clad himself in the robes of his rank, and now stood alone in one of the splendid apartments of his marble house, looking through an opening in the shutters at the passing of the Triumph. He was soon joined by old Nehushta. She also was clad in clean, white robes that the slave woman had found for her.

"Have you any news?" asked Marcus impatiently.

"Some, lord, which I have pieced together from what is known by the slave woman, and by your steward, Stephanus. A beautiful Jewish captive is to walk in the Triumph and afterwards to be sold with other captives in the Forum. It is said that there has been a quarrel between Titus and his brother Domitian, and Vespasian also, on account of this woman."

"A quarrel? What quarrel?"

"They could tell me little of it, but they have heard that Domitian demanded the girl as a gift, whereon Titus told him that if he wished for her, he should buy her. Then the matter was referred to Vespasian Caesar, who upheld the decree of Titus. Domitian was furious, and declared that he would purchase the girl and remember the affront that had been put to him."

"Surely the gods are against me," said Marcus, "if they have given me Domitian for a rival."

"Why so, lord? Your money is as good as his, and perhaps you will pay more."

"I will pay to my last piece, but will that free me from the rage and hate of Domitian?"

"Why need he know that you are the rival bidder?" she asked.

Marcus looked at her sideways. "In Rome everything is known—even the truth sometimes."

"Time enough for trouble when trouble comes. First let us wait and see whether this maid is Miriam."

"Aye," he answered, "let us wait—since we must."

So they waited, watching with anxious eyes as the great parade rolled by them. They saw the cars painted with scenes of the taking of Jerusalem and the statues of the gods fashioned in ivory and gold. They saw the purple hangings of the Babylonian broidered pictures, the wild beasts, and the ships mounted upon wheels. They saw the treasures of the temple and the images of victory, and many other things. The pageant seemed to be end-less, and still the captives and the Emperors had not come.

There was one sight that caused Marcus to shrink as though fire had burned him, for set in the midst of a company of jug-glers and buffoons that gibed and mocked at them, were the two unhappy men who had been taken prisoner by the Jews. On they tramped, their hands bound behind them, clad in full armor but wearing a woman's distaff where the sword should have been, and round their necks the placards that proclaimed their shame. The brutal Roman mob hooted at them, calling them cowards. One of the men, a bull-necked, black-haired fel-low, suffered it patiently, knowing that at evening he would be set free to vanish where he would. The other, blue-eyed and finer featured, having gentle blood in his veins, seemed to be maddened by their talk, for he glared about him, gnashing his teeth like a wild beast in a cage. Before the very gate of Marcus's house the scene came to its climax.

"Cur," yelled a woman in the mob, casting a pebble that struck him on the cheek. "Cur! Coward!"

The blue-eyed man stopped, and, wheeling round, shouted in answer, "I am no coward, I who have slain ten men with my own hand, five of them in single combat. You are the cowards to taunt me. I was overwhelmed, that is all, and afterwards in the prison I thought of my wife and children and lived on. Now I die and my blood be upon you."

Behind him, drawn by eight white oxen, was the model of a ship with the crew standing on its deck. Eluding his guard, the man ran down the line of oxen and suddenly cast himself upon the ground before the wooden wheeled car, which rolled over his neck, crushing the life out of him.

"Well done! Well done!" shouted the crowd, applauding this unexpected spectacle. "Well done! He was brave after all." The body was carried away and the procession moved forward. But Marcus, who watched, hid his face in his hands.

Now the prisoners began to go past, marching eight by eight, hundreds upon hundreds of them, and once more the mob shouted and rejoiced over the unfortunates, whose crime was that they had fought for their country to the end. The last files passed, and then at a little distance from them, plodding forward wearily, appeared the slight figure of a girl dressed in a robe of white silk blazoned at its breast with gold. Her bowed head, from which her curling tresses fell almost to her waist, was bared to the fierce rays of the sun, and on her naked bosom lay a necklace of great pearls.

"Pearl Maiden, Pearl Maiden!" shouted the crowd.

"Look!" said Nehushta, gripping the shoulder of Marcus with her hand.

He looked, and after so many long years once more beheld Miriam, for though he had heard her voice in the old tower in Jerusalem, her face had been veiled by the darkness. There was the maid from whom he had parted in the desert village by Jordan. The same maid, and yet changed. She had been a lovely girl then, now she was a woman on whom sorrow and suffering had left their mark. Her features were finer, her deep, patient eyes were frightened and reproachful; her beauty was like a figure from a dream, not altogether of the earth.

"Oh! My darling, darling, child" murmured Nehushta, stretching out her arms towards her. "Christ be thanked, that I have found you." Then she turned to Marcus, who was devouring Miriam with his eyes, and said in a fierce voice, "Roman, now that you see her again, do you still love her as much as of old time?"

He took no note and she repeated the question. Then he answered, "Why do you trouble me with such idle words. Once she was a woman to be won, now she is a spirit to be worshipped."

"Woman or spirit, or woman and spirit, beware how you deal with her, Roman," snarled Nehushta, quickly withdrawing her hand from his shoulder.

"Peace, peace!" said Marcus. As he spoke the procession came to a halt before his windows. "How weary she looks. And sad," he went on speaking to himself. "Her heart seems crushed. Oh, that I must stay here and see her thus! If she could but know!"

Nehushta thrust him aside and took his place. Fixing her eyes upon Miriam she made some effort of the will, so fierce and concentrated that beneath the strain, her body shook and quivered. See! Her thought seemed to reach the captive, for she looked up.

"Stand aside," she whispered to Marcus. She unlatched the shutters and slowly pushed them open. Between her and the air there was now nothing but the silken curtains. Very gently she parted them with her hands, for some few seconds allowing her face to be seen between them. Then laying her fingers on her lips she drew back and they closed again.

"It is well," she said, "she knows."

"Let her see me also," said Marcus.

"Nay, she can bear no more. Look, she is too weak."

Groaning in bitterness of spirit, they watched Miriam, who seemed about to fall. A moment later, a woman from the crowd moved swiftly to Miriam's side and gave her a cup of wine. She drank and recovered herself.

"Note that woman," Marcus said, "so I may reward her."

"It is needless," answered Nehushta, "she seeks no reward.

She is more than a Roman. She is a Christian. As she lifted the cup, she made a sign of the cross."

The wagons creaked, the officers shouted, and the procession moved forward. From behind the curtain the pair kept their eyes fixed upon Miriam until she vanished in the dust and crowd. When she had gone, they seemed to see little else; even the sight of the glorious Caesars could not hold their eyes.

Marcus summoned the steward, Stephanus.

"Go into the city," he said, "and discover when and where the captive Pearl Maiden is to be sold. Then return to me swiftly. Be secret and silent, and let none suspect from where you come or what you seek. Your life hangs upon it. Go."

The sun was sinking fast, staining the marble temples and colonnades of the Forum blood red with its level beams. For the most part the glorious place was deserted now, for the Triumph was over, and the hundreds of thousands of the Roman populace, wearied with pleasure and excitement, had gone home to spend the night in feasting. But round one of the public slave markets, a small building with a marble ring fenced about by rope, where the slaves were sheltered until the moment of their sale, a mixed crowd was gathering, some of them bidders, some idlers drawn there by curiosity. Others were in the house behind examining the wares before they came to the hammer. Presently, an old woman presented herself at the door of the house, humbly clad and with her face veiled, bearing on her back a heavy basket like those used to carry fruit to the market.

"What do you want?" asked the gatekeeper.

"To inspect the slaves," she answered in Greek.

"Go away," he said roughly, "you are not a buyer."

"I may be if the stuff is good enough," she replied, slipping a gold coin into his hand.

"Pass in, old lady, pass in." In another second, the door had closed behind her, and Nehushta found herself among the slaves.

The light in the building was already so low that torches had been lit for the convenience of visitors. By their flickering glow, Nehushta saw the unfortunate captives—there were but fifteen—seated upon marble benches, while slave women moved from the one to the other, washing their hands, feet, and faces in scented water, brushing and tying their hair and removing the dust of the procession from their robes, so that they might be more pleasing to the eyes of the purchasers. A fair number of bidders were present, twenty to thirty of them, strolling from girl to girl discussing the points of each and at times asking them to stand up, or turn round, or show their arms and ankles, that they might judge them better. At the moment when Nehushta entered, one of them, a fat Eastern man with greasy curls, was endeavoring to persuade a dark and splendid Jewess to let him see her foot. Pretending not to understand, she sat still and sullen until at length he stooped down and lifted her robe. Then in an instant, the girl dealt him such a kick in the face that amidst the laughter of the spectators, he rolled backwards on the floor and rose with a cut and bloody lip.

"Very good, my beauty, very good," he muttered in a savage voice, "before twelve hours are over you shall pay for that."

But still the girl sat sullen and motionless, pretending not to understand.

Most of the buyers, however, were gathered about Miriam, who sat upon a chair by herself, her hands folded, her head bent down, a picture of disgraced and outraged modesty. One by one as their turns came and the attendant allowed them to approach, the men advanced and examined her closely, though Nehushta noted that none of them were allowed to touch her with their hands. Placing herself at the end of the line, she watched and listened keenly. Soon she had her reward. A tall man, dressed as a merchant of Egypt, went up to Miriam and bent over her.

"Silence!" said the attendant. "I am ordered to permit none to speak to the slave called Pearl Maiden. Move on, sir, move on."

The man lifted his head, and although in the gloom she could not see his face, Nehushta knew its shape. Still she was not sure, until presently he moved his right hand so that it came between her and the flame of one of the torches, and she perceived that the top joint of the first finger was missing.

"Caleb," she thought to herself, "Caleb in Rome! So Domitian has another rival." Then she went back to the doorkeeper and asked him the name of the man.

"A merchant of Alexandria named Demetrius," was the answer.

Nehushta returned to her place. In front of her, two men, agents who bought slaves and other things for wealthy clients, were talking.

"One might hold a dog sale," grumbled one, "after sunset when everybody is tired out. Not the sale of one of the fairest women who ever stood upon the block."

"Hah!" answered the other. "The whole thing is a farce. Domitian is in a hurry, that's all, so the auction must be held tonight."

"He means to buy her?"

"Of course. I am told that his purchaser, Saturius, has orders to go up to a thousand *sestertia* if need be," he said, nodding toward a quiet man dressed in a robe of some rich, dark stuff, who stood in a corner of the place watching the company.

"A thousand *sestertia*! For one slave girl! Ye gods! A thousand *sestertia*!"

"The necklace goes with her, that is worth something. And there is her property at Tyre."

"Property in Tyre," said the other, "property on the moon. Come on. Let's look at something a little less expensive. I am not bidding against the prince. I, at least, wish to keep my head about my shoulders."

"I think many are of like mind. I expect he will get his fancy pretty cheap after all."

Then the two men moved away, and a minute afterwards, Nehushta found that it was her turn to approach Miriam.

"Here comes a curious sort of buyer," said one of the attendants.

"Don't judge the taste of the fruit by the look of the rind, young man," answered Nehushta, and at the sound of that voice, for the first time Pearl Maiden lifted her head, then dropped it quickly.

"She is good-looking enough," Nehushta said aloud, "but there used to be prettier women when I was young. In fact, though dark, I was myself," a statement at which those within hearing, noting her gaunt and aged form bent beneath the heavy basket, laughed aloud. "Come, lift up your head, my dear," she went on, trying to entice the captive to consent by encouraging waves of her hand.

They were fruitless. Still, had any known what to look for, there was meaning in them. On Nehushta's finger shone a ring that Miriam knew, for she had long worn it on her own. With the recognition, her bosom and neck grew red and a spasm passed across her face, which even the falling hair did not suffice to hide. The ring told Miriam that Marcus lived and that Nehushta was his messenger.

Now the doorkeeper called a warning, and the buyers flocked from the building. Outside, the auctioneer, a smooth-faced, glib-tongued man, was already mounting the rostrum. Calling for silence, he began his speech.

"On this evening of festival," he said, "I shall be brief. The lots I have to offer to this select body of connoisseurs I see before me, are at present the property of the Imperator Titus, and the proceeds of the sale will not go into Caesar's pocket, but are to be equally divided between the poor of Rome and deserving soldiers who have been wounded or have lost their health in the war. So you patriotic citizens out there, be quick to bid!

"These lots are unique, being nothing less than the fifteen most beautiful girls, believed all of them to be of noble blood, among the many thousands who were captured at the sack of Jerusalem, the city of the Jews. All were especially selected to adorn the great conqueror's Triumph. No true judge, who desires a charming memento of the victory of his country's arms, will wish to neglect such an opportunity. I am informed," he added with a wink, "that Jewish women are affectionate, docile, well instructed in many arts, and very hard working.

"Be patient. I have but two more points to address. First, I ... regret that this important sale should be held at so strange an hour. But there is really no place that these slaves can be comfortably kept without risk of their maltreatment or escape, so it has been decided that they should be removed at once to the seclusion of their new homes, a decision, I'm sure, that will meet the wishes of you buyers.

"Finally, among the fifteen is one specimen of surpassing interest, Pearl Maiden. This young woman, who cannot be more than twenty years of age, is the last representative of a princely family of the Jews. She was found exposed upon one of the gates of the holy house of that people, where it would seem she was sentenced to perish for some offence against their barbarous laws. As the clamors of the populace today have already testified, she is of the most delicate and distinguished beauty, and the collar of great pearls she wears about her neck give evidence of her rank. If I know anything of the tastes of my countrymen, the price paid for her will prove a record even in this ring. I am aware that among the vulgar, a great, almost a divine name has been coupled with that of this captive. Well, I know nothing of it, except this, I am certain that if there is any truth in the matter the owner of that name, as becomes a noble and a generous nature, will wish to obtain his prize fairly and openly.

"The bidding is as free to the humblest here as to Caesar himself—provided, of course, that he can pay, and not an hour's credit will be given except to those who were known to me. Now, as the light is failing, I shall order the torches to be lit and commence the sale. The beauteous Pearl Maiden, I might add, is lot number seven."

So the torches were lit, and the first victim was led out and placed upon a stand of marble in the center of the flaring ring. She was a dark-haired child of about sixteen years, who stared round her with a frightened gaze.

The bidding began at five *sestertia* and ran up to fifteen, at which price she was knocked down to a Greek, who led her back into the receiving house, paid the gold to a clerk who was in attendance, and took her away, sobbing as she went. Then followed four others, who were sold at somewhat better prices. Number six was the dark and splendid Jewess who had kicked the greasy-curled Eastern in the face. As soon as she appeared

upon the block, this brute stepped forward and bid twenty *sestertia* for her. An old gray-bearded fellow answered with a bid of twenty-five. Then some one bid thirty, which the Eastern capped with a bid of forty. So it went on until the large total of sixty *sestertia* was offered, whereon the Eastern advanced two more, at which price, amidst the laughter of the audience, she was knocked down to him.

"You know me and that the money is safe," he said to the auctioneer. "It shall be paid to you tomorrow. I have enough to carry without burdening myself with so much gold. Come on, girl, to your new home, where I have a little score to settle with you," and grasping her by the left wrist he pulled her from the block and led her unresisting through the crowd and to the shadows beyond.

Already number seven had been summoned to the block and the auctioneer was taking up his tale, when from out of these shadows rose the sound of a dreadful yell. Some of the audience snatched torches from their stands and ran to the spot from where it came. There, on the marble pavement the Easterner lay dead or dying, while over him stood the Jewess, a red dagger in her hand—his own, which she had snatched from its scabbard—and on her noble face a look of vengeful triumph.

"Seize her! Seize the murdering witch! Beat her to death with rods," they cried, and at the command of the auctioneer slaves ran up to take her.

She waited until they were near, then, without a word or a sound, lifted her strong, white arm and drove the knife deep into her own heart. For a moment she stood still, until suddenly she stretched her hands wide and fell dead, facedown upon the body of the brute that had bought her.

The crowd gasped and was silent. Then one of them, a sickly looking patrician, called out:

"Oh! I did well to come. What a sight! What a sight! Blessings on you, brave girl, you have given Julius a new pleasure."

After this there was tumult and confusion while the attendants carried away the bodies. A few minutes later, the auctioneer climbed back into his rostrum and alluded in moving terms to the "unfortunate accident" which had just happened.

"Who would think," he said, "that one so beautiful could be so violent? I weep when I consider that this noble purchaser, whose name I forget at the moment, but whose estate, by the way, is liable for the money, should have thus suddenly been transferred from the arms of Venus to that of Pluto, although it must be admitted that he gave the woman some provocation. Well, gentlemen, grief will not bring him to life again, and we who still stand beneath the stars have business to attend. Bear me witness, all of you, that I am blameless in this affair. Slaves, bring out that priceless gem, Pearl Maiden."

CHAPTER XXIV
MASTER AND SLAVE

A hush of expectancy fell upon the crowd, until presently two attendants appeared, each of them holding in his hand a flaming torch, and between them the captive Pearl Maiden. So beautiful did she look as she advanced thus with bowed head, the red light of the torches falling upon her white robe and reflecting in a faint, shimmering line from the collar of pearls about her neck, that even that jaded company applauded as she came. In another moment, she had mounted the two steps and was standing on the block of marble. The crowd pressed closer, among them the merchant of Egypt, Demetrius, and the veiled woman with the basket, who was now attended by a little man dressed as a slave and bearing on his back another basket, the weight of which he seemed to find tedious, since from time to time he groaned and twisted his shoulders. Also the chamberlain, Saturius, secure in the authority of his master, stepped over the rope and against the rule began to walk round and round the captive, examining her critically.

"Look at her!" said the auctioneer. "Look for yourselves. I have nothing to say, words fail me—unless it is this. For more than twenty years I have stood in this rostrum, and during that time I suppose that fifteen or sixteen thousand young women have been knocked down to my hammer. They have come out of every part of the world. From the farthest East, from the Grecian mountains, from Egypt and Cyprus, from the Spanish plains, from Gaul, from the people of the Teutons, from the island of the Britons, and other barbarous places that lie still further north. Among them were many beautiful women, of every style and variety of loveliness, yet I tell you honestly, my patrons, I do not remember one who came so near perfection as this maiden whom I have the honor to sell tonight. I say again—look at her, look at her, and tell me with what you can find fault.

"What do you say? Oh! Yes, I am informed that her teeth are quite sound, there is no blemish to conceal, none at all, and the hair is all her own. That gentleman says that she is rather small. Well, she is not built upon a large scale, and to my mind that is one of her attractions. Little and good, you know, little and good. Only consider the proportions. Why, the greatest sculptors, ancient or modern, would rejoice to have her as model, and I hope that in the interests of the art-loving public"—here he glanced at the Chamberlain, Saturius—"that the fortunate person into whose hands she passes will not be so selfish as to deny them this satisfaction.

"Now I have said enough, but I must add this, that by the special decree of her captor, the Imperator Titus, the beautiful necklace of pearls worn by the maiden goes with her. I asked a jeweler friend of mine to look at it just now, and judging as well as he could without removing it from her neck, which was not allowed, he values it at least at a hundred *sestertia*. Also, there goes with this lot considerable property, situated in Tyre and neighboring places, to which, had she been a free woman, she would have inherited. You may think that Tyre is a long way off and that it will be difficult to take possession of this estate, and, of course, there is something in the objection. But the title to it is secure enough, for here I have a deed signed by Titus Caesar himself, commanding all officials, officers and others concerned, to hand over without waste or deduction all property, real or personal, belonging to the estate of the late Benoni. This Jewish merchant of Tyre was a member of the Sanhedrin—and the maiden's grandfather. I am assured, gentleman, that her purchaser, who has only to fill in his own name in the blank space, may appoint any representatives over the property that he pleases. Anyone wish to see it? No? Then we will take it as read. I know that in such a matter, my patrons, my word is enough for you.

"Now I am about to come to business, with the remark that the more liberal your bidding the better will our glorious general, Titus Caesar, be pleased; the better will the poor and the invalided soldiers, who deserve so well at your hands, be pleased; the better will the girl herself be pleased, who I am sure will know how to reward a generous appreciation of her worth; and the better shall I, your humble friend and servant, be pleased, because, as I may inform you in strict secrecy, I am paid, not by fixed salary, but by commission.

"Now, gentlemen, what shall I say? A thousand *sestertia* to begin with? Oh, don't laugh, I expect more than that. What! Fifty? You are joking, my friend. But the acorn grows into the oak, doesn't it? And I am told that you can stop the sources of the Tiber with your hat, so I'll start with fifty. Fifty—a hundred. Come, bid up, gentlemen, or we shall never get home to supper. Two hundred—three, four, five, six, seven, eight—ah! That's better. What are you stopping for?" he demanded of a heavily scarred man who had thrust himself forward over the rope of the ring.

The man shook his head with a sigh. "I'm done," he said. "Such goods are for my betters," a sentiment that seemed to be shared by his rivals, since they also stopped bidding.

"Well, friend Saturius," said the auctioneer, "have you gone to sleep, or have you anything to say? Only in hundreds, now, gentlemen, mind, only in hundreds, unless I give the word. Thank you, I have nine hundred," and he looked round rather carelessly, expecting that this bid would be the last.

Then the merchant from Alexandria stepped forward and held up his finger.

"A thousand, by the Gods!"

Saturius looked at the man indignantly. Who was this that dared to bid against Domitian, the third dignitary in all the Roman Empire, Caesar's son, Caesar's brother, who might himself be Caesar? Still he answered with another bid of eleven hundred.

Once more the finger of the Egyptian went up.

"Twelve. Twelve hundred!" said the auctioneer, in a voice of suppressed excitement, while the audience gasped, for such prices had never been heard of.

"Thirteen," said the Chamberlain.

Again the finger went up.

"Fourteen hundred. I have fourteen hundred. Against you, worthy Saturius. Come, come, I must knock the lot down, which perhaps would not please some whom I could mention. Don't be stingy, friend, you have a large purse to draw on, and it is called the Roman Empire. Now. Thank you, I have fifteen hundred. Well, my friend yonder. What! Have you had enough?" and he pointed to the Alexandrian merchant, who, with a groan, had turned aside and hidden his face in his hands.

"Knocked out, knocked out, it seems," said the auctioneer, "and though it is little enough under all the circumstances for this lot, who is as lovely as she is historical, I suppose that I can scarcely expect—" and he looked around despondently.

Suddenly the old woman with the basket glanced up and, speaking in a quiet matter-of-fact voice but with a foreign accent, said, "Two thousand."

A titter of laughter went around the room.

"My dear madam?" queried the auctioneer, looking at her dubiously, "might I ask if you mean *sestertia or sestertii?** Your pardon, but it has occurred to me that you might be confounding the two sums."

"Two thousand *sestertia*," repeated the matter-of-fact voice with the foreign accent.

"Well, well," said the auctioneer, "I suppose that I must accept the bid. Friend Saturius, I have two thousand *sestertia,* and it is against you."

"Against me it must remain, then," replied the little man in a fury. "Do all the kings in the world want this girl? Already I have exceeded my limit by five hundred *sestertia.* I dare do no more. Let her go."

"Don't vex yourself, Saturius," said the auctioneer, "bidding is one thing, paying another. At present I have a bona fide bid of fifteen hundred from you. Unless this liberal but unknown lady is prepared with the cash I shall close on that. Do you understand, madam?"

*A single *sesterium* (plural is *sestertia*) was equal to one thousand *sestertii.*

"Perfectly," answered the veiled old woman. "I am a stranger to Rome, so I thought it well to bring the gold with me, since strangers cannot expect credit."

"To bring the gold with you!" gasped the auctioneer. "To bring two thousand *sestertia* with you! Where is it then?"

"Where? Oh! In my servant's and my own baskets, and something more as well. Come, good sir, I have made my bid. Does the worthy gentleman advance?"

"No," shouted Saturius. "You are being fooled, she has not got the money."

"If he does not advance and no other worthy gentleman wishes to bid, then will you knock the lot down?" said the old woman. "Pardon me if I press you, noble seller of slaves, but I must ride far from Rome tonight, to Centum Cellae, indeed, where my ship waits. I have no time to lose."

Now the auctioneer saw that there was no choice, since under the rules of the public mart he must accept the offer of the highest bidder.

"Two thousand *sestertia* are bid for this lot number seven, the Jewish captive known as Pearl Maiden, sold by order of Titus Imperator, together with her collar of pearls and the property to which, as a free woman, she would have been entitled. Any advance on two thousand *sestertia?*" and he looked at Saturius, who shook his head. "No? Then—going—going—gone! I declare the lot sold, to be delivered on payment of the cash to the person named—by the way, madam, what is your name?"

"Mulier."

At this, the company burst into a loud laugh.

"*Mulier?*" repeated the auctioneer, "*Mulier*—'Woman'?"

"Yes, am I not a woman, and what better name can I have than is given to all my sex?"

"In truth, you are so peculiar that I must take your word for it," replied the auctioneer. "But come, let us put an end to this farce. If you have the money, follow me into the receiving house—for I must see to the matter myself—and pay it down."

"It would be my pleasure, sir. But be so good as to bring my property with you. She is too valuable to be left here unprotected amongst these distinguished but disappointed gentlemen."

So Miriam was led from the marble stand into an office annexed to the receiving house, where she was followed by the auctioneer and by Nehushta and her servant, whose backs bent beneath the weight of the baskets that were strapped upon them. The door was locked, and with the help of her attendant Nehushta loosened her basket, letting it fall upon the table with a sigh of relief.

"Take it and count, he said to the auctioneer, untying the lid.

He lifted it and there met his eye a layer of lettuces neatly packed.

"By Venus!" he began in a fury.

"Softly, friend, softly," said Nehushta. "These lettuces will grow only in yellow soil. Look," and lifting the vegetables she revealed beneath row upon row of gold coin. "Examine it before you count," she said.

He did so by biting pieces randomly with his teeth and causing them to ring upon the marble table.

"It is good," he said.

"Quite so. Then count."

So he and the clerk counted, even to the bottom of the basket, which was found to contain gold to the value of over eleven hundred *sestertia*.

"So far well," he said, "but that is not enough."

The buyer beckoned to the man with her who stood in the corner, his face hidden by the shadow, and he dragged forward the second basket, which he had already unstrapped from his shoulders. Here also were lettuces, and beneath the lettuces gold. When the full two thousand *sestertia* were counted, the second basket still remained more than a third full.

"I ought to have run you up, madam," said the auctioneer, surveying the shining gold with greedy eyes.

"Yes," she replied calmly, "if you had guessed the truth you might have done so. But who knows the truth, except myself?"

"Are you a sorceress?" he asked.

"Perhaps. What does it matter? The gold will not vanish when I leave the room. And, actually, it is troublesome carrying so much of the stuff back again. Would you like a couple of handfuls for yourself, and say ten pieces for your clerk? Yes? Well, please first fill in that deed with the name that I shall give you and with your own as witness? Here it is—'Miriam, daughter of Demas and Rachel, born in the year of the death of Herod Agrippa.' Thank you. You have signed, and the clerk also, I think. Now I will take that roll.

"One thing more, there is another door to this receiving house? With your leave I should prefer to go out that way, as my newly acquired property seems tired, and has had enough public notice for one day. You will, I understand, give us a few minutes to depart before you return to the rostrum, and your clerk will be so courteous as to escort us out of the Forum. Now help yourself. Man, can't you make your hand larger than that? Well, it will suffice to pay for a summer holiday. I see a cloak there, which may serve to protect this slave from the chill air of the night. In case it should be claimed, perhaps these five pieces will pay for it. Most noble and courteous sir, again I thank you. Young woman, throw this over your bare shoulders and your head. That necklace might tempt the dishonest.

"Now, if our guide is ready, we will be going. Slave, bring the basket, and you, young woman, strap on this other basket; it is as well that you should begin to be instructed in your domestic duties, for I tell you at once that having heard much of the skill of the Jews in those matters, I have bought you to be my cook and to attend to the dressing of my hair. Farewell, sir, farewell; may we never meet again."

"Farewell," replied the astonished auctioneer, "farewell, my lady Mulier, who can afford to give two thousand *sestertia* for a cook! Good luck to you, and if you are always as liberal as this, may we meet once a month, say I. Yet have no fear," he added meaningly, "I know when I have been well treated and shall not seek you out—even to please Caesar himself."

Three minutes later, under the guidance of the clerk, who was as discreet as his master, they had passed, quite undisturbed, through various dark colonnades and up a flight of marble stairs.

"Now you are out of the Forum, so go your way," he said.

They went, and the clerk stood watching them until they were round a corner, for he was young and curious, and to him this seemed the strangest comedy of the slave market of which he had ever even heard.

As he turned to go, he found himself face to face with a tall man, in whom he recognized the merchant of Egypt that had bid for Pearl Maiden up to the enormous total of fourteen hundred *sestertia*.

"Friend," said Demetrius, "which way did your companions go?"

"I don't know," answered the clerk.

"Come, try to remember. Did they walk straight on, or turn to the left, or turn to the right? Fix your attention on these, it may help you," and once more the clerk found five gold pieces thrust into his hand.

"I don't know that they help me," he said, for he wished to be faithful to his hire.

"Fool," said Demetrius in a changed voice, "remember quickly, or here is something that will—" and he showed him a dagger glinting in his hand. "Now then, do you wish to go the same road as they carried the Jewish girl and the Easterner?"

"They turned to the right," said the clerk sulkily. "It is the truth, but may that road you speak of be yours who draw knives on honest folk."

With a bound, Demetrius left his side, and for the second time the clerk stood still, watching him go.

"A strange business," he said to himself, "but perhaps my master was right and that old woman is a sorceress. Or perhaps the young one is the sorceress. All men seem ready to pay a tribe's tribute to get hold of her. Or, perhaps they are both sorceresses. A strange story, of which I should like to know the meaning, and so, I fancy, would the Prince Domitian when he comes to hear of it. Saturius, the chamberlain, has a fat place, but I would not take it tonight if it were given to me."

Then the young man returned to the mart in time to hear his master knock down lot thirteen, a sweet looking girl, to Saturius himself, who proposed, though with a doubtful heart, to take her to Domitian as a substitute.

Meanwhile, Nehushta, Miriam and the steward Stephanus, disguised as a slave, went on as swiftly as they dared toward the palace of Marcus in the Via Agrippa. The two women held each other by the hand but said nothing; their hearts seemed too full for speech. Only the old steward kept muttering—"Two thousand *sestertia!* The savings of years! Two thousand *sestertia* for that bit of a girl! Surely the gods have smitten him mad."

"Hold your peace, fool," said Nehushta at length. "At least, I am not mad. The property that went with her is worth more than the money."

"Yes, yes," replied the aggrieved Stephanus, "but how will that benefit my master? You put it in her name. Well, it is no affair of mine, and at least this accursed basket is much lighter."

Now they were at the side door of the house, which Stephanus was unlocking with his key.

"Quick," said Nehushta, "I hear footsteps."

The door opened and they entered, but at that moment a man passed by them, pausing to look until the door closed again.

"Who was that?" asked Stephanus nervously.

"He whom they called Demetrius, the merchant of Alexandria, but once I knew him by another name," answered Nehushta in a slow voice while Stephanus barred the door.

They walked through the archway into an antechamber lit by a single lamp, leaving Stephanus still occupied with his bolts and chains. Here, with a sudden motion, Nehushta threw off her cloak and tore the veil from her brow. In another instant, uttering a low, crooning cry, she flung her long arms about Miriam and began to kiss her again and again on the face.

"My darling," she moaned, "my darling child."

"Tell me what this all means, Nou," said the poor girl faintly.

"It means that God has heard my prayers, permitted my old feet to overtake you in time, and provided the wealth to preserve you from a dreadful fate."

"Whose wealth? Where am I?" asked Miriam.

Nehushta made no answer, but unstrapped the basket from Miriam's back and unclasped the cloak from about her shoulders. Then, taking her by the hand, she led her into a lighted passage and through a door into a great and splendid room spread with rich carpets and adorned with costly furniture and marble images. At the end of this room was a table lighted by two lamps, and on the further side of this table sat a man as though he were asleep, for his face was hidden upon his arms. Miriam saw him and clung to Nehushta trembling.

"Hush!" whispered her guide, and they stood still in the shadow.

The man lifted his head so that the light fell full upon it, and Miriam saw that it was Marcus. Marcus grown older and with a patch of gray hair upon his temple where the sword of Caleb had struck him, very worn and tired, but still Marcus and no other. He was speaking to himself.

"I can bear it no longer," he said. "Thrice have I been to the gate and still no sign. The plan has failed. By now she must be in the palace of Domitian. I will go and learn the worst," and he rose from the table.

"Speak to him," whispered Nehushta, pushing Miriam forward.

She advanced into the circle of the lamplight, but as yet Marcus did not see her, for he had gone to the window to find a cloak that lay there. Then he turned and saw her. Before him in her robe of white, the soft light shining on her gentle loveliness, stood Miriam. He stared at her bewildered.

"Do I dream?" he said.

"No, Marcus," she answered in her sweet voice, "you do not dream. I am Miriam."

In an instant, he was at her side and held her in his arms, nor did she resist him, for after so many fears and sufferings they seemed to her a home.

"Loose me," she said at length, "I am faint, I can bear no more."

At her entreaty, he let her to sink upon the cushions of a couch that was at hand.

"Tell me, tell me everything," he said.

"Ask it of Nehushta," she answered, leaning back. "I am spent."

Nehushta ran to her side and began to chafe her hands. "Let be with your questions," she said. "I bought her, that is enough. Ask that old huckster, Stephanus, the price. But first, in the name of charity, give her food. Those who have walked through a Triumph to end the day on the slave block need sustenance."

"It is here, it is here," Marcus said confusedly, "such as there is." Taking a lamp, he led the way to a table that was placed in the shadow, where stood some meat and fruit with flagons of rich colored wine and pure water and shallow silver cups from which to drink.

Putting her arm about Miriam's waist, Nehushta supported her to the table and sat her down upon one of the couches. Then she poured out wine and put it to her lips, and then Nehushta cut meat and made Miriam swallow it until she would touch no more. Now the color came back to her face, and her eyes grew bright again, and resting there upon the couch, she listened while Nehushta told Marcus all the story of the slave sale.

"Well done," he said, laughing in his old merry fashion, "well done, indeed! Oh! What favoring god put it into the head of that honest old miser, Stephanus, from year to year to hoard up all that sum of gold against an hour of sudden need, which none could foresee!"

"My God and hers," answered Nehushta solemnly, "to Whom you should be thankful as well, which, by the way, is more than Stephanus is, who has seen so much of your savings squandered in an hour."

"Your savings?" said Miriam, looking up. "Did you buy me, Marcus?"

"I suppose so, beloved," he answered.

"Then . . . I am your slave?"

"Not so, Miriam," he replied nervously. "As you know well, it is I who am yours. All I ask of you is that you should become my wife."

"That cannot be, Marcus," she answered in a kind of cry. "You know that it cannot be."

His face turned pale.

"After all that has come and gone between us, Miriam, do you still say so?"

"I do."

"You could give your life for me, and yet you will not give your life to me?"

"Yes, Marcus."

"Why? Why?"

"For the same reason I gave you by the banks of Jordan. My vow and charge has not changed. How then can I marry you? I would rather join my parents than break their command."

Marcus gave the problem a moment's consideration and spoke.

"Well, then, since I must, I will become a Christian."

She looked at him sadly and answered, "It is not enough simply to say so. Have you forgotten what I told you in the village of the Essenes? This is no matter of casting incense on an altar, but one of a changed spirit. When you can say those words from your heart as well as with your lips, then, Marcus, I will listen to you. But not until then."

"What then do you propose?" he asked.

"I? I have not had time to think. To go away, I suppose."

"To Domitian?" he asked sullenly, then checked himself. "Forgive me, but a sore heart makes bitter lips."

"I am glad you ask forgiveness for those words, Marcus," she said quivering. "What need is there to insult a slave?"

Her words seemed to suggest a new thought to Marcus.

"Yes," he said, "a slave—my slave whom I have bought at a great price. Well, why should I let you go? I am minded to keep you."

"Marcus, did you not once tell me that you would offer me no station lower than that of wife? You can keep me if you will, but then your sin against your own honor will be greater even than your sin against me."

"Sin!" he said, passionately. "What sin? You say you cannot

marry me, not because you do not wish it, if I understand you right, but for other reasons that have weight, at any rate with you. But the dead give no command as to whom you should love."

"No, my love is my own, but if it is not lawful, it can be denied."

"Why should it be denied?" he asked softly and coming towards her. "Is there not much between you and me? Did not you, brave and blessed woman that you are, risk your life for my sake in the Old Tower at Jerusalem? Did you not for my sake stand there upon the gate Nicanor to perish miserably? And I, though it be little, have I not done something for you? Have I not so soon as your message reached me, journeyed here to Rome, at the cost, perhaps, of what I value more than life—my honor?"

"Your honor?" she asked. "Why your honor?"

"Because those who have been taken prisoner by the enemy and escaped are held to be cowards among the Romans," he answered bitterly, "and it may be that such a lot awaits me."

"Coward! You a coward, Marcus?"

"Aye. When it is known that I live, that is what my enemies will call the man who lived on for your sake, Miriam—for the sake of a woman who denies me."

"Oh!" she said, "that is cruel. Now I remember and understand what Gallus meant."

"Then will you still deny me? Must I suffer thus in vain? Had it not been for you I could have stayed afar until the thing was forgotten. If I still chose to live. But now, because of you, things are thus, and yet, Miriam—you deny me," and he put his arms about her and drew her to his breast.

She did not struggle, but she wrung her hands and sobbed, saying, "What shall I do?"

"Do?" said the voice of Nehushta, speaking clear as a clarion from the shadows. "Do your duty, girl, and leave the rest to Heaven."

"Silence, accursed woman!" gasped Marcus, turning pale with anger.

"Nay," she answered, "I will not be silent. Listen, Roman. I like you well, as you have reason to know, for it was I who nursed you back to life, when for one hour's want of care you would have died. I like you well, and above everything on earth I wish that, ere my eyes shut for the last time, they may see your hand in her hand, and her hand in your hand, man and wife before the face of all men. Yet I tell you that now, indeed, you are more a coward than the Romans could ever dream of. You are a coward for trying to work upon the weakness of this poor girl's loving heart, for trying in the hour of her sore distress to draw her from the spirit, if not from the letter, of her duty. So great a coward are you that you remind her even that she is your slave and threaten to deal with her as you heathen deal with slaves. You put a gloss upon the truth. You try to filch the fruit you may not pluck. You say 'you may not marry me, but you are my property, and therefore if you give way to your master it is no sin.' I tell you it is a sin, and doubly so, for you would bind the weight of it on her back, as well as on your own. And in the end, it would bring its just reward to both of you."

"Have you finished?" asked Marcus coldly, as he allowed Miriam to slip from his arms back upon the couch.

"No. I have not finished. I spoke of the fruits of evil. Now as the Spirit prompts me I speak of the promise of good. Let this woman go free as you have the power to do. Strike the chains off her neck and take back the price that you have paid for her, since she has property that will repay it to the last farthing. It stands today in her name and can be conveyed to you. Then, go search the Scriptures and see if you can find no message in them. If you find it, well and good, then take her with a clean heart and be happy. If you find it not, well and good, then leave her with a clean heart and be sorrowful, for so it is decreed. Only in this matter do not dare to be double-minded, lest the last evil overtake you and her, and your children and hers. Now I am done, my lord Marcus. Be so good as to signify your pleasure to your slave, Pearl Maiden, and your servant, Nehushta the Libyan."

Marcus began to pace up and down the room, out of the light into the shadow, out of the shadow into the light. At length, he halted, and the two women saw that his face was drawn and ashen, like the face of an old man.

"My pleasure," he said vacantly. "That is a strange word on my lips tonight, is it not? Well, Nehushta, you have the best of the argument. All that you say is quite true, if a little overdone. Miriam is quite right not to marry me if she has scruples, and I should be quite wrong to take advantage of the accident of my being able to purchase her in the slave ring. I think that is all I have to say. Miriam, I free you, as indeed I remember I promised the Essenes that I would do. Since no one knows you belong to me, I suppose that no formal ceremony will be necessary. It is manumission *inter amicos,* but quite valid. As for the title to the Tyre property, I would accept it in payment of the debt, but I ask that you keep it a while on my behalf. At present, there might be trouble about transferring it into my name. Now, goodnight. Nehushta will take you to her room, Miriam, and tomorrow you can depart where you will. I wish you all fortune, and . . . can you not at least thank me? Under the circumstances, it would be kind."

But Miriam only burst into a flood of tears.

"What will you do, Marcus?" she sobbed.

"In all probability, things which I would rather you did not know of," he answered bitterly. "Or I may take it into my head to accept the suggestion of our friend, Nehushta, and begin to search those Scriptures of which I have heard so much, though they seem specially designed to prevent the happiness of men and women." Then he added fiercely, "Go, girl, go at once, for if you stand there weeping before me any longer, I tell you that I shall change my mind, and as Nehushta says, imperil the safety of your soul, and of my own—which does not matter."

So Miriam stumbled from the room and through the curtained doorway. As Nehushta followed her, Marcus caught her by the arm.

"I have half a mind to murder you," he said, quietly.

The old Libyan only laughed.

"All I have said is true and for your own good, Marcus," she answered, "and you will live to know it."

"Where will you take her?"

"I don't know yet, but Christians always have friends."

"You will let me hear of her."

"Surely, if it is safe."

"And if she needs help, you will tell me?"

"Surely, and if you need her help, and it can be done, I will bring her to you."

"Then I hope I may soon need help," he said. "Begone."

Chapter XXV
The Reward of Saturius

Meanwhile, in one of the palaces of the Caesars not far from the Capitol, another more stormy scene was being enacted. Such was the palace of Domitian, where the bewildering pomp of the Triumph had finished at last, and the prince had withdrawn himself in no happy mood. That day, many things had managed to vex him. First and foremost, as had been brought home to his mind from minute to minute throughout the long hours, its glory belonged not to himself, not even to his father, Vespasian, but to his brother, the conqueror of the Jews. Titus he had always hated, Titus, who was as beloved of mankind for his virtues, such as virtues were in that age, as he, Domitian, was despised for his vices. Now Titus had returned after a brilliant and successful campaign to be crowned as Caesar, to be accepted as the sharer of his father's government, and to receive the ovations of the populace, while his brother Domitian must ride almost unnoted behind his chariot. The plaudits of the roaring mob, the congratulations of the Senate, the homage of the equestrians and subject princes, the offerings of foreign kings, all laid at the feet of Titus, filled him with a jealousy that went nigh to madness. Soothsayers had told him, it was true, that his hour would come, that he would live and reign after Vespasian and Titus had both gone down to Hades. But even if they spoke the truth, that hour seemed a long way off.

And there were other things. At the great sacrifice before the temple of Jupiter, his place had been set too far back where the people could not see him; at the feast that followed, the master of the ceremonies had neglected to pour a libation in his honor.

Furthermore, the beautiful captive, Pearl Maiden, had appeared in the procession unadorned by the costly girdle he had sent her. Last of all, the different wines that he had drunk had disagreed with him, so that because of them, or because of the heat of the sun, he suffered from headache and sickness. Pleading this indisposition as an excuse, Domitian left the banquet very early and, attended by his slaves and musicians, retired to his own palace.

There, his spirits revived somewhat, for he knew that before long his chamberlain Saturius would appear with the lovely Jewish maiden upon whom he had set his fancy. This at least was certain, for he had arranged that the auction should be held that evening and instructed him to buy her at all costs, even to a thousand *sestertia*. Indeed, who would dare to bid for a slave that the Prince Domitian desired?

Learning that Saturius had not yet arrived, he went to his private chambers and, to pass away the time, commanded his most beautiful slaves to dance before him, inflaming himself the more by drinking wine of his favored vintage. As the fumes of the strong liquor mounted to his brain, the pains in his head ceased for a while, at any rate. Soon he became half drunk and, as was his nature when in drink, savage. One of the dancing slaves stumbled and, growing nervous, stepped out of time, whereon he ordered the poor half-naked girl to be scourged before him by the hands of her own companions. Happily for her, before the punishment began, a slave arrived with the message that Saturius waited outside.

"What, alone?" said the prince, springing to his feet.

"Nay, lord," said the slave, "there is a woman with him."

At this news, his ill temper was immediately forgotten.

"Let that girl go," he said, "and bid her be more careful next time. Away, all the lot of you, I wish to be in private. Now, slave, bid the worthy Saturius enter with his charge."

Presently the curtains were drawn apart, and Saturius came through them rubbing his hands and smiling somewhat nervously, followed by a veiled woman wrapped in a long cloak. He began to offer the customary salutations, but Domitian cut him short.

"Rise, man," he said. "That sort of thing is very well in public, but I don't want it here. So you have got her," he added, eyeing the draped form in the background.

"Yes," replied Saturius doubtfully.

"Good. Your services shall be remembered. You were ever a discreet and faithful agent. Did the bidding run high?"

"Oh! My lord, enormous. Ee-*nor*mous. I never heard such bidding," and he stretched out his hands.

"Impertinence! Who dared to compete with me?" exclaimed Domitian. "Well, what did you have to pay?"

"Fifty *sestertia*, my lord."

"Fifty *sestertia?*" Domitian remarked with an air of relief. "Well, of course it is enough, but I have known beautiful maidens to fetch more. My dear one," he went on, addressing the veiled woman, "I fear you must be tired after all that weary, foolish show."

The "dear one" made no audible reply, so Domitian went on. "Modesty is pleasing in a maid, but now I pray you, forget it for awhile. Unveil yourself, most beautiful, that I may behold that loveliness for which my heart has ached these many days. Nay, that task shall be my own," and he advanced somewhat unsteadily towards his prize.

Saturius thought that he saw his chance. Domitian was so intoxicated that it would be useless to attempt to explain matters that night. Clearly he should retire as soon as possible.

"Most noble prince and patron," he began, "my duty is done, with your leave I will withdraw."

"By no means, by no means," hiccupped Domitian, "I know that you are an excellent judge of beauty, most discriminating Saturius, and I should like to talk over the points of this lady with you. You know, dear Saturius, that I am not selfish, and to tell the truth, which you won't mind between friends—who could be jealous of a wizened, last year's walnut of a man like you? Not I, Saturius, not I, whom everybody acknowledges to be the most beautiful person in Rome, much better looking than Titus is, although he does call himself Caesar. Now for it. Where's the fastening? Saturius, find the fastening. Why do you

tie up the poor girl like an Egyptian corpse and prevent her lord
and master from looking at her?"

As he spoke the slave did something to the back of her head
and the veil fell to the ground, revealing a girl of very pleasing
shape and countenance, but who, as might be expected, looked
most weary and frightened. Domitian stared at her with his
bleared and wicked eyes, while a puzzled expression grew upon
his face.

"Very odd!" he said, "but she seems to have changed! I
thought her eyes were blue, and that she had curling black hair.
Now they are dark and she has straight hair. Where's the necklace, too? Where's the necklace? Pearl Maiden, what have you
done with your necklace? Yes, and why didn't you wear the girdle I sent you today?"

"Sir," answered the Jewess, "I never had a necklace—"

"My lord Domitian," began Saturius with a nervous laugh,
"there is a mistake—I must explain. This girl is not the Pearl
Maiden. The Pearl Maiden fetched so great a price that it was
impossible for me to buy her, even for you—"

He stopped, for suddenly Domitian's face had become terrible. All the drunkenness had left it, to be replaced by a mask
of savage cruelty through which glared those pale and glittering
eyes. The man appeared half satyr and half fiend.

"A mistake—" he said. "Oh! A mistake? And I have been count-
ing on her all these weeks, and now some other man has taken
her from me—the prince Domitian. And you—you dare to come
to me with this tale, and to bring this slut with you instead of
my Pearl Maiden—" and at the thought, he fairly sobbed in his
drunken, disappointed rage. Then he stepped back and began to
clap his hands and call aloud.

Instantly slaves and guards rushed into the chamber, thinking that their lord was threatened with some evil.

"Men," he said, "take that woman and kill her. No, that would
draw attention. She was one of Titus's captives. Don't kill her,
throw her into the street."

The girl was seized by the arms and dragged away.

"Oh! My lord," began Saturius.

"Silence, man, I am coming to you. Seize him, and strip him. Oh! I know you are a freedman and a citizen of Rome. Well, soon you shall be a citizen of Hades, I promise you. Now, bring the heavy rods and beat him until he dies."

The servants hurried to obey the dreadful order, and for a while, nothing was heard save the sound of heavy blows and the smothered moans of the miserable Saturius.

"Wretches," yelled the Imperial brute, "you are playing, you do not hit hard enough. I will teach you how to hit!" He snatched a rod from one of the slaves and rushed at his prostrate chamberlain, the others drawing back to allow their master to show his skill in flogging.

Saturius saw Domitian come, and knew that unless he could change his purpose in another minute the life would be battered out of him. He struggled to his knees.

"Prince," he cried, "hearken ere you strike. You can kill me if you will who are justly angered, and to die at your hands is an honor that I do not merit. Yet, dread lord, remember that if you slay me, you will never find the Pearl Maiden whom you desire."

Domitian paused, for even in his fury he was cunning. Doubtless, he thought, the knave knows where the girl is. Perhaps even he has hidden her away for himself.

"Ah!" he said aloud, quoting the vulgar proverb, "'the rod is the mother of reason.' Well, can you find her?"

"Surely, if I have time. The man who can afford to pay two thousand *sestertia* for a single slave cannot easily be hidden."

"Two thousand *sestertia!*" exclaimed Domitian astonished. "Tell me the story. Slaves, give Saturius his robe and fall back— no, not too far—he may be treacherous."

The chamberlain threw the garment over his bleeding shoulders and fastened it with a trembling hand. Then he told his tale, adding, "Oh, my lord, what could I do? You have not enough money at hand to pay so huge a sum."

"Do, fool? Why you should have bought her on credit and left me to settle the price afterwards. Oh, never mind Titus, I could have outwitted him. But the mischief is done, now for the remedy, so far as it can be remedied," he added, grinding his teeth.

"That I must seek tomorrow, lord."

"Tomorrow? And what will you do tomorrow?"

"Tomorrow I will find where the girl's gone, or try to, and then—why he who has bought her might die and—the rest will be easy."

"Die, he surely shall, who has dared to rob Domitian of his darling," answered the prince with an oath. "Well, hearken, Saturius, for this night you are spared, but be sure that if you fail for the second time, you also shall die, and after a worse fashion than I promised you. Now go, and tomorrow we will take counsel. Oh! Ye gods, why do you deal so hardly with Domitian? My soul is bruised and must be comforted with poesy. Rouse that Greek from his bed and send him to me. He shall read to me of the wrath of Achilles when they robbed him of his Briseis, for that hero's lot is mine."

So this new Achilles departed, now that his rage had left him, weeping maudlin tears of disappointed passion, to comfort his bruised soul with the immortal lines of Homer, for when he was

not merely a brute, Domitian fancied himself a poet. It was perhaps as well for his peace of mind that he could not see the face
of Saturius, as the chamberlain comforted his bruised shoulders
with some ointment. Nor could he hear the oath which that
useful and industrious officer uttered as he sought his rest, face
downwards, since for many days he was unable to lie upon his
back. It was a very ugly oath, sworn by every god who had an
altar in Rome, with the divinities of the Jews and the Christians
thrown in, that in a day to come, he would avenge Domitian's
rods with daggers. Had the prince been able to do so, there might
have risen in his mind some foresight of a scene in which he was
destined to play a part on a distant night. He might have beheld
a vision of himself, bald, corpulent, and thin-legged, but wearing the imperial robes of Caesar, rolling in a frantic struggle for
life upon the floor of his bedchamber, at death grips with one
Stephanus, while an old chamberlain named Saturius drove his
dagger again and again into his back, crying with each stroke,
"Oho! That for thy rods, Caesar! Oho! Do you remember the
Pearl Maiden? That for thy rods, Caesar, and that—and that—
and *that*—!"

But Domitian, weeping himself to sleep over the tale of the
wrongs of the godlike Achilles, which did but foreshadow those
of his divine self, as yet thought nothing of the rich reward that
time should bring him.

On the day following the great Triumph, the merchant
Demetrius of Alexandria sat in the office of the storehouse he
had hired for the bestowal of his goods in one of the busiest
thoroughfares of Rome. Handsome and noble as he was, his
countenance was a sorry sight. From hour to hour during the
previous day, he had fought a path through the dense crowds
that lined the streets of Rome, to keep as near as he could to
Miriam while she trudged her long route of splendid shame.

Then came the evening, when, with the other women slaves,
she was put up to auction in the Forum. To prepare for this sale
Caleb had converted almost all his merchandise into money, for
he knew that Domitian was one of the purchasers, and guessed
that the price of the beautiful Pearl Maiden, of whom all the city

was talking, would run high. He had bid to the last coin he possessed, only to find that others with even greater resources were in the market. Even the agent of the prince had been beaten, and Miriam was at last knocked down to some mysterious stranger woman dressed like a peasant. The woman was veiled and disguised; she spoke with a feigned accent and in a strange tongue, but from the beginning Caleb knew her. Incredible as it might seem that she should be here in Rome, he was certain that she was Nehushta, and no other.

That Nehushta should buy Miriam was understandable, but how had she come by so vast a sum of money, here in this far-off land? In short, for whom had she been buying? Indeed, for whom would she buy? He could think of one only—Marcus.

But he had made inquiries, and Marcus was not in Rome. Indeed he had every reason to believe that his rival was long dead, that his bones were scattered among the tens of thousands that whitened the tumbled ruins of the Holy City in Judea. How could it be otherwise? He had last seen him wounded, as he thought to death—and he should know, for the stroke fell from his own hand—lying senseless in the Old Tower in Jerusalem. Then he had vanished, and where Marcus had lain, Miriam had been found. To where had he vanished, and if it was true that she succeeded in hiding him in some secret hole, what chance was there that he could have lived on untended and without food? And if he lived, why had he not appeared long before? Why had so wealthy a patrician and so distinguished a soldier not ridden in the triumphant train of Titus?

With black despair raging in his breast, Caleb had seen Miriam knocked down to the mysterious basket-laden stranger. He had seen her depart together with the auctioneer and a servant, also basket-laden, to the office of the receiving house, where he had attempted to follow upon some pretext, only to be stopped by the watchman. After this, he hung about the door until he saw the auctioneer reappear alone, and it occurred to him that the purchaser and the purchased must have departed by some other exit, perhaps in order to avoid further observation. He ran round the building to find himself confronted only by the empty, starlit spaces of the Forum. Searching them with his eyes, for one instant it seemed to him that far away he caught sight of a little knot of figures climbing a black marble stair in the dark shadow of some temple. He sped across the open space and ran up the great stair to find at its head a young man whom he recognized as the auctioneer's clerk, gazing along a wide street as empty as the stairway.

He followed, and twice perceived the little group of dark robed figures hurrying round distant corners. Once he lost them altogether, but a passerby on his road to some feast told him courteously enough which way they had gone. On he ran, almost at hazard, to be rewarded in the end by the sight of them vanishing through a narrow doorway in the wall. He came to the door and saw that it was tall and massive. He even tried it, but it was locked. Then he thought of knocking, only to remember that to state his business would probably be to meet his death. At such a place and hour, those who purchased beautiful slaves might have a sword waiting for the heart of an unsuccessful rival who dared to follow them to their haunts.

Caleb walked round the house, to find that it was a palace that seemed to be deserted, although he thought he saw a light shining through one of the shuttered windows. Now he recognized the place. It was here that the procession had halted and one of the Roman soldiers who had committed the crime of being taken captive escaped the taunts of the crowd by hurling himself beneath the wheel of a great pageant car. Yes, there was no doubt of it, for his blood still stained the dusty stones and by it lay a piece of the broken distaff with which, in their mockery, they had girded the poor man. They were gentle folk, these Romans! Why, measured by this standard, the same doom would have fallen upon his rival, Marcus, for he had also been taken prisoner. The thought of Marcus being branded a coward made Caleb smile at the irony, as he knew well that no braver soldier lived. Then came other thoughts that pressed him closer. Miriam was somewhere in that great dead looking house, as far off from him as though she were still in Judea. Miriam was there—and who was with her? The newfound lord who had spent two thousand *sestertia* on her purchase? The thought of it turned his brain.

Until now, the life of Caleb had been ruled by two passions—personal ambition and his desire for Miriam. He had aspired to be ruler of the Jews, perhaps their king, and to this end had plotted and fought for the expulsion of the Romans from Judea. He had taken part in a hundred desperate battles. Again and again he had risked his life; again and again he had escaped. For one so young, he had reached high rank, until he was numbered among the first of their captains.

Then came the end, the last hideous struggle and the downfall. Once more his life was spared. Where men perished by the hundred thousand, he escaped, winning safety, not through the desire of it, but because his love of Miriam had driven him on to follow her. Happily for himself, he had hidden money, which, after the gift of his race, he had been able to turn to good account, so that now he who had been a leader in war and council walked the world as a merchant in Eastern goods. All that glittering past had gone from him. He might become wealthy, but Jew as he was, he could never be great nor fill his soul with the glory that it craved. There remained to him, then, nothing but this passion for one woman among the millions who dwelt beneath the sun, the girl who had been his playmate, whom he had loved from the beginning, and whom he would love until the end, though she had never loved him.

Why had she not loved him? Because of his rival, that accursed Roman, Marcus, the man whom time upon time he had tried to kill, but who had always slipped like water from his hands. Well, if she was lost to him, she was lost to Marcus also, and from that thought he would take such comfort as he might. Indeed, he had no other, for during those dreadful hours the fires of all Gehenna raged in his soul. He had lost—but who had found her?

Throughout the long night, Caleb lingered round the cold, desolate palace, suffering in his spirit as he had never suffered before. At length, the dawn broke and the light crept down the splendid street, showing here and there groups of weary and half-drunken revelers staggering homewards from the feast, flushed men and disheveled women. Others appeared also, humble and industrious citizens going to their daily trade. Among them were people employed in cleaning the roads, abroad early this morning, for after the great procession, they thought that they might find articles of value lost by the spectators or even by those who had walked in the Triumph. Two of these scavengers began sweeping near the place where Caleb stood and lightened their toil by laughing at him, asking him if he had spent the whole night in the gutter and whether he knew his way home. He replied that he waited for the doors of the house to be opened.

"Which house?" they asked. "The House Fortunatus?" and they pointed to the marble palace, which, as Caleb now saw for the first time, had these words blazoned in gold letters on its portico.

He nodded.

"Well," said one of them, "you will wait for some time, for that house is no longer fortunate. Its owner is dead, killed in the wars, and no one knows who his heir may be."

"Fortunatus," he repeated with an acrid suspicion. "What was his full name?" he asked.

"Marcus Carius Fortunatus," the sweeper replied.

With a bitter curse upon his lips, Caleb turned and walked away.

CHAPTER XXVI
THE JUDGEMENT OF DOMITIAN

Two hours had gone by, and Caleb, with fury in his heart, sat brooding in the office attached to his rented warehouse. At that moment he had but one desire—to kill his successful rival, Marcus. Marcus had escaped and returned to Rome; of that, there was no longer any doubt. He, one of the wealthiest of its patricians, had furnished the vast sum that had enabled old Nehushta to buy the coveted Pearl Maiden in the slave ring. Then his newly acquired property had been taken to this house, where he had awaited her. This then was the end of their long rivalry. This was the conclusion to the affair for which Caleb had fought, toiled, schemed, and suffered. In that dark hour of his soul, he would rather have seen her cast to the foul Domitian, for at least Domitian she would have hated. But Marcus, she loved.

There remained nothing to him but vengeance. He must be avenged, but how? He might shadow Marcus and murder him, but then his own life might be forfeit, for he knew the fate that awaited the foreigner, particularly the Jew, who dared to lift his hand against a Roman noble. If he hired others to do the work, they might bear witness against him. Caleb had no wish to die. Life was the only thing left to him. And while he lived, he might still win Miriam—after his rival had been eliminated. If Marcus died, then she would be sold with his other slaves, and he could buy her at the common rate of used goods. No, he would do nothing to run himself into danger. He would wait, wait and watch for his opportunity.

It was nearer at hand than he could have guessed, for even as Caleb sat there in his office, there came a knock upon the door.

"Open!" he cried savagely, and through it entered a small man with close-cropped hair and a keen, hard face that seemed familiar to him. Just now, however, that face was somewhat damaged, for one of the eyes had been blackened and a wound upon the temple was strapped with plaster. The man walked lame and continually twitched his shoulders as though in discomfort. The stranger opened his lips to speak, and Caleb knew him at once. He was the chamberlain of Domitian who had been outbid by Nehushta in the slave ring.

"Greeting, noble Saturius," he said. "Be seated, I pray, for it seems to pain you to stand."

"Yes, yes," answered the chamberlain, "but I had rather stand. I met with an accident last night . . . a most unpleasant accident," and he coughed as though to cover up some word that leapt to his lips. "You also, worthy Demetrius—that is your name, is it not?" he added, eyeing him keenly, "look as though you have not slept well."

"No," answered Caleb, "I also met with an accident—oh, nothing you would see—a slight internal injury which is, I fear, likely to prove troublesome. Well, noble Saturius, how may I serve you? Anything in the way of Eastern shawls, for instance?"

"I thank you, friend, no. I come to speak of shoulders, not shawls," and he shrugged his own. "Women's shoulders, I mean. A remarkably fine pair for their size that Jewish captive had, by the way, in whom you seemed to take an interest last night—to the considerable extent, indeed, of fourteen hundred *sestertia*."

"Yes," said Caleb, "they were well shaped, were they not?"

There was a pause.

"Perhaps, as I am a busy man," suggested Caleb pointedly, "you would not mind coming to the point."

"Certainly, I was but waiting for your leave. As you may have heard, I represent a very noble person—"

"Who, I think, took an interest in the captive to the extent of fifteen hundred *sestertia*," suggested Caleb.

"Quite so—and whose interest unfortunately remains unabated, or rather, I should say, that it is transferred."

"To the gentleman whose deep feeling induced him to provide five hundred more?" queried Caleb.

"Precisely. What intuition you have! It is a gift with which
the East endows her sons."

"Suppose you put the matter plainly, worthy Saturius."

"I will, excellent Demetrius. The great person to whom I have
alluded was so moved when he heard of his loss that he actually
burst into tears. He even reproached me, whom he loves more
dearly than his brother—"

"That is easy enough to believe, if all reports are true," said
Caleb dryly, adding, "Is that when you met with your accident?"

"It was. Overcome at the sight of my royal master's grief, I
fell down."

"Into a well, I suppose, since you managed to injure your eye,
your back, and your leg all at once. I understand. These things
will happen in households of the Great, where the floors are so
slippery that the most wary feet may slide. But that does not
console the sufferer whose hurt remains, does it?"

"No," answered Saturius with a snarl, "but until he is in a
position to relay the floors, he must find chalk for his sandals
and ointment for his back. I want the purchaser's name, and
thought perhaps that you might have it, for the old woman has
vanished, and that fool of an auctioneer knows absolutely nothing."

"Why do you want his name?"

"Because Domitian wants his head. An unnatural desire
indeed that devours him, but one which, to be frank, I find it
important to satisfy."

Suddenly a great light seemed to shine in Caleb's mind, it
was as though a candle had been lit in a dark room.

"Ah!" he said. "And supposing I can show him how to get this
head, even how to get it without any scandal, do you think that
in return he would leave me the lady's hand? You see I knew her
in her youth and take a brotherly interest in her."

"Oh, yes, I am sure," Saturius sneered. "Just like Domitian
and the two-thousand-*sestertia* man, and, indeed, half the male

population of Rome, who were moved by the same familial affection when they saw her yesterday. Well, I don't see why he wouldn't. You see, my master never cared for pearls that were not perfectly white, nor admired ladies upon whom report cast the slightest breath of scandal. But he is of a curiously jealous disposition, and it is, I think, the head that he requires, not the hand."

"Had you not better make yourself clear upon the point before we go any further?" asked Caleb. "Otherwise, I do not feel inclined to undertake a very difficult and dangerous business."

"With pleasure. Now would you let me have your demands, in writing, perhaps? Of course, I understand—to be answered in writing."

So Caleb took parchment and pen and wrote:

> A written promise, signed by the person concerned, that if the head he desires is put within his reach, the Jewish slave named Pearl Maiden shall be handed over at once to Demetrius, the merchant of Alexandria, whose property she shall become absolutely and without question.
>
> A free pardon, with full liberty to travel, live, and trade throughout the Roman Empire, signed by the proper authorities, to be granted to one Caleb, the son of Hilliel, for the part he took in the Jewish war.

"That is all," he said, handing the paper to Saturius. "The Caleb spoken of is a Jewish friend of mine to whom I am anxious to do a good turn, without whose help and knowledge I should be quite unable to perform my share of this bargain. He is very shy and timid—his nerves were much shattered during the siege of Jerusalem—he will not stir without this authority, which, by the way, will require the signature of Titus Caesar, duly witnessed. Well, that is merely an offering to friendship. Of course, *my* fee is the conferral of the lady. I desire to restore her to her relations, who mourn her loss in Judea."

"Precisely—quite so," replied Saturius. "Pray do not trouble to explain further. I have always found those of Alexandria most excellent merchants. Well, I hope to be back within two hours."

"Mind you come alone. As I have told you, everything depends upon this Caleb, and if he is in any way alarmed, that is the end of the matter. He is the only one with a possible key to the mystery. Should it be lost, your patron will never get his head, and I shall never get my hand."

"Oh! Bid the timid Caleb have no fear. Who would wish to harm a dirty Jewish deserter from his cause and people? Let him come out of his sewer and look upon the sun. The Caesars do not war with carrion rats. Most worthy Demetrius, I go swiftly, as I hope to return again with all you require."

"Good, most noble Saturius, and for both our sakes—remember that the palace floor is slippery, and do not get another fall, for it might finish you."

"I am in deep waters, but I think that I can swim well," reflected Caleb as the door closed behind his visitor. "At any rate it gives me a chance, and I have no other. The prince plays for revenge, not love. What can Miriam be to him beyond the fancy of an hour, of which a thief has already robbed him? Doubtless, he wishes to kill the thief, but kings do not care for faded roses, which are only good enough to weave the chaplet of a merchant of Alexandria. So I cast for the last time. Let the dice fall as it is fated."

Very shortly afterwards, in the palace of Domitian, the dice began to fall. Humbly, most humbly, that faithful chamberlain, Saturius, laid the results of his mission before his august master, Domitian, who was suffering from a severe bilious attack that had turned his ruddy complexion a dingy yellow and made the aspect of his pale eyes even more unpleasant than usual. He was propped up among cushions, sniffing the essence of roses and dabbing vinegar water upon his forehead.

He listened indifferently to the tale of his jackal, until the full meaning of the terms asked by the mysterious Eastern merchant penetrated his sodden brain.

"So," he said, "the man wants Pearl Maiden. That's his share, while mine is the life of the fellow who bought her, whoever he may be. Are you still mad, man, that you should dare to lay such a proposal before me? Don't you understand that I need both the woman and the blood of him who dared to cheat me out of her?"

"Most divine prince, I understand perfectly, but this fish is only nibbling. He must be tempted or he will tell nothing."

"Why not bring him here and torture him?"

"I have thought of that, but those Jews are so obstinate. While you were twisting the truth out of him, the other man would escape with the girl. Much better promise everything he asks and then—"

"And then—*what?*"

"And then forget your promise. What can be simpler?"

"But he needs them in writing."

"Let him have them in writing—my writing—which your divine self can repudiate. Titus can sign merely the pardon to Caleb, who I suppose is this Demetrius himself. It will not affect you whether a Jew has the right to trade in the Empire, if thereby you can win his services in an important matter. Then, when the time comes, you can net both your unknown rival and the lady, leaving our friend Demetrius to report the facts to her relatives in Judea, for whom, he claims, is his only concern."

"Saturius," said Domitian, growing interested, "you are not so foolish as I thought you were. That trouble last night has quickened your wits—we should make it a custom. Be so good as to stop wriggling your shoulders, will you, it makes me nervous, and I wish that you would have that eye of yours painted. You know that I cannot bear the sight of black. It reminds me of melancholy things, and I am by nature joyous and lighthearted as a child. Now forge a letter for my—or rather for your—signature, promising the conferral of Pearl Maiden to this Demetrius. Then bear my greetings to Titus, begging his signature to an order granting the desired privileges to one Caleb whom I desire to favor, a Jew who fought against him at Jerusalem—with less success than I could have wished."

Three hours later Saturius presented himself for the second time in the office of the Alexandrian merchant.

"Most worthy Demetrius," he said, "I congratulate you.

Everything has been arranged as you wish. Here is the order, signed by Titus and duly witnessed, granting to you—I mean to your friend, Caleb—pardon for whatever he may have done in Judea, and permission to live and trade anywhere that he may wish within the bounds of the Empire. I may tell you that it was obtained with great difficulty. Titus, worn out with toil and glory, leaves this very day for his villa by the sea, where he is ordered by his physicians to rest three months, taking no part whatever in affairs. Does the document satisfy you?"

Caleb examined the signatures and seals.

"It seems to be in order," he said.

"It is in order, excellent Demetrius. Caleb can now appear in the Forum, if it pleases him, and lecture on the fall of Jerusalem for the benefit of the vulgar. Well, here also is a letter from the divine—or rather the half divine—Domitian to yourself, Demetrius of Alexandria, also witnessed by myself and sealed. It promises to you that if you give evidence enabling him to arrest that miscreant who dared to bid against him—do not be alarmed for yourself, the lady was not knocked down to you— you shall be allowed to take possession of her or to buy her at a reasonable price, not to exceed fifteen *sestertia*. That is as much as she will fetch now in the open market. Are you satisfied with this document?"

Caleb read and scrutinized the letter.

"The signatures of Domitian and of yourself as witness seem much alike," he remarked suspiciously.

"Somewhat," replied Saturius, with an airy gesture. "In royal houses it is customary for chamberlains to imitate the handwriting of their imperial masters."

"And their morals—no, they have none—their manners also," commented Caleb.

"At the least," went on Saturius, "you will acknowledge the seals—"

"Which might be borrowed. Well, I will take the risk, for if there is anything wrong about these papers, I am sure that the prince Domitian would not like to see them exhibited in a court of law."

"Good," answered Saturius, with a relief which he could not altogether conceal. "And now for the culprit's name."

"The culprit's name," said Caleb, leaning forward and speaking slowly, "is Marcus Carius, who served as one of Titus Caesar's prefects of horse in the campaign of Judea. He bought the lady Miriam, known as Pearl Maiden, by the agency of Nehushta, an old Libyan woman, who conveyed her to his house in the Via Agrippa, which is known as the House Fortunatus. Doubtless, she is there even now."

"Marcus," said Saturius. "Why, he was reported dead, and the matter of the succession to his great estates is now being debated, for he was the heir of his uncle, Caius, the proconsul, who amassed a vast fortune in Spain. After the death of the said Caius, this Marcus was a favorite of the divine Nero, who made him guardian of some bust of which he was enamored. He is a great man, if, as you say, he still lives. Even Domitian will find it hard to meddle with him. How do you know all this?"

"Through my friend Caleb. Caleb followed the black hag, Nehushta, and the beautiful Pearl Maiden to the very house of Marcus, which he saw them enter. Marcus, who was her lover in Judea—"

"Oh, never mind the rest of the story, I understand it all. But you have not yet proved that Marcus was in the house. And if he was, bad taste as it may have been to bid against the prince Domitian, at a public auction it is not illegal."

"Yes, but if Marcus has committed a crime, could he not be punished for that crime?"

"Without doubt. But what crime has Marcus committed?"

"The crime of being taken prisoner by the Jews and escaping from them with his life, for which, by an edict of Titus, whose laws are as those of the Medes and Persians, the punishment is death—or at the least, banishment and degradation."

"Well, and who can prove all this?"

"Caleb can, because he took him prisoner."

"And where," asked Saturius in exasperation, "where is this thrice accursed cur, Caleb?"

"Here," answered Demetrius. "I am Caleb, O thrice blessed

chamberlain, Saturius."

"Indeed," said Saturius. "Well, that makes things more simple. And now, friend Demetrius—you prefer that name, do you not—what do you propose?"

"I propose that the necessary documents should be procured, which, to your master, will not be difficult, that Marcus should be arrested in his house, put on trial, and condemned under the edict of Titus, and that the girl, Pearl Maiden, should be handed over to me, who will at once remove her from Rome."

"Good," said Saturius. "Titus is gone, leaving Domitian in charge of military affairs. That part is easy, though Caesar himself must confirm any sentence that may be passed. And now, farewell again. If our man is in Rome, he shall be taken tonight, and tomorrow your evidence may be wanted."

"Will the girl be handed over to me then?"

"I think so," replied Saturius, "but of course I cannot say for certain, as there may be legal difficulties in the way which would hinder her immediate resale. However, you may rely upon me to do the best I can for you."

"It will be to your advantage," answered Caleb significantly. "Shall we say . . . fifty *sestertia* on receipt of the slave?"

"Oh! If you wish it, if you wish it, for gifts cement the hearts of friends. On account? Well, to a man with many expenses, five *sestertia* can always be useful. You know how it is in these palaces, so little pay and so much to keep up. Thank you, dear Demetrius, I will give you and the lady a supper out of the money—when you get her," he added to himself as he left the office.

When, early on the following morning, Caleb came to his warehouse from the dwelling where he slept, he found two men dressed in the livery of Domitian waiting for him, who demanded that he accompany them to the palace of the prince.

"What for?"

"To give evidence in a trial," they said.

Then he knew that he had made no mistake, that his rival was caught, and in the rage of his burning jealousy, such jealousy as only an Eastern can feel, his heart bounded with joy. Still, as he trudged onward through streets glittering in the morning sunlight, Caleb's conscience told him that this rival should not be overcome in this way, that he who went to accuse the brave Marcus of cowardice was himself a coward, and that from the lie that he was about to act, if not to speak, could spring no fruit of peace or happiness. But he was mad and blind. He could think only of Miriam—the woman whom he loved with all his passionate nature and whose life he had preserved at the risk of his own—fallen at last into the arms of his rival. He would wrench her away, even at the price of his own honor and of her life-long agony, and if it might be, leave those arms cold in death, as often already he had striven to do. When Marcus was dead, perhaps she would forgive him. At least he would occupy his rival's place. She would be his slave, to whom, notwithstanding all that had passed, he would give the place of wife. Then, after a little while, seeing how good and tender he was to her, surely she must forget this Roman who had taken her girlish fancy and learn to love Caleb.

Now they were passing the door of the palace. Saturius met them in the outer hall and motioned to the slaves to stand back.

"So you have them," said Caleb, eagerly.

"Yes, or to be exact, one of them. The lady has vanished."

Caleb staggered back a pace.

"Vanished! Where?"

"I wish I could tell you. I thought perhaps you would know. We found Marcus alone in his house, which he was about to leave, apparently to follow Titus. But come, the court awaits you."

"If she has gone, why should I come?" said Caleb, hanging back.

"I really don't know, but you must. Here, slaves, escort this witness."

Then seeing that it was too late to change his mind, Caleb waved them back and followed Saturius. Presently they entered an inner hall, lofty, but not large. At the head of it, clad in the purple robes of his royal house, sat Domitian in a chair, while to his right and left were narrow tables, at which were gathered five or six Roman officers, those of Domitian's own bodyguard, helmless, but arrayed in their mail. In addition, there were two scribes with their tablets, a man dressed in a lawyer's robe, who seemed to fill the office of prosecutor, and some soldiers on guard.

When Caleb entered, Domitian, who, notwithstanding his youthful, ruddy countenance, looked in a very evil mood, was engaged in talking earnestly to the lawyer. Glancing up, he saw him and asked, "Is that the Jew who gives evidence, Saturius?"

"My lord, it is the man," answered the chamberlain. "And the other witness waits without."

"Good. Then bring in the accused."

There was a pause, until presently Caleb heard footsteps behind him and looked round to see Marcus advancing up the hall with a proud and martial air. Their eyes met, and for an instant, Marcus stopped.

"Oh," he said aloud, "the Jew Caleb. Now I understand." Then he marched forward and gave the military salute to the prince.

Domitian stared at him with hate in his pale eyes, and said carelessly:

"Is this the accused? What is the charge?"

"The charge is," said the lawyer, "that the accused Marcus Carius Fortunatus, a prefect of horse serving with Titus Caesar in Judea, allowed himself to be taken prisoner by the Jews when in command of a large body of Roman troops, contrary to the custom of the army and to the edict issued by Titus Caesar at the commencement of the siege of Jerusalem. This edict commanded that no soldier should be taken alive, and that any soldier taken alive and subsequently rescued, or who made good his escape, should be deemed worthy of death, or at the least, of degradation from his rank and banishment. My lord Marcus, do you plead guilty to the charge?"

"First, I ask," said Marcus, "what court is this before which I am put upon my trial? If I am to be tried, I demand that it shall be by my general, Titus."

"Then," said the prosecutor, "you should have reported your-

self to Titus upon your arrival in Rome. Now he has gone to where he may not be troubled, leaving the charge of military matters in the hands of his Imperial brother, the Prince Domitian, who, with these officers, is therefore your lawful judge."

"Perhaps," broke in Domitian with bitter malice, "the lord Fortunatus was too much occupied with other pursuits on his arrival in Rome to find time to explain his conduct to the Caesar Titus."

"I was about to follow him to do so when I was seized," said Marcus.

"Then you put the matter off a little too long. Now you can explain it here," answered Domitian.

The prosecutor took up the tale, saying that it had been ascertained on inquiry that the accused, accompanied by an old woman, arrived in Rome upon horseback early on the morning of the Triumph, that he had gone straight to his house, where he lay hid all day, that in the evening he sent out the old woman and a slave, carrying on their backs a great sum of gold in baskets, with which he purchased a certain fair Jewish captive, known as Pearl Maiden, at a public auction in the Forum. This Pearl Maiden, it would seem, was taken to his house, but when he was arrested on the morrow, neither she nor the old woman were found there. The accused, he might add, was arrested just as he was about to leave the house, as he stated, in order to report himself to Titus Caesar, who had already departed from Rome. This was the case in brief, and to prove it, he called a certain Jew named Caleb, who was now living in Rome, having received an amnesty given by the hand of Titus. This Jew was now a merchant who traded under the name of Demetrius.

Then Caleb stood forward and told his tale. In answer to questions that were put to him, he related how he was in command of a body of the Jews that fought an action with the Roman troops at a place called the Old Tower, a few days before the capture of the Temple. In the course of this action, he parleyed with a Roman officer, the Prefect Fortunatus, who now stood before him, and at the end of the parley challenged him to single combat. As Marcus refused the encounter and tried to run away, he struck him on the back with the flat of his sword. A fight ensued in which he, the witness, had the advantage. Being wounded, the accused let fall his sword, sank to his knees and asked for mercy. The fray having now become general, he, Caleb, dragged his prisoner into the Old Tower and returned to the battle.

When he went back to the Tower, he found that the captive had vanished, leaving in place a lady who was known to the Romans as Pearl Maiden, and who was afterwards taken by them and exposed for sale in the Forum, where she was purchased by an old woman whom he recognized as her nurse. He followed the maiden, having bid for her and being curious as to her destination, to a house in the Via Agrippa, which he afterwards learned was the palace of the accused Marcus. That was all he knew of the matter.

Then the prosecutor called a soldier, who stated that he had been under the command of Marcus on the day in question. There he saw the Jewish leader, whom he recognized as Caleb, at the conclusion of a parley strike the accused, Marcus, on the back with the flat of his sword. After this ensued a fight, in which the Romans were repulsed. At the end of it, he saw their commander, Marcus, being led away prisoner. His sword had gone and blood was running from the side of his head.

The evidence being concluded, Marcus was asked if he had anything to say in defense.

"Much," he answered proudly, "when I am given a fair trial. I desire to call the men of my legion who were with me, none of whom I see here today, except that man who has given evidence against me, a rogue whom, I remember, I ordered to be scourged for theft and dismissed from his company. But they are in Egypt, so how can I summon them? As for the Jew, he is an old enemy of mine, who was guilty of murder in his youth, and whom once I overcame in a duel in Judea, sparing his life. It is true that when my back was turned he struck me with his sword, and as I flew at him, he smote me a blow upon the head, and I fell unconscious. In this state, I was taken prisoner and lay for weeks sick in a vault, in the care of some of the Jews, who nursed me. From them I escaped to Rome, desiring to report myself to Titus Caesar, my master. I appeal to Titus Caesar."

"He is absent and I represent him," said Domitian.

"Then," answered Marcus, "I appeal to Vespasian Caesar, to whom I will tell all. I am a Roman noble of no mean rank, and I have a right to be tried by Caesar, not by a packed court, whose overseer has a grudge against me for private matters."

"Insolence!" shouted Domitian. "Your appeal shall be laid before Caesar, as it must—that is, if he will hear it. Tell us now, where is the woman whom you bought in the Forum? We desire her testimony."

"Prince, I do not know," answered Marcus. "It is true that she came to my house, but then and there I granted her freedom and she departed from it with her nurse. I don't know where she went."

"I thought that you were only a coward, but it seems you are a liar as well," sneered Domitian. Then he consulted with the officers and concluded, "We judge the case to be proved against you, and for having disgraced the Roman arms, when, rather than be taken prisoner, many a meaner man died by his own hand, you are worthy of whatever punishment it pleases Caesar to inflict. Meanwhile, until his pleasure is known, I command that you be confined to the private rooms of the military prison beside the Temple of Mars, and that if you attempt to escape, you shall be put to death. You have liberty to draw up your case in writing, that it may be transmitted to Caesar, my father, together with a transcript of the evidence against you."

"Now," replied Marcus bitterly, "I am tempted to do what you say I should have done before and die by my own hand, rather than endure such shameful words and this indignity. But my honor will not allow it. When Caesar has heard my case and Titus, my general, gives his verdict against me, I will die, but not before. You, Prince, and you, officers, who have never drawn sword outside the streets of Rome. You call me coward. I, who have served with honor through five campaigns, who from my youth until now have been in arms. All this upon the evidence of a renegade Jew who, for years, has been my private enemy, and of a soldier whom I scourged as a thief. Look now upon my breast and say if it is that of a coward!" And tearing his robe, Marcus exposed his bosom, scarred with four white wounds. "Call my comrades, those with whom I have fought in Gaul, in Sicily, in Egypt, and in Judea, and ask them if Marcus Carius is a coward. Ask that Jew, to whom I gave his life, whether Marcus is a coward."

"Have done with your boasting," said Domitian, "and hide those scratches. You were taken prisoner by the Jews—it is enough. You have your wish. Your case shall go to Caesar. If the tale you tell is true, you would produce that woman who is said to have rescued you from the Jews and whom you purchased as a slave. When you do this, we will take her evidence. Until then, to your prison with you. Guards, remove the man Marcus Fortunatus, once a Prefect of Horse in the army of Judea."

Chapter XXVII
The Bishop Cyril

O n the morning after the day of the Triumph, Julia Gallus's wife was seated in her bedchamber looking out at the yellow waters of the Tiber that ran almost beneath her window. She had risen at dawn and attended to the affairs of her household, and now she retired to rest and pray. Mingled with the Roman crowd the previous day, she had seen Miriam marching wearily through the streets of Rome. Then, able to bear no more, she had gone home, leaving Gallus to follow the last acts of the drama. About nine o'clock that night, he joined her and told her the story of the sale of Miriam for a vast sum of money, since, standing in the shadow beyond the light of the torches, he had witnessed the scene at the slave market. Domitian had been outbid, and their Pearl Maiden had been knocked down to an old woman who looked like a witch with a basket on her back, after which she vanished with her purchase. That was all he knew for certain. Julia could shed no light upon the matter and reproached her husband for not learning more. Still, although she seemed to be vexed, at heart she rejoiced. Into whomever's hand the maid had fallen, for a while, at least, she had escaped the vile Domitian.

Now, as she sat and prayed, Gallus being abroad to gather more tidings if he could, she heard the courtyard door open, but took no notice of it, thinking that it was but the servant returning from market. Presently, however, as she knelt, a shadow fell upon her, and Julia looked up to see none other than Miriam and with her a dark skinned, aged woman, whom she did not know.

"How have you come here?" she gasped.

"Oh! Mother," answered the girl in a low and thrilling

voice, "Mother, by the mercy of God and by the help of this Nehushta, of whom I have often told you, and . . . and of another, I have escaped from Domitian and return to you, free and unharmed."

"Tell me the story," said Julia, "for I do not understand. It sounds incredible."

So Miriam told her tale. When it was done, Julia said, "Heathen though he is, your Marcus must be a noble-hearted man. May Heaven reward him."

"Yes," answered Miriam with downcast eyes, "may Heaven reward him, as I wish I could."

"As you would have done had I not stayed you," put in Nehushta. Her voice was severe, but for an instant Julia saw something that she took to be a smile on her grim features.

"Well, friend, well," said Julia, "we have all fallen into temptation from time to time."

"Pardon me, lady," answered Nehushta, "but speak for yourself. I never fell into any temptation—from a man. I know too many men."

"Then, friend," replied Julia, "return thanks for the good armor of your wisdom. For my part, I say that like the lord Marcus, this maid has acted well, and my prayer is that she also may not lose her reward."

"Mine is," commented Nehushta, "that Marcus may escape the payment which he will doubtless receive from the hand of Domitian, if he can hunt him out," a remark at which the face of Miriam grew very troubled.

Just then Gallus returned, and to him the whole history had to be told anew.

"It is wonderful," he said. "Wonderful! I have never heard the like of it. Two people who love each other and who, when their hour comes, separate over some question of faith, in obedience to a command laid upon one of them by a lady who died years ago. Wonderful—and wise, I hope, though had I been the man concerned I should have taken other counsel."

"What counsel, husband?" asked Julia.

"Well—to get away from Rome with the lady as far as possible, and without more delay than necessary. It seems to me that under the circumstances it would have been best for her to consider her scruples in another land. You see, Domitian is not a Christian any more than Marcus is, and our maid here does *not* like Domitian but *does* like Marcus. No, it is no good arguing. The thing is done. And now to breakfast, which we all need after so much night duty."

So they went and ate. But during that meal, Gallus was very silent, as was his custom when he set his brain to work. Presently he asked, "Tell me, Miriam, did any see you or your companion enter here?"

"No, I think not," she answered. "The door of the courtyard was ajar, and the servant has not yet returned."

"Good," he said. "When she does return, I will meet her and send her out on a long errand."

"Why?" asked his wife.

"Because it is as well that none should know what guests we have until they are gone again."

"Until they are gone again!" repeated Julia, astonished. "Surely you would not drive this maid, who has become to us as our daughter, from your door?"

"Yes, I would, wife, for the dear maid's sake," and he took Miriam's little hand in his great palm and pressed it. "Listen now," he went on, "Miriam, the Jewish captive, has dwelt in our care these many months, has she not, as is known to all, is it not? Well, if anyone wants to find her, where will they begin looking?"

"Aye! Where?" echoed Nehushta.

"Why should anyone wish to find her?" asked Julia. "She was bought in the slave market for a great price by the lord Marcus, who of his own will has set her at liberty. She is a free woman whom none can touch."

"A free woman!" answered Gallus with scorn. "Is any woman free in Rome upon whom Domitian has set his mind? Surely, you Christians are too innocent for this world. Peace now, for there is no time to lose. Julia, take your cloak and go seek that high priest of yours, Cyril. Tell him the tale, and say that if he

would save her from great danger, he had best find some secret
hiding place among the Christians, for her and her companion,
until means can be found to ship them far from Rome. What
think you of that plan, my Libyan friend?"

"I think that it is good, but not good enough," answered
Nehushta. "I think that we had best depart with the lady, your
wife, this very hour, for who can tell how soon the dogs will be
laid upon our scent?"

"And what say you, maid Miriam?" asked Gallus.

"I? I thank you for your thoughtfulness, and I say—let us
hide in any place you will, even a drain or a stable, if it will save
me from Domitian."

Two hours later, in a humble and densely populated quarter
of the city where folk were employed making articles to minister to the comfort or the luxury of the wealthy, a certain master
carpenter known as Septimus was seated at his midday meal in
a little chamber above his workshop. His hands were rough with
toil, and the dust of his trade clung to his garments and powdered
his long gray beard so that, at first sight, it would not have been
easy to recognize him as Cyril, bishop among the Christians. Yet
it was he, one of the foremost of the Faith in Rome.

A woman entered the room and spoke with him in a low voice.

"The lady Julia, wife of Gallus, and two others with her?" he
said. "Well, we need fear none whom she brings. Bring them in."

The door opened moments later and Julia appeared, followed
by two veiled figures. He raised his hands to bless her, then
checked himself.

"Daughter, who are these?" he said.

"Declare yourselves," said Julia, and at her bidding, Miriam
and Nehushta unveiled.

At the sight of Miriam's face, the bishop drew a startled
breath, then turned to study that of her companion.

"Who vouches for this woman?" he asked.

"I vouch for myself," answered Nehushta, "for I am a
Christian who received baptism a generation ago at the hands of
the Apostle John, and was condemned to pay the price of faith
in the arena of Caesarea."

"Is this so?" asked the bishop of Miriam.

"It is so," she answered. "This Libyan was the servant of my grandmother. She nursed both my mother and myself, and many times has saved my life. Have no fear, she is faithful."

"Your pardon," said the bishop with a grave smile and addressing Nehushta, "but you who are old will know that the Christian who entertains strangers sometimes entertains a devil." Then he lifted up his hands and blessed them, greeting them in the name of their Master.

"So, Miriam," he said, still smiling, "it would seem that I was no false prophet, and though you walked in the Triumph and were sold in the slave ring—for this much I have heard—still the Angel of the Lord went with you."

"Father, he went with me," she answered, "and he leads me here."

Then they told him all the tale, and how Miriam sought refuge from Domitian. He looked at her, stroking his long beard.

"Is there anything you can do?" he asked. "Anything useful, I mean? But perhaps that is a foolish question. Well-favored women rarely learn a trade."

"I have learnt a trade," answered Miriam, flushing a little. "Once I was held of some account as a sculptor. Indeed, I have heard that your Emperor Nero decreed divine honors to a bust from my hand."

The bishop laughed outright. "The Emperor Nero! Well, the madman has gone to his appointed place, so let us say no more of him. But I have heard of that bust. I saw it once. It was a likeness of Marcus Fortunatus, was it not? In its fashion, it was a great work. But our people do not make such things. We are artisans, not artists."

"An artisan *should* be an artist," said Miriam, setting her mouth.

"Perhaps, but as a general rule, he isn't. Do you think that you could mould lamps?"

"There is nothing I should like better," she smiled, adding as afterthought, "as long as I am not forced to copy a pattern."

"Then, daughter," said the bishop, "I think I can show you

how to earn a living where none are likely to seek for you."

Not a hundred paces from the carpenter's shop where the master craftsman Septimus worked, there was another workshop in which vases, basins, lamps, and such articles were designed, fashioned, and baked. The customers who frequented the place, mostly wholesale merchants, noted from that day on the skill of a new workwoman who, so far as her rough clothing permitted them to judge, seemed to be young and pretty. She sat in an isolated corner beneath a window laboring by the light of the sun. In time, those with artistic taste also observed that, among the lamps produced by the factory, some of singular and charming design began to appear. They were so fine that although the makers reaped little extra benefit, the resellers found no difficulty in selling these pieces at five times their cost. All day long, Miriam sat fashioning them, while old Nehushta, who had learnt something of the task years ago by Jordan, prepared and tempered the clay and carried the finished work to the furnace.

Now, though none would have guessed it, in this workshop all the laborers were Christians, and most of the profit of their toil was cast into a common treasury from which all drew their livelihood, each of them taking a share as the elders decreed and giving the surplus to the sick or to brethren in need. Adjoining these shops were lodging houses, plain enough in appearance, but clean and orderly. At the top of one of them, three stairways high, Miriam and Nehushta dwelt in a large attic that grew very hot when the sun shone on the roof and very cold in the bitter winds and rains of winter. In other respects, however, the room was not unpleasant, for the din of commerce in the streets and the stench of the city did not reach so high, and the breeze that blew in at the windows was fresh and scented of the open lands beyond the city.

So they dwelt there in peace, for none came to search for the costly Pearl Maiden in those squalid courts. By day they labored, and at night they rested, ministering and holding fellowship in the community of Christian brotherhood. Despite their fears and anxieties for themselves and for one another, they were happier than they had been for years. And the weeks went by.

Tidings came quickly to them, for the Christians knew of all that passed in the great city, and when they met at night in the catacombs, as was their custom, Julia gave them news. They learned from her that they had done wisely to flee her house. Within three hours of their departure, indeed before Julia had returned, the palace guards had arrived to inquire whether they had seen anything of the Jewish captive named Pearl Maiden, who had been sold in the Forum on the previous night and, as they said, escaped from her purchaser, on whose behalf they searched. Gallus received them and lied as boldly as a senator, vowing that he had seen nothing of the girl since he delivered her into the charge of Caesar's servants on the morning of the Triumph. So the guards suspected no guile and departed, to trouble his household no more.

Marcus was taken from the palace of Domitian to his prison near the Temple of Mars. There, because of his wealth and rank, and because he made appeal to Caesar and was not yet condemned of any crime, he found himself well treated. Two well-furnished rooms were given him to live in, and his own steward, Stephanus, was allowed to attend him and provide him with food and all he required. When he had given his word that he would attempt no escape, he was allowed to walk in the gardens between the prison and the Temple and to receive his friends at any hour of the day. His first visitor was the chamberlain, Saturius, who began by sympathizing with him over his misfortune and most undeserved predicament. Marcus cut him short.

"Why am I here?" he asked.

"Because, most noble Marcus, you have been so unlucky as to incur the displeasure of a very powerful man."

"Why does Domitian persecute me?" he asked again.

"How innocent you soldiers are!" said the chamberlain. "I will answer your question by another. Why do you buy beautiful captives upon whom royalty chances to have set its heart?"

Marcus thought a moment, then said, "Is there any way out of this trouble?"

"My lord Marcus, I come to show you one. Nobody really

believes that you of all men failed in your duty out there in Jerusalem. The thing is absurd, as even those carpet captains before whom you were tried knew well. But your situation is most awkward. There is evidence against you—of a sort. Vespasian will not interfere, for he is aware that this is some private matter of Domitian's, and having had one quarrel with his son over the captive, Pearl Maiden, he does not wish for another over the man who bought her. No, he will say, 'this prefect was one of the friends and officers of Titus, let Titus settle the affair as it may please him, when he returns.'"

"At least Titus will do me justice," said Marcus.

"Yes, without doubt, but what will that justice be? Titus issued an edict. Have you ever known him to go back on his edicts, even to save a friend? Titus declared throughout his own camps that Romans who were taken prisoner by the Jews were worthy of death or disgrace, and two of them, common men and cowards, have already been publicly disgraced in the eyes of Rome. You were taken prisoner by the Jews and have returned alive, unfortunately for yourself, to incur the dislike of Domitian, who has aggravated a matter that otherwise would never have been noticed.

"'Now,' he says to Titus, 'Show justice and no favor, as you showed in the case of the captive Pearl Maiden, whom you refused to the prayer of your only brother, saying that she must be sold according to your decree.' Even if he loves you dearly, as I believe he does, what can Titus answer to that argument, especially if he also seeks no further quarrel with Domitian?"

"You said you came to show me a way to safety—yet you tell me that my feet are set in the path of disgrace and death. Must this way of yours, then, be paved with gold?"

"No," answered Saturius dryly, "with pearls. Oh! I will be plain. Give up that necklace and its wearer. What do you answer?"

Now Marcus understood, and a saying that he heard on the lips of Miriam arose in his mind, though he knew not how it came to him. "I answer," he said with set face and flashing eyes, "that I will not cast pearls before swine."

"A pretty message from a prisoner to his judge," replied the chamberlain with a curious smile. "But have no fear, noble Marcus, it shall not be delivered. I am not paid to tell my royal master the truth. Think again."

"I have thought," answered Marcus. "I do not know where the maiden is and therefore cannot deliver her to Domitian, nor would I if I could. I would rather suffer disgrace and Hades."

"I suppose," mused Saturius, "that this is what they call true love, and to speak plainly," he added with a burst of candor, "I find it admirable and worthy of a noble Roman. My lord Marcus, my mission has failed, but I pray the Fates may order your deliverance from your enemies and, in reward for these persecutions, bring back to you unharmed that maiden whom you desire, but whom I go to seek. Farewell."

Two days later Stephanus, Marcus's steward who waited upon him in his prison, announced that a man identifying himself as Septimus wished speech with him, but would say nothing of his business.

"Admit him," said Marcus. "I grow weary of my own company." And letting his head fall upon his hand he stared through the bars of his prison window.

Presently he heard a sound behind him and looked round to see an old man clad in the robe of a master workman, whose pure and noble face seemed a strange contrast to his rough garments and toil-scarred hands.

"Be seated and tell me your business," said Marcus courteously, and with a slight bow his visitor obeyed.

"My business, my lord Marcus," he said in an educated and refined voice, "is to minister to those who are in trouble."

"Then, sir, your feet have led you aright," answered Marcus with a sad laugh, "for this is the house of trouble and you see I am its inhabitant."

"I know, and I know the cause."

Marcus looked at him curiously. "Are you a Christian, sir?" he asked. "Do not fear to answer. I have friends who are Christians," he sighed, "nor could I harm you if I wished. But I wish to harm none, least of all a Christian."

"My lord Marcus, I fear hurt at no man's hand, and the days of Nero have gone by. Vespasian gives us little trouble. I am Cyril, bishop of the Christians in Rome, and if you will hear me, I am come to preach to you my faith, which, I trust, may yet be yours."

Marcus stared at the man. It was to him an amazing thing that this leader of so great a people should undergo so much trouble for a stranger. Then a thought struck him and he asked, "What fee do you charge for these lessons in your new religion?"

The bishop's pale face flushed. "Sir," he answered, "if you wish to reject my message, do it without insult. I do not sell the grace of God for lucre."

Again Marcus was impressed.

"Your pardon," he said. "But I have known priests to take money, though it is true they were not of your faith. Who told you about me?"

"One, my lord Marcus, whom you have treated well," answered Cyril gravely.

Marcus sprang from his seat. "Do you mean—?" he began and paused, looking round him warily.

"Yes," replied the bishop in a whisper, "I mean Miriam. Fear not, she and her companion are in my charge, and for the present, safe. Seek to know no more, lest their secret might be wrung from you. I and her brethren in the Lord will protect her to the last."

Marcus began to pour out his thanks.

"Thank me not," interrupted Cyril, "for what is both my duty and my joy."

"Friend Cyril," said Marcus, "the maid is in great danger. I have just learned that Domitian's spies hunt throughout Rome to find her. If she is found, they will take her to his palace and to a fate that you can guess. She must escape from Rome. Let her fly to Tyre, where she has friends and property. There, if she lies hidden a while, she will be harmed by none."

The bishop shook his head.

"I have thought of that," he said, "but it is scarcely possible. The officers at every port have orders to search all ships that sail with passengers, and to detain any woman on them who matches the description of the one called Pearl Maiden. I know this for certain, for I also have my officers, more faithful perhaps than those of Caesar," and he smiled.

"Then is there no way to get her out of Rome and across the sea?"

"I can think of only one, which would cost more money than we poor Christians can command. A ship must be purchased in the name of some merchant and manned with sailors who can be trusted. Then she could be taken aboard at night, for on such a vessel there would be no right of search nor any to betray."

"Find the ship and men and I will find the money," said Marcus, "for I still have gold at hand and the means of raising more."

"I will make inquiries," answered Cyril, "and speak with you further on the matter. Indeed, it is not necessary that you should lose money. The ship and her cargo should sell at a great profit in the Eastern ports if she arrives safely. Meanwhile, have no fear; in the protection of God and in the company of her brethren, the maid is safe."

"I hope so," said Marcus. "Now, if you have the time to spare, tell me of this God of whom you Christians speak so much but who seems so far away from man."

"But who, in the words of my master, the apostle Paul, in truth is not far from any who call upon Him," answered Cyril. "Now hearken, and may your heart be opened."

Long they spoke. At first, the tenets of the Christian faith rung hollow upon the ears of the Roman. The religion seemed strange and, in all ways, different from those of the Romans and the Greeks. Whereas the civilized Greek mind required one to use reason in the pathway to heaven, it seemed that Cyril asked him to abandon all that was reasonable. One God in three persons, maker of all things, and arbiter in the affairs of men. And yet, he had deigned to be born in great humility so he might die for his enemies.

At length Marcus shook his head in amazement that approached derision. "I spoke rightly all those years ago by

Jordan. The religion of your Christ is truly one for whom all else has failed."

"What," inquired Cyril pointedly, "has availed you thus far, O Fortunatus?"

The one called Fortunatus fell silent for a moment, and after that, he no longer looked upon Cyril's faith with the old contempt. And he recognized something else at work in him, causing his heart and mind to begin to toil heavily at the strange truths and ideas that were presented to him.

Cyril spoke of the truth of man's innate corruption—a fact that Marcus could do nothing but confirm, not only from the vice he saw in the world, but also from what he knew was in his own heart. With remorse, he remembered the test of love he had once put to Miriam, the shameful solicitation of her affections by the Jordan.

The notion of a just God was foreign to the Roman mind, whose gods were as depraved and immoral as the beings that worshipped them. And he saw truly that though Rome claimed to uphold justice, the truth was otherwise. Money and power ruled the courts of Rome.

"What of the good that men do?" Marcus sought to reason. "How can one be judged for solitary actions if his greater tendency is that of good?"

"First, they are not solitary actions, but a reflection of man's very nature. Man's tendency is to evil, and not good. But even if it were otherwise . . . Marcus, you have done much for Rome," the bishop continued, knowing that to the Roman, dishonor was the most terrible of all crimes. "You have fought her wars, you have vanquished her enemies. But if you should commit a single crime worthy of death—if, for instance, you *had* in your moment of weakness knelt before a Jew to beg in dishonor for mercy, would all your courage in the past compensate for your action of cowardice? And should it?"

"No, it would not. Nor should it," Marcus replied finally, and with conviction. "What then can man do? You have said it, and now I see the truth in it—all mankind is wicked, and justice is required. We are all condemned. So do you worship a God of anger who will scourge all of mankind?"

To this, Cyril replied, "He is a God of holy anger and righteous judgment, certainly. He cannot abide evil unpunished. But He is also a God of mercy, and does not wish that any man should perish."

"Mercy and justice," Marcus mused. "Well, I hope He may prove more merciful than Caesar has thus far. But justice must be satisfied—you have said so yourself. Where, then, is the chance for mercy?"

To this Cyril answered, "Our sin, our wickedness, is as a debt that must be paid. Until it is paid, the noblest of us are slaves to our sin. Our lives and our very souls are forfeit. But for the one who believes, that debt has been paid in full. We are like those enslaved because of our debts. When the debt is paid, the slavery is ended."

"Paid. In what way?"

"Why, by the raising up of Jesus, whom we call Christ. He paid our debt upon a Roman cross. And so we are free from our slavery to sin."

Marcus nodded. "I have heard of your Jesus. He was said to be a troublemaker. And so they crucified him. So all your hopes are staked upon a dead man, is that it?"

"Not upon the dead, Marcus," Cyril answered gravely, "but upon the living. For this same Jesus rose from the grave and lives today."

"A man rose from the grave?"

"He was the Son of God. How could the grave hold him? He paid our debt to God, and so we are free. Because he lives, we have hope of life. So of all men, it is only the Christian who is truly free."

There was a great pause as Marcus tried to understand. "Why," asked Marcus finally, "would your God do all this?"

The bishop's answer was simple. "Because He loved us."

"Loved us?" Marcus remarked incredulously. "Slaves? How can that be?" The idea of gods looking down upon mankind with affection or lust was not unknown, but the sacrificial love that Cyril described was entirely foreign to him.

"Marcus, you noted the slaves marching in Triumph of Titus Caesar, did you not? All were in bonds. Afterward, some were condemned to the block or to the cross. Some were sold to masters, who shall treat them cruelly for years to come. But there was one slave among them all that was not. One slave, among them all, found freedom."

He knew at once of whom the bishop spoke, for she was ever near to his heart. "Miriam. Pearl Maiden went free."

Cyril sucked air in through his teeth, drawing back and lifting his eyebrows in a fair imitation of Marcus's own disbelief. "But how can that be so? All who marched in the Triumph were condemned by Titus to death or bondage. How did Pearl Maiden escape?"

"I bought her," Marcus said slowly, suddenly beginning to see clearly.

Cyril smiled. "Yes! That is so. You redeemed her, paid the price for a slave, bidding against the devil himself, and here you are imprisoned because of it. Do you regret the deed?"

"Of course not."

"And so it is with us. But your love for Miriam is but a feeble likeness of God's love for His redeemed. For Pearl Maiden, who was desirable to all, you paid two thousand *sestertia*. To buy us, who are desirable to none, God sent His only Son to die. For your love, you suffer prison, dishonor, and the wrath of Domitian. For *His* love, Jesus, Son of God, suffered himself to be made man, to be nailed to a cross, and to undergo the wrath of His own Father. If through your love you redeemed her who was innocent before man, how much more did Jesus love, who redeemed those who were guilty before God?"

The sun was sinking, and at length, it was time for the prison gates to close.

"Come to me again," said Marcus as they parted, "I would hear more."

"Of Miriam or of my message?" asked Cyril with a smile.

"Of both," answered Marcus, and he was almost surprised to realize that he sincerely meant it.

Four days passed before Cyril returned. They were heavy

days for Marcus, for on the day following the bishop's visit he had learned that as Saturius had foretold, Vespasian refused to consider his case, saying that it must await the decision of Titus when he returned to Rome. Meanwhile, he commanded that the accused officer should remain in prison, but that no judgment should be issued against him. There, Marcus was doomed to lie, fretting out his heart like a lion in a cage.

From Cyril, Marcus learned that Miriam was well and sent him her greetings, though she dared neither visit him nor write. The bishop told him also that he had found a certain Grecian mariner, Hector, who was a Roman citizen and a faithful Christian. This man desired to sail for the coasts of Syria and was competent to command a vessel. And he thought that he could collect a crew of Christians and Jews who might be trusted. Lastly, he knew of several small galleys that were for sale, one of which, named the *Luna*, was a sturdy ship and almost new. Cyril told him, moreover, that he had seen Gallus and his wife Julia, and that these good people, having no more ties in Rome, partly because they desired to leave the city, and partly for love of Miriam—though more the second reason than the first—were willing to sell their house and goods and to sail with her to Syria.

Marcus asked how much money would be needed, and when Cyril named the sum, he sent for Stephanus and commanded him to raise it and to pay it over to the craftsman Septimus, taking his receipt in discharge. This Septimus promised to do readily enough by an appointed day, believing that the gold was needed for his master's ransom. Then having settled all as well as might be, Cyril again took up his tale with great earnestness and power and preached to Marcus of the Savior of lost sinners.

Thus the days went on, and two or three times a week, Cyril visited Marcus, giving him tidings and instructing him in the Faith. The ship *Luna* was bought and the most of her crew hired, and a cargo of goods salable in Syria was being laid into her hold at Ostia. The Greek captain, Hector, spread the rumor that this was a private venture of his own and some other merchants.

As the man was well known as a bold trader who had bought and sold in many lands, his tale caused neither wonder nor suspicion, none knowing that the capital was furnished by the steward of Marcus through the master craftsman and contractor called Septimus. Indeed, Miriam herself did not know this, for it was kept from her by the special command of Marcus, and if Nehushta guessed the truth, she held her peace.

Two full months had gone by. Marcus still languished in prison, for Titus had not yet returned to Rome, but as he learned from Cyril, Domitian wearied somewhat of his fruitless search for Miriam, although he still vowed vengeance against the rival who had robbed him. The ship *Luna* was laden and ready for sea, and if the wind and weather were favorable, she was to sail within a week. Gallus and Julia, having concluded their affairs, had moved to Ostia, where Miriam was to be brought secretly on the night of the *Luna*'s sailing.

Marcus, his heart guided by the light of Cyril's preaching and softened by the Spirit who is greater than the words of men, had become a changed man. Three times the bishop had put forward the sacrament of baptism, but there was yet one thing that prevented Marcus from accepting it.

"You believe, Marcus. You have told me so, and I see it in your life. Why are you so reluctant to accept that which is commanded of the Lord?" wondered the bishop. "Do you still doubt God's readiness to receive you?"

"No. It is not so much that I am unwilling, but unready," Marcus tried to explain, though he kept the true reason hidden.

"They are both one and the same thing," answered Cyril with his stern demeanor. "But I shall be patient as God is patient. I must not force the water of baptism on any man that would refuse it."

Thus matters stood when Cyril visited the prison bringing with him Miriam's farewell message to her love. It was very short.

"Tell Marcus," she had said, "that I go because he bids me, and I know not whether we shall meet again. Perhaps it is best that we should not meet, for even if he should still wish it, we cannot be together. But in this life I am his, and his only, and until my last hour my thought and prayer will be for him. May he be delivered from all the troubles that I have brought upon him, through no will of mine. May he forgive me for them and let my love and gratitude make some amends for all that I have done amiss."

To this, Marcus replied, "Tell Miriam that from my heart I thank her for her message, and that my desire is that she should be gone from Rome so soon as may be, for danger dogs her steps here. Tell her that though my love has brought to me shame and sorrow, still I give her love for love, and if ever I come living from my prison, I will follow her to Tyre and we may speak further of these matters. If I die, I pray that Providence may attend her and that from time to time she will make the offering of an hour's thought to the spirit that once was Marcus."

Chapter XXVIII
The Lamp

If Domitian slackened in his fruitless search for Miriam, Caleb, whose whole heart was in the hunt, proved more diligent. But he could find no trace of her. At first, he was sure that if she was in Rome, she would return to visit her friends and protectors, Gallus and his wife, and in the hope of thus discovering her, Caleb caused a constant watch to be kept upon their house. But Miriam was never seen there, and although their footsteps were dogged from day to day, they did not lead him to her, for Julia and Miriam met only in the catacombs, where he and his spies dared not venture. But Gallus soon discovered that his home was under observation and its household tracked from place to place. It was this knowledge, more than any other fact, that brought him to determine to leave Rome and dwell in Syria, for he said he would no longer live in a city where, night by night, he and his were hunted like jackals. But when he left for Ostia to wait there for the *Luna*'s departure, Caleb followed him, and in that small town, he soon learned all the old centurion's plans. But as he heard nothing of Miriam, he returned to Rome.

In the end, he discovered her whereabouts by accident, and not through his own cunning. Needing a lamp for his chamber, he entered a shop where such things were sold and examined those that the merchant offered to him. Presently he noticed one with the strange design of two palms, the trunks intertwined and the feathery heads nodding apart. It was furnished with two lamps, each hung by little chains from the topmost fronds. The shape of the trees struck him as familiar, and he let his eyes run down their stems until they rested upon the base, constructed wide to support so tall a piece. The palms grew upon a little bank, and the water rippled gently at it shores, while between bank and water was a long, smooth stone, pointed at one end. In an instant, Caleb recognized the place, as well he might, for on many and many an evening, he and Miriam had sat side by side upon that stone, angling for fish in the muddy stream of Jordan. There was no doubt about it, and, lo! Half hidden in the shadow of the stone lay a great fish, the biggest that ever he had caught—he could swear to it, for its back fin was split.

A mist came before Caleb's eyes and, across the years, he saw himself a boy again. There he stood, his rod of reed bent double and the thin line strained almost to breaking, while on the waters of Jordan the great fish splashed and rolled.

"I cannot pull him in," he cried. "The line will never bear it and the bank is steep. Oh! Miriam, we shall lose him!"

Then there was a splash, and, behold! The girl at his side had sprung into the swiftly running river. Though its waters, reaching to her neck, washed her down the stream, she hugged to her young breast that great, slippery fish and gripped its back fin between her teeth, until with the aid of his reed rod he drew them both to land.

"I will buy that lamp," said Caleb presently. "The design pleases me. What artist made it?"

The merchant shrugged his shoulders.

"Sir, I do not know," he answered. "These goods are supplied to us with many others, such as joinery and carving, by one Septimus, who is a contractor. They say he is a leader of the Christians, employing many hands at his shops in the poor streets. One or more of them must be designers of taste. Lately we have received from him some lamps of great beauty."

Then the man was called away to attend to another customer, and Caleb paid for his lamp.

That evening at dusk, bearing the lamp in his hand, Caleb found his way to the workshop of Septimus, only to discover that the part of the factory where lamps were molded was already closed. A girl, who had just shut the door, saw him standing perplexed before it and asked courteously if she could help him.

"Maiden," he answered, "I am in somewhat of a dilemma. I wish to find the maid who molded this lamp, so that I may order more, but am told that she has left her work for the day."

"Yes," said the maiden, looking at the lamp, which she evidently recognized. "It is pretty, is it not? Well, cannot you return tomorrow?"

"Alas! No, I expect to be leaving Rome for a while, so I fear that I must go elsewhere."

The girl reflected to herself that it would be a pity if the order were lost, and with it the commission, which she might divide with the maker of the lamp. "It is against the rules, but I will show you where she lives," she said, "and if she is there, which is likely enough, for I have never seen her or her companion go out at night, you can tell her your wishes."

Caleb thanked the girl and followed her through narrow streets to a court surrounded by old houses.

"If you go in there," she said, pointing to a certain doorway, "and climb to the top of the stairs—I forget whether there are three or four flights—you will find the maker of the lamp in the roof rooms—oh! Sir, I thank you, but I expected nothing," she exclaimed as Caleb pressed a whole *sestertia* into her hand. "Goodnight."

At length, Caleb stood at the head of the stairs, which were steep, narrow, and in the dark difficult to climb. Before him, at the end of a rickety landing, a small ill-fitting door stood ajar. There was light within the room beyond, and from it came a sound of voices. Caleb crept up to the door and listened, for as the floor below was untenanted he knew that none could see him. He bent down to look through the space between the door and its framework, and his heart stood still. There, standing full in the lamplight, clothed in a pure white robe, her rough working dress laid upon a stool beside her, was Miriam herself, leaning against the curtained window frame. She was talking to Nehushta, who was bent over a little charcoal fire, engaged in cooking their supper.

"Think," she was saying, "only think, Nou, our last night in this wretched city, and then, instead of that stifling workshop and the terror of Domitian, the open sea and the fresh salt wind and nobody to fear but God. *Luna*! Is it not a beautiful name for a ship? I can see her, all silver—"

"Peace," said Nehushta. "Are you mad, girl? Do not talk so loud. I thought I heard a sound upon the stairs just now."

"It is only the rats," answered Miriam gleefully. "No one ever comes up here. Were it not for Marcus, I could weep with joy."

Caleb crept back to the head of the stairs and down several steps, which he began to reascend noisily, grumbling at their gloom and steepness. Then, before the women even had time to shut the door, he thrust it wide and walked straight into the room.

"Your pardon," he began, then added quietly, "Why, Miriam, when we parted on the gate Nicanor, who could have foretold that we should live to meet again here in a Roman attic? And you, Nehushta. We were separated in the fray outside the Temple walls, though, indeed, I think that I saw you in a strange place some months ago. The slave ring on the Forum?"

"Caleb," asked Miriam in a voice hollow with sudden fear, "what is your business here?"

"Well, Miriam, it began with a desire for a replica of this lamp, which reminds me of a spot familiar to my childhood. Do you remember it? Now that I have found who the lamp's maker is —"

"Oh, cease your foolishness," broke in Nehushta. "Bird of ill omen, you have come to drag your prey back to the shame and ruin that she has escaped."

"I was not always called thus," answered Caleb, flushing, "when I rescued you from the house at Tyre, or when I risked my life, Miriam, to throw you food upon the gate Nicanor. Nay, I come to save you from Domitian—"

"And to take her for yourself," answered Nehushta. "Oh! We Christians also have eyes to see and ears to hear, and, black-hearted traitor that you are, we know all your shame. We know of your bargain with the chamberlain of Domitian, by which the body of the slave was to be the price of the life of her buyer. We know how you swore away the honor of your rival, Marcus, with false testimony, and how from week to week you have quartered Rome as a vulture quarters the sky seeking your quarry. Well,

she is helpless, but there is one who is strong, and may His vengeance fall upon your life and soul."

Suddenly Nehushta's voice, which had risen to a scream, died
away, and she stood before him, threatening him with her bony
fists and searching his face with her burning eyes, a vengeance
incarnate.

"Peace, woman, peace," said Caleb, shrinking back before
her. "Spare your reproaches. If I have sinned much it is because
I have loved more—"

"And hate most of all," added Nehushta.

"Oh, Caleb," broke in Miriam, "if as you say you love me, why
do you deal with me like this? You know well that I cannot love
you as you would wish. Even if you keep me from Domitian,
who is using you, how could you delight to take a woman who
leaves her heart elsewhere? Would you make a slave of your old
playmate, Caleb? Would you bring her to the level of a dancing
girl? Let me go in peace."

"Upon the ship *Luna*," said Caleb sullenly.

Miriam gasped. So he knew their plans.

"Yes," she replied desperately, "upon the ship *Luna*, to find
such a destiny as Heaven may give me, at least to be free and at
peace. For your soul's sake, Caleb, let me go. Years ago you swore
that you would not force yourself upon me against my will. Will
you break your oath today?"

"I swore also, Miriam, that it should go ill with any man who
came between you and me. Shall I break that oath today? Give
yourself to me of your own will and save Marcus. Refuse and I
will bring him to his death. Choose now between me and your
lover's life."

"Are you such a coward that you would lay such a choice upon
me, Caleb?" she whispered, the color draining from her face.

"Call me what you will. Choose."

Miriam clasped her hands and for a moment stood looking upwards. Then a light of purpose grew in her eyes and she
answered, "Caleb, I have chosen. Do what you must. Marcus's
life is not in my hands, or your hands, but in the hands of God,
and unless God wills it, not one hair of his head can be harmed
by you or Domitian. For is it not written, 'the King's heart is in

the hand of the Lord, he turneth it wherever he wills.' But my honor is my own, and to stain it would be a sin for which I alone must answer to Heaven, and to Marcus, dead or living—Marcus, who would curse and spit upon me did I attempt to buy his safety at such a price."

"Is that your last word, Miriam?"

"It is. If it pleases you by false witness and by murder to destroy the man who once spared you, then have your will and reap its fruit. I will make no bargain with you, for myself or for him—do your worst to both of us."

"So be it," said Caleb with a bitter laugh, "but I think that the ship *Luna* will lack her fairest passenger."

Miriam sank down upon a seat and covered her face with her hands, a piteous sight in her misery and terror that, despite her bold words, she could not conceal. Caleb walked to the door and paused there, while the white-haired Nehushta stood by the brazier of charcoal and watched them both with her fierce eyes. Presently Caleb glanced round at Miriam crouched by the window and a strange new look came into his face.

"I cannot do it," he said slowly, each word falling heavily from his lips like single raindrops from a cloud.

Miriam let her hands slip from her face and stared at him.

"You are right," he said. "I have sinned against you and Fortunatus. I will expiate my sin. Your secret is safe with me, but I can no longer bear your hate for me. You shall not see me again, Miriam. We look upon each other for the last time. And if I can, I will see your Marcus released from prison to follow you to Tyre—that is where the *Luna* is bound, is she not? Farewell."

Once again he turned to go, but it seemed that his eyes were blinded, or his brain was dulled by the agony that worked within. Caleb caught his foot in the ancient uneven boards, stumbled, and fell heavily upon his face. Within moments, with a low hiss of hate, Nehushta was upon him, seizing the nape of his neck with her left hand. With her right hand she drew a dagger from her bosom.

"Stop!" cried Miriam. "Touch him with that knife and we part forever. I mean it. I myself will hand you to the officer, even if he hales me to Domitian."

Nehushta rose stiffly to her feet, her momentary vigor of desperation gone.

"Fool!" she said, "fool, to trust to this man of double moods, whose mercy tonight will be vengeance tomorrow. Oh, you are undone! Alas, you are undone!"

Regaining his feet Caleb looked at her contemptuously.

"Had you stabbed me she might have been undone indeed," he said. "Now, as of old, there is little wisdom in that gray head of yours, Nehushta. Your hate cannot suffer you to understand the intermingled good and evil of my heart." Then he stepped quickly toward Miriam, lifted her hand and kissed it. She inclined her head to offer him her brow.

"No," he said, "tempt me not, it is not for me. Farewell."

Another instant and he was gone.

It would seem that Caleb kept his word, for three days later, the vessel *Luna* sailed unmolested from the port of Ostia in the charge of the Greek captain Hector, bearing on board Miriam, Nehushta, Julia, and Gallus.

They sailed south along the Italian coast on favorable winds, but as they neared the port of Rhegium, the sea heaved in turmoil beneath the gusts that whipped up into a fury. The *Luna* was tossed upon the waves, and her passengers were thrown to and fro in the cabins within her hull. Her captain, Hector, saw that they could not hope to weather the storm or push through it to their destination at Rhegium, and so he began to make their way south. But the gale had no intention of allowing them to escape its clutches.

Within their cabin, Miriam and Nehushta sat as still as they could, doubled over with nausea at the constant surging of the ship. They had lit no lamps, for it was dangerous to light oil when a sudden jarring might upset it and set the cabin aflame. So they waited in the complete darkness, clinging to each other and listening to the thudding of sailor's boots above as they raced across the decks, securing lines and struggling to keep the *Luna* afloat.

The ship was thrown sideways beneath a mighty swell of the sea, and Miriam fell heavily against the hull of the ship. For a moment, she feared the ship would overturn, but at length the *Luna* righted herself again. But Miriam could no longer bear waiting in the darkness. With a cry, she flung herself toward the door of the cabin.

"Where are you going, Miriam?" Nehushta called after her. But her voice was not heeded.

Miriam threw open the door, filling the cabin with a sickly, gray light, and climbed the stairs toward the deck. She was met at the top by Gallus, who was soaked to the skin. He noted her shortly and waved her away. "Back down to the hold with you! This deck is no place for a woman."

"I cannot face my end down there!" she replied. The old centurion offered no word of encouragement, nor did he deny that all might be lost. Instead he offered her his hand, and she took it readily, leaning on him as they were jolted again by the sea. Upon the deck, sailors were hauling the *Luna*'s cargo to the deck and throwing it overboard, hoping thereby to lighten the load and keep the craft from sinking. But it seemed a hopeless battle. Already, several of their number had been lost to the sea when the ship had been nearly capsized.

She felt another firm grip upon her left arm, and she turned to see that Nehushta had joined them.

"It is as you say," the Libyan woman cried above the howling of the wind. "I will not meet my end in the belly of a ship. It is better to be thrown into the sea than to sink, trapped beneath the decks. But do not lose hope. God is able to save. Pray for the *Luna* and for her crew!"

Neither Gallus nor Miriam answered her, for their eyes were transfixed upon the majesty of the storm. The sea seemed as a living thing bent on destruction, shrieking at them as waves the height of Jerusalem's walls hurled them about. At the top of one such wave, Miriam thought she caught a glimpse of another ship in like distress, but the swell quickly plummeted, and she saw it no more.

Titus had returned to Rome, and in due course, Marcus's case was brought before him by the prisoner's friends, together with a demand that he should be granted a new and open trial for the clearing of his honor. Titus, who for his own reasons refused to see Marcus, listened patiently and gave his decision.

He rejoiced, he said, to learn that his close friend and trusted officer was still alive, for he had long mourned him as dead. He grieved that, in his absence, his friend had been put on trial with the charge of having been captured alive by the Jews. If upon his arrival in Rome Fortunatus had at once reported himself, the trial would not have gone forward. He dismissed all accusations against his military honor and courage as mere idle talk, as he had a hundred times proved himself to be the bravest of men, and Titus knew something of the circumstances under which he had been captured. But, however willing he might be to do so, he was unable for public reasons to disregard the fact that he had been duly convicted by a court martial under the Prince Domitian of having broken the command of his general and suffered himself to be taken prisoner alive. To do so would be to proclaim himself, Titus, unjust, who had caused others to suffer for the same offence, and to offer insult to the prince, his brother, who in the exercise of his discretion as commander in his absence had thought fit to order the trial. However, his punishment would be as lenient as possible. Titus commanded that, on leaving his prison, Marcus should go directly to his own house by night, so that there might be no public talk or demonstration among his friends, and there make such arrangement of his affairs as seemed good to him. Within ten days, he must leave Italy, to dwell or travel abroad for a period of three years, unless the time should be shortened by special decree. After the lapse of these three years, he would be free to return to Rome. This was his judgment and it could not be altered.

As it happened, it was the chamberlain Saturius who first communicated the Imperial decree to Marcus. Hurrying straight from the palace to the prison, he was admitted into the prisoner's chamber.

"Well," said Marcus, looking up, "what evil tidings have you now?"

"None, none," answered Saturius. "I have very good tidings, and that is why I run so fast. You are only banished for three years, thanks to my secret efforts," and he smiled craftily. "Even your property is left to you. A fact which will, I trust, enable you to reward your friends for their labors on your behalf."

"Tell me all," and the rogue obeyed, while Marcus listened with a face of stone.

"Why did Titus decide thus?" he asked when it was finished. "Speak frankly, man, if you wish for a reward."

"Because, noble Marcus, Domitian had been with him before-hand and told him that if he reversed his public judgment, it would be a cause of open quarrel between them. This, Caesar, who fears his brother, does not seek. That is why he would not see you, lest his love for his friend should overcome his reason."

"So the prince is still my enemy?"

"Yes, and more bitter than ever before, for he cannot find the Pearl Maiden, and he is sure that you have spirited her away. Take my advice and leave Rome quickly, lest worse things befall you."

"Yes," said Marcus, "I will leave Rome quickly, for how can I abide here when I have lost my honor. But first it may please your master to know that by now the lady whom he seeks is far across the sea. Now get you gone, you fox, for I desire to be alone."

The face of Saturius became evil.

"Is that all you have to say?" he asked. "Am I to win no reward?"

"If you stay longer," said Marcus, "you will win one you do not desire."

Then Saturius went, but outside the door he turned and shook his fist towards the chamber he had left.

"Fox!" he muttered. "He called me fox and gave me nothing. Well, foxes may find some pickings on his bones."

The chamberlain's road to the palace ran past the place of business of the merchant Demetrius. He stopped and looked at it. "Perhaps this one will be more liberal," he said to himself, and entered.

In his private office he found Caleb alone, his face buried

in his hands. Seating himself, he plunged into his tale, ending it with an apology to Caleb for the lightness of the sentence inflicted upon Marcus.

"Titus would do no more," he said. "Indeed, were it not for the fear of Domitian, he would not have been brought to do so much, for he loves the man, who has been a prefect of his bodyguard, and was deeply grieved that he must disgrace him. Still, disgraced he is—aye, and he feels it. Therefore I trust that you, most generous Demetrius, who hate him, will remember the service of your servant in this matter."

"Yes," said Caleb quietly. "Fear not, you shall be well paid, for you have done your best."

"I thank you, friend," answered Saturius, rubbing his hands. "And, after all, things may be better than they seem. That insolent fool let out just now that the girl about whom there is all this bother has been smuggled away somewhere across the seas. When Domitian learns that, he will be so mad with anger that he may be worked up to take a little vengeance of his own upon the person of the noble Marcus, who has thus contrived to trick him. Marcus shall not get the Pearl Maiden, for the prince will cause her to be followed and brought back—to you, worthy Demetrius."

"Then," answered Caleb, slowly, "he must seek for her, not across the sea, but in its depths."

"What do you mean?"

"I have tidings that Pearl Maiden escaped in the ship *Luna* a month ago. This morning, the captain and some mariners of the galley *Imperatrix* arrived in Rome. They report that they met a great gale off Rhegium and, towards the end of it, saw a vessel sink. Afterwards, they picked up a sailor clinging to a piece of wood, who told them that the ship's name was *Luna* and that she foundered with all hands."

"Have you seen this sailor?"

"No. He died of exhaustion soon after he was rescued, but I have seen the men of the galley, who brought me note of certain goods consigned to me in her hold. They repeated this story to me with their own lips."

"So, after all, she whom so many sought was destined to the arms of Neptune, as becomes a pearl," reflected Saturius. "Well, well, as Domitian cannot be revenged upon Neptune, he will be the more wroth with the man who sent her to that god. Now I go to tell him all these tidings and learn his mind."

"You will return and acquaint me with it, will you not?" asked Caleb, looking up.

"Certainly, and at once. Our account is not yet balanced, most generous Demetrius."

"No," answered Caleb, "our accounts are not yet balanced."

Two hours later the chamberlain reappeared in the office.

"Well," said Caleb, "how does it go?"

"Ill, very ill for Marcus, and well, very well for those who hate him, as you and I do, friend. Oh! Never have I seen my Imperial master so enraged. Indeed, when he learned that Pearl Maiden had escaped and was drowned, so that he could have no hope of her this side of the Styx, it was almost dangerous to be near to him. He cursed Titus for the lightness of his sentence, he cursed you, he even cursed *me*. But I turned his wrath into the right channel. I showed him that for all these ills, Marcus alone is to blame, Marcus who is to pay the price of them with a three years' pleasant banishment from Rome, which doubtless, will soon be remitted. I tell you that Domitian wept and gnashed his teeth at the thought of it until I showed him a better plan—knowing that it would please you, friend Demetrius."

"What plan?"

Saturius rose, and having looked round to see that the door was fastened, came and whispered into Caleb's ear.

"After sunset tonight, within two hours, Marcus is to be released from prison and escorted to the door of his own house beneath the archway, where he is ordered to remain until he leaves Rome. No one lives in his house except an old man, the steward Stephanus, and a slave woman. Before he gets there, certain trusty fellows, such as Domitian knows how to lay his hands on, will have entered the house, and having bound the steward and the woman, will await the coming of Marcus beneath the archway. You can guess the rest. Is it not well conceived?"

"Very well," answered Caleb. "But would there not be suspicion?"

"None, none. Who would dare to suspect Domitian? A private crime, doubtless! The rich have so many enemies."

What Saturius did not add was that nobody would suspect Domitian because the masked bravoes were instructed to inform the steward and the slave when they had bound and gagged them that they had been hired to do the deed by a certain merchant named Demetrius, who had an old quarrel against Marcus, which he had already tried to satisfy by giving false evidence before the court martial.

"Now," went on Saturius, "I must be going, for there are one or two little things which need attention, and time presses. Shall we balance that account, friend Demetrius?"

"Certainly," said Caleb, and taking a roll of gold from a drawer he pushed it across the table.

Saturius shook his head sadly. "I expected twice as much," he said. "Think how you hate him and how richly your hate will be fed. First disgraced unjustly, he, one of the best soldiers and bravest officers in the army, and then hacked to death by cutthroats in the doorway of his own house. What more could you want?"

"Nothing," answered Caleb. "But the man isn't dead yet. Sometimes the Fates have strange surprises for us mortals, friend Saturius."

"Dead? He will be dead soon enough."

"Good. You shall have the rest of the money when I have seen his body. No, I don't want any bungling and that's the best way to make certain."

"I wonder," thought Saturius, as he departed out of the office and this history, "I wonder how I shall manage to get the balance of my fee before they have my Jewish friend by the heels. But it can be arranged—doubtless it can be arranged."

When he had gone, Caleb, who had things that needed attention and felt that time pressed, took pen to write a short letter. He summoned a clerk and gave orders that it was to be delivered two hours after sunset—not before.

Meanwhile, he enclosed it in an outer wrapping so that the address could not be seen. Then he sat still for a time, his lips moving, almost as though he were engaged in prayer. At the hour of sunset he rose, wrapped himself in a long red cloak, and went out.

CHAPTER XXIX
HOW MARCUS CHANGED HIS FAITH

Caleb was not the only one who heard the evil tidings of the ship *Luna*. It came also to the ears of the bishop Cyril, for little of any moment passed within the city of Rome that the Christians did not know.

Like Caleb, he assured himself of the truth of the matter by an interview with the captain of the *Imperatrix*. With a sorrowful heart, he departed to the prison near the Temple of Mars. There the warden told him that Marcus wished to see no one, but he answered, "Friend, my business will not wait," pushed past the man and entered the room beyond. Marcus was standing in the center of it, in his hand a drawn Roman gladius sword, which, on sight of his visitor, he cast upon the table with an exclamation of vexation. It clattered down beside a letter addressed to *The Lady Miriam in Tyre. To be given into her own hand.*

"Peace be with you," said the bishop, searching his face with his quiet eyes.

"I thank you, friend," answered Marcus, smiling strangely, "I need peace—and seek it."

"My son," asked the bishop, "what were you about to do?"

Marcus answered, "If you wish to know, I was about to fall upon my sword. One more minute and I would have been dead. They brought it to me with the cloak and other things. It was thoughtful of them, and I guessed their meaning."

Cyril lifted the sword from the table and cast it into a corner of the room.

"God be thanked," he said, "Who led my feet here in time to save you from this sin. Why, because it has pleased Him to take her life, should you seek to take your own?"

"Her life?" said Marcus. "What dreadful words are these? Her life! Whose life?"

"The life of Miriam. I came to tell you. She was drowned upon the seas with all her company."

For a moment Marcus stood swaying to and fro like a drunken man. Then he said, "Is it so indeed? Well, the more reason that I should make haste to follow her. Begone and leave me to do the deed alone," and he stepped towards the sword.

Cyril set his foot upon the blade.

"What is this madness?" he asked. "If you did not know of Miriam's death, why do you desire to kill yourself?"

"Because I have lost more than Miriam. Man, they have robbed me of my honor. By the decree of Titus, I, Marcus, am branded as a coward. Yes, Titus, at whose side I have fought a score of battles—Titus, from whom I have warded many a blow—has banished me from Rome."

"Tell me of this," said Cyril.

So Marcus told him all. Cyril listened in silence, then said sternly:

"Is it for this that you would kill yourself? Is your honor lessened by a decree based on false evidence and given for reasons of politics? Do you cease to be honorable because others are dishonorable, and would you—a soldier—fly from the battle? Now, indeed, Marcus, you show yourself a coward."

"How can I live on who am so shamed?" he asked passionately. "My friends knew that I could not live, and that is why they wrapped a sword in that cloak and sent it me. And now . . . you say Miriam is dead."

"Satan sent that cloak to you, Marcus, desiring to fashion of your foolish pride a ladder down which you might climb to hell. Cast aside this base temptation that wears the mask of false honor. Face your trouble like a man, and conquer it by innocence and faith."

"But Miriam! What of her?"

"Yes, what of Miriam? How would she welcome you yonder, who come to greet her with your own blood upon your hands? Oh! Son, do you not understand that this is the trial laid upon you? You have been brought low that you might rise high. Once the world gave you all it had to give. You were rich, you were a noble among nobles, and you were highborn. Men called you Fortunatus. Then the message of Christ appealed to you in vain, and your heart rejected Him. What had you to do with the cruci-fied carpenter of Galilee? Now, by the plotting of your foes, you are brought low. No longer do you rank high in your trade of blood. You are dismissed from its service and an exile. The real-ity of life is now upon you, so you seek to escape from life rather than bide in it to do your duty through good and ill, heedless of what men may say, and finding your peace in the mercy of God. Let Him whom you rejected in your hours of pomp come to you now. Carry your cross with your shame as He carried His in His shame. In His light find light; in His peace find peace. And at the end you will find her who has been taken from you awhile. Has my spirit spoken in vain with your spirit during these many weeks, Marcus? Already you have told me that you believe, and now at the first breath of trouble will you forget what you know to be the Truth? Once more listen to me, that your eyes may be opened before it is too late."

"Speak on, I am listening," said Marcus with a sigh.

So Cyril pleaded with him in the passion of one inspired, and as Marcus hearkened his heart was softened and his pur-pose turned.

"I understood it all before, I believed it all before," he said at length. "And yet—"

"And yet you will not accept baptism to become a member of the Church," Cyril finished. "Why?"

"Because had I done so she might have thought, and you might have thought, and perhaps I myself might have thought that I did it only to win her whom I desired above all things on earth. In ignorance, I once offered to do as much. But now she is dead, and there is no more reason for doubt. So baptize me now, and do your office."

So there, in the prison cell, the bishop Cyril took water and baptized the Roman Marcus Carius into the body of the Christian Church.

"What shall I do now?" Marcus asked as he rose from his knees. "Once Caesar was my master, now you speak with the voice of Caesar. Command me."

"I do not speak, Christ speaks. Listen. I have been called by the Church to go to Alexandria in Egypt, and I must sail within three days. Will you who are exiled from Rome come with me? There I can find work for you to do."

"I have said that you are Caesar," answered Marcus. "Now it is sunset and I am to be set free. Accompany me to my house, I pray you, for much business in which I need counsel awaits me there."

So presently the gates were opened as Titus had commanded, and they went forth, attended only by a guard of two men, walking unnoted through the streets to the palace in the Via Agrippa.

"There is the door," said the sergeant of the guard, pointing to the side entrance of the house. "Enter with your friend and fare you well, noble Fortunatus."

So they went to the archway and finding the door ajar, they passed through and shut it behind them.

"For a house where there is much to steal, this is ill guarded," said Cyril as he groped his way through the darkness of the arch. "In Rome an open gate ought to have a watchman."

"My steward Stephanus should be at hand. The jailer advised him of my coming—" Marcus began, then he stumbled heavily on a shrouded heap lying in the street.

"What is that?" asked Cyril, eyeing the bundle in the dim light.

"A drunkard—or a dead man. Some beggar, perhaps, sleeping off his liquor here."

By now Cyril was through the archway and in the little court-yard beyond.

"A light burns in the window," he said. "Come, you know the path, guide me to it. We can return to this vagrant later."

"He seems rather hard to wake," added Marcus, as he led the way across the courtyard to the door of the offices. This door was also open, and they entered through it into the room where the steward kept his books. Upon the table, a lamp was burning, that which they had seen through the casement. Its light revealed a dreadful sight. An ironbound box that was chained to the wall had been broken open and its contents rifled, for papers were strewn here and there, and on the floor lay an empty leathern moneybag. The furniture also had been overturned as though in some struggle, while among it, one in the corner of the room and one beneath the marble table, which was too heavy to be moved, lay the two figures of a man and a woman.

"Murderers have been here," said Cyril with a groan.

Marcus snatched the lamp from the table and held it over the face of the man in the corner.

"It's Stephanus," he said, "Bound and gagged, but he's alive, and the other is the slave woman. Hold the lamp while I loose them." He drew his sword and cut away the bonds, first of the one and then of the other. "Speak, man, speak!" he said, as Stephanus struggled to his feet. "What happened here?"

For some moments, the old steward stared at him with round, frightened eyes. Then he gasped, "Oh! My lord, I thought you dead. They said they had come to kill you by command of the Jew Caleb, who gave evidence against you."

"They! Who?" demanded Marcus.

"I know not, four men whose faces were masked. They said that though you must die, they were commanded to do me and the woman no harm, only to bind and silence us. Then they took all the money they could find and went out to waylay you. I heard a scuffle near the arch and well nigh died of sorrow, for I could neither warn nor help you, and I was sure that you were perishing beneath their knives."

"Thank God for this strange deliverance," murmured Cyril, lifting up his hands.

"Presently, presently," answered Marcus. "First follow me." And taking the lamp in his hand, he ran back out the door. The steward and the bishop followed his steps hastily.

Beneath the archway a man lay upon his face—the one across whom Marcus had stumbled, and about his body blood flowed from many wounds. In silence, they turned him over so that the light fell upon his features. Then Marcus staggered back in shock, for they were Caleb's. Blood and wounds marred him, but he was still dark and handsome, even in death.

"Why," he said to Stephanus, "that is the very man whose bloody work the murderers came to do. It would seem that he has fallen into his own snare."

"Are you certain?" asked Cyril. "His gashed face might deceive you."

"Draw his hand from beneath the cloak," answered Marcus. "If I am right the first finger will lack a joint."

Cyril obeyed and held up the stiffening hand. It was as Marcus had said.

"Caught in his own snare!" repeated Marcus. "Well, I knew he hated me, and more than once we have striven to slay each other in battle and single combat, but I never would have believed that Caleb the Jew would sink to hired murder. He is well repaid, the treacherous dog!"

"Let us not be so quick to judge," answered Cyril. "What do you know of how or why this man came by his death? He may have been hurrying here to warn you."

"Against his own paid assassins! No, Bishop, I know Caleb better, only he was viler than I thought."

They carried the body into the house and took counsel what they should do, for every path seemed full of danger. While they reasoned together, there came a knock upon the archway door. They hesitated, not knowing whether it would be safe to open, until the knock was repeated more loudly.

"I will go, lord," said Stephanus. "I need not fear, for I am of no account to anyone."

So he went, presently to return.

"What was it?" asked Marcus.

"Only a young man, who said that he had been strictly charged by his master, Demetrius the Alexandrian merchant, to deliver a letter at this hour. Here it is."

"Demetrius, the Alexandrian merchant," Marcus mused as he took it. "Caleb used that name while he was in Rome."

"Read the letter," said Cyril.

So Marcus cut the silk, broke the seal, and read:

To the noble Marcus,

In the past I have worked you evil and often striven to take your life. Now it has come to my ears that Domitian, who hates you even more than I do, if for less reason, has devised a plot to murder you on the threshold of your own house. Therefore, by way of amends for the evidence I gave against you that stained the truth, since no braver man ever breathed than you, Marcus, it has come into my mind to visit the Palace Fortunatus wrapped in the cloak of a Roman officer. There, before you read this letter, perhaps we shall meet again. But mourn me not, Marcus, nor speak of me as generous, or noble. For Miriam is dead, and I who have followed her through life desire to follow her through death, hoping that there I may find a kinder fortune at her hands, or if not, then at least forgetfulness. You will live long, and so you must drink deep of memory—a bitterer cup. Farewell, Marcus. Since I must die, I would that it had been in single combat beneath your sword, but Fate, who has given me fortune, but no true favor, appoints me to the daggers of assassins that seek another heart. So be it. You tarry here, but I travel to Miriam. Why should I grumble at the road?

Caleb,
Written at Rome upon the night of my death.

"A brave man and bitter," said Marcus when he had finished reading. "Know, my friend, that I am more jealous of him now than ever I was in his life's days. Had it not been for you and your preaching," he added angrily, "when he came to seek Miriam, he would have found me at her side. But now, how can I tell?"

"Peace to your heathen talk!" answered the bishop. "Is the land of spirits then as your poets picture, where the dead turn to each other with eyes of earthly passion? Yet," he added more gently, "I shall not blame you, for like this poor Jew, from childhood you have been steeped in superstitions. Have no fear of his rivalry in the heavenly fields, Marcus. For there, they do not marry nor are given in marriage. And think not that self-murder can profit a man anything. What the end of this tale may be does not yet appear. But I am certain that Caleb will take no gain in hurrying to his own death, unless indeed he did it for a nobler cause than he says."

"I trust that it may be so," answered Marcus, "although in truth that another man should die for me gives me no comfort. I would rather he had left me to my doom."

"As God has willed so it has befallen, for man's goings are of the Lord. How then can a man understand his own way?" replied Cyril with a sigh. "Now let us consider other matters, for time is short and you would do well to be clear of Rome before Domitian finds that Caleb fell in place of Marcus."

Nearly three more months had gone when, at length, one night as the sun vanished, a galley crept wearily into the harbor of Alexandria and cast anchor just as the light of Pharos began to shine across the sea. Her passage through the winter gales had been hard, and for weeks at a time, she had been obliged to shelter in harbors by the way. Now, short of food and water, she had come safely to her haven, a mercy for which the bishop Cyril, with the Roman Marcus and the other Christians aboard her, gave thanks to Heaven upon their knees in their little cabin near the forecastle, for it was too late to attempt to dock that night.

Then they went on deck, and as all their food was gone and they had no drink but spoiled water, they leaned upon the bulwarks and looked hungrily towards the shore, where the thousand lights of the mighty city gleamed. Near to them, not a bowshot away indeed, glided another ship. Presently, as they stared at her black outline, the sound of singing floated from her decks across the still, starlit waters of the harbor. They listened to it idly enough at first, until at length some words of the song reached their ears, causing them to look at each other in wonder.

"That is no sailor's ditty," said Marcus.

"No," answered Cyril, "it is a Christian hymn, and one that I know well. Listen. Each verse ends, 'Peace, be still!'"

"Then," said Marcus, "that must be a Christian ship, or they would not dare to sing that hymn. The night is calm, let us hail the boat and visit it. I am thirsty, and those good folk may have fresh water."

"If you wish," answered Cyril. "They may have tidings as well as water."

A while later, Cyril and Marcus embarked upon a small boat and rowed to the side of the strange ship, asking leave of the watchman to board.

"What sign do you give?" asked the officer.

"The sign of the cross," answered Cyril. "We have heard your hymn and are of the brotherhood of Rome."

A rope ladder was thrown down to them, and the officer bade them make fast and be welcome.

They climbed aboard and went to seek the captain at the aft of the ship, where an awning was stretched over the deck. And there beneath the awning, lit with lanterns, stood a woman in a white robe, singing the refrain of the hymn in her sweet voice, the others of the company, joining in its choruses from time to time.

"From the dead am I arisen," rang her voice, and there was something in the thrilling notes that gripped Marcus's heart, some tone and quality that was familiar.

Side by side with Cyril, he climbed onwards across the rowing benches, and the noise of their stumbling footsteps reached the singer's ears, causing her to pause in her song. Then stepping forward a little, as though to look, she moved under the lantern so that its light fell full upon her face. But she saw nothing, and so once more took up her chant.

Oh ye faithless, from the dead am I arisen.

"Look, look!" gasped Marcus, clutching Cyril by the arm. "Look! It is Miriam!"

In another instant, he came into the circle of the lamplight, so that his eyes met the eyes of the singer. She saw him then, and with a little cry, sank to her knees upon the deck.

Thus the story ended. They soon learned that the tale that had been brought to Rome of the *Luna's* sinking had been false. When the great gale had descended upon her, she had escaped to